"WE BOTH HAVE OUR OWN REASONS FOR THIS MARRIAGE, YOUR GRACE."

"I merely wish to point out that even though we are wed, nothing need change. You have your life and your friends, and I mine."

Devon smiled devilishly. "Ah, but then you have failed to take into consideration the fact that I might actually be looking forward to this marriage."

"Please release me," she said through clenched teeth.

"Rest easy, love," he whispered in her hair as she tried to pull away from his arms. He let his leg brush against hers. "You wouldn't want the whole countryside to know how I coerced you into this marriage, would you?"

"You wouldn't reveal that," she gasped.

He grinned down at her. "You're more than likely correct. But I'd not let it go to my head, if I were you," he advised, holding her more possessively now.

Scandal's Darling

Anne Caldwell

AVON BOOKS ◆ NEW YORK

AVON BOOKS
A division of
The Hearst Corporation
105 Madison Avenue
New York, New York 10016

Copyright © 1991 by Jean Anne Caldwell
Published by arrangement with the author
Library of Congress Catalog Card Number: 90-93418
ISBN: 0-380-76110-6

First Avon Books Printing: April 1991

AVON TRADEMARK REG. U.S. PAT. OFF. AND IN OTHER COUNTRIES, MARCA REGISTRADA, HECHO EN U.S.A.

Printed in the U.S.A.

RA 10 9 8 7 6 5 4 3 2 1

Chapter 1

Westbryre, England
1811

An ancient oak stood guard at the corner of the orphanage. Its barren branches swayed with the chill winter wind, scratching its signature into the building's mellow pink brick. Leaves that had sought shelter among its gnarled roots were plucked from their bed and scattered across the lawn, coming to rest against a large wooden sign that said:

WESTBRYRE ORPHANAGE
FOUNDED 1775 BY ALEXANDER STANTON
THIRD DUKE OF BURNSHIRE
Hope for the Homeless

A grim smile touched Danielle Wakefield's lips as she crept closer. Given the well-kept grounds and the outward condition of the home, it was no wonder people believed the false words. Taking refuge behind the sign, she ran her slim fingers under the band of her woolen cap, tucking in the loose strands of her auburn hair. This was no time to be recognized. The new Duke of Burnshire had returned to England, and the vicar was sure to have informed him of the abductions.

Danielle's green eyes searched the front of the orphanage. The windows on the lower level were ablaze with light that splashed across the panels of the vicar's

1

dark carriage standing in the drive. His team of black horses stamped impatiently, their breath pale clouds of vapor in the brisk night air.

Amy's message had said nothing of the vicar's visit. Had something gone amiss, or worse still, was this a trap? Danielle had lodged countless complaints against the vicar's policies in overseeing the orphanage, and knew that he would dearly love to discover her part in the disappearance of the orphans.

Reason told Danielle to return to her coach and forget tonight's plan, but Amy was inside waiting for her. Amy had been helping her abduct orphans for over two years now. Danielle couldn't leave without at least making a try.

Carefully avoiding the vicar's footman beside the carriage, she made her way to the back of the orphanage. The cloud-streaked moon cast eerie shadows across the path, and Danielle pulled her borrowed coat tighter. She would never get used to the winters of England. Even the warm fires on the hearths did little to dispel the cold dampness that seemed to cling to everything.

Quietly, she opened the heavy door that led to the cellar. A rush of dank, stale air assailed her. Danielle swallowed hard. Where was the candle Amy normally left for her? She knew she was late. She'd had a difficult time hiring a coach. But surely Amy knew she would come.

Moving inside, she counted her footsteps into darkness. *One . . . two . . .* The door slammed shut behind her. Danielle jumped. Only the wind, she thought, mocking her fears.

She remained motionless, waiting for her eyes to grow accustomed to the dark. Her nostrils filled with the smell of rotted food and discarded clothing.

Plunk! She stiffened. *Plunk! Plunk!* The dead, hollow sound of dripping water echoed off the cellar walls.

Don't let your imagination get the better of you, she told herself. You've made this trip enough times to find your way blindfolded.

Placing her hand along the cold, damp bricks, Danielle slowly moved up the stairs. Something sleek and furry ran across the toe of her doeskin boot. She swallowed the impulse to scream. It was impossible to see in the smothering darkness, but she reassured herself with the thought that it was more than likely one of the loathsome rats she had encountered on her earlier trips. Taking a deep, steadying breath, she moved on.

Finally, Danielle attained the first landing. *Two more flights*, she thought, before she would reach Amy's room under the eaves.

The unexpected sound of loud, angry voices stopped her. They seemed to come from the stairs above her. Despite the cold draft, she could feel tiny pricks of perspiration on the back of her neck, and her throat grew dry. She was being foolish. The doors to the stairway had long since been boarded up. Only she and Amy used it now. Even so, Danielle slipped her trembling hand into the pocket of her coat. The solid feel of her father's pistol gave her the courage to continue.

Step by slow step, Danielle made her way through the spiderwebs that spanned the staircase. She passed the second landing. The orphans' rooms were on this floor. How she longed to rescue all the children tonight, but the chance of such a plan succeeding would be poor. She must console herself with the few she was able to abduct. Someday, she vowed, she would return to storm the walls and save them all—including Amy.

The door above her opened, and a shaft of light sliced through the darkness of the stairwell. Danielle pressed against the wall, willing herself into invisibility. Air returned to her lungs when a small boy was thrust through the opening.

"Stay here until Miss Danny comes," she heard Amy whisper. "Tell her she must leave quickly. There is trouble afoot tonight." The lad's short blond curls bobbed in agreement.

Before Danielle could call out, the door shut, shrouding her once more in darkness. She climbed the last steps to the small, huddled figure, then gently touched him. The boy jumped. "I'm Miss Danny," she whispered, wrapping her arms around his thin shoulders. "What do they call you?"

"Jeremy, miss," he murmured shyly, then pulled away. "Amy said we'd best hurry." His words came in a rush. "The vicar is here tonight and he's fit to be tied. She's 'fraid he might be onto her. She said—"

Danielle rose abruptly and turned to the door, but Jeremy stopped her. "She said we must hurry, miss," he pleaded, tugging at the corner of her jacket. "She's 'fraid for the others."

Danielle stood with her hand on the door. She had to honor Amy's wishes. She must not do anything to jeopardize her position at the orphanage. If that happened, there would be no hope of helping the others.

Slowly, they made their way down the stairs. The sound of running feet and angry voices grew louder as they reached the first landing. The light of a candle filtered through the cracks in the boards that crisscrossed the wooden door. Danielle paused. Instinctively, she held her breath, afraid that even the sounds of their heartbeats would give them away.

"He has to be here," said a low, gravelly voice from the other side of the door.

Danielle easily recognized the raspy voice of the vicar. She gave Jeremy's hand a reassuring squeeze.

" 'E can't 'ave gone far," answered another. "Ol' Myrtle says 'e was down to supper less than 'n hour ago. That cup o' gruel she serves won't keep 'em warm for long. Ye takes my word for it. 'E gets cold and 'ungry, 'e'll come 'ome right enough."

"You'd best find him. He's sold, and I don't wish to explain to Lord Carruthers that you let the boy slip through your hands. I want him found. Now!"

"The swine!" Danielle muttered. The boy looked no more than five years old. To sell him for work at such a young age was unpardonable. With renewed determination, she grabbed Jeremy's arm and continued down the steps. I *will* return, she vowed again, and rescue them all. And somehow I'll find a way to punish the fiends responsible for this outrage.

Reaching the bottom, Danielle cautiously eased open the door. The sky was still dark with threatening storm clouds as she stepped out into the cold night air. Keeping to the shadows, Danielle motioned the lad to follow. She ran for the high shrubs lining the grounds of the orphanage.

"Who goes there?" a deep voice cried out.

Danielle stopped and quietly pulled Jeremy to her side. The light from a lantern swung a wide arc over the side yard where the two fugitives stood, poised for flight.

"I've found him!" the man shouted.

Danielle tugged on Jeremy's arm, pulling him with her. They reached the bushes, but the thick brambles formed an effective barricade. They couldn't go back. They had no choice but to crawl beneath the intertwining limbs. Danielle pushed Jeremy into a small opening, then followed, inching along on her hands and knees, the twisted briars plucking at her clothing. Someone grabbed at her boot. She screamed and plunged deeper into the thicket. Her cap was torn from her head, and her long auburn curls caught in the branches. Desperately, painfully, she managed to free herself, giving little heed to the silken strands she left behind. At last she was through to the other side.

Freedom! Scrambling to her feet, she took Jeremy's hand and headed down the road. The boy stumbled along beside her, his short legs moving twice to each of her strides. Danielle could hear their pursuers' footsteps on the far side of the hedge.

Too close!

Much too close. She could not afford to get caught now, for the lad's only hope rested with her.

Stopping, she picked up Jeremy, then continued. If only she could put a greater distance between them, but her sides ached and her breath came in short, ragged gasps. She and Jeremy had to reach the coach!

"M-miss," Jeremy panted. "They're gaining on us."

His small, frightened voice urged Danielle on. Behind her she could hear branches breaking underfoot, clothes ripping, muffled oaths . . .

Closer, ever closer, they came, until the two men crashed through the bushes behind them.

A shaft of moonlight broke through the clouds and Danielle spied her coach up ahead. She shouted. Immediately, the driver snapped his whip over the horses and the coach moved forward. As it drew near, a pale hand opened the door. Using her last ounce of strength, Danielle pulled herself and Jeremy aboard the carriage.

Not ready to admit defeat, the two men lunged for the horses as the coach sped by. One lost his hold and fell, but the other clung to the leather harness.

Crack! The tip of the driver's whip lashed out at the man's hand. Losing his grip, he fell and rolled to the roadside.

When the coach was safely away, Danielle leaned back in the worn seat, a sigh of relief trembling on her lips. She had more than tempted fate this time.

"Danielle Wakefield!" scolded the gray-haired woman sitting across from Danielle and the little boy. "You continue in this manner and you'll be the death of me yet."

"Brodie, meet Jeremy," Danielle said, determining to ignore the older woman's comment. "He has decided to live with us at Haverly House."

Brodie nodded her greeting. Her argument was with Danielle, not the boy. "Danielle—"

"Jeremy, this is Brodie. She's my companion," Danielle explained as she tucked the carriage robe around the boy. "Brodie was once my governess. I hope you like her as much as I do, for she teaches you ever so many wonderful things."

Jeremy smiled shyly.

Brodie would not be dismissed so easily. "None of your fine talk, missy," she said. "When I think of how close they were to catching you . . ."

She paused, her eyes suddenly narrowing. Danielle's cheeks were flushed a bright pink, and her hair, matted with twigs and dead leaves, had fallen to her shoulders. "Where's your cap?" Brodie demanded.

"I lost it crawling through the bushes. But that's not important, Brodie."

"Not important!" she growled. "If anyone saw that red hair of yours, we're as good as caught."

Danielle gave Jeremy a broad wink. "Pay no mind to Brodie's grumblings. She would be bored to distraction if I ever gave up my life of crime."

"Hah!" Brodie snorted in exasperation. "Whatever possessed me to think that coming to England would help you learn to be a lady? We might as well have stayed in Virginia. After twelve of these abductions, I think I could adjust quite easily to the quiet life of a governess again. That is, if I live that long."

"I was never any good at being a lady." Danielle took Jeremy's small hand and gave it a squeeze. "I'm much better at rescuing little ones from the mean old vicar, aren't I, Jeremy?"

His innocent blue eyes and trusting smile warmed her heart. This was why it was so difficult to convince herself that she should quit. But she had to admit the risks were becoming greater.

"Are you warm enough, lad?" she asked, trying to coax him to talk. He only continued to smile shyly. "When we get to Haverly House, Brodie and I will get you some decent clothes and a pair of shoes with no holes. Won't we, Brodie?"

"Best worry about covering those breeches of yours before we arrive," she answered as she tossed Danielle a blue traveling gown. "And do something with your hair. It looks a fright. If your aunt were to see you now, your life as an abductress would come to an abrupt end."

Removing her jacket, Danielle slipped the garment over her head. "If Aunt Margaret should try to stop me, it would upset you too," she mumbled from within the heavy wool fabric. "We both know you wouldn't have it any other way. You care about what happens to these children as much as I do."

Brodie winked at Jeremy. "She's right, you know. The difficulty is, she knows it."

Brodie rummaged through the portmanteau on the seat beside her until she found the small box of chocolates she had tucked away. Pulling out one of the sweets, she handed it to the lad. "Miss Danny purchased these for her aunt Margaret, but I'm sure Lady Bradford wouldn't mind sharing them with you." She watched him take a small bite, then devour the treat with gusto. "Did Amy instruct you that you were not to tell anyone about coming from the orphanage?"

He nodded solemnly.

"Not even Lady Bradford," she stressed. "Miss Danny's aunt would never understand. We'll tell her you are an orphan we found during our stay in London. She would have an absolute fit if she even suspected Miss Danny had abducted the entire lot of you."

"You need not frighten the lad, Brodie," Danielle scolded as she finished pulling the gown down to cover her breeches.

"My intention was only to warn him," Brodie answered. "It wouldn't do for Lady Bradford to discover our secret."

The speed of the coach suddenly quickened and Danielle found it difficult to fasten the small ivory buttons across her linen bodice. "Even if Aunt Margaret were to discover the truth, I would never allow the children to return to the orphanage. I may not have two farthings to rub together, but as long as Haverly House is mine, they will have a home."

"How long do you think the authorities will allow them to stay there once they know?" Brodie admonished, leaning with the sway of the coach. "You got away without being caught this time, but you can't expect to be so fortunate forever."

Danielle refused to dwell on Brodie's dire predictions and reached down to help the boy. "Hold onto the side strap, Jeremy. It will keep you from sliding off the seat. The coachman will slow as soon as he feels we've put enough distance between us and Westbryre,'' she said as she secured her bonnet over her disheveled curls.

He answered her with a nod, a weak grin curving his lips. ''That's a brave boy.'' She cupped his small face in her hand, then straightened and leveled a glance at Brodie. ''There would have been no problem this time had the vicar not come early for the boy.''

Suddenly, the carriage listed to one side, forcing everyone to grab for a firm hold. Danielle and Brodie exchanged glances as the coach gathered speed again. Whatever was the driver thinking of? Surely they were well away from their pursuers by now. Danielle reached behind Brodie and pounded on the coachman's trap. He appeared not to hear, for the vehicle only picked up its pace.

Danielle handed Jeremy across to Brodie before lowering the window. The night had suddenly turned bitter cold. Ignoring the sharp wind that stung her face, Danielle poked her head out the window, but it was too dark to see if they were being followed. She thought about the pistol still tucked in her breeches. Yet what good would it be if she could not see her target?

The coach hit another bump in the road, forcing Danielle to withdraw her head. ''I didn't see anyone,'' she said. She knew without asking that she and Brodie were thinking the same thing. A runaway carriage could be every bit as dangerous as being caught by the vicar's men.

Desperately, they held on as the coach rounded a curve. Faster and faster it went, threatening to split its seams with each rut in the road. How much more could the carriage take?

She was reaching to help Brodie with Jeremy when they were suddenly slammed against the side of the coach. Tanner's Corner! It was a difficult spot in the road under the best of conditions. How would they ever clear it at this speed?

Danielle could hear the horses squeal in their traces as the driver attempted to negotiate the sharp turn. Their anguished cries were soon joined by the splintering of wood.

The coach balanced precariously on two wheels. For a heart-stopping moment, it seemed suspended in air. Finally, the ancient vehicle shuddered, then crashed to its side. Screams exploded in Danielle's head as she was thrown against one of the carriage lamps. Then all was quiet, except for the distant beat of the horses' hooves as they continued down the lane, their traces flapping behind them.

"Is anyone hurt?" Brodie demanded.

Waves of pain washed over Danielle. Gently she fingered the lump on the back of her head. Thankfully her bonnet had served to soften the impact.

"Danielle!" Brodie demanded once more. "Are you hurt?"

"A few bumps," she answered, thankful the darkness hid her grimace of pain. She had worried Brodie enough. She slowly gathered her legs beneath her and tried to stand. Her head throbbed as she fought back the nausea that threatened with each movement, but she managed to get to her feet. Bringing her hands up, she opened the door. The rush of cold air helped quell the ringing in her head.

The horses were gone, but where was the driver? Finding a foothold, Danielle started to ease her way out of the coach when she saw him lying in the road, his body contorted in an unnatural pose.

How had this happened? She had only meant to rescue a child, and now someone was dead. Her stomach twisted into a knot. A hired coach and a hired driver . . . She didn't even know his name, and with the nearest inn miles away, there was no one she could summon to care for the body.

"The driver's dead and the horses are gone," she said, retreating into the carriage.

"No!" Brodie cried. "The poor man! And we'll be caught for sure."

Danielle was well aware of that. Not only Jeremy would be returned to the orphanage, but the others as well. The two years of risks would be for naught. Was she really willing to give up?

"If the vicar followed us, I for one do not plan to make it easy for him." Her mind worked quickly to formulate a plan. She carefully considered their options and, one by one, discarded them. It was too cold to walk. There was no telling how far they would have to go before they found shelter. But was staying in the coach any better? Just then she heard the sound of an approaching carriage, bringing her worse fears to life.

"Someone is coming. You'll have to go out and greet them, Brodie. If they're from the orphanage, pretend you're alone until you can get help."

Brodie stared at Danielle, her eyes wide. "I'm no good at this. If it is the vicar, I'll never get him to believe me."

"Then we'd best pray it isn't."

His Grace, Devon Alexander Stanton, fifth Duke of Burnshire, leaned back against the velvet squabs of his roomy coach. The oil lantern within cast a harsh glow on the rugged lines of his profile. No one would guess from the frown that creased his brow that his Grace was about to become one of England's wealthiest men.

The terms of his late father's will were simple enough. He had a year from his father's demise to marry. If he refused, all he would inherit was Burnshire, his ancestral home. His father had had no control over that, for it was entailed to whoever held the title. It was the other, vast holdings the Stantons had acquired over the years that remained in question.

Even considering all the benefits, Devon was reluctant to comply with the dictates of a father he had not seen since their bitter quarrel seven years ago. Then too, the duke had demanded that his son marry, causing Devon to storm out of Burnshire, vowing never to return. With an inheritance left to him by his godfather, he had purchased a ship and left England.

Though dead, his father was still attempting to govern Devon's life. Yet if he didn't marry, his cousin, the Reverend Nathan Holmes, would be the one to inherit. Devon's fingers curled into a fist. His entire life had been haunted by Nathan's greed. It was ironic that the person most responsible for driving the wedge between him and his father would end up being the reason for Devon agreeing to accept the terms of the will.

A cynical smile formed on his lips. It hadn't been two days after Giles, his father's agent, had tracked Devon down in Jamaica to tell him of the duke's death that someone had tried to kill him. There was no doubt the man had been sent by Nathan. His cousin had made no secret of the fact that he wanted everything that was rightfully Devon's—the title, Burnshire, the lands.

Even so, had Devon not discovered that the same man who had tried to stab him in the back in Jamaica had also attempted to force his mother's carriage off the road, Devon would not have returned to England. The inheritance meant nothing to him—but his mother did.

For his entire life, Lady Julia had been one person who had always believed in him. When Nathan had sought to discredit him, she had stood by Devon.

Now, Nathan's reasons for wanting to murder him were obvious, but his motives for making an attempt on Lady Julia's life were harder to fathom. Other than a generous allowance paid from the estate, she received nothing. But as far as Devon was concerned, until he was able to solve the mystery, Lady Julia's protection came first. Even her near solitary existence in Bath worried him. Once he had her safely tucked away at a friend's estate in Scotland, he could concentrate on Nathan.

He would begin by marrying and claiming the inheritance. If he was fortunate, that would be enough to force Nathan's hand.

Having made the decision, he had returned to England to select his bride. After reviewing the available candidates with his mother, he had settled on Lady Emily Chalmers. She was beautiful and would be a good hostess for Burnshire; but most importantly, other than the exchange of marriage vows, she would require no additional commitments from him. Devon's sardonic smile deepened. As long as Lady Emily had his wealth at her fingertips, she would not care that he had no intention of remaining in England once he'd dispensed with Nathan.

Still, he was not entirely pleased with the selection, and had done everything possible in the past two weeks to postpone the proposal. The Lady Emily he remembered was spoiled and selfish, but he had little choice if he wanted to carry out his plans. With the anniversary of his father's death approaching in just ten days, time was running out.

"Whoa! Blimey, wha's this?" shouted Jem, the coachman, as he fought to bring his Grace's horses under control. "There's a ruddy coach what missed the turn, your Grace. She's going to need some help. Looks like a bad 'un."

Lord Stanton, shaken from the contemplation of his own problems, pulled back the heavy fabric covering the window. A closed carriage lay on its side, its crippled wheels spinning helplessly in the wind. The snow that had been holding off for most of the day was just beginning to fall, filtering through the trees and sparkling against the blackness of the overturned conveyance.

As a footman went forward to secure the horses, Jem climbed down from his perch. The wind had taken on a chill, and he pulled his cloak tighter about his wizened frame as he held the door open for his passenger.

Lord Stanton climbed down. A patch of lamplight spilling out from the open coach door found the unfortunate driver of the disabled vehicle. "Appears to have broken his neck," Devon said.

"The bloke's done for all right," Jem confirmed.

"Have the footmen put him atop our carriage, then

come with me," Devon instructed as he approached the toppled coach.

"Help me," a cry came from inside.

His coachman stopped dead in his tracks, his eyes wide. "It's one o' them bloomin' haunted coaches, it be," Jem whispered. "I 'eared tell they were along this road. Why, me friends at the Beef and Biscuit told me about this 'ere very thing only last week."

"A ghost carriage?" Devon laughed. "Best be changing the alehouse you frequent, Jem, if those are the tales they serve with their draught."

Jem dipped his head in embarrassment. Despite his reluctance, the old man climbed upon the side of the coach and opened the door.

"For pity's sake, get me out of here," echoed a woman's voice from inside.

Even from where he stood, Devon could see that Jem hadn't changed his mind about the carriage. The coachman kept his eyes closed as he reached inside for the woman, which made Devon smile.

"Are you hurt?" Devon asked the small, gray-haired woman Jem pulled from the carriage.

Brodie looked hesitantly at the imposing figure before her. The fact that he was not the vicar did little to dispel the spark of fear his presence ignited. She was no good at this. Danny should have taken the speaking part in this charade.

Nonetheless, she fixed the tall gentleman with a stern eye. "I'm not injured," Brodie answered, "but I thought I was going to freeze to death before anyone came along."

"I'm sorry to have made you wait," he apologized with a broad smile.

Brodie dropped her eyes from his look of amusement. "It was a blessing you happened our way," she said hurriedly. "The boy and I are only a bit bruised, but my companion has been injured."

"Get the others out, Jem," Devon instructed over the rising wind. "I'll help the lady down."

"Thank you, sir," Brodie said as he lifted her to the ground.

Jem climbed into the coach with a great deal more enthusiasm than he had shown a moment ago, and it wasn't long before he handed out a small boy. Devon took him from Jem. The child's clothes were ragged and smelled strongly of woodsmoke, which made Devon wonder why the lad had been inside the coach. Most servants traveled on the box.

But he abandoned the thought when his attention was drawn to a movement in the woods across the road. One man, perhaps two, were taking cover behind the trees. Were the pickings so slim in England nowadays that highwaymen would stoop to rob even such a nondescript coach as this?

Hurrying back to his own conveyance, Devon placed the child inside, then opened a compartment under the seat. Taking care to avoid the eyes of the boy, he removed a pistol, and went to have a word with the footmen.

"Ready your firearms," he whispered. "If the men watching our progress from the trees intend to rob us, the sight of an armed guard might help dissuade them." Tucking the pistol into the band of his breeches so that it was plainly visible, Devon returned to assist Jem with the other passenger.

"This is the last of 'em," Jem informed him.

Devon was taken aback by the beauty of the young lady Jem lowered into his arms. With great interest, his gaze traveled from the long dark lashes that rested softly on her pale cheeks to the soft contours of her pink lips.

As if she sensed his scrutiny, she shifted in his arms. The movement dislodged her fur-trimmed bonnet and it fell to the ground, exposing a luxurious head of reddish-brown curls. What a delightful bundle, he thought, as he watched the sequins of snow settle in her hair and across the front of her blue traveling gown. Quickly the older woman picked up the bonnet and jammed it back on the red-maned lovely's head.

The young girl fluttered her eyelashes and allowed a moan to escape her lips. "Brodie, Brodie. Where are you?"

"I'm here, Danielle." Brodie's words were full of concern.

"Where's . . ." Danielle's speech trailed off as her gaze rested on the man who held her. His chiseled good looks came as a surprise, and she tried not to dwell on how his deep blue eyes contrasted so strikingly with a face that had been bronzed by the sun. The pair of strong arms that encircled her most certainly belonged to the impressive set of broad shoulders encased in the black multi-caped coat that rubbed against her cheek. Holy Hannah! If her heart didn't stop beating so fast, he was sure to hear it.

The wind whipped about his dark hair, stirring up an image of a swashbuckler dressed in fine clothes, and her mouth went powder-dry. Instinct told her they shouldn't accept his help. This was not the type of man liable to be fooled for long.

"Jeremy's fine, Danny," Brodie broke in. What was wrong with the girl? This was no time for daydreaming. "You mustn't worry. The lad's in this gentleman's coach. You *need* to rest."

Danielle recognized her rehearsed cue, and fainted.

Devon continued to stare at the slim bundle he carried. As he gazed at her delicate beauty, the idea of postponing his trip to London for another day began to appeal to him. Hell and damnation! It wasn't as if Emily would turn him down if he was a day late. Besides, it wouldn't do to leave this green-eyed beauty unattended at some inn. It was his duty as a gentleman to see to her needs.

The wind snatched the folds of Danielle's skirt and set them swirling around her ankles, providing Devon with a glimpse of her buckskin breeches. He cocked a dark brow, but made no comment as he motioned Brodie to precede him. He had noticed quite a few changes since his return to England. The fear of an invasion by Napoleon had everyone up in arms. Why, even the locals had taken to drilling. But unless England had begun recruiting young women in its volunteer militias, there was more to this lady than mere loveliness.

"My home's not far," he said, dismissing his suspicions. "I shall see you settled there first; then, when the weather clears, my driver will see you home."

"That's very kind of you," Brodie replied, still uneasy.

Leading the way, Brodie suddenly stopped a few feet from the coach. The crest emblazoned on its door drove home her fears for the safety of their secret. This was Lord Stanton's coach. The new Duke of Burnshire. The very man who owned the orphanage.

Devon, his head bowed against the snow, almost collided with her. "Jem, over here, please," he called to his coachman. "Could you open the door for us? It wouldn't do for the footmen to lower their firearms until we're on our way. Those men watching us from the trees might be tempted to make their move."

Devon was somewhat surprised to feel the unconscious woman stiffen in his arms. He studied her face carefully, but her eyes remained firmly closed.

With Jem's help, he managed to get her in the carriage and propped up on the seat across from the lad. Standing aside, he assisted Brodie, then climbed aboard.

It was difficult for Brodie to maintain a calm demeanor as the duke took his seat beside Jeremy, but she had no choice but to brazen it out.

As the coach moved forward, they exchanged introductions. Lord Stanton had barely gotten his name out when Brodie felt Danielle's hand grab her knee under the carriage rug. "Perhaps it would be more convenient to take us to an inn," she suggested, wishing once more she could exchange roles with Danielle. "We wouldn't want to inconvenience your household in any way, your Grace."

"My housekeeper would never forgive me if I turned away someone who was stranded on a night such as this. Unless, of course, you live near here?"

Brodie hesitated. Giving him directions to Haverly House was out of the question. If he were to hear of the abduction later, he was bound to know they were the ones responsible. "Actually, we are from Virginia, your Grace. Miss Wake—Walker—is staying with relatives here." It wasn't a *total* lie. They *were* from Virginia and Danielle's aunt, Lady Bradford, *was* staying with them.

Devon was intrigued. First, a woman who is supposed to be unconscious responds when he mentions highwaymen. Now, from the clumsy way in which Mrs. Brodie had stumbled over her companion's name, it was evident the appellation had been only recently acquired. Wondering what other surprises were in store for him, he studied his fellow passengers.

"And the boy?" His question startled even him. A tantalizing glimpse of emerald-green eyes was not an excuse to delve into the personal affairs of others. He rarely discussed his own private life and had always tried to respect the need for privacy in others.

"We were fetching him home," Brodie answered. "His parents are dead and the streets of London are no place for a boy to grow up." Oh dear, she hadn't meant to tell him so much. The little white lies were beginning to accumulate.

"Quite commendable." Lord Stanton ran a critical eye over the lad. "Did you check with the proper authorities? It's possible his parents aren't dead and he has merely run away from home."

At the unexpected turn of the conversation, Danielle ventured a peek at their rescuer. Brodie was giving him entirely too much information. Had her normally practical nature been shaken by this man's piratical good looks?

She studied him through lowered lashes, her gaze once again drawn to the sun-browned features. A lock of unruly black hair fell slowly down his forehead, coaxing the other strands to follow, and the piercing blue eyes, sheltered beneath his dark brows, were strangely entrancing.

"I see you're awake." His husky voice acknowledged her intimate perusal. "Would you care to tell me the purpose of this little tragedy?"

A flush gradually stained Danielle's cheeks. She considered a dramatic swoon, then quickly dismissed the idea. His smile told her what she had already begun to suspect. He hadn't believed their act for a moment! Never one to bemoan the loss of a skirmish, she lowered the carriage robe from her shoulders, sat up straight, readjusted the folds of her skirt, and returned his smile with one of her own.

Chapter 2

I sabel Pickett watched her husband pace the narrow office of the orphanage. "Why should you get yourself in a fuss over one of them brats?" she snapped. "Others have run off before. As long as we continue to collect our share for their care, why should we fret?"

"The 'brat' happens to be sold to one of the vicar's best customers."

The display of impatience was rare for her husband. Isabel pursed her lips. "Well, it ain't like we don't have others he can choose from."

Pickett bestowed a tight smile on his plump wife. "The vicar's customer took a particular liking to the boy."

"What was so special about this one?" she demanded, jerking her lace robe across her ample bosom. "They all look alike to me—a lot of snot-nosed, filthy little animals."

Mr. Pickett considered telling her, then decided against it. She would have no interest in Lord Carruthers' special tastes. Better to point out how the loss of the child would directly affect her. "Our share of the sale should pay for that new dress you ordered from London."

The pout on Isabel's face was immediately replaced with a familiar mask of efficiency. "Well, what are you doing to see that the boy is caught?" She yanked aside the drapes at the window and peered outside. "He won't be going far. The weather looks to be turning

bad, and I doubt he has a pair of shoes to his name.
More than likely, he'll be hiding in the shrubbery."
She turned away from the window. "You'd do well
to—"

The door to the office slammed back against the wall,
and the Reverend Nathan Holmes, Vicar of Westbryre,
stepped into the warm room. "I need to talk with
you, Pickett." He looked at Isabel coldly. "In private."

She returned his haughty stare before leaving. He
needn't be so high-and-mighty about it, she grumbled
silently. As soon as he left, she would learn the details.
There were no secrets between Mr. Pickett and her.

"They've escaped the grounds, Pickett!" Nathan
stormed after the door was closed.

"They?" Pickett sniveled. "Did more than one of
them get by us?"

"The lad had help." Nathan paused. "It's bad
enough that my cousin's return to England is costing
me the old duke's fortune, but now my position as
administrator is being placed in jeopardy by these abductions. I need not point out that affairs at Westbryre
will not withstand close scrutiny."

Pickett could understand the vicar's concern. The
new duke might very well put an end to their profitable ventures. They could easily curtail a great many of
their activities for a short time, but the sale of the child
to Lord Carruthers was an important one. His taste for
young boys had lined their pockets well over the past
few years, and it wouldn't do to disappoint him now.

"I've spoken with Lord Carruthers and informed him
of the delay."

"There's that new boy George brought in today,"
Pickett offered. "He's kind of pretty."

"Don't be so quick to replace the lad." The vicar
opened his hand over Pickett's desk.

Pickett watched in fascination as pieces of twigs and
dried leaves fell onto the scarred surface. Long strands
of red hair still clung to them.

"Once again, Pickett, I've saved your position. I now
know who took the lad." Nathan's thin lips curved

into a triumphant smile. "Miss Wakefield has opposed us once too often."

"It cannot be." Pickett fingered the tangle of hair and twigs. "Surely you are not suggesting that this belongs to Lady Bradford's niece."

"That's precisely what I am suggesting. I know of no other woman more determined to present us in a bad light. But after this evening, she'll not meddle in our affairs again. I've sent Chilton and Faris after the lad. We'll have him back in his bed before morning."

The triumphant smile faded from Nathan's lips as just then Chilton and Faris walked in—alone.

"Where's the boy?" Nathan demanded.

They shuffled their feet under the vicar's keen stare. "We don't 'ave 'im," Faris mumbled.

"What do you mean you don't have him?" Nathan thundered. Was he forever destined to put up with their bungling ways? "What's your excuse this time?"

"The coach overturned at Tanner's Corner, jus' this side of Squire's Meadow," Chilton explained. "Turned that carriage plumb over, they did. We—"

"Was the boy hurt?" Nathan broke in.

Chilton cringed from the dark look that crossed the vicar's normally bland features. "No, 'e looked to be fine. It was that Wakefield chit all right," he added with more confidence than he felt. "Messed 'er up some. 'er and that dragon of a woman what's always telling us 'ow we don't care for the children properly. We was about to nab 'em when this big coach comes 'round the turn. That fancy cousin of yours gets out, puts 'em in 'is carriage, and drives off."

Nathan grabbed the front of Chilton's coat. Hatred burned in his eyes as he slammed the man against the wall. "You let them leave with the duke?"

"Didn't let 'em, Vicar," Chilton choked. " 'E 'ad 'is men ready with their guns. 'Ad 'em things pointed square at 'em trees where we was 'id."

"I don't give a tinker's damn about what could have happened to you! You've lost the boy. That's all that matters."

"I could tell by the way 'e acted, the duke wanted the boy for 'isself," Chilton said, hoping to appease the vicar. "Wouldn't surprise me iffen she 'ad sold the boy to 'im."

"You fool!" Nathan snarled. He shoved Chilton away from him. "What would he want with the boy? Now get back to your duties. Surely you two can see to it that no other orphans disappear tonight."

Dismissed, Chilton and Faris hurried from the room.

"So she means to put me out of business, does she?" Nathan said, twisting the large diamond ring on his finger. A cold, calculating smile crossed his face. "Well, I shall beat her at her own game. The time has come to inform my dear cousin of what Miss Wakefield has been up to. Let Devon convince her she would do better to spend her evenings sewing samplers."

Having enjoyed the luxury of a warm bath, Danielle slipped her arms into the thick robe the housekeeper had brought. Lord Stanton had been most generous in their accommodations. The rooms were large and beautifully decorated in shades of yellow and rose. The pattern of small flowers intricately worked into the woven fabric of the counterpane reminded Danielle of her bedchamber in Virginia; but after two years, such memories no longer carried the pain they once had. She still missed the closeness she had shared with her father, but she had finally come to terms with his death.

Danielle had been too young to remember her mother, who had died in childbirth when Danielle was only a year old. She knew her parents had sailed for the colonies when their own parents had disapproved of their marriage, but she had often wondered why her father had chosen to remain in Virginia after he had inherited Haverly House.

Now Haverly House was hers. To be sure, it would never be as grand as Burnshire. But had it been properly managed over the years, it might have been a profitable estate. As it was, it would take years of hard work and scrimping and saving to make it financially sound again.

In the meantime, money might be tight, but at least she was able to make a home for herself and the orphans. Danielle sank down in one of the large cushioned chairs and tucked her bare feet beneath her. Sometimes the tasks she had set for herself seemed overwhelming.

Even now her head ached, and she wanted nothing so much as to be able to crawl into bed and pull the covers up over her, but she had other things to consider. Had the men in the woods tonight followed them from the orphanage? And what if Aunt Margaret were to learn of her escapades? She would be furious.

Danielle knew she wasn't being entirely fair to her aunt. When they had come to England, Lady Bradford had abandoned her own social life in Bath to supervise her niece's London debut and had done everything possible to see that she became a lady. How could Danielle tell her that she was fighting a losing battle? Besides, it wasn't as if Danielle wanted things as they were. She dearly wished she could conform to what society expected of a young lady in her eighteenth year.

Danielle leaned forward and held out her hands to the warm fire. Most ladies her age were concentrating on finding wealthy husbands. What was so bad about that? She was a woman after all, and heaven only knew, Haverly House was in dire need of repairs. A husband could take some of the burden off her shoulders. It wasn't as if she hadn't had her fair share of suitors during her London season. But wasn't that where the problem lay? She had yet to meet a man who'd accept a household of children along with a bride, as well as an exceedingly slim dowry.

The bold image of Lord Stanton came uninvited to her thoughts, but she quickly abandoned the foolish notion. He was not to be considered. He was the enemy, and she would do well to keep that in mind when she found herself dwelling on his beguiling smile. Oh, he was charming, to be sure, but he was also a cursed

Stanton. The Stantons owned the orphanage, and it was under their direction that the unspeakable conditions there were allowed to continue. If he were ever to learn of her involvement, she very much doubted he would tolerate her behavior.

The bedchamber door opened and Brodie joined her by the fire. "The boy's asleep," Danielle's companion said. "You'd best try to get some also."

"How can I sleep?" Danielle slid her feet to the floor and stood. "Of all the carriages to happen by, it would have to be the duke's that came to our rescue. What is he doing at Burnshire anyway? Aunt Margaret said he left for London. Everyone knows he plans to ask Lady Emily to be his bride. He'll not get her answer sitting by his fire."

"Perhaps she refused."

An unexpected rush of relief confused Danielle. The man was totally without honor. Lady Emily and Lord Stanton were suited to each other. "The Lady Emily I met in London may make him wait for her answer, but she would never turn him down. She's well aware of the fortune he inherits once he marries."

"She'd better not make Lord Stanton wait too long. He might ask another."

Danielle's shoulders drooped. "Will it really make a difference?"

"Would you rather he forfeited his inheritance to his cousin? There would be no hope for the children then. The vicar would have complete control of everything. Even the orphanage."

"I refuse to dwell on that possibility, Brodie. All these months when the late duke's business agent was searching for Lord Stanton, I prayed each night he would find him before it was too late. Now I can only pray Lord Stanton will be different from his father." She raised a hand to her head and gently massaged her throbbing temples. She was so tired. Tired of fighting the indifference. Tired of fighting alone. Tears of frustration welled in her large green eyes.

"Hush, child," Brodie soothed, taking Danielle in her arms. "It will all work out for the best."

"Is it too much to hope that Lord Stanton will see what his cousin is doing and have him replaced?"

Brodie handed Danielle a handkerchief. "No, just unrealistic. Lady Bradford assures me it would take nothing short of an order from the bishop himself to oust a vicar from his position."

"But what of the children? Isn't their plight sufficient to warrant his removal?"

"What's happening at Westbryre happens at most of the orphanages. Some are better, some worse. You've done what you could. It's time to put an end to these abductions before you're caught."

Danielle pulled away. "I don't care if I am caught. I'll never stop!"

"And then what will become of the ones you have already saved?" Brodie asked calmly.

"You would have to return to Virginia with them." Danielle began to pace the room. "The house there will need some work after having been closed up for so long, but it's better than returning them to the orphanage."

"You talk as if you will be caught tomorrow," Brodie scolded.

"We have to face the fact that those men watching from the trees tonight may have followed us from the orphanage."

"Then all the more reason to call an end to this ludicrous misadventure."

"I know you're right, Brodie," Danielle conceded. "I guess I should stop feeling sorry for myself and do something about finding a way out of this mess."

She reached under the bed, pulled out the breeches she had stashed there earlier, and slipped them on under her robe. It was time she saw to getting them a carriage.

"Can you see if the lights are still lit in the stables?" she asked as she stuffed the bottom of her linen shirt into the buckskin breeches. "If the men on the road were from the orphanage, we haven't much time."

"What are you planning, Danny?" Brodie asked as she drew back the heavy drapes at the window. "You're not going to steal the horses again, are you? The stables are lit bright enough for a party. Someone will see you."

"I'll wait until everyone has retired." Danielle shoved her feet into her boots. "Besides which, I didn't steal horses the last time we found ourselves stranded. I merely borrowed them."

"Well, the last time you *borrowed* them, it took us most of the night to get home, and it was a week before I could open my mouth without my teeth rattling."

"I couldn't very well take prime stock or they would have been out beating the bushes for us. As it was, I had a devil of a time returning the nags without being caught."

Brodie sighed. She felt responsible for what was happening. Since Danielle's father died, she had tried to guide the young girl. When they had learned of Mr. Wakefield's estate in England, Brodie encouraged Danielle to go there.

It was time the girl met her father's relatives and established herself in a civilized world. Her father had spoiled her terribly, encouraging her wild, tomboyish ways. England was where Danielle belonged. The type of gentleman a lady should marry was hard to find in Virginia.

Brodie's frown deepened. She should never have let Danielle become involved with the situation at the orphanage. It was proving much too dangerous. She must put her foot down and insist Danielle stop.

A light knock sounded at the door. Brodie dropped the drapes back in place, then waited until Danielle scrambled into bed. Once the covers were pulled up to Danielle's chin, Brodie opened the door.

Mrs. Talbut, the housekeeper, stood in the hall. "I trust the accommodations meet with your satisfaction?"

Brodie nodded. "They are most adequate, thank you."

"His Grace would like the pleasure of your company for supper."

"Thank him for us, but Miss Walker was quite worn out by the accident and has already retired. Tell him the tea provided was more than enough."

Devon smiled when Mrs. Talbut delivered the message. So they thought to avoid him, did they? He had to admit they were clever. They seemed to have a well-rehearsed answer for everything, but he was no amateur when it came to intrigue.

He reopened the note his footman had taken from the dead driver's pocket. It was addressed to a stable in London requesting the hire of a coach-and-four to take them to a small village west of Norwich. Although the signature was difficult to read, the number of letters following the large W told him the name wasn't Walker.

It was obvious Mrs. Brodie had lied about the young lady's identity. But why did they feel the need to conceal it? If they knew him better, they wouldn't waste the effort. Given time, he would learn their secret.

After instructing Andrews, the butler, to have someone sent to retrieve his guests' luggage from the coach, Devon relaxed with a good supper. He didn't usually dwell on the concerns of others, but for the first time in days, he had something besides his upcoming marriage to occupy his mind.

Had the young lady been on her way to a clandestine meeting with her lover? But as quickly as the suspicion formed, he dismissed the idea. It was unlikely the companion would be a party to it.

Retiring to his study for an after-dinner brandy, Devon sat down at his oak desk. Emily would be wondering about his delay. He should at least send her a note of apology. Yet why bother? It wasn't as if she would refuse his offer.

A harsh smile darkened his handsome features. Distractedly, he pulled at his cravat. The carefully tied ends gave way and tumbled down the front of his gray embroidered waistcoat. Why wasn't he addressing the real problem? His business agent, Giles, had been right. In his absence, his cousin had been systematically draining the estates of huge sums of money. The discovery came as no surprise. Devon had learned at an early age not to trust Nathan.

His dark brows drew together in a frown. Would his father have continued to believe in Nathan's innocence had he known that someone had attempted to kill Devon to keep him from returning to England? What did it matter now? In the end, his father had turned to Nathan. But this was one time his cousin was not going to profit from his schemes. It was one of the few compensations Devon had for claiming his inheritance. The other was the fulfillment of one of his dreams. For the last several years, he had wanted to add the India trade routes to his voyages. Maybe it was time. With the extra funds now available to him, he would purchase the new ships needed.

He sipped his brandy and, as he'd done so many times of late, turned his thoughts to Emily. She was attractive, but her self-centered ways easily outweighed her blond good looks. Odd, how life's nightmares have a way of returning. She had been his father's choice seven years ago . . .

Reaching into his desk drawer, he pulled out a list of eligible young ladies his mother had prepared not long after she learned of the conditions of her husband's will. Devon's eyes once again scanned the names. Halfway down the first page, he stopped. Disgusted with himself, he crumpled the list and tossed it onto the desk. Why was he wasting his time? During the nine months his agent had spent finding him and the two it had taken Devon to return to England, most of those on the list had married and his mother had already crossed out a good many of the names.

His fingers touched the crumpled list. What would it be like to be married to Lady Emily Chalmers? Her greed reminded him strongly of Nathan's. Would her greed also prompt her to send someone to his bedchamber to plunge a knife in his heart as he slept? He leaned forward, resting his arms on the desk. Without realizing it, he had reopened the list and smoothed its pages. What would it hurt if he went over it again?

Methodically, Devon reviewed those who remained. Dipping a sharpened quill in the crystal inkwell, he drew a line through Lady Patricia's name. The announcement of her engagement had been carried in the morning's *Gazette.*

Miss Hester came next. Like most of the names, it had a comment written beside it. *Pleasant enough, but too weepy,* his mother had written. *Would more than likely faint dead away when faced with a husband who expected her to fulfill her wifely duties.* For a moment he seriously considered her, then dismissed the idea. He hadn't the patience to deal with such a wife.

Lady Emily Chalmers. It always came down to her. Was there truly no one else? He continued to study the pages, reevaluating each entry and the reason it would not do. He stopped at Wakefield.

Wakefield! That was the red-haired beauty's name! He opened the note to the London stables and studied the signature. There was no doubt in his mind. The name was Wakefield.

What was it his mother had told him about her? He slowly read the words written after her name. *Lady Bradford's niece.*

Lady Bradford was one of his mother's closest friends. It was no wonder Miss Wakefield's name was on the list. But wasn't Lady Bradford staying at Haverly House to chaperone her niece? Yet his guests had made a point of saying they were from Virginia. Devon read on.

A green-eyed, red-haired beauty. Independent. Strong-willed. Would never willingly accept a marriage under these terms.

That was what he was trying to remember. As his mother had told the story, old Lord Smythe had offered Miss Wakefield marriage, stating he needed an heir. If she married him, he would see that she wanted for nothing the rest of her days. Apparently, the feisty miss had calmly asked if he could also provide her with a new brain, since, if she accepted such an offer, she was sure to have lost the one God had given her. Lord Smythe retired to his country estate, where it was later rumored he had found a spouse to fit his specifications in his housekeeper.

Devon smiled. Yes, that tale aptly described the chit behind the little drama he had seen performed this evening. Having met Miss Wakefield, he was now intrigued by his mother's notation. So she would never *willingly* accept an offer of marriage under his terms? The word rang with its own challenge. If he only had more time, he might consider taking up the gauntlet.

Laying his quill aside, he leaned back in his chair. The room was growing dim. The candles, beginning to burn low, sputtered in pools of their own wax. Devon considered ringing for fresh ones, but it was late and he knew he should be getting to bed. Still, he continued to sit as each candle, one by one, flickered and went out.

Resting his elbows on the cushioned arms of his chair, he steepled his fingers before him. It had stopped snowing, and the moonlight threw vague silvery patterns across the carpet as it spilled through the squares of glass in the door that led to the back gardens.

The green fire of emerald eyes continued to illuminate his thoughts. Miss Danielle Wakefield was certainly different from the young women he had known in his youth. Yet he had a difficult time accepting that any lady would turn down an offer to become the next Duchess of Burnshire.

A slim figure moved along the path outside the study doors, and it took him a moment to realize the image was not conjured out of his own thoughts. The clothes of the trespasser might be those of a boy, but the curls pinned high on her head could belong to none other than Miss Wakefield. With a devilish grin on his face, he rose to follow.

With the house at last dark, Danielle slipped outside. Although the snow had stopped hours ago, the night had grown colder. Her boots made crunching sounds as she hurried along the snowy path to the stables. Slowly she eased open the heavy door and stepped inside. The stables were cloaked in black except for the pale light of an oil lamp hanging on a wooden peg over the grain bins. Its pierced tin cover set beads of light dancing along the straw-covered corridor, like stars tossed across the heavens. After a moment's hesitation, Danielle moved forward into the shimmering rays.

The horses shifted uneasily in their stalls as she crept along the dim passageway to the back. It was as she'd hoped—there was a small carriage in the last stall. Lacking the family crest, it was more than likely used by the servants to do the household shopping and wouldn't be immediately missed.

Devon, hidden in the deep shadows, slipped through the door behind her. The boy's clothing hung loosely on her slim frame. Whatever she had in mind, she obviously didn't want to be recognized. His blue eyes darkened with interest. Even the dim interior of the stables could not hide the enticing curves that pushed at her clothing when she moved.

He watched her circle the small coach, inspecting each wheel in turn. Next, she stooped to examine the undercarriage. An amused grin spread across his face. Her innocent gestures afforded him a most tantalizing view of a firm, rounded derriere.

"This one should do nicely," she said as she stood and wiped her dusty hands on the seat of her breeches.

Devon stepped up behind her. "Do nicely for what?"

Danielle spun around only to face the one person whose company she most wanted to avoid. "Must you sneak up on someone and scare them half out of their wits?" she demanded.

Devon appraised her lazily. Anger was most becoming to her. "Why do I have a strong feeling that you were just about to steal a pair of my horses?"

His sarcasm made Danielle tilt her chin defiantly. "I did not plan to steal anything, your Grace. They would have been returned within the week."

The lantern light danced within the lustrous strands of her rich auburn hair and Devon longed to run his fingers through the glowing ringlets. "Then you only meant to *borrow* the coach and horses?" he prompted, stepping toward her.

Danielle swallowed hard as she backed into the carriage. "Yes, your Grace."

"Yet you waited until everyone was bedded down for the night." He took another step closer.

Danielle could feel the heat of his body, his breath a whisper of warmth on her face. But she stood her ground, greeting his innuendos with silence. If the vicar had already been here and told him all about her exploits, then let him say so. She refused to rise to his bait.

Cupping her chin in his fingers, Devon searched her face. "Do I detect disappointment in those large green eyes?"

Danielle jerked her head away. "If Tom were—" Was she daft? Tom was younger than she was. He had been the first child to run away from the orphanage and come to Haverly House. Danielle had let him stay. It was through him that she had met Amy. He still carried messages to Amy, but she had no intention of involving him further.

"Tom?" Devon raised a questioning brow. "A lover perhaps?"

His sarcasm was not lost on Danielle. The arrogance of the man! The arrogance of all men! She had dealt with others of his kind the whole of her London season. It was always the same. If you spurned their advances, their egos couldn't accept it. They would attribute your lack of interest to an imagined attraction for another—a secret lover, one with whom you shared stolen kisses in the gardens. But what did she care what he thought of her? If the vicar had discovered her identity, she would be forced to leave England with the children. His Grace's assumption might prove the easiest explanation she could give for her reasons for being here.

"You'll not tell on me, will you?" she asked, flashing him one of her brightest smiles.

Although he had blatantly accused her of meeting a lover, Devon found himself disappointed at her answer. Thomas? The only Thomas he knew in the area was Lord Carruthers, but that was impossible. Even as a lad, he had heard the whispers about the man's household. But then she hadn't called him Thomas, had she? Tom was the name. Lady's Bradford's niece involved with a servant? The thought unsettled him. Didn't she realize that what she was doing would hurt Lady Bradford deeply? Her bold grin held no hint of conscience. She obviously cared for no one but herself. The lady definitely needed to be taught a lesson.

"And what do I get for my silence?" he asked, running a finger along her cheek.

Her entire body flamed at the thought. His purpose was clear. Why hadn't she considered the consequences of the lie? Her fictitious lover presented a variety of new problems, the least of which was Lord Stanton's lack of obligation to treat her like a lady. But it was too late to worry about that now. She needed the coach. If he thought her a tart, then she would play the part.

"A kiss in exchange for the coach," she offered, almost choking on the proposal. Determined to bluff her way through, Danielle batted her dark lashes at him flirtatiously. "I must have your answer before . . ." His intense gaze caused her to pause. Even in the dim light of the stables, his eyes seemed to burn through her.

"You must pay your debts first," he said, acknowledging her offer. She was no better than any of the other young ladies he knew. Their double standards on morals had always put him off. Yet he was strangely drawn to the minx. He pulled her into his arms.

"It grows late. I shall pay on my return . . ." Danielle began.

"But how am I to know if your kiss is worth the loan of my coach?" he interrupted, his voice growing husky.

His eyes raked over her, assessing her with a familiarity that was unsettling. Her cheeks grew warm under his bold perusal. Were dukes known to ravish their guests? Nervously, she ran her tongue over her lips. What was wrong with her? She had offered a kiss, no more. Since when had a kiss become fatal? Best to get the foul duty over with. Bravely, she threw back her head, closed her eyes, and offered her mouth to his. "Then be done with it."

His lips twitched at her attitude of martyrdom, but he was not about to cry off now. He'd not pass up the opportunity of tasting her kiss—not after the fire she had sparked in his loins.

He wrapped his arms around her. Lowering his head to hers, he covered her mouth with his own. She smelled of lavender. Her lips were soft, moist; the kiss she returned, shy. Her inexperience was evident. Either her lover was truly incompetent or she had lied.

Danielle stood stiff in his arms, mentally struggling against a kiss that could stir such strange emotions within her. His mouth moved against hers and she quickly forgot her earlier resolve to remain passive. Instinctively, she gave in to the sensations that his touch awakened and twined her arms about his neck.

He seemed to sense the change in her, for he pulled her closer, his lips demanding more—and she willingly gave. The kiss deepened and her legs threatened to give way. Hungrily, she savored the masculine scent of him, the feel of his strong arms. He shifted her within his embrace, his fingers working their way under her jacket. Possessively, he ran his hand up the back of her linen shirt.

Devon's advances met with no resistance. She didn't have a thing on under her shirt, and her skin was as smooth as velvet beneath his fingertips. He couldn't remember when a woman had felt so right to him—so absolutely perfect. He usually sailed clear of virgins, but how was he to know how strongly her simple kiss would affect him? He raised his head from hers. Her slumberous green eyes glowed with passion.

Suddenly, he wanted to be the one to teach her how to love a man, the one to nurture these passions that had surfaced from within her. He ran his hands up her slim, naked back. She trembled at his touch but didn't pull away. Her fingers, buried in the curls at the back of his neck, pulled his head down as she leaned into him. Was she aware of what she was risking, offering her lips to him? He was only human. How could he deny her? Crushing her to him, Devon demanded that her desire match the sudden intensity of his own unexpected need for her.

She did not disappoint him, but molded her body to his. Her soft moan against his lips tore at his conscience. This was Lady Bradford's niece. His mother would never forgive him. He would never forgive himself.

He pulled her arms from his neck and stepped back. He could see the confusion—the hurt—in her eyes. Never had he wanted someone as much as he wanted her. He should never have encouraged her. He was no better than a pirate. He had lured her out to sea, then cast her adrift. He couldn't just leave her there, or, to be sure, she would accept a lifeline from the next ship that passed her way. No, he must head her back to shore and crash her on the rocks. That way she would be much more prudent about testing the waters next time.

He slowly ran his fingertips across his lips as if tasting her kiss. "Adequate," he said. "Yes, adequate. You may borrow the coach."

A wave of humiliation washed over Danielle at her wanton response to his kiss. The warm flush on her face was sure to tell him all, but this was no time for self-incrimination. They must get home. "Which horses may I borrow?"

"There was nothing mentioned in our bargain of a pair of horses."

"But a coach is of little use without the horses."

"In much the same manner, a young woman is of little good without her reputation. A *lady* knows better than to trade her favors."

"You blackguard! What of my reputation must I sacrifice to obtain the horses?"

"You have nothing to offer that could compensate for my having to endure Lady Bradford's wrath should I let her niece leave dressed as she is. My driver will see to your return tomorrow."

The color drained from Danielle's face. It was all the confirmation he needed. He would wash his hands of the whole affair. It was time he took care of his own problems. Turning, he shouted for his head groom.

Danielle leaned back against the wooden slats of the stall. He knew who she was! What was she to do? Aunt Margaret would never forgive her for this.

Distractedly, she watched a small man come running down between the stalls, rubbing the last vestige of sleep from his eyes. She straightened, resigning herself to the humiliation of exposure when his Grace stepped between her and the groom.

"I'm leaving for London. Have my horse readied," he said.

"The dark bay, your Grace?"

"Yes, he should do. And, Hines," he instructed, raising his voice slightly, "there was someone on the path outside my window earlier. Have two stableboys watch the grounds. I'll not have any of the horses disappearing this evening."

The groom hurried away. Devon took Danielle by the arm and led her back to the house. Despite his evident disgust at her behavior, Danielle couldn't banish the kiss from her thoughts. She wondered if similar feelings tumbled through his mind. But without a word or a look in her direction, he left her at the door to her room.

Slumped against the door, Danielle watched as he strode down the hall, her heart in his pocket. True, she was too impulsive by far, always jumping into a situation before she thought it through, but never before had she questioned her ability to keep a tight rein on her heart. Well, she had surprised herself this time, and Brodie was right. If she didn't change her ways, there would be the devil to pay . . . or a dark-haired duke.

Tossing a heavy cloak about his shoulders, Devon returned to the stables. It was high time he put aside his irrational reluctance to take a wife. If he continued to put off the marriage, he would find himself sitting helplessly by while Nathan carted off all of Burnshire's wealth. But apparently even that wasn't enough for Nathan. Devon's fingers massaged the spot where the assailant's knife had pierced his side. He must not forget—Nathan wanted Burnshire and he would stop at nothing until it was his.

Devon mounted the dark stallion the groom held for him. The bite of the icy wind would help him keep everything in perspective. Lady Emily would be a perfect mistress for Burnshire. She would say and do all the right things. Everyone would approve of her—even his dead father. But he wanted more from his bride. When he looked into her eyes, he wanted the fires that burned there to be for him, not his wealth or title.

He sighed. No such woman existed. They had all been reared to grace their husbands' homes, perform their wifely duties like Christian martyrs, and produce heirs. Was there no woman in all of England with the spirit to spit in the eye of his wealth and the fire to warm his bed—and his soul?

Devon pulled his mount to an abrupt stop as the image of Danielle appeared in his head. A deep ache flared in his loins. Danielle had given him a glimpse of the flames that burned within her and he had turned her away. Yet what else could he have done? He would have been a cad to take advantage of her innocent response to what had obviously been her first taste of passion. It would be best to forget the seductive way she had looked at him through those dark, thick lashes. Anyway, despite what she had appeared to offer, it was all a charade. She had been interested in acquiring the coach only. He would be wise not to involve himself with whatever trouble she might have gotten herself into. He had enough problems of his own, the least of which was to soothe Lady Emily's feathers about his tardiness.

A smile broke across his rugged features. He almost wished she would turn him down. Then he'd visit Miss Wakefield and lay the blame for losing Lady Emily at her feet. Her coach accident had detained him, he would point out. To be sure, the red-haired beauty would rave at his accusations. But he would patiently wait until she had vented her anger. Then he would insist she marry him to rectify her guilt.

Devon laughed aloud at the scenario. Of course she would never agree, but the prospect of trying to convince her was most pleasant. Too pleasant.

Enough, he chastised himself. He was on his way to ask Lady Emily to be his wife. Why was he tormenting himself with Danielle's kiss?

Despite the cold, a calm warmth spread through him. He could almost feel her in his arms again, his lips seeking hers. Her body began to respond to the thought, to the taste of her lips, the feel of her body melting into his. He closed his eyes and the vision was so real he could almost see her standing before him, fresh from her bath. The scent of lavender water swirled around them. He swept her up in his arms and carried her off to his bedchamber. She was his.

"Hell and damnation!" he shouted. "She *will* be mine." Then, with a flick of his whip, he wheeled his mount about and urged him home.

Chapter 3

"**A** body always needs warm water on a chilly morning such as this, miss," the chambermaid said as she sat the pitcher on the pine table along the wall. Moving to the window, she drew open the heavy drapes.

Sunlight spilled across the polished floor and Danielle turned from the bright reflection. Whatever had possessed her to strike that ridiculous bargain with Lord Stanton last night? Her cheeks flushed warm at the thought. Never in all her eighteen years had one of her stunts failed so miserably. She had misjudged the situation and acted foolishly. Aunt Margaret would be horrified to learn that her only niece had sunk beyond all redemption.

But turning the incident over in her mind would not change anything. As soon as she could get her hands on a carriage, they would be on their way. There would be no Lord Stanton to stop her this time!

The maid laid out a fresh towel and a bar of scented soap. "Your fire's gone down, miss. I'll have it roaring again in no time." She knelt and placed a fresh log on the warm ashes.

"Who would I see about dispatching a note to the nearest inn?" Danielle asked. "I'll be needing to hire a carriage."

"That would be the groom, miss. He can send one of the stable lads. But you needn't worry about your coach, miss. When his Grace returned this morning, he told the coachman, Jem, to ready one for you and your companion this afternoon."

"Returned? His Grace returned this morning?" Danielle asked the girl, barely able to conceal her shock. Did that mean the duke hadn't left for London after all?

The maid leaned forward, her voice lowered to a whisper. "Toby says as how his Grace left late last night."

"Toby?"

The girl blushed as she rushed to explain. "Me and Toby are stepping out, you might say. He works in the stables. He says as how his Grace's face was as black as a thundercloud when he left, and when he came back this morning it was all sunshine. Toby thinks he went to ask Lady Emily to be his wife and she accepted."

Danielle couldn't explain the strange tightening of her chest at the thought. The possibility of the duke's marriage should please her. Let him marry the ravishingly beautiful Lady Emily. It was nothing to her.

The maid gave the fire a final inspection. "I told him how that was all a bit of nonsense. His Grace would never go asking a lady to marry him in the middle of the night."

Danielle combed her slim fingers through her tousled curls. Then why had he come back? she wondered. Surely he didn't expect to keep them here forever. No. He said he was going to London. Something must have happened to make him change his plans. *Oh, please, dear God, let it have been the condition of the roads and not the Vicar.*

"Would you like a hot cup of chocolate, miss?" the maid asked.

"Please, and a breakfast tray for my companion and the boy."

"The boy had breakfast with my Toby earlier, miss. One of the old duke's bitches had a litter of little ones, and Toby brought one in for the boy. They was sitting on the kitchen floor getting acquainted when I left, miss." She retrieved the empty water jug. "I'll bring a tray of chocolate and scones. His Grace is with one of the tenants now, but that shouldn't take long; then he'll be wishing to speak with you."

Danielle pushed the breakfast tray from her. Standing, she began to pace the large bedchamber. She could feel her companion's gaze on her, but it was impossible to concentrate on Brodie's questions when her thoughts kept returning to what the maid had said. *He'll be wishing to speak with you.*

It was unlike her not to confide in the older woman, but what could she say? That she had stood in the stables last evening and encouraged the Duke of Burnshire to kiss her? Brodie would think she'd taken leave of her senses.

At first, she had worried that he would tell Lady Bradford of her behavior. But upon reflection, she realized that if he exposed her, he would have to reveal his part in the misadventure.

Yet what was a mere kiss after all? Had the ploy been successful, she wouldn't be sitting here now. No! She would have taken the coach without another thought of what she had forfeited in the bargain to get it.

Danielle set her cup down with a force that threatened to crack the china saucer. She'd settle with him now! If her coach repairs were going to take too long, she would demand the loan of another—with a team of horses. A bargain was a bargain. She rose to her feet.

"What are you planning now?" Brodie asked suspiciously.

"You mustn't worry," Danielle answered. "You won't have to face his Grace this morning. We shall be leaving as soon as I collect on a debt."

She swept from the room before Brodie could ask questions she would rather not have to answer. She hadn't quite reached the stairs when she heard an angry voice from the foyer below.

"Where is he, Andrews?" someone demanded of the butler.

Danielle stopped dead in her tracks. It was the vicar! Careful not to be seen, she peeked over the banister.

"His Grace is with someone at the moment and has asked that he not be disturbed."

Danielle didn't have to see Andrews' face. The butler's rigid back and terse words clearly told her that he was displeased with the visitor's demands.

"I'll wait," the vicar snapped, dumping his greatcoat in the butler's arms as he pushed his way past. "Bring me a brandy!" he shouted over his shoulder as he entered the drawing room. "And not that bilge water you tried to pass off on me the last time."

Danielle clutched the banister. How was she to get the coach before the vicar spoke with the duke? Last night was humiliating enough. Now this. She could already envision the smug smile on Lord Stanton's face when his cousin told him of the abduction.

Was she always to be at a disadvantage where the man was concerned? Surely Lord Stanton had an Achilles' heel of his own. Danielle's eyes suddenly brightened and a grin spread across her face. He did indeed have one. He had to have a bride and that fact might just help her convince the vicar to leave.

A movement below distracted her and she watched in horror as Jeremy, chasing a small, spotted spaniel, crossed the hall and entered the drawing room. She rushed down the steps, laying her plan as she went. The vicar would not get the lad! She forced herself to slow her pace.

Calm. She must remain calm if he was to believe her story—at least until she could return to Haverly House. She'd have to hide the children before he came after them. She couldn't let him take them now. She drew a deep, steadying breath and entered the large room.

Her sudden appearance startled the vicar and he loosened his hold on the struggling boy. Free, Jeremy ran to Danielle's side.

"Go up to Brodie, dear," she calmly instructed,

pushing the lad toward the door. "I need to speak with the vicar."

Jeremy needed no coaxing. He turned and ran, the spaniel following close on his heels. With Jeremy out of immediate danger, she faced her adversary.

"Good morning, Vicar," Danielle greeted him, fighting back her anger. "His Grace's butler informed me you were here."

"I see you've found the lad." His words were clipped, cold.

How very civil of him not to come right out and accuse her of abducting the boy. More than likely, if she hadn't been staying at Burnshire, he would have arrived with the constable. And if her suspicions were correct, he would do nothing until he determined Lord Stanton's feelings on the matter. Perhaps she could be of help there.

"I understand you wish to speak with Devon," Danielle said, putting her plan in motion.

The vicar's eyebrows shot up. She prayed that the warmth that spread through her at her familiar use of Lord Stanton's Christian name did not wash her complexion in a telltale blush. "I'm afraid he's been detained, but perhaps I can be of assistance."

Nathan's cold gray eyes narrowed. "I've come on a personal matter my cousin wished me to handle." He slowly removed his gloves. "As it is, I've been most fortunate. Since you are here, I will be able to dispense with something else as well."

Reaching into the front of his frock coat, he withdrew the woolen cap Danielle had lost in the hedges and tossed it to her.

She caught it neatly. Determined that his threat not shake her resolve to get rid of him before the duke concluded his business with the tenant, Danielle carried it across the room and placed it calmly on one of the side tables. She turned back to the vicar, meeting his gaze with one of her own. "And that is?" she asked.

A footman entered with the brandy and Danielle was

forced to wait while he poured Nathan a healthy portion. *Hurry!* she wanted to scream, but that would not do. Her plan would certainly fail if she were to appear rushed. Instead, she sat down and carefully rearranged the folds of her skirt. Finally, the footman withdrew.

Nathan swirled the amber liquid, watching it slowly climb the crystal sides of the goblet. At last, his eyes rose to meet hers. "I will be taking the lad with me when I leave."

"Then your trip has been wasted, Vicar. You see, I've taken a liking to Jeremy."

Nathan strode across the room and slammed his glass down on the small table beside Danielle. "It's too late. He's sold!"

"We'll see what his Grace has to say about that."

Nathan grabbed Danielle's arm and pulled her to her feet. "And what will my cousin say when he finds out you abducted the lad?" he growled in her face.

Neither heard Devon step into the room. Standing quietly inside the door, he watched the drama unfolding before him. So the lad was from the orphanage. Had Nathan hoped to turn a tidy little profit on the boy?

Devon smiled. Miss Wakefield was certainly capable of handling Nathan on her own. Damn, the lady was even more beautiful when she was angry. And if the fire in her eyes continued to burn, he didn't envy Nathan his punishment.

"Devon is a decent man. He will be pleased with what I've done."

"Decent!" Nathan shouted. "Is it decent to burn down the croft of a tenant while in your cups?"

Devon's curiosity about how Danielle would respond to Nathan's lies was the only thing that kept him from letting his presence be known. If Danielle was to be his wife, she would have to know from the beginning that Nathan was not to be trusted.

Danielle met Nathan's vicious anger without flinching. She had all but forgotten the rumor that purported to explain why his Grace had left England. But hadn't there been more to it than just the fire?

"Take your hands off me!" she seethed. "How dare you discuss decency with me after the way you supervised the welfare of the children under your care."

"And you believe my cousin's hands are any cleaner than mine?" he asked, tightening his grip on her arm.

"It was a mere prank of a young man," Danielle said. Although, for the life of her, she didn't know why she felt she had to defend Lord Stanton.

"Prank?" Nathan dropped her arm. "Did I forget to mention that a man was asleep in the cottage when it burned?"

The color drained from Danielle's face.

"You see. My dear cousin cares for no one but himself. Not that the fellow who died was worth a second thought." A sly smile flitted across Nathan's face. "But the old duke was quite upset with Devon."

Danielle stood mesmerized by the exaltation on the vicar's face. Suddenly she knew. Nathan had set the fire, then made sure Lord Stanton was accused of it.

"Spare me your lies," she said calmly. "I might believe it of you, but not of his Grace."

Devon was pleased with her answer, even though he knew it came more from her distrust of Nathan than from her faith in him.

Nathan pushed his livid face into hers. "And what makes you think him so innocent?"

Danielle stood quietly. She would not be intimidated. "It is only natural that a wife should have faith in her husband."

Devon's decision to step forward was halted by her words. It was difficult to believe the prize was being dropped in his lap. To be sure, it was only an act, but this was one performance he would personally see Danielle carry through to its conclusion.

"You and my cousin married? Th-this cannot be," Nathan stammered. "I would have heard of it."

Devon had to give Danielle her due. She handled the

part of the blushing bride with all the subtlety of an accomplished actress.

WIth just the right touch of maidenly innocence, Danielle lowered her head. "We haven't exchanged our vows yet, but surely you are aware that it will have to be soon. We were—"

"Then you are not married," Nathan sneered.

"No, not as yet, but—"

"No more lies!" he snapped. "I have it on very good authority that his Grace plans to marry Lady Emily Chalmers."

Danielle's eyes misted with the appropriate unshed tears. "Lady Emily? Who is this Lady Emily?"

Nathan grabbed her wrist, twisting it as he pulled her up against him. "I am not the dupe you think me, Miss Wakefield," he snarled down at her. "I've had enough of your interferences. Either give the lad to me now or you and that companion of yours will not live long enough to plan the abduction of another child."

Danielle stared up into his eyes. He meant it. He would kill her for the boy.

Devon could not let this continue. He would never forgive himself if Nathan's anger were to become focused on Danielle. He cleared his throat. "How ungentlemanly of you, Nathan. I cannot turn my back without finding my future wife in your arms."

Nathan quickly released Danielle and turned to the doorway, wondering how long his cousin had been standing there, casually leaning against the doorjamb.

"I was merely congratulating the bride," he offered.

Devon sauntered across the room to Danielle's side. "It is I who is to be congratulated. Little did I know that the young lady I met in the colonies all those years ago would turn out to be such a beauty."

It took all her resolve to look him in the eye. Oh, piffle. Lord Stanton *would* have to conclude his business before she had finished with the vicar. One glimpse of that devilish twinkle in his eye and she knew she was in for it now.

Before she could step back, he pulled her into his

arms, knowing full well there was nothing she could say or do in front of the vicar. Danielle wanted nothing so much as to be able to kick his Grace in the shin, but that would have to wait until the vicar left.

"Nathan, Andrews said you wished to speak with me," Devon said, moving his hand up Danielle's back.

Nathan smiled thinly. Pulling a lace handkerchief from his cuff, he dabbed the side of his nose. To involve his cousin now would be foolish. "It being less than two weeks until you must marry, I thought to bring you the news that I was able to secure the special license. I meant only to check before I took the liberty of putting your intended's name on the document." He carefully replaced the handkerchief.

Devon smiled down at Danielle. "By all means, Nathan. I see no reason to wait until the wedding. You may write in Miss Wakefield's name."

Danielle lowered her eyes before his bold ones. He was clearly challenging her to deny the engagement. "Should we be discussing this before we have Aunt Margaret's permission?"

He cupped her chin in his long fingers and forced her to meet his gaze. "Do you truly believe Lady Bradford will object to her niece marrying the Duke of Burnshire?"

That beguiling lopsided grin of his told it all. He was not going to drop this. She would have to bide her time until Nathan left. Surely she could put up with his attempts to discomfort her until then. It was only his way of punishing her again. And, to be fair, she deserved it. No sooner had the thought formed in her mind than he lowered his head to hers. Danielle swallowed hard.

Holy Hannah! He was going to kiss her. Right here in front of God and everyone. She quickly turned in his arms. "Vicar, perhaps it would be better to leave the license with his Grace's agent and let him take care of it."

"Nonsense, love," Devon whispered into the ear she had turned to him. "Nathan will be performing the ceremony," he continued. "So it only seems right that he fill out the license."

Danielle trembled at the huskiness in his voice. His warm breath teased the sensitive lobe. There was no denying the unfamiliar feelings his nearness stirred in her. Brazenly, he nibbled at the tip of her ear, sapping her of the will to argue with him. It was hard to believe all he had to do was touch her and she turned into a bowl of watery mush. If she didn't get a hold on her emotions, she would soon be melting at his feet.

"Perhaps we should let Nathan return to his parish, love," Devon said. "We have a tremendous number of details to resolve before the wedding." He stepped back but still did not release Danielle. "Unless there is something else you require, Nathan, I must ask you to excuse us. I'm sure you understand that we have much to discuss."

The tight hold he maintained on her arm as Nathan strode angrily from the room left little doubt in Danielle's mind that he did indeed have many matters he wished to take up with her. She had to admit it had been gallant of him to back up her little white lie—even if he had taken unfair advantage of her in the process. And it was only fair that she express her gratitude. "Tha—"

"Not yet," he whispered, taking her arm again. "Breakfast has been laid in the morning room. We'll talk there."

He took her down a long hallway to the back of the house. A footman seemed to appear out of nowhere and opened the door for them. The breakfast room was delightful, with leaded glass doors that opened onto a secluded courtyard. In the center of the table was a bowl of fresh cut flowers. The heady scent of the hot-house blooms filled the room, reminding Danielle of all the luxuries money could buy.

"I apologize for cutting you short, but my dear cousin has a bad habit of listening behind closed doors," Devon explained as he seated her.

Danielle offered no reply. When would he ask her about the lies?

"You must try the fruit," he advised, taking his own place across from her. "It's from our greenhouses. Andrews fancies himself a gardener and is constantly badgering me for the space to grow more trees."

"Thank you, but I've eaten."

"So your maid told me." He unfolded his napkin and placed it across his lap. "But since estate matters have taken up most of my morning, please grant me the pleasure of your company while I partake of mine."

It was evident from his immaculate appearance that he hadn't spent the whole morning on estate matters. And she did rather like the way his fawn-colored coat of corduroy stretched across his broad shoulders, the lapels coming together over a white linen shirt and an intricately tied cravat.

Danielle suddenly felt dowdy in her rumpled traveling gown. She was happy to have broken her fast earlier. Lord Stanton's presence across the table would have prevented her from swallowing a bite.

"Do you have a particular day in mind?" Devon asked, picking up his knife.

"Day?"

"Given your conversation with Nathan, am I to assume you know about the provisions of my father's will?"

Embarrassed, she only nodded.

"Then you realize I must be wed by the end of next week, or Nathan inherits everything which should be mine." He waited for her acknowledgment, but she merely returned his direct gaze. Lord, but those green eyes had a way of distracting him. He busied himself with cutting his meat. "Given the date," he continued, "our wedding must be soon. In the meantime, you will return to Lady Bradford. You may inform her that I will be calling on her within the next day or two."

Danielle straightened in her chair. She would not allow him to get the better of her again. Last night in the stables was more than enough. "I wish to thank you for your support of my little lie, but—"

"Lie?" Devon looked up from the piece of ham he was cutting, his dark eyebrows rising in a quizzical arch.

"You surely didn't expect that I would actually marry you."

"It has been my experience that when someone says they are going to do something, they generally do it. Especially when it comes from the lips of a *lady*."

Her cheeks grew warm. "My words were meant for the vicar's ears only. I never intended that they go any further. As soon as I am gone, you may send a message to him explaining that it was all a mistake."

"I'm afraid it's a little late for that. At this very moment, I suspect Nathan is on his way to Lady Emily with the news that I plan to take another as my bride."

Danielle's brow furrowed. She had not thought to ruin his chances of marriage. "You'll have to tell her your cousin was mistaken," she said. "If she's the Lady Emily I met in London last season, I can safely say she'll believe anything, if only it's to her advantage."

"She has her own reasons for making me suffer, and I fear her pride is running a close second to greed in this matter. Another blow to her ego might be all that is needed for her to throw my offer of marriage back in my face."

"But she would be giving up her chance to become the next Duchess of Burnshire."

He leaned across the table and took Danielle's hand in his. "Let's not quibble. You are to be my bride."

She jerked her hand away. Her eyes met his, then flew to the door as she judged the possibility of opening it before he reached her.

"Don't try it," Devon stated calmly.

"You can't mean to keep me here against my will."

"Since you went out of your way to scotch my chances with Lady Emily, I think it only fair that you be the one to rectify my loss."

"And for that you expect me to marry you?" she asked, attempting to match his nonchalance. "Do you think me some naive country miss who will accept whatever you propose? I meant no harm and I appreciate your not giving me away to your cousin, but a small white lie is hardly justification for marriage."

"But I'm sure you'll agree that my silence on the abduction of the lad is."

Danielle's hopes were shattered. He knew. "You would use the welfare of a child to get what you want?"

"You needn't make it sound so awful. I would rather view it as the solution to both our problems. Unless, of course, there is someone else who holds your interest."

"No," she replied. "But then neither do you."

"As most young ladies marry without love, I see no problem. You'll find marriage to me has many advantages." He appraised her boldly, but lazily. "I have a reputation for being most generous with my women."

"Then I suggest you point that out to Lady Emily. I cannot but feel it will weigh more with her than it does with me."

Danielle stood and marched from the room, his laughter ringing behind her.

Danielle and Brodie remained in their rooms while the repairs were made on their coach. Danielle's only hope was that his Grace hadn't learned that they were staying at Haverly House. She would give the coachman directions to Aunt Margaret's home in Bath; then, when they were safely on their way, she would stop at the nearest inn, dismiss the duke's coachman, and hire a carriage. If the ruse worked, the duke would not learn of their true destination until she and Brodie had the children packed and away from Haverly House. Returning to her home in Virginia was the only option open to her now.

Though she saw no more of Lord Stanton that morning, Danielle could not keep him from her thoughts. It was ludicrous to think he would hold her to such a bargain, she kept telling herself. He had merely meant to scare her. It was his idea of punishment for her lies. Even so, she was relieved when the housekeeper appeared at her door to inform her the coach was ready.

The driver offered no objections when Danielle ordered him to head for Bath. Fortune was finally on their side. Lord Stanton was unaware that they were staying at Haverly House, and she could put aside her worries that he would carry his tales to Aunt Margaret. For the first time in hours, she could relax.

The horses were fresh and it wasn't long before they reached the first posting inn. Danielle asked one of the footmen to come forward and let down the steps. With her head held high and Brodie and Jeremy in tow, she climbed from the coach and swept across the straw-covered cobbles.

Slapping the last of her coins on the counter, Danielle hired the rig and driver she needed. Having dispensed with that, she confronted the duke's coachman. "Thank his Grace for his generous hospitality, but we will continue on our own from here."

Although the coachman offered no objections, Danielle suffered a twinge of conscience as she watched him leave. She hoped her actions wouldn't bring Lord Stanton's wrath down on him, but she had others to think of at the moment.

She watched as the fresh horses were hitched up to the rented coach. If only the first coach hadn't overturned, none of this would have happened. Now they could no longer remain at Haverly House. Aunt Margaret would be disappointed they were leaving England, and Danielle could only hope that she was doing the right thing. Returning to Virginia would be difficult. The house there had been standing vacant for over two years. But they would be safe. That was what was important.

When the horses were finally ready, Danielle stood aside as the steps were lowered once again. Brodie and Jeremy climbed aboard. With a quick prayer on her lips, ·

Danielle stepped up to the coach. Lifting the hem of her gown, she placed her gloved hand on the door. It was immediately covered by another.

Her heart caught in her throat as she slowly turned to confront a tall figure in a black cloak. Her eyes traveled from the hand-painted buttons of an embroidered waistcoat, past the silver clasp at the throat of a multicaped cloak, to the solid lines of a bronzed jaw. She stopped at the curved edges of his smile. She knew if she continued her perusal, she would have to deal with the boldness of a familiar pair of blue eyes.

Lord Stanton lowered his head to hers. "A lot of things have changed since I left England seven years ago, but I doubt very much if the road to Haverly House can be named among them."

"Sniveling snappers!" Danielle hissed. He'd known all along where she was staying.

"My, my. I don't know where it is that you pick up these expressions."

"What are you doing here?"

"Surely you didn't expect me to allow my fiancée to return home without a proper escort once I learned she thought to get the better of me by heading for Bath."

"I am not your fiancée," Danielle snapped, ignoring the gasp that came from Brodie, inside the coach.

Devon lowered his voice. "Are you willing to repeat that to Nathan and the constable?"

Danielle's heart sunk to her toes. He truly meant to turn Jeremy over to the vicar if she didn't marry him.

Devon lifted her chin, forcing her to meet his gaze. She stiffened, her green eyes ablaze with fire. He had expected as much. Miss Wakefield was not one to admit defeat. But she should also realize her announcement to Nathan had sealed her fate. He had but to secure Lady Bradford's consent. The note one of his servants had carried to Haverly House earlier should smooth the way.

"Shall we?" he said, motioning to the open carriage door.

She pulled away from him, spun around, and climbed into the coach.

"Tie my horse to the back," she heard him instruct the driver. "We're off to Haverly House. It's along the Old Church Road, north of Westbryre."

Taking her seat across from Brodie and the boy, Danielle prepared herself for Brodie's sharp reprimand. She most definitely deserved it. After all, Brodie had warned her time and again that if they continued with the abductions, it was only a matter of time before they were caught. But the rebuke didn't come. Brodie merely sat staring at her, apparently assessing the situation. A niggle of fear began to crawl up Danielle's spine. Brodie's wrath she could deal with, but this? It was almost as if Brodie had washed her hands of Danielle. Please, God, no. Brodie was more than just a governess. She was the closest thing to a mother that Danielle had. She started to protest her innocence when Lord Stanton climbed in and took the seat beside her.

This was all his fault. Damn him and his inheritance! Danielle cast a scathing glance at Lord Stanton. If the orphanage didn't depend so heavily on the Stanton funds, she could almost hope that when he did marry, the estate would prove to be worthless.

"Such a frown for such a lovely face," he mocked her as the coach lurched forward. "And 'tis I who should be wearing it. For, I swear, it felt as if you had cut my heart out when you left without so much as a by-your-leave."

"I only wish I had," she said between clenched teeth.

Devon pulled off his leather gloves. "Tut, tut. And to think of the mess that would have made on the carpets."

"The lad." Brodie finally spoke up. "If your conversation isn't too bloodthirsty for him, it certainly is for me."

"My apologies, Mrs. Brodie. I fear my broken heart got the better of me."

Brodie smiled at the absurdity.

Devon leaned across with an exaggerated guise of confidentiality and said, "Mrs. Brodie, I ask you. What is your opinion of a young lady who proclaims to the world she will be your bride and then, on the very same day, leaves without a word?"

"Is this true, Danielle?"

Danielle's fingers itched to slap that grin from Lord Stanton's face. "I proclaimed no such thing *to the world*. I merely mentioned to the vicar th—"

"The vicar!" Brodie choked. "When did you talk with the vicar?"

"He arrived at Burnshire this morning."

Brodie placed her arm protectively around Jeremy and stared in disbelief at her former student. "Heaven help us. What have you gotten us into now? And do not dance around the issue with me, young lady. Did you or did you not tell the vicar you were to marry his Grace?"

Danielle shifted uneasily in her seat, giving serious thought to carving Lord Stanton's *broken* heart out with a very dull knife. She glanced at Jeremy. Instead of being upset, he appeared only to be interested in what was being said.

"The vicar meant to take Jeremy back with him. It was the only way I had of stopping him. There was nothing more to it. Had it not been overheard by this . . . this . . ."

"Careful now, love," Devon taunted. "Bear in mind how that tongue of yours gets you into trouble."

". . . this Duke from Duck Water!" she continued.

"Danielle!" Brodie scolded. "Whatever has gotten into you?"

"She is a mite disrespectful, isn't she? She must have been quite a handful for you, trying to teach her manners and all."

Brodie's lips twitched. The man obviously knew he was waving a red flag in front of Danielle, but he seemed to enjoy baiting her. Of course, the idea of holding Danielle to the marriage was ludicrous. Even

Danielle should realize that. Yet she appeared to take his teasing seriously. This was delightful. His Grace was the first gentleman who had evoked more than casual indifference from her charge. If Danielle was beginning to form an attachment, it would certainly be an answer to Brodie's prayers. Marriage to the Duke of Burnshire would certainly put an end to the abductions. Brodie grinned broadly. If anyone could put a stop to Danielle's impulsive ways, this handsome duke would be first on her list of candidates.

Brodie wasn't above waving a few red flags of her own and proceeded to do so. "Her father was one for sparing the rod, your Grace."

"Brodie!" Danielle gasped.

"I suspected as much," Devon offered solemnly. "But you need not worry further. Once Danielle and I are wed—"

"We shall never be wed! I would rather marry a goat! I would even marry a—"

"But you are most fortunate to be marrying me instead," Devon said with stern indulgence before turning to the boy. "How long have you been at the orphanage, lad?"

Danielle bit back the rest of her words. It was evident what was behind his question to Jeremy. He was not going to drop his threat, and Brodie appeared to be falling in with his schemes. But once she got Brodie to herself and pointed out Lord Stanton's true character, he would soon lose his following. Let them talk about her as if she weren't there. It did not upset her.

As the miles sped by, Danielle remained silent, refusing to take part in the conversation as Devon regaled Brodie and Jeremy with tales of his life as a sea captain. She pointedly pulled the heavy drape back from the window and stared out at the white countryside.

The winter sun sank lower in the sky. Enveloped in a tangle of lavender-and-rose-ribboned clouds, it was soon lost to Danielle's view. Melancholy settled over Danielle like a cold blanket as the horses at last turned into the lane that led to Haverly House. This had become her home, but all that was changed now. She had little more than a day to pack only what was necessary and then . . .

Devon watched her lips curve in a smile. He was not totally insensitive. He would allow her to hatch her little schemes. It would keep her occupied while he continued to arrange their wedding.

He took Danielle's hand as the coach pulled to a stop in front of the steps of Haverly House. "Do not fret. I do not intend to intrude on your homecoming. You are free to give your own explanation for your tardy return."

He cast a conspiratorial glance at Brodie. "I will trust you to inform Lady Bradford that I will be calling on her."

"Brodie is not one of your servants, your Grace," Danielle snapped. "If you wish to speak with Aunt Margaret, you may send a note around tomorrow. I do not know of her plans. She may grant you the time."

Devon bowed his acknowledgment. "Should you have need of me sooner," he whispered, "I shall be staying at the Hat and Crown."

Despite the bright pink that painted her countenance, Danielle breathed a sigh of relief. He was giving her the opportunity she needed. By tomorrow morning, she, Brodie, and the children would be gone.

"Don't look so devastated," he said, deliberately misreading the gleam that leapt to her eyes. "I have every intention of doing this up proper, love. First I must ask Lady Bradford for your hand; then we will set the date."

"The first cold day in Hades," she mumbled as he climbed from the coach to retrieve his mount. He was trying to take over her life as if she had no choice in the matter. Well, she would show him.

Tom held the door for them as they stepped from the coach. She would need a few words with him. Amy must be warned that their exploits at the orphanage might have been discovered. It would be Tom's last visit.

As they climbed the front steps, the oak doors opened and a thin lad greeted them. Pockets stood silently in front of a stately butler.

Pockets was the only one of Danielle's orphans to come directly from the streets of London, where he had acquired his name because of an unusual article of clothing he wore. Wrongly accused by a merchant who believed his multi-pocketed coat to be the mark of a thief, Pockets welcomed the offer to work at Haverly House. He had taken an immediate liking to Danielle's butler, Dobbs, whose manners he put all his efforts into mimicking.

But now the sight of the huge stallion caused Pockets to forget himself for a moment. His eyes grew round as the big bay horse attempted to unseat the gentleman on his back. Pockets did not step back quickly enough when Dobbs threw the door open wide for Danielle to enter, and it crashed into him. Picking himself up off the floor, Pockets shyly lifted his eyes to the disapproving countenance of his idol. Danielle was both surprised and pleased to see the butler's stern demeanor appear to thaw at the sight of Pockets' tentative smile.

"So you have finally returned," Aunt Margaret boomed as she bore down on the weary travelers.

"I'll take Jeremy to his room," Brodie whispered. "You deal with Lady Bradford. Perhaps the news of your upcoming marriage will distract her from our late arrival."

Danielle glared back. "You're deriving entirely too much enjoyment from this."

"Aren't you?" Brodie asked innocently.

Danielle pasted a smile on her face and greeted her aunt. "Good afternoon, Aunt Margaret."

"None of your polite good afternoons. What, may I ask, happened? You were to be home last evening. Do you know the worry you caused me? What with me ailing and all, I could have suffered a relapse."

Danielle smiled at the rebuke. Green eyes only a

shade lighter than her own failed to reflect an illness Aunt Margaret was attempting to lay at her door.

Time had treated Lady Margaret kinder than most. Although she had seen the better part of sixty summers come and go, her skin remained smooth, and the gray that had begun to thread its way through the auburn strands of her thick hair only served to lend her a distinguished air of pattern-card gentility Danielle feared she herself would never acquire. Lady Bradford was a strange dichotomy of featherheaded feminine vagueness and instinctive shrewdness. Her innate ability to detect a mystery kept Danielle awake many a night. It would be no easy task explaining the delay to Aunt Margaret's satisfaction. "I'm sorry for the worry I must have caused you," Danielle apologized dutifully. "We had a slight delay. Then the weather turned bad."

Lady Bradford accepted the apology but remained untouched by her niece's display of meekness. She was well aware of the stubborn nature hidden behind those angelic smiles. "None of your excuses, young lady. You should be more careful. This is not the colonies, where everyone seems to be disgustingly robust. This is England. A lady must protect herself from the elements. I send you off to London for a short visit with Lady Montgomery and you fail to come home. I've no doubt it was the fault of those spirited horses you insist on hiring. When you failed to arrive last night, I knew you'd been left stranded somewhere. I've warned you many a time the fast pace you set would come to no good end."

Danielle attempted to look contrite. For a person who had a difficult time remembering what she had for breakfast, Lady Bradford had an uncanny way of making her case. "I am home safe now. You see, you need not have worried."

"I think I know my duty," Lady Bradford continued. "When you still hadn't returned this morning, I summoned Paddy—which I might point out was barely better than nothing. If you would only allow me to hire you a decent staff, I wouldn't be forced to deal with all these children you insist on employing. Paddy couldn't even recall where you had gone.''

''His name is Pockets, Aunt Margaret,'' Danielle corrected.

Lady Bradford dismissed Danielle's objection with a vague wave of her hand. ''I daresay, with a name such as that, he would prefer I call him Paddy.''

''For someone who is forever keeping me on my toes lest my every secret be known, you have an unbelievable ability to forget a name moments after it's been given.''

''It's always been a dreadful curse of mine,'' she said, giving the corner of her shawl a tug. ''Everyone knows I have a devil of a time with names, but after all, what does it matter? You need only get them right if there's a chance of mistaking who you're addressing or, perhaps, if they happen to belong to Prinny's latest mistress. And since you insist on burying yourself here in this drafty old house, trying to manage an estate best left to its creditors, neither you nor I will ever get the opportunity to address the latter.''

Danielle toyed with the strings of her reticule, feeling thankful that Aunt Margaret had been so easily distracted. ''Then you will be pleased to know I have decided to take your advice and repair to Bath. Do you think you can be ready by morning?''

''Morning? Why the hurry, child? And what of our guest?''

''Our guest?''

''We're expecting a guest for supper. Don't tell me you know nothing of the note I received earlier,'' Lady Bradford exclaimed.

''If we are expecting a guest, I'm sorry. But I see no problem. I'll have my maid get started packing immediately.''

Though puzzled at the sudden hurry, Lady Bradford turned to Pockets.

''Paddy,'' she said, ''bring down the trunks from the

attic. We will start packing at once—before Danielle changes her mind.''

"His name is Pockets, Aunt Margaret."

''Whoever,'' she countered as she patted Danielle's arm. ''If we are to entertain this evening and still be ready to leave tomorrow, you'd best get some rest. Why don't you lie down until supper?''

''Thank you, Aunt Margaret. I think I will.''

Lady Bradford watched her niece climb the stairs. ''What a shame,'' she muttered to herself. ''A beautiful girl like that and unmarried. Refused every one of her suitors. Will I ever find one to satisfy her?''

To be fair, Lady Bradford could sympathize with Danielle to some degree. She herself had little patience for the young men today. All they seemed to have on their minds was how fast their horses could run. She cringed at the thought of some of the conveyances they drove. Absolutely unsafe. She much preferred to ride in the same coach that had served her so well all these years. Most would say she should get something more fashionable, but she was not about to risk life and limb as many others did.

Her eyes lit on the gilt-edged missive she had received earlier. Surely Devon had not come all this way to ask after the welfare of an old lady. A suspicion began to form in her mind. Haverly House wasn't so remote that she hadn't heard the terms of the old duke's will. Everyone was talking about the fact that Devon would finally be marrying Lady Emily. Was it possible she had turned down his offer? Or had someone put the notion into his head that Danielle was available? Well, if that happened to be the case, she wasn't about to let this opportunity for matchmaking slip through her fingers.

Chapter 4

W arm strong arms . . . a ruggedly handsome face.
Haunting blue eyes stared down at Danielle.
Dark brows arched seductively. Slowly a pair of soft
lips lowered to hers. The kiss left her weak, yet at the
same time strangely fulfilled. The thought that she
should resist skipped across her mind, but like a bright
flicker of sunlight through the trees, it lived for just a
moment.

Do you, Danielle Wakefield, take this man to be . . . The
words broke the spell woven around her, and Danielle
struggled to wake from the nightmare. Despite the
coldness of the room, a fine sheen of perspiration clung
to her body.

She opened her eyes. The bedchamber looked
strangely small and empty. Then she remembered. She
had taken the room across the hall from hers so Mary
could start packing while she slept.

And then the dream came rushing back. It seemed
so vivid—so real. Whatever had she been thinking to
tell the vicar she was to be the next Duchess of Burnshire?

"Miss Danny," her maid called from the door.

"Come in, Mary."

"Lady Bradford said as how I was to make sure you
were up. It's time to dress for supper," Mary chatted
as she helped Danielle into a robe. "There's to be a
special guest this evening." She ventured a glance at
her mistress. Danielle wasn't generally known to give

in to the dictates of fashion while staying at Haverly House, and Mary wondered what proportions the battle would take before she had her mistress properly dressed.

Mary followed Danielle across the hall. No objections were made as she helped Danielle prepare for her bath. Danielle didn't appear to notice the soft woolen gown Mary had laid out on the bed. The maid sighed. Perhaps she was to be spared. "Once you're finished with your bath, I'll do your hair."

Danielle stepped into the tub. "Have you completed the packing?"

"The small trunk is packed, but I still have the dresses in the large wardrobe to prepare."

"The small trunk will be sufficient."

"Oh no, Miss Danny. Lady Bradford said as how I was to be sure your London gowns were packed."

Danielle sighed. She didn't have time to argue with Aunt Margaret over the necessity of a few ball gowns. It was more important that they be on their way before first light tomorrow.

"I'll try to get away early and help, Mary."

"That won't be necessary, Miss Danny. You just enjoy your supper. It won't take me long to finish in here. I'll get a few of the children to help me."

Danielle leaned back against the tub and closed her eyes. A small frown creased her forehead. She wasn't pleased with her decision to leave Haverly House, but it was too dangerous to remain. Once the vicar discovered the lie about the engagement, he was sure to inform Lord Stanton of the other abductions. What if, after learning the extent of her involvement, Lord Stanton decided to summon the constable after all? What purpose would all her efforts have served then? Aunt Margaret would feel betrayed by Danielle's prevarications. The children would be returned to the orphanage, and she would have hurt all those she cared for.

Her toilette complete, Danielle made her way to the stairs. She placed her hand on the banister, which curved gracefully along the stairs to the foyer below. The large, sweeping stairway had always been a favorite of hers. Even though the wood was dry and cracked, she would miss it when she left.

The sound of voices coming from the drawing room reminded her of their guest, and she quickened her pace. Aunt Margaret would be displeased that she was late.

"Danielle?" Lady Bradford turned as her niece entered. "There you are. Come meet our guest. You've heard me speak of his Grace, the Duke of Burnshire."

He was the guest? Too late to retreat, Danielle stepped forward. She longed to wipe the self-satisfied smile from his lips. He had known when he left them at the door that he would be returning in a few hours, yet he had let her think she wouldn't have to deal with him until tomorrow.

"I was just telling Devon how sorry we were to learn of his mother's failing health," Aunt Margaret said. "Lady Julia and I have been bosom bows since, well . . . well, forever."

Lady Julia. Danielle could have kicked herself for her stupidity. She should have put it together sooner. That was how Lord Stanton knew so much of her affairs. Lady Julia must have mentioned her in her letters to her son. Danielle bit her lip and reluctantly curtsied.

Devon gave a small nod. "There's no need for introductions, Lady Bradford," he said, bestowing Danielle a smug grin. "She's my—"

"We've met, Aunt Margaret." Danielle cut him short. "It's a pleasure to see you again, Lord Stanton," she lied as she extended her hand.

"Don't be so formal, Danielle. Call me Devon. I insist. Since we're—"

"Our acquaintance isn't of such long standing that I would feel it proper." She lowered her eyes demurely.

Devon took her hand. He was rather enjoying her efforts to keep him silent, but he did not intend to make it easy for her. Gently turning her hand over, he brought it to his lips. He felt her stiffen as they brushed her exposed wrist. "Yes, alas, we've only met once. But I knew, within those few hours, that our lives were destined to become one."

Ever the dutiful chaperone, Lady Margaret cleared her throat, effectively cutting short the exchange. "Would you care for a glass of ratafia, Devon?"

"I would be most pleased, Lady Bradford—particularly because it will enable me to keep two beautiful ladies within my sight."

"Ah, Devon," Aunt Margaret preened as she took a seat on the settee. "I'm delighted to see a pirate's life hasn't changed you. You're still quite the charmer."

Danielle glared at him. He was quite the charmer all right. But she'd had enough of his beguiling ways. The man was absolutely insufferable. Even after all this time, the warmth of his kiss still lingered on the edge of her lips—taunting and teasing. She had thought herself rid of him, yet here he was again. Did he really think all he had to do was show up at her door and she would willingly fall in with his schemes?

"Danielle, do come and sit down," Lady Bradford said.

Danielle crossed the room and took the seat beside her aunt. With the elegantly dressed duke standing in front of her hearth, the room suddenly appeared shabby. Despite all she'd done to restore the old drawing room, it was not enough. Nothing short of new draperies and carpets would brighten the room. She frowned at her guest. If he so much as hinted that marriage to him would enable her to take care of all this, she would have his head. What was more, though she might be forced to play the hostess for Aunt Margaret's sake, she'd be switched if she'd enjoy it.

If only to let him know of her displeasure, Danielle forced herself to meet Devon's gaze as he handed Aunt Margaret a goblet of the cordial. Yet he merely smiled that infuriating lopsided grin of his, setting her heart to racing again.

"Thank you, Devon," Lady Bradford said.

"Think nothing of it," he replied, next handing Danielle a drink. He purposely let his fingers trail along hers as he relinquished the glass, noting the delicate touch of pink that washed her face. "It is the least I can do after being forced to give you such short notice of my visit."

"Nonsense, Devon. We are fortunate to have you." Lady Bradford inclined toward her niece. "Devon dispatched a note saying he had a small matter of business he wished to discuss. I was so thrilled to hear from him. It isn't often we get to entertain a duke, is it, Danielle?"

"Business, Lord Stanton?" Danielle turned a critical eye on Devon. "Surely your agent could have handled it for you."

He smiled down at her, wondering whether he would ever get enough of her beauty. "I felt this was something which required my *personal* attention."

Danielle's eyes narrowed into bright green slits. She opened her mouth to speak, when Brodie entered the room with Pockets. Holy Hannah! She had forgotten all about the children. From the expression on Brodie's face, it was evident the possible consequences had occurred to her also.

Pockets straightened his shoulders and proudly announced that dinner was served. Then, turning on his heel, he marched out of the room. Danielle tried to excuse herself on the pretext of having a word with the cook, but Aunt Margaret would have none of it.

"Don't fuss so, Danielle. I've taken care of everything."

She had no alternative but to trail along with Brodie as Lord Stanton escorted Lady Bradford in to supper. She breathed a sigh of relief to see that the butler was serving the meal without the assistance of Pockets. The meal went rather smoothly, but Danielle could not say what she ate as one course followed another.

The last of the dishes had been cleared when the door behind Lord Stanton opened. Danielle cringed on seeing Sara and Molly enter with dessert. Knowing how proud the two orphan girls were of their accomplishments, Danielle managed to swallow the lump that had risen to her throat and attempted a smile. "Would you care for a raspberry tart, your Grace, or would a caramel cake confection be more to your liking?" Danielle asked before the little girls could open their mouths.

Lord Stanton impaled her with his piercing blue eyes. "It would seem you are having a difficult time acquiring servants in this area."

Lady Bradford leaned forward. "Danielle is forever hiring these urchins for positions much better filled by those who are qualified. I'm beginning to think there's not a servant in this house over four feet tall. Why, each day the butler threatens to quit. He feels it is beneath him to have to train a troop of—as he puts it—'ankle biters.' "

Devon glanced at Danielle, but she appeared to have developed a sudden interest in her dessert and would not meet his gaze. "Have you perhaps taken on a new charity, Lady Bradford?"

"I assure you, the project is my niece's alone," the older woman was quick to answer. "It's gotten so that Danielle and Brodie can't leave without bringing back another one."

Danielle cleared her throat dramatically. "I'm sure Lord Stanton doesn't wish to hear about our projects, Aunt Margaret."

"You're wrong, Danielle," Devon objected. "I suddenly find myself extremely fascinated by the subject. Let me ask you a question. Given the children you are . . . acquiring, shall we say, are you perhaps considering starting an orphanage of your own?"

He wasn't prepared for the deep emerald fire that ignited in the depths of her eyes. What would it be like to make them burn for him? The thought definitely merited further study. "Since the Stanton funds sponsor one, I would be more than willing to have my man of business give you a few tips."

"Have you visited your orphanage in Westbryre since your return?" Danielle asked.

If truth be known, he hadn't intended to involve himself with the home, but Danielle's note of sarcasm and Brodie's obvious discomfort in discussing the subject piqued his interest. To be honest, everything about Danielle was beginning to intrigue him. "Recent developments have convinced me that I should make an effort to do so immediately."

"I would hope you would also find it necessary to put forth an effort to know those you have in charge."

"You don't care for the Picketts?" He made a mental note to have his agent arrange for him to meet them. "They came highly recommended. I'm sure they would be more than happy to assist you in finding a place for the orphans you seem to have acquired."

"More than you can imagine," Danielle mumbled to herself.

"What an excellent idea, Devon," Lady Bradford added enthusiastically.

Danielle was on the brink of expressing her opinion of the idea when the butler entered with the port.

"Come along, ladies," Lady Bradford said. "We shall leave Lord Stanton to his port."

She stood and turned, the black lace of her gown majestically sweeping the floor behind her as she left the others to follow. After issuing orders for the card table to be set up in the drawing room, Lady Bradford took a place on the sofa, next to Brodie. "Danielle, will you please find a spot and light? Your pacing puts my delicate nerves on edge."

"I'm sorry, Aunt Margaret. I seem to have a lot on my mind lately."

"It's a shame husband hunting isn't one of them."

"Aunt Margaret!"

Brodie, who had chosen to while away her time sewing, bent over her sampler frame and tried to hide her amusement in the rhythm of her steady stitches.

Now that Lady Bradford had introduced the subject, she was not about to let it drop. "I'm well aware that you think marriage is not for you. Given the gentlemen you had to choose from last season, I can't say I blame you. But there are other men to be had. Consider Lord Stanton . . ."

"You consider him." Immediately, Danielle blushed at her own curtness. After a moment she went on. "I did not mean to sound harsh, Aunt Margaret, but surely it's clear his Grace and I would never suit. He seems egotistical, overbearing, and altogether too dictatorial for my taste."

"Listen to what you've said. If you would but consider it, I'm sure you would see that those are the qualities you should search for in a husband." Lady Bradford carefully rearranged the lace on the front of her gown before continuing. "I understood when you turned up your nose at the young bucks you met in London, but Devon's different. You would never see him bowing to someone to put himself in their good graces. He'd as soon tell them all to go to the devil. And, I might remind you, he is on the lookout for a wife."

"Is marriage all you and Brodie think about? I'm not a piece of produce, Aunt Margaret, to be displayed on market day."

"Land's sake, child, as if we would."

Danielle knelt before her. "I know that, Aunt Margaret. But you see, marriage doesn't seem to appeal to me. I have you and Brodie. That's all I need."

"Nonsense, child. There will come a time when you will tire of us. You'll want a home and children."

Danielle took Lady Bradford's hand in hers. "I will never tire of you. And as for children, I have them all around me."

"You have a generous heart, Danielle, but it's not the same as having a husband and children of your own."

"Aunt Margaret, I love these children as if they were my own."

"I'm aware of that, but it isn't natural. Maybe you should consider Westbryre for them," suggested Lady

Bradford. "After all, this Mr. Pickett sounds most competent."

Danielle rose to her feet. "Mr. Pickett is a . . . a . . ." She turned and strode to the card table. Getting a tight hold on her emotions, she turned back to her aunt. "The children deserve more than a bowl of watery gruel and a cold bed to go to at night. With us, they will be educated and sufficiently trained to secure *suitable* positions . . ." Danielle stopped her lecture when the butler arrived with the tea tray. Devon stood behind him.

One look at the broad grin on his face and Danielle knew he had heard everything. It was just like him to be sneaking around corners, listening to her conversations. Afraid her anger would get the better of her, Danielle took her seat beside the tea tray and busied herself rearranging the cups and saucers.

"Devon," Lady Bradford said, "talk some sense into this impetuous young niece of mine while we have our tea. If she continues, she'll have every orphan in England on her doorstep."

Devon moved a chair next to Danielle's and sat down. "What would be your solution, Miss Wakefield, since apparently you have so many criticisms of the conditions at Westbryre. Would you enter the orphanage in the dead of night and abduct the children from their beds?"

Concentrate on pouring the tea! Danielle commanded herself. He knew about Jeremy. Had he guessed about the others as well? *Please, dear God, don't let my hand shake now.* She gave Lord Stanton his cup. "Your Grace," she answered, her gaze locking with his, "given the opportunity, I would abduct them all."

"Nonsense, Danielle!" Lady Bradford broke in. There was no mistaking the stubborn set of her niece's slim jaw. It was time she put a stop to this before Devon got the wrong impression. "My niece is merely teasing, Devon—she would do no such thing. Now, Danielle, let's hear no more of orphans or orphanages. All that is over now. Danielle has decided to leave for

Bath in the morning, and there will be no room for any additional children.''

"Bath?" Devon said. So she thought to escape him? Pounds to pence her decision to leave was an exceedingly recent one. "When you retire to Bath, will you be leaving the children here?"

Danielle searched his face. Was he genuinely concerned or merely attempted to discomfort her? "Your Grace, these children are more than just servants. We teach them to read, write, and cipher—which, I might add, is more than most wives can do."

"A point well taken, Danielle, but then those skills are seldom required of wives. Generally they need do little more than act as hostesses in their husbands' homes and mothers to their children. Wouldn't you agree?"

Danielle forced herself to remain calm. "You talk as if a wife were a possession to be set on a shelf until her services are needed. A wife should share in all facets of her husband's life, not just his home. She should be able to dispense advice and comfort, should her husband have need of it. A wife is a partner—one who gives as well as takes."

"And is that the type of wife you will be, Danielle?"

She shifted uneasily in her chair. Drat the man. He had done it again. "The type of wife I plan on being is none of your concern, Lord Stanton," she stated.

"Danielle!" Lady Bradford scolded. "We'll have no more such talk. If you wish to punish Devon for his views, do so at the card table, for he and I shall attempt to take on you and Brodie at a game of whist."

Seeing the challenging light in Lord Stanton's eye and the it's-no-more-than-you-deserve smile on Brodie's face, Danielle agreed. She was quite skilled at cards and was more than prepared to give the man a much-needed setdown.

The cards were dealt and the playing began. As game followed game, Danielle found it more and more difficult to hold her own. Not only was the man playing havoc with her concentration, but he had the devil's own luck, and Brodie certainly wasn't helping the situation. It was almost as if Lord Stanton's skills pleased her. Danielle laid down her last card and took the game. She would need a lot more hands like that one to win back the points they had lost on the previous games.

Lady Bradford picked up the cards and began to deal. She stole a quick glance at her niece, but Danielle's attention remained diligently on her cards. "Devon, I've been meaning to ask you. Did you find yourself a bride?" she said, in an attempt to liven up the conversation.

"Aunt Margaret!" Danielle interjected frantically. "If Lord Stanton wished to discuss his marital plans, I'm sure he would have enlightened us on his own."

Lady Bradford waved the objection aside. "Now, Danielle, don't be prudish. Gentlemen are notoriously shy about such things and it generally takes a woman to coax the information from them." She turned a hopeful eye to Devon. "Well?"

Devon grinned broadly. "Alas, my father left me with little choice."

Danielle focused her attention on her cards and calmly rearranged them. She would not give him the satisfaction of knowing the unsettling effect this conversation was having on her.

Lady Bradford leaned forward. "Then you intend on asking for someone. Excellent. Excellent. I was concerned you would let pride make your decision. I hope whoever you have settled on is someone worthy of you?" she asked coyly.

"Worthy? Let me think on that a moment."

At that, Danielle's head popped up, and Devon paused to appreciate the way she lifted her chin defiantly, and the deep jade of her dark-lashed eyes. She was daring him to say more.

Devon kept his eyes on Danielle. He didn't bother checking his hand. He placed his bid, then answered. "When marriage is a necessity, does the worthiness of the bride really matter?"

Brodie quickly passed.

Lady Bradford studied her cards for a moment. "I cannot imagine whatever possessed your father to put that dreadful stipulation in his will," she stated, trying to keep the disappointment from her voice. She made her bid. "No one was more surprised than Lady Julia and I to hear the terms. She was furious. I can't say that I blame her. To run the risk of Burnshire going out of the family is insane. And to the parish of Westbryre of all things."

"Burnshire was never in jeopardy of that, Lady Bradford. It's entailed to the one holding the title. Only the surrounding lands and the funds would go to Westbryre."

"It's unforgivable. What good is Burnshire without the lands or the wealth to support it? Why, if everything were to go to Westbryre, that pompous ass of a cousin would be in complete control and . . ."

Danielle's mind closed to the rest of Aunt Margaret's words. Had her impulsive announcement to the vicar truly ruined Lord Stanton's chance of marrying Lady Emily?

"It's your play, Danielle," Lady Bradford stated for the second time.

"What?"

"I played the queen. It is your play now."

"Yes . . . I see."

She had started to lay down her card when she felt someone's foot nudge hers. Her eyes flew to Lord Stanton. Amusement crept wantonly across his features as he moved the toe of his boot up her ankle.

"Perhaps you are willing to admit defeat and concede the game," he suggested.

Danielle shifted in her chair, casually moving her foot out of his reach, but his boot seemed to find her again. She fixed him with a stern eye. "Lord Stanton, Brodie and I are still capable of besting you."

"Do not speak for me, Danielle," Brodie protested. "I passed."

Danielle ignored the protest. "Do your worst, Lord

Stanton. We are prepared." She laid down a card, then moaned when Devon played the king.

Devon boldly ran his foot along her trim ankle, finding it all too easy to forget there were others in the room. "Danielle, it's obvious your partner cannot support you in this game." He smiled at her scowl and moved the toe of his boot higher. "Though heaven forbid that I should appear a villain. I would not wish my luck to discourage you from continuing," he added.

Danielle once again moved her foot. "Do not burden yourself with the thought that anything you've said could cause me to do something I do not wish to do. If you knew me, you would know I play to win and usually succeed."

Lady Bradford, who had been watching this verbal exchange with interest, turned to the young man and said, "I must warn you, Devon, my niece is a most formidable player. Her father taught her to be as skilled as a man at the game. And most other things," she casually added.

Devon placed his hand on his chest in mock despair, his eyes never leaving Danielle's. "Why, Lady Bradford, I'm disappointed in you. I thought us fast friends. Now you inform me that you have pitted me against a veritable gamester. And at your own table. Did you hope to ruthlessly fleece me of my meager funds?"

"Meager funds! Hah!" Lady Bradford laughed. "Devon, you were forever warm in the pockets. I'd have no qualms about setting you up for a royal fleecing. If you have found your bride, you can well afford to spare a few coins to us women."

His toe once more caressed the top of Danielle's slipper. "I have found my bride, Lady Bradford."

"Has Lady Emily accepted?" the older woman asked. "I swear, I heard nothing."

"Do not feel as if the gossips have let you down. I only learned of my intended's acceptance this morning."

"This morning?"

"Yes. Didn't Danielle tell you?"

Lady Bradford looked at her niece. "Danielle?"

"I'm sorry, Aunt Margaret. I did not know Lady Emily had accepted his offer," Danielle said, feeling sure that she had at last ended his cat-and-mouse game.

"Don't tease your aunt, Danielle," Devon said, taking a firm hold on her hand. "Don't you think it's time we told her?"

Danielle's refusal to answer had nothing to do with the lump that had formed in her throat. Lord Stanton's boot was now slowly making its way well above her ankle.

"With your permission, Lady Bradford," he continued, "Danielle has consented to be my wife."

Chapter 5

"I've brought your morning chocolate, Miss Danny," Mary said as she set down the tray. "You'd best hurry. The maids will be wanting to clean this room soon." Mary lifted the linen napkin from the tray and opened it with a quick snap.

"Maids?" Danielle mumbled irritably. Another night with but brief snatches of sleep was doing little for her temperament.

"Why, a whole army of them arrived just before light this morning." Mary clutched the napkin to her breast. "Isn't it romantic?"

"Romantic?" Had the entire household gone mad? Danielle wondered.

"Oh my, yes," the maid cooed. "A handsome gentleman like Lord Stanton sweeps you off your feet. Him a duke and all and still he doesn't want to put a burden on us. Why, when the carriages arrived with all the food, cook said as how she could marry him herself. Why, there was . . ."

"And she can very well have him," Danielle mumbled as she tried to ignore Mary's cataloging of Lord Stanton's attributes. Anger boiled within her. So, he was so sure of her acceptance that he'd come fully prepared. Waltzing in here last evening—all confidence and smiles. Her opinion of the matter didn't appear to count. She should never have let it reach this point.

She had been dumbfounded when he had told Aunt Margaret of the proposal. Then, seeing the look of im-

77

mense pleasure on Lady Bradford's face, Danielle had hesitated in making her denial, and before she knew it, it was too late. Aunt Margaret was welcoming Lord Stanton into the family, even inviting him to stay until after the wedding. Clearly, she'd let this farce continue long enough.

"Please tell Tom I wish to see him."

"But, Miss Danny, he left for London hours ago."

"Left?"

"Don't look so surprised. Someone had to deliver the announcement to the *Gazette*."

"He goes too far," Danielle muttered, tossing aside the covers. She would deal with Lord Stanton now—before Aunt Margaret woke up. "Where is his Grace now?"

"The butler was preparing to serve him breakfast when I collected your chocolate from the kitchen."

"Help me dress, Mary. It's time someone informed Lord Stanton just who is in charge of this household. Oh, and fetch me my riding boots."

"Your riding boots?"

Danielle smiled to herself. "Yes, the ones with the hard heels."

She burst into the breakfast room less than an hour later, only to find Lady Bradford seated at the table instead of Lord Stanton.

"Good morning, Danielle."

Danielle swallowed her frustration. "Good morning, Aunt Margaret. You're up unusually early." After placing a kiss on the older woman's cheek, she slid into the chair Pockets held for her at the other end of the table.

"We haven't much time, Danielle. The invitations must go out, not to mention the fact that I have to go over a menu with cook. The ballroom is yet to be readied. Your gown . . ." Lady Bradford paused. "It's a shame we haven't time to arrange the wedding I had planned to give you."

Danielle lowered her head. Once again she was about

to disappoint her aunt. It had never occurred to Lady
Bradford that Danielle might not accept the duke's proposal. Taking a deep breath, she let the words spill
out. "Aunt Margaret, there will be no wedding."

"No wedding? Such nonsense, child! The thought
merely overwhelms you now. Once you become accustomed to the idea, you will realize how fortunate you
are."

Fortunate! Danielle bit down on her lip to keep from
lashing out. She would never be the grateful, willing
bride. But her argument was with his Grace, not Aunt
Margaret. She very much doubted that he even realized he was forcing her into something he might very
well regret. After all, wives had been known to poison
their husbands . . .

"Where is Lord Stanton this morning?" she asked.

"Why, here he is now." Lady Bradford leaned forward and whispered, "I was a bit chilled, and what
with the maids being so busy, he fetched my shawl for
me."

"How very thoughtful," Danielle said, hoping her
aunt did not notice the bitter edge to her words.

Devon paused for a moment in the doorway as if he
were a man who knew the value in being cautious.
Except for his white linen shirt, he was dressed all in
dark blue, a color that went well with his eyes. He
looked at Danielle and her heart seemed to leap in her
throat. It should be a sin for someone to be so handsome. How was she ever going to convince Aunt Margaret that she had no wish to marry him? If she could
only hold her tongue, it would be best to settle this
with his Grace in private.

"Good morning, my dear," Lord Stanton said, seating himself at Danielle's right. "You look particularly
lovely. Is it for my benefit?"

She cast him a withering glance. "I dress to please
myself, your Grace."

A broad smile creased his handsome face. "I trust
you slept well?"

"Quite well, considering the viper that crept into our

midst last night," she mumbled as she shoved her spoon into a particularly fat coddled egg.

"A snake!" Lady Bradford shrieked.

Danielle's spoon slipped, sending a warm river of yolk across her plate. She hadn't realized her aunt would hear what was meant for Lord Stanton's ears only. "Now, Aunt Margaret, please don't upset yourself. I should never have mentioned the incident."

Lady Bradford fanned her flushed face. "There was a snake in the house last evening? I knew it. We should never have stayed here. I should have insisted the place remained closed."

Danielle rolled her eyes. Her attempt to put Lord Stanton in his place was going awry. Turning, she bestowed him one of her coldest stares, but he merely gave her that smug grin of his and continued to spread a generous portion of jam on his muffin. The man was infuriating. "I'm sure you've seen them before, your Grace," Danielle said. "It was one of those disgusting ones you sometimes see behind the stables. Nothing dangerous, just annoying."

She was sure he had gotten the meaning of her comment, yet it didn't appear to bother him in the least. His laughing blue eyes mocked her efforts.

"All the more reason, Lady Bradford, that we move forward with the plans for the wedding. Wouldn't you agree, Danielle?"

"Good heavens, yes," Lady Bradford interjected. "Brodie and I have already begun a guest list. Nothing large, mind you. A few neighbors, a few friends."

"The wedding is set for the end of this week," Devon added as he watched the intriguing way Danielle's green eyes darkened when she was angry. "There was no time for the posting of banns," he continued, "but under the circumstances, I'm sure everyone will understand."

"Enough!" Danielle leapt from her chair, knocking her cup of coffee to the floor. She'd had all she could take of Lord Stanton's high-handed interference. "The circumstances be hanged!"

"Danielle!" Lady Bradford was visibly shocked.

"I'm sorry, Aunt Margaret, but there will be no wedding."

Turning slightly in his chair, Devon leaned back and stared up at her. The draperies were opened behind her and she stood bathed in the morning light, her hair an enchanting halo of red.

"We haven't much time, love," Devon stated calmly. "I expect Nathan will be returning tomorrow to claim Jeremy."

Danielle's legs felt as if they'd suddenly turned to water, and she slowly sank back down in her chair.

"Returning?" Lady Bradford asked. "I'm surprised he would absent himself from Westbryre on account of a child."

"It came as quite a surprise to me also. Especially after learning of the problem he encountered at the orphanage." Devon ventured a glance at Danielle. Deep emerald pools of green glittered back at him from beneath her dark lashes. Her undivided attention pleased him and he continued. "It all started with a troupe of players I came upon two nights ago. An accident left them stranded. One appeared to be injured and I offered them the hospitality of Burnshire until my man could make the necessary repairs on their coach. In exchange, the actress insisted on giving a demonstration of her talents. Nathan arrived quite unexpectedly, and upon reflection, I feel the drama was enacted solely for his benefit."

This tickled Lady Bradford's sense of the ridiculous and she laughed. "My boy, are you telling me she preferred the attention of that self-righteous idiot to you?"

A smile tilted the corners of Devon's lips. "What can I say? The performance was brilliant. She had his full attention. Nathan was so taken by her that he felt compelled to rush to Lady Emily Chalmers with the details."

"Fiddlesticks, Devon," Lady Bradford snorted. "Nathan would never be taken in by a pretty face. And

I can't even begin to imagine his reasons for sharing the performance with Lady Emily.''

Devon lifted his hands in mock despair. "I'm only relating what I observed. I must say, I was surprised myself. I've never seen a woman have quite that effect on him." Casting Danielle a significant glance, he continued. "I can only justify his behavior by adding that the woman was most attractive.''

"Hum! I find it hard to believe any woman, no matter how beautiful, could melt Nathan's heart.''

"But that was not the most surprising thing." Devon brought his cup of coffee to his lips. Boldly, he smiled over the rim, daring Danielle to object.

She returned the smile with a tight one of her own. She wasn't about to let him suspect that the conversation was having a shattering effect on her. Yet what could she do or say to stop him from exposing her crimes? "Aunt Margaret, don't you think it's time we started on the invitations?" she said, desperately hoping to distract her aunt.

"As soon as Devon finishes his story, child." Lady Bradford smiled at the duke. "Do not keep us dangling. What happened next?''

Devon's gaze met and held Danielle's as he lowered his cup. "When she left, she took something of great importance belonging to Nathan." The sudden paleness of Danielle's face meant Lady Bradford knew nothing of the abduction. His suspicions were confirmed. Danielle would not want her secret known.

"He knew this and he let her leave?" Lady Bradford demanded.

"He knew she had what was his. She did everything but wave it under his nose. He sat there, wanting it back more than anything. Yet at the same time he did not wish to challenge her. It was a pleasure to watch.'' Having delivered the bit of fluff and nonsense, Devon leaned back to observe its effect.

Lady Bradford shook her head in amazement. "Had this not come from you, Devon, I would never have believed it. Nathan in love.''

"Did I say love?" Devon stretched his long legs out before him. "No. It was more as if he was entranced by what she had to say."

Danielle sat stiffly in her chair. How could such a handsome man be such a devil? "A most interesting tale, your Grace," she said coolly, revealing none of the emotions that raged within her. "From the little I have heard of your cousin, he probably deserved to lose what was taken from him. I heartily applaud your actress friend."

He weighed her calm demeanor against the risks she had taken with Nathan. Surely he was not mistaken. Convinced the child was the key to obtaining her co-operation, he proceeded. "Don't misunderstand. The move was brilliant. Unfortunately, my cousin is not one to be dazzled for long. Once the shine of her scheme dulls, he will know it for the lie that it is and follow her to the ends of the earth to claim what is his."

It had never occurred to Danielle that Nathan might actually follow her to Virginia to retrieve Jeremy. The thought appalled her. Could he be that set on revenge? Or had Lord Stanton read her thoughts and meant to scare her? "And what would you suggest the actress do, your Grace?" she asked skeptically.

Devon placed his napkin on the table. "I see that she has but three choices. One, she can return what she has taken. Two, she can wait until Nathan comes to collect it. In which case, she will be forced to return it or . . ." He paused deliberately.

His toe touched hers. This was the moment she had hoped for. "And three, your Grace?" she asked innocently as she attempted to concentrate on the exact position of his foot.

"Oh, that's the simplest solution," he said, boldly rubbing his foot against hers. "She has but to seek the protection of someone Nathan fears. Then she can keep what she has taken."

Lady Bradford reached for her coffee cup and didn't see the pain that etched itself on Devon's face when Danielle brought the heel of her boot down on his toe.

After a delicate sip, she returned her cup to its saucer. "I can think of no one he should fear more than you, Devon. Now that you will be taking over the affairs of Burnshire, Nathan would be a fool to cause you to look closely into his affairs. But enough of Nathan. We have a wedding to plan. Come along, Danielle."

"I shall be with you shortly, Aunt Margaret. There are a few things I need to discuss with Lord Stanton."

Lady Bradford considered the advisability of leaving the two of them alone. True, they were to be married, but a girl had to be so careful of her reputation. Servants did talk. Still, would their pint-sized versions of domestics know the difference? she wondered. "Danielle, don't be too long. I will be with Brodie going over the guest list when you finish here."

Danielle waited until Pockets had closed the door behind her aunt before turning to Devon. "You mean to go through with this, don't you?"

He reached down to rub his toe. "You hurt my foot."

"Excellent," she replied. "I meant to hurt it. Now tell me, surely you do not plan on actually marrying me."

"Don't look at me as if I were some type of monster. I meant what I said. Without me, Nathan will have no difficulty getting Jeremy back. The constable will not look on your actions with favor."

"Why would Nathan back away if you were to become involved? From all I have heard, it's next to impossible to have him removed."

"As the Duke of Burnshire, I hold the purse strings of the parish." Devon straightened and took her hand. "Given the right persuasion, I might be convinced to stir myself sufficiently to make Nathan's life at Westbryre so unbearable that he requests a parish elsewhere."

"The right persuasion?" she repeated warily. He was dangling another bargain in front of her. She knew from experience to beware of the string he most certainly had tied to it.

"You needn't look as if I plan on asking for your

head on a platter. You have but to marry me and I will take care of Nathan for you.''

The wide-eyed look of innocence Devon was beginning to recognize crossed Danielle's face. She was accepting this much more calmly than he had dared hope.

''This influence you have over Nathan,'' she asked, ''is it sufficient to allow me to keep *all* I have taken from the Vicar?''

He slowly perused this new Danielle. The deceptive serenity of her face was negated by the smug delight that danced within the spring-bud green of her eyes. Yet despite his doubts, he fully intended to take advantage of the situation. After all, how many children could she have abducted? Three, at the most four? ''Nathan wouldn't dare challenge your right to keep Jeremy—and the others—after you become my wife.''

''Yes,'' Danielle said thoughtfully. ''I can see that marriage might prove to be a most effective measure.''

Danielle sat atop a large trunk which had been brought down from the attic. Thirteen solemn faces stared back at her, each one reflecting its own fear at her announcement that she would soon be marrying the Duke of Burnshire.

''You need not worry that this will change anything, children. When I leave for Burnshire, I will be taking you with me.'' Danielle paused.

Pockets stood up. ''All of us?'' he asked.

''I would not have agreed to the marriage otherwise. But I must be honest and say the duke does not know how many children we have, and until the wedding is over, I wouldn't want him to find out.''

''Ye want us to 'ide, Miss Danny?''

''I think it would be best,'' she said. ''Perhaps we can make a game of it. We can pretend we are on a special mission for the king and must be careful not to be seen by Napoleon's spies.''

''And if the duke captures us, we'll attack,'' Pockets shouted, waving his arms as if he wielded a great sword.

Danielle laughed. "I think it best if we merely avoid being captured."

"I rather fancied runnin' 'im through," Pockets grumbled as he lowered his imaginary sword.

"Well, try to curb the urge. I know that makes for a very dull game, but it will only be for a few days, I promise."

"Wat about me 'orses, Miss Danny?" Tom asked.

"You and Pockets may go about your duties as usual, Tom. The only ones I wish to keep from the duke's notice are those he has not seen."

" 'E'll not be sending us back, will 'e?" one of the younger boys asked.

Danielle reached out and took his hand. "No one goes back to the orphanage," she said as she stood. She wrinkled her face into an evil grin. "And if anyone tries to return you, I shall take Pockets' sharp sword and run them all through."

She left the children giggling at her absurdity.

"The wedding's tomorrow, Brodie. He's not going to cancel it now."

"He'll never agree to it!" Brodie declared.

"But you see, he already has." Danielle folded the last of the children's garments and placed them in the trunk.

"And you're going to tell me now that he knew the bargain included thirteen children?"

"I don't recall that a specific number was mentioned."

"And you don't plan on mentioning one until it's too late. That's the real reason for all this deception, isn't it?" Brodie placed her hands on her broad hips. "Lord Stanton will never accept this."

"I am not the villain, Brodie. He is. He was the one to barter a child's welfare for my agreement to this marriage."

"That doesn't mean he will allow you to keep all the young ones."

"He can hardly refuse in front of the wedding

guests.'' Danielle jerked a small nightdress from its hook behind the door and dropped it into the trunk. ''To be sure, it will not be a marriage he will be pleased with. But if it's a wife he wants, it's a wife he shall get.''

''And you intend to be his wife in all respects?'' Brodie asked suspiciously.

''I do not intend to grace his bed, if that's what you're suggesting. I will gladly leave that to his mistress.''

''Danielle!''

''Do not look so shocked. He should be grateful I am willing to manage his household.''

''A husband will never permit such an arrangement.''

In truth, Danielle had worried over that very thing ever since she had agreed to this farce. ''What more can the man expect?'' she said with more conviction than she felt. ''After all, I am marrying him. That alone should be sufficient. And I plan on telling him so.''

Brodie didn't appear convinced. ''Lord Stanton does not look the type to be manipulated, no matter how cleverly.''

Danielle paused in folding the last garment. ''He does rather resemble a pirate, doesn't he?''

''You'd do well to consider that.''

''Brodie, that's nonsense. What can he do? Make me walk the plank?''

''I'd not set foot on one of his ships if I were you. After he discovers what you've been up to, the temptation to throw you overboard might prove too great.''

''I admit, when the idea first occurred to me, I had my reservations also. But then I remembered that his only concern is that he have his bride.''

''Do not lay the full blame on his Grace. It was your own impulsive behavior with the vicar that got you into this situation to begin with.''

''The duke knew very well that it was all a sham, and when I think of how he maneuvered me into agreeing to this marriage, I cannot help but feel he should expect something like this.''

"I can only hope you're right," Brodie sighed.

Danielle scooped up the small array of keepsakes on one of the bedside tables. After placing them atop the clothes, she closed the trunk. "Have Mary help you get the items we discussed. You'll find most of what you need in the attic. Be sure to use the white and blue lace. We don't have enough of the green. Then, when Tom returns, Mary is to help him prepare the coaches."

"Did the neighbors agree to lend us theirs?"

"As soon as I mentioned they were needed for the wedding procession, they were more than willing to help out." Danielle threw her arms around Brodie. "Don't fret so. All you have to do is make sure the children are there to say good-bye when his Grace and I are ready to leave. I'll take care of everything else."

It was the "everything else" that bothered Brodie.

Danielle lifted her arms as Mary slipped the blue wedding gown over her head. She tried not to think about the horde of butterflies that were doing battle in her stomach as the fabric settled in graceful folds around her.

"I wish we'd had time to make you a proper wedding dress," Mary said as she adjusted the gown's shimmering white overlay.

"We haven't the funds to waste on such things. The one you have chosen will do quite nicely." Assuring herself that the pearl drops that trimmed the fragile material hung properly, Danielle stepped back to view the effect in the mirror.

"Oh, Miss Danny, you look beautiful," Mary exclaimed, clasping her hands to her breast.

Danielle studied her reflection. The bodice, although snug, was discreetly trimmed with a narrow ruffle of the same white iridescent material that drifted down from the blue satin ribbon tied under her bust.

In a few moments, she would be marrying a man she knew nothing about. Yet the memory of his kiss in the stables was still strong enough to bring a warm flush to her cheeks. This was ludicrous. How did she expect to keep him at arm's length when a mere kiss had left her knees trembling and her heart racing? Think of the children, she reminded herself. She mustn't lose sight of her reasons for going through with this dangerous game.

Slowly, she turned in front of the mirror, trying to maintain her fragile control. The reflection brought a frown to her countenance. This had always been one of her favorite gowns. Now, suddenly everything appeared to be wrong. Its vibrant blue no longer pleased her, and seemed to call undue attention to her auburn hair, dramatically accentuating the red highlights. It was no wonder Lord Stanton had seen through her performance on that snowy night. With her flamboyant coloring, she strongly resembled an actress painted for the part.

Danielle moved away from the mirror. As she did so, the ruffle at her breast shifted. Instinctively, her fingers rose to readjust it. Odd, she had not noticed the bodice being so low before. Considering her decision to keep the door of her bedchamber locked against Lord Stanton, it wouldn't do to encourage his amorous side. She must quickly dispel any misconceptions he had that this marriage was anything other than a way to help the orphans, an arrangement of advantage to both participants. How could he possibly expect more? She wasn't in love with the man. She wasn't in love with anyone. And she certainly hadn't encouraged him to think otherwise. Aside from the kiss, she hadn't so much as held his hand. Nevertheless, she had to admit the kiss had been foolish error on her part. But surely he was aware her response was nothing more than the excitement of experiencing something new, something forbidden. It meant nothing beyond that. Nothing to her or him, she bravely told herself. And that's what the marriage would be as well—nothing!

Most of the furniture had been moved against the back wall to accommodate the chairs that had been set up in two perfect rows on each side of the drawing room. The vicar stood beside Devon at the end of the long aisle cleared for the bride's entrance.

Nathan muttered under his breath, silently cursing his father for starting the tradition that required him, as the Vicar of Westbryre, to perform this ceremony. Then he cursed his mother, Lavinia Stanton, for having invalidated her status as the eldest child of the third Duke of Burnshire by being born a woman.

Lavinia's mother had died giving her birth, and after no baby appeared to bless the duke's second marriage, it seemed that Lavinia was destined to be an only child. As the sole heir, she could have married anyone, but she fell in love with the elderly Reverend Jeremiah Holmes. Then, two years after Lavinia's marriage, the duke's second wife presented him with a son, William Stanton, and Burnshire finally had a male heir. Resentment festered within Nathan at the quirk of fate that had cost him everything. First, Devon's father; now, Devon. He should be the one inheriting the title and fortune. Nathan had worked too hard and come too close to getting what was rightfully his. He had no intention of giving up now. He had bided his time before and he would again.

All eyes turned as the bride entered the drawing room. Nathan was forced to admit Miss Wakefield was beautiful. Too beautiful. If Devon were to form an emotional attachment to her, it might present a complication later.

Nathan leaned toward Devon. "Your Grace, I must protest," he whispered. "You cannot be serious about this wedding. You know nothing of the bride."

"You're wrong, Nathan," he answered, his eyes never leaving Danielle. "I'm very serious about this wedding. We *will* be married. That is," he continued slowly and deliberately, "unless you plan on collecting my inheritance."

The bride moving up the aisle prevented Nathan from answering. He lowered his gray eyes.

Devon stepped forward and took Danielle's hand. More shaken than she cared to admit, Danielle listened uneasily as the vicar began the ceremony. Seeing the hatred in Nathan's eyes, she knew even her marriage to Lord Stanton would not guarantee her safety. It would only be a matter of time before . . .

Lord Stanton gave her hand a firm squeeze, drawing her eyes to him, and she somehow felt more secure. With his towering height and broad shoulders, he certainly looked quite capable of protecting her. He gave her a reassuring smile as if he had read her thoughts.

A cold chill crept up her spine. Could the threat of Nathan's revenge be any more frightening than telling the Duke of Burnshire that his marriage to her would be in name only?

The vows were exchanged and Devon slipped a large sapphire ring on her finger. Odd, she had thought it would be an emerald—to match her eyes. Perhaps there hadn't been time to consider such things. The ring winked at her. Of course, it had been purchased for Lady Emily. How silly of her to have forgotten. Lady Emily's eyes were blue.

"I now pronounce you man and wife."

Lord Stanton turned to her. He was now her husband, and she his wife. A crazy mixture of hope and despair washed through her as he lowered his head to hers. She closed her eyes in expectation, but his kiss was brief, almost cold.

"Later," he whispered against her lips. Embarrassed, Danielle turned away. Had he sensed her disappointment? Disappointment! Whatever was happening to her?

The marriage supper passed all too slowly for Danielle's taste. Afterward the guests assembled in the large ballroom. Aunt Margaret had outdone herself. Rich blue satin ribbons and white lace caught up with large silver rosettes trimmed the windows and doorways, while narrow banners of matching material streamed across the ceiling to meet at the large chandeliers at each end. The lights from a multitude of candles reflected off the satiny surfaces, turning the room into the romantic illusion of a crystal palace.

The strains of a waltz sounded and Devon took Danielle into his arms. "Shall we open the dancing?"

He didn't wait for her answer, but whirled her out across the newly polished floors. His steps were confident, his execution graceful, and Danielle had no difficulty following. The dance floor soon filled as others joined them.

"I wish to thank you for your thoughtfulness concerning the preparations," Danielle offered sweetly. "Left to our own resources, Aunt Margaret and I could not have done half so well."

"It was the least I could do for my betrothed."

He smiled that cat-in-the-cream smile and Danielle nearly stepped on his foot. She was willing to be civil about their relationship, but that grin hinted at things she'd do well to nip in the bud. But she'd best be careful about broaching the subject. It wouldn't do to get his back up here.

"I would imagine, after being gone from England for so long, you must be very busy with the estates."

"I've yet to find it a burden," he answered.

Vexed, Danielle tried again. Perhaps she was being too subtle. "But surely you'll be spending most of your time reacquainting yourself with your properties. I mean, I don't want you to feel that you need to remain at Burnshire to entertain me."

"I will never be too busy for you," he replied, pulling her closer as he guided her across the dance floor.

Danielle could feel the warmth of embarrassment wash over her. He had deliberately misunderstood in order to intimidate her.

"We both have our own reasons for this marriage, your Grace. I merely wished to point out that even though we are wed, nothing need change. You may have your life, your friends, and I mine."

He squeezed her hand. "Ah, but then you have failed to take into consideration the fact that I might actually be looking forward to this marriage."

Her eyes flew to his, and she missed a step. A knowing smile tugged at the corners of his lips. Drat him anyway! He was forever seeing through her. Before Danielle realized what he had in mind, he clasped her tighter.

"Please release me," she said through clenched teeth.

"Rest easy, love," he whispered in her hair as she tried to pull away from his arms. Lord, he thought, she smelled good. "You might find you enjoy having my arms around you." He let his leg brush against hers.

"Unhand me this minute," she said firmly.

He grinned down at her. "You wouldn't want the whole countryside to know how I coerced you into this marriage, would you?"

"You wouldn't reveal that," she gasped.

"You're more than likely correct. But I'd not let it go to my head if I were you. I was thinking of Lady Bradford."

"No doubt that would be the only factor to deter you."

He smiled at her and she could feel herself growing faint.

"You needn't paint me so black," he said. "I did, after all, assist in removing you from a embarrassing situation." He drew her closer, forcing her to lay her head against his chest.

Her head filled with the masculine scent of him. Her treacherous heart started beating wildly. Holy Hannah! Would he always have this effect on her? And he talked of removing her from an embarrassing situation. Hah!

"A situation not half as embarrassing as this," she breathed into the lace at the front of his shirt.

"You needn't worry, love. We *are* married." He gently ran his fingers up her back. "Consider the alternative and you must agree your decision was an intelligent one."

"How intelligent could it have been when, if you

recall, I was faced with two equally unpleasant choices," she whispered. "Being pursued by a heartless toad or mauled by a bloody pirate."

He threw back his head in laughter. The music stopped, but he didn't release her.

"Ah, love," he said, his voice husky. "If you've never been mauled by a pirate, you're in for a rare treat."

Danielle was sure her heart had stopped beating. A hard knot formed in her chest. Then suddenly, he dropped his hand from her back and stepped away. She could breathe again.

Danielle stared after his retreating form. She felt like a fool. Why did she let him upset her so? Instead, she should be concentrating all her efforts on their departure for Burnshire. But before she had the chance to berate herself for long, another dance partner claimed her.

Devon turned back. Like a starving man who sees his last crust of bread being carried away, he watched her progress across the dance floor. How could he tell her he had coerced her into this marriage because he wanted her? Even now the tantalizing lavender scent of her clung to the front of his shirt, stirring up a dangerous caldron of emotions. His blue eyes darkened. Was she even aware of how his body responded to the way her gown appeared to caress her slim figure with every step she took?

Despite his resolve to avoid any emotional commitment to this marriage, Devon found himself fantasizing about the night he would soon spend with his wife. With a smile on his lips, he joined Lady Bradford and her lady friends.

Surrounded by old acquaintances, Danielle's aunt fairly beamed. But there was no mistaking the humble grace with which she accepted Beatrice Hadden's congratulations for her niece's good fortune.

"Danielle looks positively stunning tonight, Lady Bradford," Beatrice forced herself to say.

"Thank you. I will be sure to tell her," Margaret

said, knowing full well Beatrice was disappointed because her own daughters had not been as successful in their marriages. "I only wish Julia could have been here to meet Danielle, but she has not been feeling at all well lately."

Beatrice shook her head. "Such a shame to miss your own son's wedding."

Devon stepped up and introduced himself.

"Ah, your Grace, I was hoping we would meet," Beatrice cooed. "I was telling Lady Bradford how lovely Danielle looks." She leaned forward and tapped Lord Stanton's wrist with her fan. "My son has always been quite taken with her, you see. Had you not snatched her from beneath his very nose, Russell would have asked for her hand. They would have made such a nice couple." Beatrice sighed. "And with both of them blessed with such lovely shades of red hair, I could truly envision the children their union would have produced." Patting her own head of brassy curls, she continued. "To be sure, the coloring is most rare."

Devon could envision them also, but "beautiful" was not the word that came to mind to describe a blending of Danielle's deep auburn curls with the carrot-red ones of young Hadden. Lady Bradford's indignant "Hum!" told him he was not alone in his assessment.

The dance continued as partners were exchanged. It wasn't long before Danielle was claimed by the vicar.

His hooded eyes regarded her coldly. "It's a pleasure to see you again, Miss Wakefield." He bowed before her as the music began. "But how very remiss of me. I must now call you your Grace."

The steps of the dance separated them and Danielle was spared the necessity of responding, but after a few more turns he was back at her side. "Such a shame that Devon will more than likely return to his ships now that he has secured his inheritance. The parishioners were so looking forward to having the Stanton pews filled again."

Danielle smiled sweetly. She doubted the vicar even suspected that the thought of Lord Stanton leaving was more of a relief than a threat. Beyond the protection of the Stanton name, she didn't need Devon, she reminded herself. She could more than handle the vicar. Indeed, it was time the he learned she could be a formidable adversary.

"I've never been one to take my duties lightly, Vicar. Rest assured, even if Devon should decide to go to sea, I shall always be at Burnshire. As the new duchess, I plan on taking an avid interest in all matters concerning my husband's lands."

Once more the dance steps separated them. Unfortunately, they also eventually brought them back together.

The vicar moved close. "You will not be upset when I advise Devon to return the children to the orphanage, where they belong?"

She would not be intimidated. "I'm surprised, Vicar. I would not have thought you would want to broach the subject. You might have to explain how I came by them. And that would put you in the embarrassing position of also having to explain why the orphanage continues to collect a quarterly stipend for children no longer under your care."

She was pleased to see a touch of pink color the vicar's pale face. Her suspicions were correct. Nathan had not reported the disappearances. The rest of the dance was completed in stony silence, and at its end he left the ballroom.

Danielle breathed a sigh of relief. His early departure suited her just fine.

She sipped at a glass of champagne, her eyes searching the dance floor for her husband. He was dancing with one of the neighbors, a young girl with lovely blond curls pinned high on her head. She was smiling up at Lord Stanton, her eyes alight with laughter at something he had said. Danielle's stomach tightened at the scene. The man was hopeless. Was no one exempt from his charms? Forever the pirate. A conquest a minute. Didn't he realize it wasn't necessary to conquer everything that sailed his way?

Danielle tossed her head. What did she care, anyway? The sooner the man returned to his ships, the sooner her life would be her own. There would be no more delving into her affairs. No more sleepless nights, wondering what he was going to discover next. Danielle took a deep breath. No more piercing blue eyes searching her soul. No more disconcerting smiles wreaking havoc with her peace of mind. And no more bold kisses leaving her knees as weak as a newborn foal's.

The music stopped and Devon handed the petite blond over to her next partner. He turned, his gaze sweeping the room until it came to rest on Danielle. His presence seemed to fill the entire room as his long strides carried him to her. He was coming to claim her for another waltz. Danielle stepped back. She didn't dare trust herself in his arms again. She was about to flee when she felt a tug on her sleeve.

"Everything's ready, Miss Danny," Pockets whispered from behind her.

The time had come. Danielle straightened her shoulders, bracing herself for what could prove to be the greatest performance of her life.

"There you are, Devon," she said. His blue eyes seemed to look right through her, and she briefly reconsidered the advisability of carrying out her plans. But he had promised her she could keep all the children, and she wasn't going to give him the chance to change his mind once he learned precisely what his promise entailed. She forced herself to smile. "I've been looking everywhere for you. Give me but a moment to change, then I think we should be on our way."

"Such impatience, my love. How flattering."

Momentarily forgetting her goal, she shot him a scathing look. "It takes so little to flatter you, Lord Stanton."

"Tut, tut," he scolded. "It would be best not to let our guests in on the circumstances of our marriage."

The smile that suddenly appeared on Danielle's face left Devon reviewing what he had said.

"An excellent idea," she said, placing her gloved hand within his. She leaned close. "A truce, then. I shall do my part to show that our motives went beyond simply fulfilling your father's will. Are you capable of doing the same?" She didn't give him much time to wonder at the meaning of her words as she hurried to change into her traveling gown.

Mary was putting the last items in the portmanteau when Danielle pushed open the door to her bedchamber. A green gown was laid out on the bed, along with a fur-trimmed cloak and hat.

"Help me change. I mustn't give Lord Stanton time—" Her words were cut short when she noticed the green negligee Mary was folding. "Where in heaven did that come from?" she asked, plucking the thin garment from the maid's hands.

"Lady Montgomery sent it. It's to be for you . . . you know. Your honeymoon."

Danielle held the thin gown out to inspect it. The silken material shimmered in the fading sunlight. "You can almost see through it, Mary. It's—it's positively sinful. Why, it makes me blush just looking at it."

Lydia Montgomery had been Danielle's first acquaintance upon her arrival in England. Despite Danielle's outspokenness and Lydia's painfully shy ways, they had become fast friends. Were it not for the fact that Lydia was expecting, she would have been at the wedding. Danielle grinned. "How unlike Lydia to send such a thing. Throw it away, Mary."

"Why, Miss Danny, it's such a beautiful gift. Lady Montgomery was kind to send it. You should at least try it on before you decide."

She tossed it over her shoulder, then unbuttoned the lace cuff of her dress. "If you like it so much, you may have it."

"Miss Danny! Whatever would I be doing with such a gown?"

"Well, I have no use for it either," Danielle returned.

"You never know when you might be needing it, Miss Danny."

Danielle didn't know whether to be annoyed or amused when Mary stubbornly packed the negligee in the portmanteau. She shouldn't expect her to understand. "We don't have much time, Mary."

The maid's fingers fumbled with the tiny pearl buttons on the back of Danielle's gown. "Oh!" she exclaimed when one of them came off in her hands. "What am I going to do now, your Grace? I can't leave until I repair the gown, and his Grace is sure to suspect something if we delay."

"Don't get yourself into a dither, Mary. The button can wait. You collect Brodie and the children. Tom will meet you at the back stairs." Danielle stepped out of the blue gown. "Remember, you are to ride with me in the front carriage. Brodie will remain with the children."

Mary helped Danielle dress. "Aren't you afraid his Grace will be upset with you?"

"Lord Stanton is a gentleman. He would never express his displeasure in front of the guests."

"Tom says his Grace has been away from England so long he doesn't have to be a gentleman now. He says sea captains live by a different code."

"Since when have you started listening to Tom?" Danielle asked with more conviction than she felt. She had wagered everything on Devon behaving like a gentleman. This certainly wasn't the time for doubts. "Hurry along, Mary. Tom will be wondering if something's gone wrong."

As soon as Mary left with the bag, Danielle retrieved her father's small pistol from the drawer of her bedside table. Stuffing it into the lining of the reticule she'd had made especially to accommodate the extra bulk, Danielle donned her cloak, bonnet, and soft leather gloves. When she was ready she grabbed up her fur muff and left the room.

All the guests appeared to have gathered in the foyer for the departure of the bride and groom. *This is it.* Throwing back her shoulders and taking a deep breath, Danielle gave them one of her brightest smiles.

"How lovely you look, my dear," Lord Stanton said as he tucked her arm in his. "Shall we go?"

The butler threw the large oak doors open wide and all eyes turned to see Lord Stanton's coach approach. Decked out in the same blue ribbons and lace as the ballroom, the coach pulled to a stop at the bottom of the steps.

"Oh, Devon," Danielle exclaimed breathlessly, turning in to his arms. "It's beautiful."

"If not ostentatious," he muttered gruffly as he viewed the gaudy display of ribbons and lace. Although he had expected that his beloved wife had some trick under her handsome bonnet, he certainly hadn't expected this. One look at his driver's red face told him the blame could not be placed on Jem.

"Ah!" rose in unison from the guests. Behind the coach came a footman leading Devon's black stallion and a procession of children. From Jeremy in front to the little girl holding Brodie's hand in the back, each child was dressed in a long white linen gown.

"Good Lord!" Devon swallowed the words as he realized there had to be more than a dozen of them. Where had they all come from?

He could hear the guests admiring the parade. He had to admit it was impressive. Danielle must have employed every servant at Haverly House to sew the elaborate blue-and-white trim on each robe. If she had planned to give the guests something to gossip about over the last months of winter, she had succeeded.

"I wish my husband cared as much for me," a lady crooned. Her maligned husband gave a disgruntled snort.

Encouraged by the approval of her guests, Danielle stood on tiptoe and bestowed a kiss on Devon's cheek. She could feel the muscles work on his clamped jaw.

"What a wonderful surprise," she exclaimed with what she hoped was a sufficiently honeyed delivery.

"And what a wonderful performance," he gruffly whispered into her hair. Blue ribbons and white lace. The entire wedding had been staged. The ballroom, the coaches, the children. Everything had been carefully planned down to the blue of her wedding gown. Had he been played for a fool from the beginning? She had used the fact that he needed a bride to get the better of Nathan. Had she counted on him walking in on the little scene? If so, he had played right into her hands.

Danielle cast him a wide, innocent-eyed stare. "This is the nicest wedding gift a bride could get." She pulled a handkerchief from the sleeve of her traveling gown and dabbed her dry eyes, giving Tom their prearranged signal.

Around the corner came two additional coaches, decked out in the same manner as the first. "And to think you did this all for me," she added between dramatic sniffles.

Devon stood silently at her side as he contemplated the significance of the extra coaches. There was no doubt in his mind. She was counting on the fact that he would not refuse to take the children. Not in front of the guests. She had won this round. The next would be his.

"Say your good-byes, Danielle," he snapped.

Danielle placed a kiss on Lady Bradford's cheek. "Good-bye, Aunt Margaret. I shall be expecting you as soon as spring arrives."

Devon took Danielle firmly by the arm and hurried her down the steps before any more surprises appeared. Casting a speculative glance over the children, he handed her into the coach. Danielle's maid sat on the far side of the banquette. He didn't miss the triumphant smile Danielle gave her, but it quickly faded when he climbed in beside her.

"But your horse," she exclaimed. "I've had him

saddled for you. We thought you would prefer to ride.''

''And deprive myself of your overwhelming gratitude for this lavish display of my affection?'' Lifting the carriage rug, he laid it across their laps, brushing her body with his as he tucked it in on the far side of her.

Danielle held her breath, hoping against hope that he could not feel the rapid pounding of her heart. But the mocking smile on his lips told her he knew exactly what effect his presence was having on her. The coach moved out and cold fingers of ice began to form around Danielle's chest. Had she truly gone too far this time?

Once out of sight of Haverly House, Devon ordered the coach to stop. ''Mary will ride in one of the other coaches.''

''But they are too crowded. What with Brodie and all the others—''

''Crowded?'' he asked, issuing a challenge he knew she was unwilling to meet. ''Then I suggest she have one of the children sit on her lap.''

Chapter 6

Danielle tucked herself into the far corner of the seat. As the coach moved out, she relaxed. At least Lord Stanton gave no indication of sending the children back, but there was no doubt in her mind that punishment would be forthcoming. He leaned toward her and Brodie's warning rose before her like the evil specter of a pirate's cutlass.

He reached out to touch her cheek. "Do I truly look like such an ogre to you?" he asked as he trailed his fingers down the side of her face. When they came to the ribbon that held her bonnet in place, he tugged at the silken ends. He'd teach her not to play games with him.

"I didn't mean to stare," she said calmly, determined that he not know how shaken she was by his actions. "It's only that there are times, such as now, when you remind me strongly of your father."

"Now that's a frightening thought." Tugging the bonnet off her head, he tossed it on the seat across from them.

"I don't mean to sound disrespectful," Danielle quickly added, her eyes following the movement of his hands. "But the few times I spoke with him, it was evident we would never see eye to eye on any issue."

Suppressing a knowing grin, he began unfastening the embroidered frogs of her cloak. "I don't see that as a problem with us. We have so much in common."

"Such as?" she asked, her voice barely a whisper.

"I'm surprised you have to ask," he said, slipping the cloak from her shoulders. "We both like children— an abundance of children."

Danielle relaxed. So that was it. He was upset about the stunt she had pulled and was baiting her. He didn't frighten her. She was prepared to play his little game. "Why, yes. The more children, the better, your Grace. Given the number of orphans England has, I can easily envision us with an additional two dozen by this time next year."

"I'm so pleased you feel that way." He unfastened the tiny button at the neck of her gown. "Then you won't object to my plans for a large family."

Danielle's eyes flew to his. The cold indifference was gone. The eyes he raised to hers had darkened into smoldering blue fires. His hand moved to the next button and the game grew serious.

Did he plan on taking her here and now? Didn't he care that she didn't love him? His arms wrapped around her, lifting her onto his lap.

Think! Think! she urged herself silently.

He lowered his head, his lips tenderly capturing hers. Frantically, Danielle searched for something to distract him, but her concentration was hampered by the forbidden sensations tumbling through her body. Suddenly she pulled away.

"I've got the disease, your Grace!" she blurted out, repeating the words she had heard the sailors use on the ship to England. The diversion produced an immediate effect. Lord Stanton's face took on the same stunned look Brodie's had when Danielle had asked about the strange illness.

"And what disease do you carry?"

Encouraged by her success, Danielle slid off his lap. "I'm not exactly sure, your Grace. But I can safely say it isn't something you would wish to catch. Why, just to kiss me might cause you terrible agony."

Devon's lips twitched at her innocence. The absurdity of the conversation was making it very difficult for him to maintain a stern demeanor. "But you seem to show no signs of sickness."

"That's the corker of it all, your Grace. It's hard to detect until it's too late," Danielle said solemnly. The sailors' slang seemed to add just the right touch. She was pleased to have listened so well and remembered so much. Odd, she'd not thought to use this disease before. It seemed to work perfectly on an overly persistent suitor.

"Have you had this affliction long?" Devon asked.

Danielle lowered her head in despair. "Only since I became a trumpet." That didn't seem quite right, but it was the word the sailors had used.

The coach suddenly rang with Lord Stanton's deep, rich laughter. "The word is 'strumpet,' I believe."

"Well, as you say, your Grace. I'll not argue the point. But I consider it very ungentlemanly for you to laugh at my plight," she scolded. "For all you know, I could be at death's door."

"I've yet to hear of someone so young dying of the disease of love."

Danielle calmly rebuttoned her gown. "Well, there you have it. I never claimed to be a bargain. But then, it was you who insisted on this marriage, wasn't it?"

"What's the price to be, then?"

"Price?"

"Yes. It was a kiss for the coach. What favors are you willing to barter for the children?"

Danielle straightened in her seat. "My favors are not for sale. Not at any price!"

"True," he said thoughtfully. "But how could I have forgotten? They're not yours to sell. You gave them to me, along with your marriage vows."

"I've surrendered nothing but my freedom to live where I choose. It was you who did the bartering to secure your inheritance. Be content with that, for it's all you're going to get out of this marriage."

"Did I say I wished anything more?"

"Then what was all this about?" she demanded.

He tugged at the lace cuffs of his shirt. "I only

wished to see for myself how far you were prepared to go in order to court my favor.''

Her green eyes flashed. ''And for that you scared me half out of my wits? Did it never occur to you that you had only to ask? I would gladly have informed you there was nothing you could possibly do to lure me to your bed.''

''Did I really frighten you, Danielle?''

She did not care for the smile that played at the corners of his lips. ''Obviously, that's what you set out to do. You are nothing but a . . . bully! If this is the way you treat your ship's crew, I'm surprised you've not had a mutiny on your hands. You're no better than your cousin!''

Devon knew he shouldn't be dismayed by the comparison. He had wanted Danielle for his bride and selfishly used the boy to get her. It was a tactic Nathan would have employed. Telling himself that, as Duchess of Burnshire, Danielle would also reap the benefits of his inheritance did little to assuage his conscience. There was no getting around the fact. And what was more, by marrying her, he might have also put her life in danger.

''Clearly you share my low opinion of Nathan.'' Devon paused, not sure how much he should tell her. ''Although I applaud your ability to see beyond the facade he presents to everyone, I must question your judgment in openly opposing him. You should never have abducted the boy. Nathan can prove a formidable enemy.''

''So you have pointed out to me before.''

This was going to be more difficult than he thought. But he couldn't withdraw now. It was imperative she know from the beginning she was not to interfere where Nathan was concerned. ''If you are expecting an apology from me on the methods I employed to secure your agreement to this marriage, you will be disappointed. What I said about Nathan is true. Once he discovered our engagement was a lie, there isn't anything he wouldn't have done to get the boy back.''

"Instead of forcing me into this marriage, why didn't you just demand I return Jeremy?"

"And have everyone know my fiancée abducted him? I would enjoy the embarrassment the announcement would cause Nathan, but what would Lady Bradford's friends think if they were to hear of it?"

Seeing the blush that painted her face, he knew she had already considered the possibilities even if she wouldn't admit it. "And before you say we were not engaged, let me remind you of your announcement to Nathan."

Danielle lifted her chin defiantly. "Are you afraid of Nathan?"

"Let's just say I have my own reasons for not openly opposing him at the moment."

"Nathan does not frighten me."

There was no mistaking the mutinous gleam in her eye. It was her dauntless spirit which had attracted her to him in the first place, but he couldn't let her continue to annoy Nathan. It was much too dangerous. "Nathan has powerful friends behind him, and I must ask that you bear that in mind. You can't keep on running around the countryside abducting children."

"Not abducting. Rescuing. Rescuing them from people like your cousin."

"If anyone is to stand up to Nathan, it will be me. I warn you now, I will not allow my wife to proceed in this manner. Either you promise to let me handle it in my own way or I'll send the children back to the orphanage."

"And what of the children at the orphanage now?"

"You will have to trust that my methods for handling the situation are best."

She had no reason to put her faith in him, but she also had no other choice. "I will give you my promise," she said, carefully searching for the exact words, "as long as I have yours that you will do everything in your power should a problem arise."

"I have your word?" he asked. "No theatrics? I would have your honest word?"

"As long as I have yours."

"Fair enough," he said, sealing the bargain. With that resolved, he moved to the other seat. He could rest now. He hadn't had a good night's sleep since he arrived at Haverly House. Each morning he had fully expected to be greeted with the news that Danielle had packed her belongings and fled. Now he realized his worries had been needless. She would never leave without the children. Closing his eyes, he lay back against the velvet squabs, a contented smile on his face.

Danielle tapped him on the shoulder with her muff. "This means, of course, you find no problem with me bringing the children to Burnshire?"

Devon opened one eye. "We will discuss it later. I'm tired and I wish to get some sleep." It wouldn't hurt to have her worry a while longer, he decided.

Seeing the smug grin on Lord Stanton's face, Danielle felt she would have fared better had he ranted and raved at her. At least then she'd know his true feelings.

With his eyes closed, she found herself studying him. His sensual good looks would have turned any woman's head, yet he had decided she was to be his bride and there was no deterring him.

He was stubborn. Yes, and egotistical. She blushed to recall how her own body had betrayed her as they danced. But that had been his fault too. He had held her shamelessly close, yet short of causing a scene and embarrassing Aunt Margaret, there had been nothing she could do. But then, he had known that, hadn't he?

A fire began to kindle in Danielle's green eyes as she watched her sleeping husband. Mile after mile, it grew brighter. What right had he to chastise her for trying to correct the vicar's wrongs, then demand she promise not to interfere? Were the vicar's actions never to be questioned?

He had no difficulty when it came to calling her every bluff. Trading a coach for a kiss when he had no intention of supplying the horses. Allowing her to leave Burnshire when he was really trapping her in a sham engagement. Permitting the children to accompany them even though she feared he'd never let them stay. The man had no conscience.

Her little white lie to the vicar might have proved a minor inconvenience to him in his attempt to win Lady Emily, but that was hardly justification to blackmail her into this marriage.

She glanced over at her husband again. The look of sweet innocence on his face angered her even more and she clasped her muff in frustration. Not married an entire day and already he was extracting unfair promises from her. Then, knowing her concern about the children, he refused to put her mind at ease. What right had he to sleep while she fretted over what his decision would be? It was easy for him. He had no worries. He had fulfilled the stipulations of his father's will. He had all he wanted.

The fire in her eyes continued to grow. Was it her imagination, or had she seen a flicker of a smile cross his lips? She could envision him standing calmly by while the vicar marched her children back to the orphanage. All because he chose to handle matters in his own way. The injustice of it filled her with rage and she raised her fur muff, bringing it down on his head.

Jolted from his nap, Devon grasped Danielle's arm.

"You . . . you blackguard!" she spat. "How dare you take his side over mine!"

Devon was taken aback by the anger he saw in her eyes. "Whatever are you carrying on about?" he asked, wrenching the muff from her grasp. The thought that he might have married a woman not entirely in control of all her faculties crossed his mind.

"Carrying on!" she croaked. "Carrying on! Why, you insensitive . . ." Frantically, she looked for something to throw. Her reticule lay on the seat. Grabbing the strings, she swung the crocheted bag at his head.

Envisioning lace handkerchiefs and a few coins tucked away in the bag's silk-lined interior, Devon made no effort to duck and it hit the side of his forehead with a thud.

Stunned, Danielle watched Lord Stanton slowly fall against the side of the coach. Dear Lord, she had forgotten about the pistol. She tugged desperately at the shoulder of his cape, trying to right him on the seat, but he was too heavy for her and the sway of the coach was not helping matters. After studying the situation for a few moments, she stood over him and, leaning down, wrapped her arms about his shoulders.

Bracing herself as best she could, she succeeded in moving him a few inches. His head fell against her breasts, and when a soft sigh escaped his lips, she almost dropped him.

She paused a moment to ease the rapid beating of her heart. At least she hadn't killed him.

The coach made a sudden turn and despite all her efforts, she was unable to hold him. Lord Stanton tumbled to the floor, taking Danielle with him.

She lay across his inert form, her hair falling in disorderly curls about her shoulders. Lord Stanton moaned again. Fidaddle! Why didn't he open his eyes? She would never get him onto the seat now. Before she could right herself, the coach pulled to a stop. The door opened and Danielle found herself looking into the startled eyes of a footman. Mustering what little dignity she had left, she picked herself up and smoothed her rumpled skirts.

"You'll have to excuse his Grace. I fear he has dipped rather deeply into his cups today," she lied, ignoring the embarrassment of the footman as his gaze traveled from her unbound hair to the moaning form of his Grace. "Your name, please."

"I am Bob, the new footman," he informed her.

"Well, Bob, could you please come around and open my door? My limbs lack sufficient length for me to step over him."

"Yes, your Grace," the footman answered tentatively.

Danielle bestowed him a small, trembling smile, designed to capture his sympathy. If the impertinent grin he returned was any indication, she'd been more than successful. He helped her from the coach. And not a moment too soon, for the moans coming from behind her were growing decidedly louder. Devon was beginning to stir. She could only hope his head would not hurt him terribly much when he came to.

Chin held high, she swept past the footman and up the steps.

"Good evening, your Grace," the butler greeted the new Duchess of Burnshire, trying not to let his gaze stray to the footmen who were assisting the duke from his coach.

"Good evening, Andrews," Danielle returned as she paused to admire the beauty of the foyer. After all the scrimping she had been forced to do at Haverly House, it was difficult to believe this was to be her new home.

"Her Grace is very tired and wishes to be taken directly to her room," Bob broke in, startling Danielle, who was not aware he had followed her to the door.

Andrews made it clear that he disapproved of the new footman's unprofessional behavior. "Mrs. Talbut, the housekeeper, will show her Grace the way. See to the luggage, Bob."

But Danielle had found an ally and wasn't about to let him get away. Warming to the role of mistress of the house, she moved forward and whispered, "If it's all the same to you, Andrews, you need not trouble Mrs. Talbut. Bob will lead me to my chamber." With that, she plopped her reticule in the footman's hands and they proceeded up the stairs. Danielle was about to bless her good fortune when she heard his Grace being helped into the foyer.

"Where is she!" the duke's voice boomed from below.

She had no trouble playing the frightened wife before the footman. It was all he needed to instruct her to lock the door behind her. Wasting not a moment, she turned the key.

Poor Bob. To be sure, his manner was a bit unorthodox for a footman in a house such as Burnshire, but nonetheless, she'd never forgive herself if he lost his position because of it.

A quick glance around brought about the discovery of another door. When she opened it, she could do nothing but stare.

The room appeared to have been converted into some type of bathing chamber. A large tub stood in the center of the small room. Never in Danielle's dreams had she ever imagined such a luxury. Why, it was positively unheard of! To be sure it would save an immense amount of time for the servants not to have to bring up the tub each time she wished to bathe, but to have an entire room devoted to bathing, somehow seemed sinful.

Seeing that it also had an entrance to the hall, she quickly locked the connecting door.

Removing her gloves and cloak, she tossed them on the wide bed. The worn items appeared out of place on the silk counterpane. Danielle sighed. It would take a lot not to look out of place in this beautiful room.

Blue watered silk covered the walls where they weren't already overlaid with carved panels of rich mahogany. A painting of yellow and pink flowers dominated the wall behind a small writing desk. Her gaze traveled to the dressing table and chair, which had been covered in matching fabric. Crystal bottles of varying sizes and shapes were set out in readiness.

The footman would be bringing her own things soon and she would have to open up. She pulled back the heavy drapes at the window and stared at the front drive below. Why wasn't Lord Stanton pounding on her door? She pressed her face against the cold pane. Surely he had not taken to his bed.

"Thank you, Robert," Devon said as he took the cold cloth his friend had brought to him.

"You have a beautiful wife. I am most impressed."

Devon glowered up at his tall, brown-haired friend. "Keep in mind you're supposed to be my footman, not my wife's cicisbeo."

"From what I just witnessed, not only would the lady benefit from my company, she appears to need someone to play her gallant."

"This from a man who has yet to contact his own father since returning to England," Devon reminded him. "Lord Miles would more than likely benefit from a visit from you."

"My father is not the issue here," Robert protested as he lifted a corner of the wet cloth to inspect the lump on the side of Devon's head. "Your wife is, and I must say I've never known you to force your attentions on a lady before."

"I didn't force my attentions on her," Devon growled. "She got a bee in her bonnet and hit me while I was sleeping."

Robert coughed to keep from laughing. "The mighty Stanton laid low by a lady," he teased, then flopped down in the other leather chair. "Had I known that others besides Nathan had designs on your life, I would not have stayed behind to ferret out your spy."

"And were you successful?" Devon asked, hoping to put an end to the discussion of how he had acquired the lump on his head. The lively twinkle in Robert's brown eyes told him it was a futile effort. "Robert!" he demanded. "The spy—what did you discover?"

Robert leaned forward, his smile gone. "Your suspicions were correct. Nathan has a spy at Burnshire."

Danielle paced the length of her room again. It had been over two hours since the servants had brought her trunks up, yet Lord Stanton had not appeared. Was he seriously hurt? She was being foolish to worry so, she told herself. Anyone that seriously hurt would not have had the strength to bellow as he had when he reached the front door.

Apparently he had no intention of confronting her. The disappointment she felt at the revelation was puzzling, to say the least. After all, didn't she want him to treat her as if she wasn't there? She shoved the conflicting thoughts aside.

She should be helping Brodie with the children, instead of hiding. But she wasn't about to leave the security of her room. Drat her temper anyway!

Her pacing finally left her standing in front of the dressing table. She fingered the ivory-backed hand mirror. Its carved surface glowed creamy white in the flickering candlelight of the sconces that flanked the silvered mirror over the dressing table. Something that exquisite must have belonged to Lord Stanton's mother.

A knock sounded at the door and Danielle spun around. "Who is it?" she asked, failing to keep the tremor of fright from her voice.

"It's me, Miss Danny . . . your Grace. Mary. Katie's with me. She claims to have a toothache and won't sleep until she's told you of it."

Danielle unlocked her door. Katie was her youngest. Abandoned at the orphanage by a proud father who could not accept her disfigurement, Katie was learning to live with the birthmark that covered the entire left side of her face. Although the mark had faded considerably in the months she had been with Danielle, its bright pink color still drew attention to it.

Danielle wasn't overly concerned about the toothache. Katie was an inveterate hypochondriac. Not that she actually experienced the pains of any of her imaginary illnesses, but, at the age of four, she was very good at endowing herself with all the outward symptoms of each new sickness she came into contact with, either directly or indirectly.

"Come in, Mary," Danielle said, opening the door wide. "Who has the toothache?"

"Bess, one of cook's helpers."

Danielle knelt in front of the child. She knew she would be wise to discourage Katie's delusions, but the little girl had already suffered so much at the hands of the Picketts. "Does it hurt terribly bad, Katie?"

"Bess says it does. She had a cloth wrapped around her head and said I must get one also." Katie lifted big, sad brown eyes to Danielle. "It will help with the swelling, Miss Danny," she added, her lower lip trembling in anticipation of the pain she was sure was yet to come.

Danielle gathered the child in her arms. "I will see what I can find, love."

Unlocking the door to the bathing chamber, Danielle quickly searched the cabinets. After opening several doors, she finally found a long starched cloth. "This should do nicely."

Returning to her room, Danielle knelt once more before Katie. "Hold still while I tie this," she said. Finishing, she placed a big kiss on Katie's pink cheek and then stood back to readjust the cloth under her chin. "There, now how does that feel?"

"Much better than the side of my head, I'd wager," came a deep voice from the door she'd forgotten to lock.

Danielle whirled around. Lord Stanton leaned casually against the doorjamb, his broad shoulders filling the doorway. A dour look she was certain he reserved mainly for his crew sent Mary scurrying from the bedchamber. Danielle tried not to let her eyes stray to the dark bruise at his temple.

Devon studied the child peering at him from behind Danielle's skirts, and she in turn studied him, seemingly fascinated by the wet cloth he raised to his temple. The child was wearing a burgundy wool dress trimmed with pink lace. She appeared delicate, almost flowerlike. Dusty black curls, peeking from a white bandage that looked suspiciously like one of his starched neckcloths, framed a pink-cheeked, porcelain-doll face.

Devon bent down and ran his thumb across Katie's jaw. "Did Miss Danny hurt you too?" he asked the child.

"Lord Stanton! I would never hurt one of these children."

Katie moved closer to Danielle. "Miss Danny would not hurt anyone," she stated, defiantly shoving back a stray curl. "It's my curse," she whispered.

"Your curse?"

"Oh, yes. But I truly hope it doesn't offend you. You see, Miss Danny assures me it gets lighter each day. Someday it will fade away completely and I will be beautiful then."

"And who might you be?" he asked.

"I'm Catherine Elizabeth," she answered in her best grown-up voice.

"Well, Catherine Elizabeth, how did such a lovely young lady come to have a curse?"

Danielle pushed Katie behind her. "Katie was born with her mark."

Katie wasn't ready to relinquish the attention she was receiving. She decided she liked the tall, handsome man. Boldly she peeked around Danielle's skirt and gave him a big smile. "I have a toothache."

"I can see that," he said before turning his attention back to Danielle. "I can also see that Miss Danny's taken quite a hand in developing your imagination. A finer pair of actresses I've yet to see."

Danielle blushed. Her only salvation was the fact that Brodie was otherwise occupied. Lord Stanton's views on her behavior were beginning to sound like echoes of those of her former governess.

"The truth can be quite painful, can't it?" he pointed out as if he had read her mind.

"Oh, quite." Katie spoke up from the folds of Danielle's skirt. "Why, Bess tells me it gets fright-ful-ee worse toward bedtime."

"And who might Bess be?"

Danielle stepped boldly in front of Lord Stanton. She might as well tell him the worst about Katie right away. "Bess works in the kitchen. Bess has a toothache, so Katie has a toothache."

"An interesting theory, Danielle. And what amazes me the most is that oddly enough, in the few short days since I met you, it makes perfect sense. My understanding appears to have grown by leaps and bounds."

"It's a shame, your Grace, that it appears to be stifled concerning matters of greater importance."

Katie grew impatient with the turn in the conversation. She was losing the tall man's attention and didn't wish for him to leave. Being of a generous nature, she was prepared to share her illness with him. Stepping forward, she tugged on his sleeve. "That's why I came to sleep with Miss Danny, you see. But if you have a toothache, I'm sure Miss Danny will allow you to share our bed also. It looks forever big enough and Miss Danny—"

Danielle clapped her hand over Katie's mouth. "His Grace has his own bed, Katie." She fixed Lord Stanton with a stern eye. "He won't be needing ours."

"But, Miss Danny," Katie whined between Danielle's fingers.

Danielle removed her hand and knelt before her. "We must not inconvenience his Grace."

"There's no inconvenience," Devon interjected.

"You must remember your toothache, Katie," Danielle pointed out, ignoring Lord Stanton's attempt to discomfort her. "The pain of it might make you moan, and that would keep his Grace awake. After all, Bess did tell you it was worse at night."

Katie's mouth turned down in a pout. Danielle could see she was carefully weighing the fascinations of her toothache against a miraculous recovery.

She was spared Katie's decision by a sudden disturbance in the hallway. To her relief, Lord Stanton left and she quickly locked the door behind him.

Devon heard the key turn, but he was more concerned to know the meaning of the spectacle before him. The butler and housekeeper were struggling with a dark-haired boy. Upon seeing his Grace, they released the youth. "Stand firm, lad," he said, grabbing the boy as he tried to run past. "What is the meaning of this, Andrews?"

"Sorry to disturb you, your Grace, but the lad insists on wearing his coat to bed."

"I see no problem with that. It seems clean enough. What's your name, lad?"

"Pockets, yer Grace."

"I can see where a lot of thought went into your choice," Devon answered, eyeing the multi-pocketed coat the boy hugged to his thin frame. "Let the lad wear the coat if he's a mind to."

Seeing Andrews' reluctance to say more, Mrs. Talbut ventured to step forward. "Your Grace, he has stuffed the entire remains of his supper into the pockets. The food will attract vermin."

Devon had seen many children like Pockets on his travels. They all had that same haunted look. He'd often wondered about the scraps of food he'd seen them hide in their clothing. Were they taking it to share with others, or was it merely a way of staving off future starvation?

"Does Miss Danny let you keep food in your coat?" he asked the boy.

"No, yer Grace."

The boy trusted Danielle, but it was evident he had yet to trust this new arrangement. "There's no need to hoard food, lad. You'll not go hungry at Burnshire."

"No, yer Grace."

"Then kindly return the food to the kitchen."

Backing away from Lord Stanton, he hugged the coat tightly. "Cook give 't to me, your Grace."

"Cook will give you more tomorrow and the day after and the day after that," Devon remarked, hoping to put an end to the discussion.

" 'At's right nice of 'er, yer Grace."

"Then will you take the food back to the kitchen?"

"No, yer Grace."

He should have anticipated what the boy's answer would be. Until the lad was willing to trust Devon, he would continue doing what he felt was necessary for survival. Reaching into his own pocket, Devon withdrew a large gold coin. "I'll make a bargain with you." It seemed as if he had spent his entire day striking bargains. "I will give you this to hold. Should cook at any time fail to provide a meal for you or the other children at Burnshire, you have my permission to take it and purchase whatever you need."

Pockets eyed the coin suspiciously.

"Take it," Devon urged. "It should be more than enough to feed everyone for several days."

Pockets cautiously extended his hand. Feeling the cold surface, he grabbed it from Devon's fingers. Taking it straight to his mouth, he bit hard on the coin. Satisfied, he stuffed it into one of his pockets, then emptied the food onto the hall table.

"Not there, young man," Mrs. Talbut protested as the crumbs tumbled onto the polished surface.

"Never mind, Mrs. Talbut. See that the lad gets to bed. The table can be cleaned later."

"Yes, your Grace," she reluctantly agreed. "Come along, boy. The others will have already gone to sleep, and I don't want you waking them."

They left Devon in the hall, contemplating the crumbs on the tabletop. Perhaps he had been too hasty in allowing Danielle to bring the children. He could see how easy it would be to get caught up in their lives, and a commitment now to anything but stopping Nathan was out of the question.

A frown creased his forehead as he walked toward his room. He had planned to take Danielle to London, but visions of her collecting orphans as they passed through the streets rose before him like a bad dream.

Chapter 7

D evon took another swallow of brandy and continued to watch his sleeping bride. He was going to
have a devil of a time controlling her and Nathan at
the same time. He knew from past experience that Nathan could be clever, and Danielle . . . Danielle was
clever also. Clever, impulsive, and . . . beautiful.

Her hair was the color of a sunset before a storm, a
gossamer cloud of red fairy dust on a white pillow.
Dark lashes cast delicate shadows across her high
cheekbones. His eyes traced her heart-shaped face,
traveling down her slim throat to the pink ribbon that
trimmed the neck of her nightdress.

Each time she shifted in bed, he fought the stab of
desire that shot through him. What was wrong with
him? Why didn't he merely crawl in beside her? Had
he married Lady Emily, he would not be spending the
night sitting in this chair.

But Danielle was different, he kept telling himself.
She was a lifetime commitment—home, children, and
nights spent with your feet stretched out before a warm
fire. He was not ready for that type of existence.

His world was the sea—where the only boundaries
were those of the water under your ship and the skill
at your fingertips. It was a world of surprises, hidden
coves, and stormy nights. It was falling to sleep with
the gentle rock of your ship's hull and the challenge of
waking to the waves crashing across her bow.

Once he had dealt with Nathan, he would return to

his world, and there wasn't a woman he knew who could stop him. Not even the beautiful vixen sleeping before him.

The pale light of dawn spilled across the room. Danielle pulled aside the blue silk panels that hung from the bed's canopy frame and slid her legs over the edge.

Shortly after Katie had fallen asleep last night, Mary had taken her to her own bed, and Danielle had locked the door behind them. She was taking no chances. With the door securely locked, Danielle had finally been able to get a decent night's sleep.

She reached for her robe. Fully rested, she was determined to make Lord Stanton listen to her plans for this marriage. Surely a man who could be as gentle as he had been with Katie last night would understand the frustrations that had driven her to hit him. If only she could hold her temper.

"I always find the early hours the most restful," said a dark figure seated in one of the chairs by the fire.

Danielle spun around and grabbed for her reticule.

"Is this what you're seeking?" Devon held the pistol out for her inspection. "Rather heavy for a lady to carry, wouldn't you say?"

She took a step forward, then stopped. The temptation to snatch it from his hand was great, but she would not give him the satisfaction should she fail.

Vexed, Danielle bit her lip. Only moments ago, she had considered a truce. She didn't want to fight, but he was forever causing her to forget her good intentions. "My father commissioned the design specially," she said.

"I should think one of those small, ivory-handled ones would be more in your line."

"My father didn't approve of them. He said if a lady was in need of a pistol, she'd best have one that could take care of the problem."

Devon fingered the dark lump on the side of his head. "Was it his intention that you pull the trigger or just club your victims to death?"

"I'm terribly sorry I lost my temper and hit you," she apologized sweetly, determined he should not rile her again. "I hope it doesn't still hurt." A thought suddenly occurred to her, and all her good intentions were cast to the winds. Danielle's green eyes narrowed with suspicion. "How did you get into my room?" she demanded.

"Don't look so shocked, my dear," he said, rising out of his chair. "After all, I am your husband."

She tried not to dwell on the way the deep blue robe hugged his broad shoulders, nor the way it hung open, exposing his dark, furred chest down to the belt tied snugly at his waist.

"Th-the door was locked," she finally managed to say.

"Have you forgotten?" He tossed a heavy ring of keys on the small table beside him. "Burnshire is my home."

"You said you wanted nothing more from me. Have you changed your mind?"

Considering the provocation in the defiant way she stood beside the bed, it was difficult for Devon not to take her here and now. The challenge she presented was not the sort he was known to ignore, and he knew, without a doubt, that it was going to take every ounce of willpower he possessed to abide by his earlier decision not to become involved. But a cold night spent sleeping in her chair had done nothing to soothe his already short temper.

Devon's eyes raked her lightly clad form coldly. "Did you wish me to change my mind?" he asked, his voice low.

Her body warmed shamelessly. Upset with her inability to remain immune to his impersonal perusal, she resolved to stand firm. She had locked her door for a reason. He would have to understand that unlocking it would change nothing. "I think the answer should be obvious. My door was locked and it will remain so."

Three long strides and he was standing in front of her. "I think not," he growled.

She glared up at him. How dared he stand there, dictating to her! "Next, you will be pointing out how fortunate I should consider myself that you chose not to ravish me in my bed while I slept."

His dark brows snapped together. "I take no woman by force!"

"What a relief to discover I truly have nothing to fear, your Grace," she answered with more conviction than her shaking knees made her feel. "If it is my consent you need, you may consider the matter closed."

Once more assured of her position, Danielle turned and scooped up the robe that had fallen to the floor.

Devon thoughtfully studied the tantalizing curves her thin gown presented to him. There was no doubt in his mind that if he reached for her, pride would make her fight him every step of the way. His blue eyes brightened at the prospect. He strongly suspected that the claws she had shown thus far were merely those of a kitten. It was the brief glimpses of a tigress he saw behind those flashing green eyes that intrigued him. Was it the adventurous side of him that wished to bring it forth—or the foolish?

"A man has certain needs, my dear," he baited her.

Danielle whirled to face him. Aunt Margaret had hinted as much, but Danielle was prepared. She had thought this out thoroughly. Although she was not entirely pleased with her decision, she had convinced herself that, given the alternative, she was more than willing to relinquish the vile duty.

"You have my permission to take your needs wherever you like," she stated with a defiant toss of her head.

Devon pulled her to him. Arching a questioning brow, he asked, "You wish me to seek my pleasures elsewhere?"

Her robe slipped once more to the floor. Swallowing hard when she found herself lying against his naked chest, Danielle was forced to look into those startling blue eyes.

"You have an excellent grasp of the situation, your Grace," she said, holding herself stiffly in his arms. "As far as I'm concerned, you may spend the rest of your days wherever it is that men go to do such things."

"That's very generous of you," he answered blithely, though his words hid a twinge of bitterness that it had to be this way. Yet what had he expected? "But you've forgotten one tiny detail, love. The children." He grinned down at her. "With me gone so much of the time 'seeking my pleasures' elsewhere, what do you suggest I do about the children?"

"I'll not stay without them," she said between clenched teeth.

"Are you saying that in order to have the bride, I must take the children?"

Too late, Danielle realized the trap he was setting for her. What would she do if he were to say that the future of the children depended on her sharing his bed? Was she prepared to pay the price? She tossed back a curl that had fallen across the front of her nightdress. She'd not give up without a fight.

"In Virginia, a man would be pleased to have a wife who could bring a household of servants to her marriage."

"Servants, yes, my dear. Children, no," he pointed out. "They make a poor substitute for a dowry."

The eyes that met his were bright pools of green. His chest tightened. Would the emerald pools deepen if she lay in his arms, aroused by the fires of passion? Regretfully, he pushed the image from his thoughts. It had never been his plan to nurture this marriage. Emotional involvement was the last thing he wanted. He only needed to create a convincing facade.

"I am prepared to overlook the absence of a dowry."

"In view of the great lengths you went to in order to make me agree to this marriage, that's very considerate. If a dowry carries such importance, your Grace, you should have married Lady Emily.''

"If you will recall, that was my original plan. It was your announcement to Nathan that put an end to that. But I am willing to accept the children, providing . . .''

"Another condition, your Grace?'' she demanded.

Unable to resist, Devon stroked the side of her face. "As I was saying, I am willing to accept the children providing you play the part of a devoted and loving wife in the presence of others.''

She swatted his hand away. "You ask that after all you have done?''

"I don't understand your reluctance. Given your acting talents, it shouldn't require a great deal of effort on your part. That little bit of nonsense you drummed up for the wedding guests should be sufficient for now.''

One delicate brow arched upward. "For now?''

He grinned down at her. "You should learn to accept the small concessions I am willing to make. Surely that's not too much to ask in exchange for the children remaining at Burnshire.''

The uncompromising set of his jaw warned her not to press the issue. "As you wish, your Grace,'' she said, abruptly turning from him. "Now, if you will excuse me, I must get dressed.''

She crossed the room to the bell cord that hung beside her dressing table. Pulling it, she turned back to dismiss her husband. "Good da—'' The words lodged in her throat and she took a step backward.

Lord Stanton stood directly in front of her, so close she had to tip her head back to look up at him. "It was my understanding that I was to be allowed a small particle of privacy when in my room.''

Devon moved closer, forcing Danielle to step farther back. How dared she dismiss him so casually! He reached up and placed a hand on the wall to either side of her. Perhaps after a small taste of what she was giving up . . .

"Have you forgotten our agreement so soon?" he asked huskily.

Danielle swallowed hard. He took such delight in causing her discomfort, but must he stand so close? "Our agreement was for the occasions when we find ourselves in the presence of others."

He stepped closer, trapping her body firmly against the wall. "I'm rather new at these acts of deception, while you have obviously had a great deal of experience. Perhaps I could benefit from a few lessons."

Danielle's heart raced. She tried to turn from him, but the attempt only made her more aware of his hard-muscled frame and the thinness of her white linen nightdress as it moved against his open shirt. "Kindly leave my room."

He curled his fingers around the pink ribbon at the throat of her nightdress. The pristine bow gave way so effortlessly that Danielle gasped. Slowly his fingers outlined the opening.

"But what of the coaching for my part?" he asked.

"The lessons your actions imply are not appropriate for the drawing room," she answered, placing her trembling hands against his chest. The warmth that spread through her as the crisp black hairs curled around her fingers made her annoyed. "Now get out of my room!"

He lowered his head to kiss the pulse that beat furiously at the base of her neck. "Don't be so hasty to discount my offer," he said. "You might find that you prefer the way I act in your bedchamber to my drawing room behavior."

"Never!" Danielle cried as his warm breath laid a path of awakening desire along her neck. Frantically, she pushed against him, only to find that he welcomed her efforts. Danielle closed her eyes. What was she to do? This was nothing like the snatches of conversation she had overheard on the woes of a wife's dreaded duties in the marriage bed. She knew from the night in the stables when he had kissed her that her body couldn't be trusted in his arms. Even now it was be-

ginning to respond as his whispered breath sent enticing chills from her head to her toes. A lump suddenly
formed in her throat and she found it very hard to get
her breath. Her knees went weak, threatening to give
way at any moment. Was this what it was like to experience the vapors? Yet she felt strangely alive for
someone who was on the verge of fainting.

"W-why are you doing this?" she asked in ragged
gasps.

"On the off chance that you might change your mind
about sharing my bed," he blatantly lied, knowing full
well he only meant to punish her for the crease she
had put in his pride.

"No-o-o," she moaned.

"Would it truly be so terrible?" he whispered in her
ear. "Does the thought of lying in my arms repulse
you so much that you would deny the desires and passions that are tugging at your very soul, crying to be
released?"

"Ple-e-e-ease don't."

"Tell me that you don't ache inside," he demanded
as he laid a fresh path of kisses down her throat. "Tell
me and I'll leave you alone."

She arched her neck to one side as the taste of sweet
agony filled her. Could she, in all honesty, say she
wanted nothing from him as a husband? His kisses had
unlocked a part of her she hadn't known existed. Was
she prepared to shut the door on those feelings forever?

"Answer me, Danielle," he demanded again.

"Your Grace," Mary called as she pushed open the
door. "I have your morning chocolate."

The sight of Lord Stanton almost caused Mary to
drop the tray. "I'll return later."

"You may stay, Mary," he said, a mocking smile on
his lips. "Her Grace will be needing you." He traced
a finger across Danielle's lips. "I shall expect to see you
downstairs later."

The place on her lips tingled long after he had left.

"The beast," she whispered over and over again. He took such delight in provoking her.

She tried to concentrate on her bath, scrubbing furiously at all the places where he had touched her, but she was unable to wash away the memories. Even fully clothed, she could still close her eyes and feel the path his fingers had taken as they traced the neckline of her nightdress. The most horrifying part was her suspicion that he was merely toying with her emotions.

Having finishing her toilette, she escaped her room to find the entire house staff lined up in the great hall below. Plastering a smile on her face, Danielle descended the steps. Her duties had already begun.

Mrs. Talbut apologized for Lord Stanton's absence. An unexpected guest had arrived from London, so he was unable to join her for breakfast. Danielle was surprised at the twinge of disappointment that came with the announcement, but she pushed it aside. She had duties to attend to.

"Lady Julia sends her love," Captain Edward Winslow said as he sank down into one of the deep leather chairs in Devon's study. "And she wanted me to remind you she's upset because you wouldn't allow her to come to your wedding."

"The risk was too great and she knew that." Devon moved to his desk. "And our friend?"

"He has agreed to the arrangement," the captain replied.

"It will not present a problem for him?"

"With his outstanding debts, he was more than anxious to take a vacation from England for a few months. He will be making a social call on Lady Julia and Lady Bradford this very afternoon."

Devon picked up his quill. "Do you think Lady Bradford will accompany Mother to Scotland?"

"I understand that she has already accepted. With her niece married to you, she was pleased to have the distraction."

"I'm forever in your debt, Edward." With a flourish

of his pen, he scrawled a note to Giles. "Give this to my agent before you leave and he will take care of the man's creditors."

"He said you would say that and stressed that you not. He wants to do this—as a friend."

"Nonsense. If he is going to act as a constant escort for my mother, I cannot have his creditors hounding him."

Edward let the subject drop. He and Devon had been close friends most of their lives, and he knew Devon would have his own way in this. "I still find it difficult to believe that Nathan would attempt to have Lady Julia murdered without a very good reason. It would have to be extremely important for him."

"I've turned it over and over in my mind and I have to agree with you. It doesn't make a lot of sense, but my agent is positive that the man who tried to kill me in Jamaica is also the one who tried to maneuver Mother's coach off the road. If I hadn't been forced to kill the man before he killed me, we might have some answers. But at the time, I didn't think sparing his life was necessary."

"Setting yourself up as Nathan's target is too risky," the captain said solemnly.

"Sitting around patiently waiting for one of his henchmen to stab me in the back again seems rather risky, too. For as long as I can remember, Nathan has wanted Burnshire and the title. Now I intend to convince him that he has truly lost them both. Let him think that my marriage will produce an heir. If his greed is all I think it is, he will try to kill me before that happens. And this time he will not catch me unprepared."

"But this is far too dangerous. Granted, Robert is here should you have need of him, but he can't be with you every minute. Let me continue to watch Nathan. He's sure to slip up sooner or later."

"The truth, Edward. What have your investigations turned up thus far?"

Edward tugged at the lace cuff of his shirt. He knew

all too well that had Devon not learned of the attempt
to harm Lady Julia, chances were that he might never
have returned to England to claim his inheritance.
Clearing his throat, Edward pulled several notes from
his pocket. "Nathan has three men he uses to do his
little errands. Chilton, Faris, and Boyd. It seems Boyd
left on a ship several months ago and hasn't been heard
from since."

"My assailant?"

"That would appear to be the case. Chilton posted
two young lads from the orphanage on the docks to
await Boyd's return."

Devon's grin matched Edward's. "They'll have a
long wait."

"That they will," Edward agreed. "And in the
meantime, Chilton is having the devil's own time
keeping the lads under control."

Devon's head lifted in interest.

"One of the lads took it upon himself to relieve one
of the ship's passengers of his purse. Turned out the
passenger was one of the king's couriers and he raised
a royal ruckus. Chilton must have decided it would be
a bit embarrassing to have the lad nabbed, because he
immediately gave up the vigil and whisked them back
to the orphanage."

The room filled with Devon's easy laughter. "That
is merely the beginning of the little irritations I intend
to make sure my dear cousin suffers."

Edward's smile quickly faded. "I still believe the
early appearance of an heir will put an end to any as-
pirations Nathan might have."

"We've discussed this before. Marriage was my father's plan, not mine."

Danielle silently opened the study door. She didn't
wish to disturb Devon and his guest unnecessarily. She
would just peek in and see if they were about finished,
but the topic of conversation fascinated her.

"Devon, you're eight and twenty," the stranger
pointed out. "If you don't settle down soon and pro-

vide your family with an heir, it's very likely that Nathan will get everything anyway."

"Enough!" Devon hadn't meant to be so abrupt, but how could he explain to his friend that, increasingly, his own thoughts had been turning in that direction of late and the indecision was keeping him awake most of the night. The more he was with Danielle, the more he was tempted to bend to his father's wishes and consummate the union. But knowing his need to return to the sea, he wondered if it would be fair to Danielle to try. Besides which, she had made it decidedly clear she'd have no part of the marriage. "The marriage will be what I wish to make it, Edward. After things are satisfactorily taken care of here, I will be returning to my ships. When it's time to leave, I won't have a wife weeping on my coattails that her child needs a father."

"And did you also tell him that your wife agrees?" Danielle asked sweetly from the doorway. Both men turned sharply to her. "I came to ask our guest if he would care to join us for breakfast."

"Danielle, come in," Devon said as he stood and offered her a chair. "I'd like you to meet Captain Winslow, an old and dear friend of mine."

"Captain Winslow," Danielle acknowledged with a nod of her head.

"Edward, this is my dear wife, Danielle, Duchess of Burnshire," Devon said.

The captain swept a deep bow. "I must say you're every bit as lovely as your husband has said."

"Is that so, Captain Winslow?" she said politely, reserving her frosty glance for her husband.

Edward quickly picked up his papers from the corner of Devon's desk. "I—I must be leaving." He stumbled over the words, embarrassed that this beautiful creature must have overheard their conversation. "It was a pleasure to meet you, your Grace." He nodded to Danielle and, after a bow to Devon, left.

It was several moments after the door closed that Danielle turned to Devon. "You self-righteous son of a sea biscuit!"

His laughter was rich and warm. "My, my, such language," he said. "I'll have to speak to Brodie about her tutelage."

"How dare you let Captain Winslow believe I would use a child to keep you tied to Burnshire? If I wanted you to remain here, I would not need a child to accomplish—"

He had her in his arms before she had finished.

His lips curved in a devilish grin. "What would you do, love? Seduce me?"

A warm flush spread through Danielle. Was the man a sorcerer that he always seemed to read her thoughts?

"Don't misunderstand me," he continued. "The thought is immensely appealing."

She pulled away from him. "You . . ."

"You have another name for me?"

Danielle clamped her mouth shut and stormed out of the room, slamming the door behind her.

"He's thrown you out on your ear, hasn't he?" Brodie accused as she watched her former pupil pace the schoolroom floor. Setting aside the books she was unpacking, Brodie sank down on one of the wooden chairs. Despite a few misgivings at first, she had come to the conclusion that the Duke of Burnshire was the husband for Danielle. In time, Danielle would realize it too. But until then, Brodie definitely had her work cut out for her. "What am I to do with you? Didn't I tell you it wasn't wise to tread on his toes? Granted, Lord Stanton wasn't your first choice—"

Danielle swung around to face her. "He was not my choice at all."

Brodie let out a long sigh. "You could have at least considered the advantages of this marriage before you angered him. Why, we won't have to scrimp and save anymore. You and the chil—"

"Why do you assume it was *I* who angered *him*?" Danielle interrupted.

Brodie crossed her arms over the front of her dust

apron. "You forget. I have known you since you took your first breath."

"You needn't talk as if we should be packing our bags," Danielle said as she resumed her pacing. "His Grace has not tossed us out as yet. He merely asks that I conduct myself as a dutiful wife in front of the servants and guests."

"Then I might just as well instruct Mary to repack the trunks and be done with it. Since the day you were born, you've yet to hold your tongue. You mark my words, we'll be gone before the week is out."

Danielle stopped at the window that overlooked the back lawns. "Must you always think the worst of me?"

"I know you too well, Danny."

"It is not always my fault," she argued, plucking absently at the hem of the curtains. "These things just seem to happen."

"Yet they always seem to happen to you," Brodie mumbled.

Danielle looked up. "Well, you shall see. Come the end of this week, we will still be here. Unless, of course, I am forced to murder my husband before then."

"Good gracious, Danielle." Brodie picked up one of the books she had unpacked and fanned her flushed face. "Don't even think such things."

"If you had heard him this morning, you would agree that the thought was justified." Danielle resumed her restless pacing. "He said the children were a poor substitute for a dowry. Well, I'll show him. We'll all earn our way."

"And how do you propose to do that?"

She took a chair across from Brodie, sat, and picked up one of the books. "There must be any number of things that need to be done around here. To begin with, I'll teach the children how to mend the linens."

"And who, may I ask, is going to teach you?"

"Don't be so disagreeable, Brodie. If I can learn how to repair a roof, I can surely learn how to mend linens."

"Mending requires a skillful needle. You would do better to concentrate your efforts on pleasing your husband," the former governess scolded.

"Brodie! How can you suggest such a thing! The man is a beast. Why, he . . . he . . ." Danielle paused, her face a bright red.

"He asked that you fulfill your duties as a wife?" Brodie finished for her as she shoved a stack of books onto the shelf.

Danielle's blush deepened. "Well, yes . . . I mean no . . . not actually."

"What did he say?"

"He said he would excuse me from them."

"I thought him smarter than that," Brodie said thoughtfully. "Hand me that small stack of books, please."

"You seem disappointed," Danielle accused. "What did you expect? That he would force his attentions on me? I had not thought you would expect me to share his bed."

Brodie straightened in her chair. "Are you going to help me with these books, or are you going to sit there talking nonsense all morning?"

"Nonsense! Why, he might force me to . . ."

"Danielle, you need not worry about that. His Grace is not the type of man to force his attentions on a woman."

"That's what he said," she answered, surprised at the note of disappointment in her voice.

"You'd do well to think on that."

Danielle had been able to think of little else all morning, but she hadn't expected Brodie to bring it up.

"Consider the possibilities," her companion said, ignoring the tug on her conscience for what she was about to do. Matchmaking had never been her forte, but Danielle's stubborn resolve had to be broken down.

"What is it you have in mind?"

Brodie pulled her chair closer and whispered, "It's so simple, I'm surprised you haven't thought of it yourself."

"Are you going to tell me, or are you going to continue talking in riddles?" Danielle asked in exasperation.

Brodie patted her hand. "Men are such predictable creatures, my dear. An intelligent woman should be able to twist any man around her little finger."

"And how do you propose I do that? By seducing my own husband?"

"That would be a beginning."

"Well, think again," Danielle shouted, jumping to her feet. "The man's thoughts are already leaning in that direction. If I so much as bat an eyelash, he would be carrying me off to his bed."

Brodie sat there calmly, looking up at her. "Ah, but if a woman is clever enough, she can promise a man everything but give him nothing."

"And what's to keep him from taking what has been promised?"

"His Grace is a gentleman. He would never force himself upon you. Flirt with him. Hint of the way things might be if only he could storm the wall you make him think you've built around yourself. That should do the trick. He will be like clay in your hands."

A smile came gradually to Danielle's lips. The idea did have its merits. She would love to twist his emotions as he had been twisting hers of late. But she would have to be careful not to become a victim of her own trap.

Chapter 8

Enlisting Mrs. Talbut's assistance, Danielle set about assigning each of the older children to a task. It was a joy to watch them, for they were thrilled Burnshire was to be their new home and eager to learn. Fortunately, the servants voiced no objections, and by lunchtime she had them all settled in their new duties. If only she could deal with her new husband half as successfully, things would be close to ideal.

Having dispensed with her morning duties, Danielle changed into her blue wool gown, then hurried down the stairs. She was pleased with what she had accomplished in only one morning. She would show her arrogant husband that she was more than capable of handling her responsibilities as mistress of Burnshire. She would be the perfect wife in every way. Well, every way except one.

But Brodie's suggestion continued to nag at her. Could she really manage to pull it off? She had never been one to flirt, although she had certainly witnessed enough of it during her London season.

Danielle stopped in front of the hall mirror at the bottom of the staircase. Skillfully, she lowered her gaze, then looked up through her lashes. Tilting her head just so, she batted her long lashes at her reflection. A smile creased the corners of her lips. He more than deserved it.

The audacity of the man, thinking she desired his attentions. She had managed quite well up to this point in her life without . . . that . . . She strode purposefully down the hall. It would serve him right if she took Brodie's advice. The man was conceited beyond all reason, and it would do her heart good to feed him a large spoonful of his own medicine.

And the absolute gall of him to mention the absence of a dowry! After everything he had done to coerce her into this marriage, how dared he even suggest such a thing? Why, the children were an asset, not a liability.

Bob stood outside the dining room and opened the door for her.

"Oh!" Danielle exclaimed when she saw the two little heads, one blond, the other black, bent over a pile of silver utensils on the dining room table.

Katie looked up. Lord Stanton's neckcloth, one side tucked rakishly behind her ear, was still tied under her jaw. "I don't have time to chat now, Miss Danny. I'm helping Jeremy polish the silver."

After a quick glance down the hall, Danielle frantically tugged at Bob's sleeve, pulling him into the room. She slammed the door behind them. Leaning back against the solid oak frame, she half expected to hear her husband's voice raised in anger.

"Bob, you must help me clear away this mess," she said, reaching for the jar of polish. "Lord Stanton will be here any moment wanting his lunch."

"You mustn't fret so, Miss Danny," Katie scolded, pushing aside a glossy black curl that had fallen across her cheek. "Lord Stanton has already been here." Jeremy's head bobbed in agreement as they both continued to rub the silver pieces.

Danielle smiled and began to clear the table. "Cook will set the pieces aside, and you may finish them tomorrow."

Katie's face twisted up in concentration. "But a few more rubs and this one should be done," she offered proudly, holding up a serving spoon for Danielle's inspection.

Great globs of gray compound coated the surface. It would take a servant hours to finish polishing the pieces the children had worked on. She ventured a look at Bob. He averted his eyes, but the suspicious twitch of his lips gave him away. Danielle groaned silently. This would have to happen, just when she was trying to prove to her husband that the children would be a help to the staff.

She took the silver ladle from Katie. "Mary has lunch ready for you in the schoolroom. You mustn't keep her waiting."

"Yes, Miss Danny," they said in unison, tossing the polishing cloths on the table and scooting off their chairs.

Danielle stood aside to avoid being trampled as they ran from the room. "Bob, I trust that word of this will go no further. I would hate to hear this tale being bandied about belowstairs."

"Yes, your Grace . . . I mean no, your Grace," he answered humbly. "No one shall hear of it from me. I will put the room in order myself."

"Thank you, Bob," she said, giving him a bright smile. At least she had someone she felt she could put her trust in. "Do you know where Lord Stanton is?"

"He asked that you join him in the breakfast room. He is expecting the vicar for lunch."

Danielle stiffened. Lunching with the vicar! Well, if Devon wished the company of his cousin for lunch, then he would not be lunching with her. She'd be switched if she'd sit down at the same table with that wall-eyed weasel.

"Please inform the housekeeper that I will be taking my lunch in my room and extend my apologies to his Grace—I fear I feel a headache coming on."

Danielle restlessly twirled the quill pen. Having already counted the flowers in the fabric of her chairs three times, which had netted her three different totals, she started a letter to Lady Bradford. But after a few sentences, her mind wandered from the words. The letter forgotten, she took to expressing her thoughts in a simple line drawing. The identities of the arrogant sea captain tied to the mast of his own ship and the young woman dressed in the clothes of a seaman lighting a fire at his feet were all too apparent. Danielle picked up a fresh piece of paper. She had to admit that Aunt Margaret would not see the humor in the sketch, but it was hard to concentrate on a letter when the only words that came to mind were those of her husband. He would be returning to his ships as soon as he had things settled. Why had he kept this from her? She might have been more willing to agree to the marriage had he told her of his plans from the very beginning. But no, he had gotten more enjoyment out of forcing her into the marriage. Yet why should she care? In a matter of months he would be gone. Somehow the prospect didn't appeal to her as much as it should.

Restless, she went to check on the children. Katie was such a scamp, there was no telling what she might get into next, and now Jeremy had taken to following her around like a puppy. Although they looked nothing alike, Jeremy's features were as delicate as Katie's, and Danielle wondered, with his obvious good breeding, what set of circumstances had brought the lad to the orphanage.

Well, she would see that they received the upbringing their parents had denied them. At the same time, she was forced to admit that, with the Stanton name behind her to give the project acceptability, it would be a lot easier to accomplish.

As she topped the stairs to the nursery, a figure at the end of the hall caught her attention. A short, thin man was opening each door, looking inside, then moving to the next. Could it be Nathan's man? she wondered.

Danielle ducked down on the stairs. He had warned her he would be sending someone after Jeremy. Well, he'd not get him. Slowly, she raised her head just as the man disappeared into the schoolroom. She didn't know how long he would be in there, but she had to take the chance. Quickly she tiptoed up the rest of the steps, then ran down the hall to the nearest bedchamber, which she searched frantically for something to use as a weapon. The only thing she could find was a child's wooden chair. She snatched it up. She would have to hurry, she told herself, because even now he might be carrying Jeremy away.

Reaching the schoolroom, she stopped and took a deep breath. She could hear voices inside. Thank goodness, she was not too late. Even as the thought crossed her mind, she heard the sound of heavy footsteps approaching the other side of the door.

"No!" she heard Brodie shout. Danielle gripped the chair firmly over her shoulder as the door opened, then swung the chair in a wide arc at the scoundrel's head. *Thwack!* It hit its mark. With a loud thump and a strange *poof*, the man and his burden fell to the floor, a black cloud exploding in the doorway. Danielle stood openmouthed as ashes rained down on her.

"Good lord, Danielle," Brodie scolded, setting down her cup of tea. "Whatever possessed you to hit Devon's servant?"

"A servant?" Danielle looked across the fallen man. Brodie was seated at a small table with Jeremy and Katie. "I heard you shout," she said, confused at the tranquil scene.

"Katie was about to scoop her dessert into Jeremy's lap."

The man groaned at Danielle's feet. "He wasn't trying to take Jeremy?" she asked.

"Good heavens, no," Brodie said. "He came to remove the ashes one of the chambermaids had cleaned from the hearths."

"He's one of the servants?" she cried. "But I thought he was trying to take Jeremy. Lord Stanton is never going to understand."

Brodie crossed the room and knelt beside the unconscious man. "Perhaps it would be best if you were to leave before he comes to his senses. With you gone, I might be able to convince him that he tripped and fell."

"He'll never believe you. I'm sure he saw the chair."

"As long as you stand there covered with ashes, I'll not have a prayer."

Danielle could see Brodie's point, and as another moan came from the man, she hurried off. Using the back stairs, she made it to her room without being seen. Careful that her skirts not soil the blue carpet, Danielle walked on tippy-toe to the tile floor of her bathing chamber. Having rung for Mary, she unfastened her dress and stepped out of the blackened gown. When Mary arrived, Danielle ordered a hot bath, but not before having to endure a scolding from her as well.

Try as they might, the ashes clung to Danielle's face and neck and arms. The water was soon covered with a black, slimy film, and it had to be emptied. Danielle sat in a chair, wrapped in her bathing blanket, while the servants emptied the tub, then returned with warm water to refill it. Thankfully, their second effort met with success and Danielle was soon clean. Emerging from the tub, she dried her hair as best she could, then reached for a fresh bathing blanket and tucked it around her. Next she took her brush and began working on the tangles.

Suddenly the door of her bathing chamber burst open behind her, slamming against the wall. Her hand, poised above her curls, trembled as she looked over her shoulder to see her husband's large frame filling the hall doorway. The brush slipped from her fingers into the tub.

"Now see what you've done," she cried, plunging her arm into the water. She cast him a disparaging glance as she knelt beside the tub and searched the bottom for her brush. Then it finally occurred to her that he hadn't said a word, and she ventured another glance at him. His blue eyes were as dark as storm clouds. Her fingers curled around the brush and she slowly eased herself up from the side of the tub. "It was an accident," she stated quickly as she backed slowly toward her bedchamber.

"An accident?" he echoed, momentarily distracted by the delightful picture his wife made, wrapped in her white bathing blanket. Entranced, he watched a drop of water fall from an auburn curl. Coursing its way down the front of her bare shoulder, the wet pearl rode the wave of her creamy breast before disappearing into the deep valley between. Involuntarily, Devon licked his lips.

"I swear," Danielle pleaded. "Had I known he was there to collect the ashes, I would never have hit him."

Confused, Devon raised his eyes to hers. A frown creased his forehead. "Hit him?" he repeated, stepping toward her.

Heaven forbid, he was going to do away with her before she had a chance to explain. Danielle turned and fled to her bedchamber, slamming and locking the door behind her.

"Daniell-l-le," he threatened. Contemplating the possibility of strangling his beautiful wife and getting away with it, he pounded on the door. When she defied him like this, he wanted to take her by the arms and shake her. Yet the fire in her eyes brought other temptations to mind that he'd do best to ignore. "Open this door!"

"Not until you promise you'll not harm me."

"This is ridiculous, Danielle. Why would I hurt you?" Not a sound came from the other side of the oak door. "I promise I'll not harm you. Now tell me. Who was hit?"

"Nathan's man. Only he wasn't Nathan's man," she babbled from inside her bedchamber. "But I thought he was Nathan's man. And it was a valid mistake," she ended defiantly.

Devon's brows knit in confusion. "You were the one responsible for the lump on my servant's forehead?"

"I'm dreadfully sorry about hurting him."

"You were the one who hit him with a chair?"

"He shouldn't have been skulking around the halls like that. Anyone would have thought he was up to no good," she said.

Danielle's confession met with a hearty laugh. Curious, she slipped the bathing chamber lock and opened the door. "What is there to laugh about? I hurt the poor man."

"He insists it was the devil, come to claim his soul. Unfortunately, my driver is encouraging the tale."

"But that's ridiculous."

"Nonetheless, he swears the chair came flying out of nowhere and refuses to return to the schoolroom."

"Then I must tell him it was I," she said, still defiant. But the gesture was lost in a gasp as the straightening of her shoulders loosened the bathing blanket she had wrapped around her. Devon's gaze followed as the blanket slipped to her feet. Shocked, Danielle's eyes flew to his. There was no mistaking the desire she saw there. Quickly she kicked the blanket aside and slammed the door again. Shoving the lock home, she lay back against the door, her face a bright shade of pink.

One thing was clear. If she had interpreted Lord Stanton's thoughts correctly, Brodie was right. If a woman was clever and brave enough, she could get anything she wanted.

Devon tapped on the door. "Danielle. Open this door," he said calmly.

"Not until I'm dressed," she answered. If only she had the courage, she would open the door and court his desire. If he were handled in just the right way, she might be able to get anything—perhaps even Nathan's head. Or better yet, her freedom.

Devon pounded on the door again. "This is ridiculous, Danielle. After all, we're married."

"Not to my way of thinking," she blurted out before she could stop herself. "Oh . . ." she moaned silently. She could have kicked herself. This was no way to cajole her husband. But what did it matter? She was a coward. She would never open the door—at least not unless she was dressed.

Suddenly, an idea tumbled into Danielle's head. A devilish grin tilted the corners of her full lips. What if she were to dress? Not in her gown. But there was always that sinfully thin green negligee Mary had insisted on packing. She rushed to the wardrobe. Where would Mary have put the thing?

"Just a moment, dear," she called sweetly over her shoulder.

Devon's brows lifted quizzically at the unfamiliar endearment. What was his bride up to now? He pressed his ear against the door. The whirl of activity assured him she hadn't left the room. He raised his hand to pound on the door once more when suddenly it opened.

His eyes widened in surprise. The woman-child he had married had suddenly been transformed into a seductress. Dark auburn curls framed her delicate face and hung to her waist in a red cloud of sensuality, offering him an enticing glimpse of a shimmering green gown that clung to the lush curves of her beautiful body. Slowly, he drank in the sight before him. She took a step forward and the gown appeared to have a life of its own. Instead of hiding her nakedness, it only served to accentuate it.

Reluctantly, he lifted his face to hers. Luminous green eyes peeked provocatively at him from beneath dark, thick-lashed eyes. Her lips curved in a bright, innocent smile and she stepped close to him, her silk-clad body brushing his. She tossed back the mass of curls covering her bare shoulders and looked longingly into his eyes. He could feel his body responding to the nearness of her, and it seemed only natural for him to slip his arms around her and pull her closer.

Boldly, she ran her fingers down the front of his shirt. "Surely you are not upset with me," she coaxed, batting her dark lashes at him. "It was only a mistake. You see, I thought he was one of Nathan's men, after Jeremy."

Devon's blue eyes narrowed. Was that what all this was about? She meant to avoid his anger? He started to tell her it wasn't necessary, then thought better of it. What would it hurt to play along? "Nathan's men?" he said, his voice husky despite the cold water of reality she had just thrown on him. "Not very likely."

"How can you be sure?" She pouted. "He could have sent someone after Jeremy." She hadn't had much practice playing the flirt. She could only cross her fingers and hope for the best.

"Had you been at lunch as I asked, you would have learned before soup was served that Nathan's man was detained."

Danielle stepped back from his arms. "Detained?" she repeated, dropping the act.

"You give me so little credit, Danielle," he said, pulling her back to him. "I've known Nathan a lot longer than you. He would never invite himself to lunch without a good reason."

She ventured another look at him. If he wasn't upset about her latest exploit, why had he come storming into her bath? "You thought Nathan would try to take Jeremy?" she asked, hoping to put an end to this confusion.

"I knew he had sold the lad and I suspect it was for a great deal more than the account books at the orphanage will show. If he planned to abduct the boy from Burnshire, lunch would be the perfect time. The servants who were not busy serving would be taking their own lunch in the kitchen."

Danielle relaxed in Lord Stanton's arms. Perhaps there was a chance to be rid of Nathan after all. If only Devon could be persuaded to cooperate. Determined that she give it a try, Danielle slipped back easily into the part of the seductress. Wantonly, she laid her body against his.

"Why not be rid of him altogether?"

The corners of Devon's lips twitched. His wife had surely missed her calling. There wasn't an actress in ten who could do as fine a job. Well, two could play this game. Let her think it was all her doing. If she was so willing to give, he was more than willing to take. Holding her in his arms, he pushed aside a stray curl. Slowly lowering his head, he placed a kiss in the hollow of her slender neck. "It might prove difficult," he whispered. "But I could more than likely be persuaded to try."

Unaware that her fate was hanging by a delicate thread, Danielle forced herself to remain relaxed as his arms tightened about her. But she would have to be careful. It would be so easy to give in to the sensations his kisses evoked. She must keep her wits about her. Instinctively, she moved against him. A small moan escaped his lips—or was it hers? No matter. Brodie was right. He fell so predictably in with her scheme. This was her opportunity. If only she could get him to agree.

Danielle slid her arms behind his head and pressed her body into his. "And what would that incentive be, your Grace?" she asked innocently.

Devon was tempted to throw all caution to the wind and claim his bride, but forced himself to resist. "Nathan will never relinquish his hope of someday having Burnshire as long as he feels we are strangers."

Danielle searched his face, but his hooded eyes gave her no clue to his thoughts. Had he changed his mind? She bit her lip in frustration. Was he now asking that she truly be his wife? "But, Lord Stanton, I already agreed to appear a loving spouse," she argued.

"Yet you insist on calling me Lord Stanton. Is the name Devon too difficult for you?" he asked, trying to concentrate on the conversation and not on the body that stood enticing within his arms.

"I will endeavor to call you Devon, your Grace."

Devon frowned at her. "And yet you forget your duties as my hostess?"

"Surely you didn't expect me to entertain your cousin?" she asked.

His lips suddenly curved in a smile. "You should have been at lunch, love. You missed a rare treat," he said, lowering his head to hers. Slowly he began nibbling at the edges of her lips.

"Yes?" she said, feeling faint at his bold participation in her game.

Devon marveled at the feel of her. Her lips were so soft and their taste so sweet. Hell, he'd help her with this seduction. Sucking gently—like an expert—Devon teased her lips apart.

"Nathan nearly choked . . ." he said between kisses, "on his soup . . . when Molly and Sara served the cold meats. I take it . . . they were . . . another acquisition . . . from the orphanage."

Danielle struggled to reply. "It was you who said I could keep all I had taken from . . ."

Devon could no longer deny the fires she had ignited deep in his loins. He crushed her to him and covered her mouth with his own. Hungrily, he drank of her kiss until he was filled with the haunting scent of her lavender fragrance. His fingers found the hem of her gown, and lifting it, he ran his hand up her naked back. Her moan of pleasure and the silken feel of her skin broke the last of his reserve, and his hands dropped to her rounded buttocks.

Danielle was drifting on a sensual cloud of forbidden desires as he boldly cupped her body in his intimate embrace. But she fell to earth with a thud when he forced her hips against the evidence of his wanton need. Frantic, she bit down hard on his lip.

"Damnation!" he cursed, pulling away. He lifted his hand to dab at the blood on his lip. "Why did you bite me?"

Danielle trembled in fury. "How dare you touch me like that!" she shouted. "I did not grant you leave."

He grabbed her by the shoulders, his eyes a dangerous shade of blue as he glared down at her. "When a man's wife aches to be bedded, it's a husband's duty to oblige."

"Your only duty is to protect the children," she said, twisting out of his grasp. "Mine was to marry you."

"And what of your duties as hostess?"

"So this is about lunch, is it? You're upset because I didn't want to sit at the same table with that toad. Well, I assure you, your cousin is no more comfortable in my presence than I am in his."

"Exactly my point, my dear," he said gruffly. "I don't wish that my cousin be made comfortable."

"Then why have him here?"

Devon reached out and curled his fingers in her hair. "So that each time he is with us, he will think on all that my marriage has cost him."

"You mean we should taunt Nathan with our marriage?" she asked, confused.

Devon held her head, forcing her eyes to meet his. "No, my intentions are that *I*, not *you*, do so."

"But I can help," she said eagerly.

He dropped his hands and groaned. "You're not going to let this rest unless I take you into my confidence, are you? At least having you working with me will be safer for the servants. After all, I can't have you going around hitting everyone on the head. Good servants are too hard to find."

"What do you wish me to do?" she asked, her green eyes alight.

Reluctantly, he stepped away from her. Crossing to the wardrobe, he pulled out a green traveling gown, a warm velvet cloak, and a matching bonnet, then held them out to her. "Let's start by you getting dressed. Then we'll tackle the Picketts."

The brilliant smile she gave him warmed him to his toes. The lady definitely had a way about her.

Danielle tapped her foot impatiently while she let her eyes travel around the orphanage's drawing room. Devon had been closeted with Mr. Pickett in the office for well over an hour, and she was rapidly losing patience with Isabel Pickett's trivial complaints. If she heard one more word about the new gowns the woman had ordered and not received, she would scream.

She would give anything to know what was being said in the office. Though she had given Devon her word that she would behave less than two hours ago, already she was finding it difficult to sit idly by while he handled everything.

". . . the most delicious shade of blue you would ever hope to see this side of Paris. Why, I just simply couldn't take my eyes off of it. I was telling Mr. Pickett as how . . ."

What was keeping them so long? After all, how long could it take to march in and demand to see the account books? Surely Pickett couldn't refuse. As sole supporter of the orphanage, wasn't Devon entitled to see them at any time?

". . . the watered silk is the most elegant. Don't you agree?"

Oh, fidaddle. What was the Pickett woman asking her now?

"Oh, my, yes," Danielle agreed, hoping she wouldn't live to regret her inattentiveness. Her eyes strayed back to the doorway.

"You mustn't worry," Mrs. Pickett said, reaching out to pat Danielle's hand. "I'm sure Mr. Pickett won't be keeping his Grace much longer. It must be very trying for you, what with your husband's time being taken up with orphanage matters."

"Devon has taken an interest in the welfare of the children, Mrs. Pickett, and I fully intend to support him."

Isabel twirled one of the dark brown sausage curls that hung down on each side of her head. "That's very gracious of you, considering all your new duties as Duchess of Burnshire. What with all the parties and all . . ."

"Any entertaining we decide to do will not interfere with my responsibilities to those who are under our care," Danielle answered. "The children must always come first, mustn't they?"

"So right you are. I always says to Mr. Pickett as how no matter what problems might plague us, we must keep our spirits up in front of the little ones."

Danielle was fascinated. Mrs. Pickett hadn't so much as twitched an eye at the blatant lie. But it wouldn't do to pluck the woman's feathers now. Perhaps, though, she'd ruffle them a bit.

"Are you having problems, Mrs. Pickett? I hadn't

heard. I wouldn't like to think you and Mr. Pickett were unhappy here."

Isabel misinterpreted the subtle threat as a show of concern and immediately expanded on her own plan to use the unexpected visit to solicit extra funds for her personal expenditures. "The shortage of funds has always been a concern. Why, there's not near enough food for the youngsters. There's been many an evening when Mr. Pickett and I have given our small portion of bread to one of them. But now that the duke is back in residence at Burnshire, we know we'll have no more such episodes."

Skeptically eyeing Mrs. Pickett's plump frame, Danielle doubted that any portion, no matter how small, had ever escaped the woman's reach. But she forced herself to answer amiably. "It's shameful, Mrs. Pickett. You should not have to give up your food. There should be enough for all. I am sure, had his Grace only known, he would have corrected the situation."

Mrs. Pickett leaned forward and again patted Danielle's hand. "You mustn't feel that this is your fault. I didn't wish to bring it to his attention, him only just returning to England and all. We'll make do with the little we have."

Danielle was not about to be put off. Not when there was the slightest possibility of being able to become involved again with the children's welfare. "But this is wrong, Mrs. Pickett. As soon as we return to Burnshire I shall have Devon instruct the servants to bring you extra bread every day."

Mrs. Pickett could see that her plan was about to come tumbling down around her and she silently cursed the new duchess's denseness. Bread was not what she wanted. The children could starve for all she cared. She wanted money. Coins she could spend on herself, not on the snotty-faced waifs.

"I wouldn't want to burden your household, your Grace. But if his Grace could spare a few extra coins each quarter . . ."

Mrs. Pickett stopped in the middle of her sentence.

Her Grace was no longer smiling. Isabel could envision the funds slipping through her fingers. She'd not have the duchess thinking she was greedy, and quickly continued. "Not many, mind you. Just enough to buy the extra grain needed to feed the poor babes properly. To send them to their beds with empty stomachs makes my heart ache, but what am I to do? There just isn't enough to—"

The return of the men interrupted Mrs. Pickett's expanding on her woes. The tea cart wasn't long in following. Danielle watched Amy carefully as she brought the cart to a halt beside Mrs. Pickett. But Amy kept her head down, not so much as venturing a glance in Danielle's direction. She looked thin. Thinner than the last time Danielle had seen her. Was she being blamed for Jeremy's disappearance? If so, Danielle would discuss the matter with Devon.

Mrs. Pickett accepted the tea tray without a comment and offered it to Danielle. Evidently, her idea of sacrificing did not extend to her afternoon tea. The tray was generously laden with food—scones sprinkled with sugar and tiny chocolate teardrop cakes circled a plate of glazed raspberry tarts.

Danielle's stomach tightened at the waste. She accepted the tea but refused the confections. She could not eat knowing the children had nothing but a thin gruel to keep them from starvation. She was surprised to see Devon take only the tea, as well.

Mrs. Pickett paid no attention to the fact that her husband sat beside her in silence, his tea growing cold in his cup. She took a generous bite of one of the scones. Thick vanilla oozed from the pastry and she hungrily licked the cream and sugar that frosted her lips.

"I apologize for keeping Mr. Pickett so long this afternoon," Devon offered as he watched Mrs. Pickett pick out a plump raspberry tart from the tray and plop it in her mouth. "We had several important matters to discuss."

Isabel looked blandly at Lord Stanton and then her

husband. His face was as white as the doily on the settee behind him. She swallowed hard, the juice from her tart forgotten as it slithered down the front of her apricot-colored gown. "Important?" she managed to ask. She took another sip of her tea, wondering why her husband just sat there looking for all the world as if he'd been caught with his fingers in the pie. Well, she knew better than to admit her guilt. She had been badgering him for months to get rid of the names of the children who had disappeared. But he had refused, saying it was imperative that they remain on the books as long as he and she were receiving a quarterly allowance to provide for them.

It couldn't be the others here at the orphanage. The children were doing as well as anyone could expect. Why, not a single one of them had died from starvation in the past two years, and there had been plenty who had deserved to, what with them not being healthy enough to pull their own load around here.

She took another tart from the tea tray. "Mr. Pickett does an admirable job with the limited funds we have. Why, it wasn't much more than a fortnight ago that he received a tidy sum for one of the boys," she proudly pointed out. "A real troublemaker the lad was, too. Cried all the time. Well, the extra money surely came in handy. That it did."

Mr. Pickett groaned helplessly beside her. He'd distinctly told her that that transaction was one he wouldn't record in the orphanage's books.

"That was very industrious of you, Pickett," Devon said as he set his teacup down. "Perhaps I have overlooked one of your talents. Is it possible I am underpaying you for your services?"

Mrs. Pickett, who was not as adept as Danielle at reading Devon's seemingly innocent remarks, saw only the chance of increasing their quarterly wages. "Bless you, Lord Stanton. It is surely time that Mr. Pickett is paid for all the duties the vicar assigns him."

Mr. Pickett grabbed his wife's hand and squeezed it. "I only do what my job requires, my sweet. We mustn't be greedy. His Grace has been more than generous.''

"Nonsense! Lord Stanton is willing to acknowledge your extra labors, and you should be gracious enough to accept his offer.''

Devon didn't give Mr. Pickett a chance to protest. "You are too modest, Pickett. You should listen to your wife. You have taken on a great deal of responsibility in my absence, and I intend to compensate you for your efforts.'' He rose to leave. "Danielle, if you are finished, I think we should be on our way.''

Mrs. Pickett jumped to her feet. "But you've barely touched your tea," she protested, ignoring her husband's tug on her gown. She was not about to allow Lord Stanton to leave before he confirmed a raise in wages.

"We will be back Thursday next, Mrs. Pickett. But you mustn't worry that I will forget what we have discussed. My agent, Giles, will be here first thing in the morning to go over the account books. Your husband's efforts will not go unrewarded.''

Isabel Pickett's face blanched as she sank back down on the stuffed sofa. Danielle had to pinch herself to keep from smiling, knowing that she must contain her joy until she and Devon were in the coach.

"You were wonderful," she exclaimed when they were on their way. "Poor Mr. Pickett. He tried so hard to get her to be quiet. I would love to know what he is saying to her now.''

"If he has a scrap of intelligence in him, he will dispatch someone to the vicarage immediately. Then he can lecture his wife on the troubles her loose tongue has brought down on them all.''

Danielle studied her husband. "Are you always so successful in your dealings with women?''

Devon smiled at her. "I never questioned my abilities until I met you.''

"Thank goodness," she bantered. "I would not like to think you could maneuver me quite as easily as you did Mrs. Pickett.''

The memory of Danielle clothed in the thin green negligee was still fresh in his mind and he couldn't keep his thoughts from drifting. "With Mrs. Pickett, it was simple. I needed only to appeal to her greed. Give me a little more time, love, and I'll discover your weaknesses as well."

"I will never dance to your tune," she said, turning away.

He took her chin in his fingers and forced her to look at him. "Do not be so quick to discount my talents," he said, his voice suddenly husky with the emotions she stirred in him. "I'm known to be quite persuasive when I put my mind to it."

"Blackmail is not considered a talent, my lord."

He let his thumb travel across the velvet softness of her lips. "Blackmail is such a common word, my dear. I much prefer to look at it as an exchange of favors."

Danielle refused to let him scare her again. "Ah! Then, as I see it, you're bound to be disappointed," she said, "for no favors were included with the marriage."

A smile lifted the corners of his lips. "Think on it a moment, love. For my protection, you agreed to the exchange of marriage vows. No other favors were specified in the bargain. The marriage vows stated it all. With them, you relinquished your right to refuse me anything—even your bed. And when I decide the time is right, you will want me every bit as much as I want you."

For once, Danielle didn't bother to deny it.

Chapter 9

It was late afternoon when they returned from the orphanage, and Devon insisted on giving Danielle a personal tour of Burnshire. She didn't trust his motives after his announcement in the coach, but she couldn't very well refuse.

Without waiting for her to decide, Devon tucked her arm in his and escorted her to the gallery in the upper hall. The long walls were covered with paintings of his ancestors. Although Devon's brilliant blue eyes were portrayed in most of the portraits, the somber look of the past lords of the manor seemed unlike those of the vibrant sea captain she had married, and Danielle was pleased when they moved on.

Seeing the beautiful rooms, she could understand why keeping his inheritance meant so much to Devon. At the moment, he seemed to be lost in a world of memories and bore the same expression she had seen on her father's face when he had fingered the few treasures he and her mother had brought to Virginia from England. Danielle suffered a small twinge of sorrow. She sometimes missed her home in America, but her involvement with the orphans had helped ease her loneliness. She knew how Devon must feel to have almost lost everything.

"And this is the music room," Devon said, standing aside for her to enter. "When Mother lived here, it was her favorite."

It wasn't difficult to imagine why. The glass French

doors led out onto a wide balcony with a view of the back. Even with the grounds covered with large patches of snow, Danielle could visualize gently rolling lawns stretching out until they met the woods. Orchards bordered one edge, and with the leaves gone she could see the frozen pond tucked away on the other side.

"It's beautiful," she exclaimed, spinning around to face him. "It's no wonder Lady Julia loves it."

That shuttered look she was beginning to recognize came over Devon's face again, and Danielle wished she could take her words back.

"Mother was pleased to have Burnshire reopened," he said as he picked up a Sevres vase that had been moved from its place on the spinet. He turned it over, looking for the distinctive signature that marked it as an original. He frowned. Another item replaced with a poor copy. If not Nathan, someone had certainly been busy.

"Is there something wrong, Devon?" Danielle leaned toward him to see what had captured his interest.

Devon quickly returned the vase to the table. "I must have a word with Mrs. Talbut. The maids seem to be lax in their dusting of this room."

Danielle resisted the urge to run her finger over the gleaming surface of the table. Before she could reflect on what Devon had just said, he ushered her out of the room and down the stairs to his study.

She'd visited Devon's inner sanctum briefly that morning, but now she was able to take it in at her leisure. Like the music room, it was located at the back of the house. But the similarities ended there. Instead of the delicate chairs with their brocade seats, massive dark furniture filled the study. Burgundy drapes covered the floor-to-ceiling windows that gave access to the gardens behind the house. But throwing them open did little to alleviate the overpowering presence of Devon's father, the man who had once run Burnshire with such a heavy hand.

Danielle moved around the large room until her gaze

came to rest on a carved chess set reposing on a marble table situated between two brown leather chairs. She crossed the room and picked up the white queen.

"What an exquisite set."

"Do you play?" he asked.

"My father and I used to play often. He would have loved a set such as this. It must be very valuable."

The hint of loneliness in her voice struck a responsive cord in him and he moved to her side. "It's quite old," he said. "My mother gave it to Father on their wedding day." He took the piece from her fingers, feeling its weight and balance. "Perhaps you'll play with me someday?" he asked, arching his dark brows suggestively.

One quick look at her pink-tinged cheeks confirmed that she understood the two-edged comment. Suddenly, he wanted to see the fire kindled behind those green eyes again.

"There are so many games we could play together if you would only change your mind about the sleeping arrangements," he murmured, at the same time wondering what had possessed him to bring up the subject. There were certainly enough others on which they could disagree.

"Never!"

"Never is a long time, love." He placed his hands on her waist and pulled her to him.

"Apparently not long enough," Danielle bantered. "Remember, we have an agreement."

"You're a beautiful woman, Danielle, and I would be lying if I said I would not like to have you in my bed, but you are right. I want no long-term commitments. I do not regret our agreement." The lie slipped out so easily, it was almost as if someone had stood at his ear whispering the words to him. "The marriage will serve us both well."

She ventured a look at him. His expression was wistful, his smile almost apologetic. Eyes that normally raked her with an unsettling boldness now assessed her thoughtfully. They spoke of forgotten memories, of lost moments. And Danielle found herself drawn to him in spite of her earlier resolve to keep him at arm's length.

His gaze slid lazily to her lips and she knew she was about to receive the wedding kiss he had promised her. Was the time right for trying again what Brodie had suggested? If she appeared to succumb to his kiss, would he be susceptible to the suggestion that the orphanage be taken away from Nathan? Her heart seemed to catch in her throat as he lowered his mouth to hers.

The kiss was gentle—seductive. Danielle had a difficult time keeping her head about her as the all-too-familiar sensations he evoked threatened to overtake her. Tentatively, she returned the kiss. Surprised yet pleased at his eager response, she mustered the courage to deepen it. Brazenly, she moved her body against his. The blatant invitation brought a moan from his parted lips and his arms tightened about her, nearly crushing her. Perhaps Brodie was right. The headiness of Danielle's success spurred her on and she melted her body into his.

At her unexpected response, a warning sounded harshly in Devon's head. How had he gotten himself into this? It was one thing to tease. Danielle had erected an emotional barrier against that. But now he had apparently stormed her defenses and changed the game. If he continued in this manner he might find himself in the position of having to choose between his ships and his wife. Reluctantly, he pulled away. "I'm sorry for that, Danielle," he said.

She appeared confused by his apology.

"Neither one of us wanted this marriage," he continued. "It was unfair of me to take advantage of you."

Danielle turned away from him. After making such a fool of herself, she couldn't face him. "How foolish of you to think you could take advantage of me. Had I not been curious as to how you would kiss your wife, I would never have allowed it," she tossed over her shoulder as she frantically scanned the room to see what she could use to divert his attention from the telltale blush suffusing her cheeks.

"This room seems rather dark and gloomy. Was it always this way?"

"If you were given the choice, what would you do to change things?"

Turning around, she was somewhat taken aback to see the warm fires still burning in his eyes. Despite all he had said, it was apparent he had been equally affected by their kiss. She quickly stepped over to the bookcases that lined the far wall. Casually, she ran her fingertips over the leather bindings as she waited for her heart to slow again. What did he expect from her? The emotions he sought from her were not standing behind some door that he could open and close at will. From this point forward, she would make sure she kept the door closed to him. With her feelings once more under control, Danielle turned back to him.

"The colors are much too dark in here. I would definitely change them."

Devon was both relieved and irritated that she had chosen to ignore what could only be looked upon as a ridiculous attempt on his part to rekindle a fire he had no business starting in the first place. He would do well to swallow his pride and follow her lead.

"What do you suggest?"

"The table covers need not be such heavy fabric. I'm not saying silk would do, but—"

"Thank heaven for that. I cannot envision myself surrounded by lavender silk," he teased.

"Lavender silk. The perfect thing," she purred, carefully avoiding the dark gleam in his eyes. "Why, I would never have thought to put lavender silk in this room, but you are quite right. It would look beautiful. Oh, and with a gossamer lace overlay. Just imagine how it would look against the—"

Devon waved a threatening finger in front of her and tried to squelch the strong impulse to pull her into his arms again.

"You had another idea?" she asked, her face a perfect study of innocence.

"Don't try my patience, vixen."

"Whatever have I done, my lord, to overset you so?" She ventured a peek at him through lowered lashes. "Could you possibly have an aversion to lavender silk?"

"Don't play the innocent with me. That smile quivering on your lips professes your guilt."

"I don't know what you're referring to. You asked me how I would change it and I told you. After all, I wasn't the one who mentioned the lavender silk."

"Don't pass that on to me. You know very well any gentleman with a grain of taste would not allow the color in his study. Unless, of course, you happen to be old and senile when you marry someone like the Ice Princess."

"The Ice Princess?" Danielle echoed, unable to hide her curiosity.

"Lady Emily."

"Why an Ice Princess?"

"She was the one my father selected as my betrothed. When I refused to follow his directive, she married a man easily four times her age. I heard later that she had his study redone in lavender silk because the color became her more than the browns her husband favored. It was rumored that she and her lover danced until dawn the night her husband died. Her heart's as cold as the ice sculptures at his Majesty's banquets. She led that poor first husband of hers around as if he had a ring in his nose."

Laughter spilled from Danielle's lips. "Did you envision yourself being led around like a prize bull?"

Once again Devon was torn by the urge to throw all caution to the wind and take her in his arms. He would show her what she would get for teasing her husband. He would make her want him as much as he wanted her.

"Excuse me, my lord," Robert interrupted. "Your agent has the papers you requested."

"Tell Giles I'll be with him in a moment."

"Begging your pardon, my lord, but he seemed most anxious that you meet with him as soon as possible."

"Bob—"

"Never mind, Devon," Danielle said. "Speak with Giles. There are several things I need to check on before we dine."

Devon watched her leave before turning back to Robert. "What was so important that Giles must speak with me now? I was finally making some progress with Danielle."

Robert stepped over to the desk and poured himself a brandy before answering. "Giles doesn't need to see you. He's busy with his account books. I thought to save you from yourself. The progress you were making could only lead to trouble when you get ready to leave."

"I think I should be the judge of that," Devon growled as he joined Robert in a brandy.

"I know you too well, Devon. The sea is in your blood. You could never give it up, and I would hate to see someone as beautiful as Danielle hurt when you leave."

An unexpected stab of jealousy pierced Devon's heart. "I'm beginning to think you are forming a *tendre* for Danielle. Perhaps you're planning to take her from my side."

Robert grinned broadly. "The notion did cross my mind."

"My friend," Devon stated calmly, a slight edge to his words, "you are here to help protect me from Nathan, not my wife."

"Ah! But it's the beautiful duchess who is most in need of my protection—from you."

Devon took a sip of brandy and stood looking out at the back lawns. "What did you find out about our thief?" he asked at last.

Robert eyed his friend for a few moments. He wasn't fooled by Devon's calm denials where Danielle was concerned. He knew Devon well enough to see all the signs of an affair in the making. It wasn't going to be easy to see that Devon behaved himself. "You were right, Dev. Things are disappearing. Andrews has been keeping a close watch on me. Since I'm the new man, so to speak, he thinks I'm the likely candidate." Robert downed his brandy and poured another.

"Take it easy on that stuff. If he suspects you've been drinking, he'll dismiss you."

"Even after you recommended that I be hired?"

"Oh, he would bring it to my attention first. Perhaps I should explain that your own butler had no doubts about your drinking," Devon said, arching an eyebrow at his friend.

Robert grinned. "That's true enough. Unfortunately, he felt the need to tell my father."

"And all this time I thought it was the love of the sea that convinced you to give all that up."

Robert lowered his voice to a whisper. "Actually it was a jealous husband."

Devon laughed. "I'll have to keep that in mind, if ever my wife disappears."

Devon had the chess set brought out after supper and challenged Danielle to a game. Although she considered herself a competent player, in the end he claimed her king. It wasn't until the game was over that apprehension set in. Brodie had retired early, and Danielle was left to cope with Devon on her own.

She raised her eyes to meet his, suddenly aware that it had been over an hour since she had seen a servant. "Shall we play another game?" she asked, not quite sure how to handle the issue of going to bed.

Devon reached across the board and took her hand. "I think it's time we retired."

Danielle's heart caught in her throat. They must maintain the facade of a loving couple. Did that extend to sharing a bed? Considering her dreadful weakness when it came to his kisses, how would she keep from disgracing herself again if he lay next to her?

Maintaining his hold on her hand, Devon rose and

circled the table until he stood before her. His blue eyes darkened as he looked down at her. Mesmerized, she let him pull her to her feet. His arm slid easily around her waist as he led her from the room and up the stairs. He didn't say a word until he was in Danielle's bed-chamber with the door closed behind them.

He dropped his arm and crossed to her bed. This would be the most difficult part of his plan, and he wasn't sure she would even consider it. Preferring to jump right in rather than paddle around the edges, he sank down on the bed.

"Which side do you prefer, love?" he asked, patting the pillow beside him.

Danielle stood rooted by the door. "I prefer this side of the room. You may have the other."

Devon was tempted to tease her further, but knew it would be wiser to have her help. "You needn't stand there like a startled fawn. I won't be staying any longer than necessary."

"Then you may leave now. Mary will be coming in at any moment to help me undress."

"Mary has been instructed to go to bed. I will serve as your maid tonight."

"This was not part of our bargain."

"But it *is* part of our bargain. You were to play the role of a loving wife. Servants talk, love, to each other and to domestics at other homes. Eventually even the mistresses of all the houses nearby will have learned about our nocturnal habits from their lady's maids. Do you want the whole countryside to know that your husband is refused entrance into his lady's chamber?"

Danielle plopped down at her dressing table. "I don't care what they think," she said flatly.

Devon lay back and appeared to study the intricately carved cornice above her. "Have you forgotten so quickly the bargain we struck earlier?" he asked. "Or did I misunderstand when you said you wished to help me thwart Nathan's ambitions?"

Danielle chewed on her lower lip for a moment. "And your sleeping in my bed will do that?"

"Nathan wants to be the next Duke of Burnshire. The thought that our marriage might produce a child has to be gnawing at him." Devon gave her a moment to think about that before going on. "Would you have him suspect all is not well between us?"

She eyed him suspiciously. "You will not touch me?"

"Not unless you want me to," he replied with a devilish grin.

Danielle frowned at him and turned back to her mirror. Pulling the pins from her hair, she ran her fingers through the thick curls. With a toss of her head, they tumbled around her shoulders. "We both know the answer to that," she said calmly, not recognizing the strain the sight of her was putting on Devon's resolve to remain a gentleman.

Devon took a deep breath. "But you'll have to get used to my presence in your bedchamber."

Danielle turned around in her chair at the hint of huskiness in his voice.

"To the servants and everyone else, it must appear that we are truly husband and wife," he quickly added.

Candlelight danced over her luscious auburn curls, and not for the first time he wondered if this whole idea wasn't ludicrous. If he didn't get a firm hold on himself, he was in grave danger of taking his wife to bed, willing or not. What a fine gentleman he would be then. In all his years at sea—with all the women he had enjoyed—he had never used force. Of course, the others had come to his bed willingly.

What a fool he was! Any other man would have insisted his wife share his bed. Why couldn't he be that way? Danielle was driving him mad. He needed her, but she was not the type to take bedding lightly. Her emotions ran deep. If he made love to her and then left her, she would not take it well. She was a woman who played for keeps. He would do well to keep that in mind whenever he looked at her with lust in his heart.

"Get dressed for bed," he stated firmly.

"Not until you leave."

"Don't be such a child."

"A child! It is not childish to want my privacy."

"It is if you are only playing a part. Think of this as your stage."

Danielle stood abruptly. "I do not play those types of parts!"

"Oh, but you do, my dear. I vividly recall a trollop dressed as a boy standing in my stables, offering a kiss for the use of my coach."

"That was different. That was necessary."

"Are you saying that it is no longer necessary to make Nathan believe we're blissfully wedded?"

"Well, you must promise to keep your head turned."

She quickly grabbed the nightdress off the bed where Mary had laid it. Thank heaven the gown she was wearing buttoned in the front. She could never have brought herself to ask for his help with the fastenings.

When she was done, she drew back the covers on her side of the bed, scrambled in, and pulled the covers up to her chin.

"Finished?" he asked as he turned toward her.

"You should at least wait until I answer before turning," she scolded.

"I knew as soon as you approached the bed you were ready."

His broad smile mocked her. She deserved it. She was such a coward at times. But did he have to look so disgustingly handsome while he taunted her?

He leaned over and gave her a kiss on the forehead. The forehead! Was she a child? One part of her wanted him to look at her as a woman—the foolish part, she decided. She knew it was imperative to keep her distance from him. But how, when she ached so to be near him? She must never let him know of the effect he had on her.

He stretched out beside her on the bed. Fluffing the pillow under his head, he closed his eyes.

"You don't plan to sleep here, do you?"

Rolling toward her, Devon pulled her to him.

"Hush," he said, wrapping his arms around her. "I will retire to my room as soon as you're asleep."

"How can I sleep with you in my bed?"

"Much better than I," he mumbled.

Time seemed to stand still as they both lay thinking the same thoughts. But the stress of the previous days had made its mark on Danielle and she finally settled in sleep.

Devon lay awake long after her breathing told him of her sleep. He raised himself up on one arm to gaze at her. Gently, he traced his finger across her lips. Oh, that things were different! Maybe someday he would give up the life he lived and return to claim this woman as his wife.

Abruptly, he sat up. Whatever was coming over him of late? If this continued, he would do better to hire guards to watch over his mother, and return to his ships straight away.

"Blast!"

Danielle nearly spilled her breakfast tray as Devon stormed into her room. She had been married a week today, yet this casual violation of her privacy still embarrassed her. The nightdresses Devon had ordered from London to replace her linen ones didn't help. The fragile material wasn't thick enough to keep a rabbit warm, let alone cover her decently, but Mary insisted she wear the pretty gowns.

"You have to do something, Danielle," Devon roared as he paced the floor beside her bed. "I'll not have the lad reviewing my body while I bathe."

Danielle listened patiently while she tried to juggle her breakfast tray and pull the bedcovers up at the same time. She had seen this storm brewing ever since she had heard how Pockets had accidentally let one of cook's raspberry tarts slip off the breakfast tray into Devon's favorite pair of boots. But she had to give Devon his due. He was trying.

"What seems to be the problem?" she said calmly, recalling that she had assigned Pockets as Devon's valet without consulting him. She could, in all honesty, understand why he might be a tad upset.

Devon stood towering over her. "Why is he in my room?"

"He wants to be a valet. He admires you. What would you suggest I do? Have him wear a blindfold?"

"And what's a blindfold to do? The lad stares whether I'm dressed or not!" Devon shouted, knowing he was being irrational to let a child upset him so.

A smile brightened Danielle's face. He thought nothing of wreaking havoc with her privacy. To see the tables turned was a delight. "I never imagined that your body would prove to be such a thing of interest."

Devon didn't find this in the least humorous and gave her a steely look. "It's not my body, woman. It's the bloody scars!"

"Scars?" she said, her curiosity piqued.

"Scars!" he shouted, opening the front of his shirt.

Danielle tried not to stare at the dark hair that furred his chest, but focused her attention instead on the pale path of a scar that ran from his shoulder and under the tangle of hair to disappear behind the band of his trousers. "A jealous husband?" she asked casually, despite the tingling that crept up her spine.

"No, a drunken sailor who thought to raise his station in life by taking over one of my ships."

"You cannot blame Pockets for being fascinated by that. If all your scars have such intriguing tales behind them, it's no wonder he stares."

"Put the boy with anyone but my valet," he demanded, not to be deterred from his complaint.

"But where else can I place him? Andrews put his foot down after only a day. I had a devil of a time convincing Pockets that the profession of gentleman's valet was every bit as prestigious as that of butler, and now you want me to reassign him again?"

"Surely there is someone who can take over his training."

"I suppose I could ask one of the footmen," she said distractedly as her eyes came to rest on a bright red scar along Devon's right side. It looked to be fairly new. She wanted to ask about it, but she wished more that he would close his shirt. "Yes, Bob might agree," she decided, dragging her eyes away from the scar.

"Not Bob."

"But Bob would not mind."

"But Andrews would object," Devon quickly improvised. "Bob works in the front hall. As you recall, Andrews does not function well with Pockets nearby."

"Can't this wait until next week? Pockets will be upset that he is to be moved again so soon."

"This morning, Danielle," he growled. "The sooner the lad's out of my chamber, the better." With the problem solved, he sank into the bedside chair. "And while we're on the subject of the children, what's wrong with Katie?"

"Katie?"

"Surely you've noticed the way she's been dogging Bob's every footstep." Only yesterday Robert had complained to him that the child wouldn't let him out of her sight, making it difficult for him to function as Devon's spy.

"Oh, that," she said, trying to decide how she could best explain it. "You know how she can be. She has a small problem."

"Small problem! In the week since our marriage, she has come up with a toothache, a broken leg, and a case of the fleas. And you say she has a small problem."

"Now, I did point out to her that it was unbecoming of a young lady to scratch in public."

"What does all this have to do with her behavior now?"

"And, if you recall," she continued, ignoring him completely, "you had but to keep the stableboy away from her to make her forget the broken leg. And she did apologize for upsetting the table of porcelain figurines with her crutch."

Devon waited patiently for her to pause. "I repeat. What does all this have to do with her behavior now?"

Danielle searched for the right words. *Heaven help all*

wives forced to endure life with a stubborn husband—or any husband, for that matter. Was he just going to sit there until she answered? With a very unladylike oath, she threw the bedcovers aside.

"You and your confounded scars!" She flung the accusation over her shoulder as she climbed from the bed and reached for her robe.

"Whatever do my scars have to do with Katie?"

Her attempt to divert his attention away from Katie had failed miserably. In the week they had been married, Devon had quickly caught on to her methods of avoiding his questions. A pity. The fire in her eyes always gave her away.

She didn't realize that the sight of her in the new nightdress was a diversion much more likely to succeed. Instead, she quickly stuffed her arms into the sleeves of her heavy robe and pulled the material tight about her.

"You're avoiding my question, Danielle. What do my scars have to do with Katie?"

"How should I know?" she tossed back at him. "You burst into my bedroom to complain that Pockets stares at your scars. It's not my fault that you have a few scars. And it's only natural that the boy would show an interest."

That was an understatement, she thought as her eyes once again strayed to his open shirt. She herself was having a difficult time keeping her eyes away from the bronzed chest.

"Daniell-e-e?"

Embarrassed, she raised her gaze to him. A broad smile creased his lips.

Fidaddle! she thought. He'd caught her surveying him. Did he always have to be so observant?

"What is wrong with Katie?" he stubbornly insisted.

Danielle lifted her chin defiantly. "First you must promise me you will not laugh."

"You want me to promise I won't laugh before hearing something you think will surely amuse me? I hardly think that's fair."

"Promise, or you'll not have your answer."

"I will promise to do the best I can. Now tell me."

Danielle eyed him skeptically. The promise didn't sound like much, but it was probably the best she would get.

"You know the young chambermaid who helps Mary?"

"The mousy one?"

"Yes, well, she has developed a *tendre* for one of the footmen."

"Which one?"

"You promised not to laugh," she reminded him.

"Continue."

"If you must know. Mary accused the maid of being lovesick and Katie overheard."

"Lovesick?" he said, still confused. Then his face lit with understanding. "Lovesick! Are you telling me Katie thought it was another disease?"

"Now don't be too hard on her. She didn't understand."

"That's why she's been casting those ridiculous glances at Bob?"

"Devon," she pleaded, "not so loud. Katie's liable to hear. If she were to find out that you've been laughing at her, she would be devastated."

He had to admit it was difficult to remember his earlier promise. The little minx had done it again. She was a lot like Danielle. Just when he thought there was nothing more the children could do to surprise him, they'd do just that. Was his household never to know peace and quiet again? Yet at the same time, it occurred to him that life at Burnshire might otherwise be dull. He could only hope Robert would agree after what he was about to propose.

"Bob may help train Pockets, but I must draw the line at him also being the object of Katie's case of lovesickness. She follows him everywhere. He doesn't have a moment to himself. You direct her attentions to someone else and I promise I'll not tease her about her new affliction. Agreed?"

"Agreed," she said.

Having resolved his immediate problem, Devon left Danielle's bedchamber. He was pleased that she was willing to compromise. It wasn't the inconvenience that he begrudged. It was the fact that Danielle's whole life seemed to revolve around the children. He felt like an outsider. Seeing her with the little ones caused a strange ache in his chest, an ache to see her with their own child, a child he would give her, a child that came from his touch—his love.

He shook off the absurdity of the thought. He wanted no more responsibilities. He desired her. That was only natural. She was his wife and she was beautiful. He chided himself for suddenly being unable to meet her emerald-green eyes.

But why should he berate himself so? He was no schoolboy in his first flush of puppy love. He was a man who had known a lot of women. And what man wouldn't desire Danielle? The fact that his thoughts turned more and more often to bedding her shouldn't surprise him. After all, what better way was there to draw Nathan out? And hadn't that been the entire reason behind this marriage?

But love? No, love was another matter. Love was giving your all until there was no separation between your soul and another's. Love was never dulled by familiarity. It was forever. He could not picture it.

Chapter 10

Elizabeth Meade did not worry that anyone she met would recognize her. She had changed drastically in the past few years. Her once dark hair was pulled back severely from her thin face and gray now threaded the limp black strands, adding years to her age of five and twenty. But she no longer cared. It somehow fit her mood nowadays.

"Mrs. Meacham?" Isabel Pickett said as she bustled into the sitting room. Light from the fading sunset outlined a dark figure standing at the window. The pristine white collar that trimmed the visitor's tailored black dress was the only thing that kept Isabel from believing she was in the presence of the Grim Reaper. "Mrs. Meacham?" she said again. "Amy said you wished to speak with me."

Elizabeth turned. She must be more careful. Daydreaming was a luxury she couldn't afford. After all this time, she should be accustomed to the name she now used.

Elizabeth extended her hand. "Mrs. Pickett, I wish to thank you for seeing me so late."

In actuality, she had picked the time as the most advantageous for her purposes. She had been on her own now for well over three years and had learned that you could have your way in most things if you did them without asking permission.

At first, she'd had her doubts as to whether she could survive without the husband she had murdered.

After all, Lord Meade had pampered her—anyway, that was what she had believed until she'd learned of his betrayal. For that she could never forgive him. For that she had pulled the trigger and shot him, walking out on a life she had once cherished.

But she'd managed. The household money she'd taken had lasted longer than she'd expected. Yet it had eventually run out, and she'd been forced to spend many a night tossing and turning on a cold bed, her empty stomach keeping her from sleep. But what was sleep? Only an avenue to the nightmares that plagued her. But her perseverance had paid off. Her small list of clients was growing, and soon she would need a helper. Her lips spread in a smile of satisfaction. It was fortunate that the need fit so well with her plans.

"I will come straight to the point, Mrs. Pickett. I am a seamstress in need of an apprentice."

Although the light was poor in the sitting room, it didn't hide the greed that flared in Mrs. Pickett's eyes. Elizabeth was correct in her evaluation of the proprietress. Mrs. Pickett would be easy to deal with.

"I am not a wealthy woman, Mrs. Pickett, but I am prepared to pay the few shillings most orphanages charge. The child will be provided with a pallet and two meals a day. The work is not strenuous, but it requires someone who can be trained to handle the special clothes my customers demand."

"Please be seated, Mrs. Meacham," Isabel offered. Her husband would be home late, and with any luck she'd complete the transaction before his return. The duke had insisted on a set of ridiculous new rules that obliged her husband to consult with him before any of the children were placed. But she was bound by no such agreement. Besides, who was to know if there was one less child?

"You must understand, Mrs. Meacham, most of our older girls are committed to their work at the factory. It would be difficult to replace them."

"Discipline is my primary concern," the visitor said. "I'm perfectly willing to take on a younger one. I find it much easier to train them before they develop the bad habits so prevalent in young girls today. Wouldn't you agree?''

"Oh, yes. Most certainly,'' Isabel promptly replied. She'd not get any extra coins from the woman, but perhaps a new gown could be added to the deal. "I have two that might do, One is—''

"Excuse me, Mrs. Pickett,'' Elizabeth interrupted, her pale lips pursed, "but I would prefer to make the selection on my own. Since I will be forced to take a child whose skills are not yet evident, I must be the one to choose. Not everyone is suited to my profession. Having a feel for fine fabrics is not something that is easily learned. Anyone can see from the lovely gown you're wearing that you have a natural talent for fashion.'' The lie came easily to Elizabeth. "I need someone with that same instinct to help me create the gowns for ladies as tasteful as you.''

Isabel's already ample bust swelled with pride. Pleased that Amy had finished the alterations on her gown, she self-consciously smoothed the front. Unless you looked close, it was impossible to see where the seams had been let out to accommodate the extra portions of dessert she had each night. Perhaps she should have a gown done up in one of those new shades of blue she'd been discussing with the duchess only last month.

"It will be a pleasure helping you find just the right girl,'' Mrs. Pickett said.

"I can see that you appreciate the problems that beset someone like me, trying to make a living during these troubled times. Due to our hostilities with France, I am already having to contend with supply shortages. It's a relief to know that I won't have to wait to procure a helper.''

"Of course not. By the time you return tomorrow, I will have our girls ready to meet with you.''

"I thought you understood, Mrs. Pickett. It is a long distance to London. I would prefer to make my selection this evening.''

"But that's impossible!" Isabel squealed. Mr. Pickett was due at any moment, and it was possible that the vicar might be with him. "I would have to drag them all from their beds."

"That won't be necessary. Because of the lateness of the hour, I am prepared to go to them."

"I would rather you returned tomorrow," Isabel pouted, glancing again at the watch pinned to her bosom. It wasn't that waking the children really bothered her, but she had hoped to make the sale when it suited her.

Elizabeth extended her gloved hand. "Thank you for your time, but if I'm unable to see the children now, I must be on my way."

"You will be returning tomorrow?" Isabel asked anxiously.

"I'm a very busy woman, Mrs. Pickett. I can't be sure whether my schedule will allow for another trip."

"Let's not be hasty. I will check with Amy. The children may be awake." Mrs. Pickett crossed to the door and yelled, "Amy! Amy, come here, you lazy girl."

Amy appeared before Mrs. Pickett had finished her tirade. "Yes, mum."

"See that the girls are awakened," she ordered. "Mrs. Meacham would like to make her selection this evening."

"Yes, mum."

A tight smile tugged at the corners of Elizabeth's lips as she followed Mrs. Pickett upstairs.

The rooms were like those in most of the orphanages she'd seen. The hearth, conspicuously devoid of a fire, dominated. The girls stood in military fashion in front of the box beds lining the walls. Their nightdresses, gray from weeks of indifferent washings, provided little warmth, and the children shifted their bare feet on the rough floorboards. Elizabeth paused before each girl as she made her way down the long line. Her heart went out to each one of them. They were so thin that it made it hard to determine their ages.

"Is this all you have?" she asked when she reached the end.

Mrs. Pickett hustled forward. "These are the best."

"Then there are others?" Elizabeth demanded.

"Yes, but only the real young ones or those too sick to work."

"Nothing contagious, I hope."

"No! No! We take good care of our children here. But some are naturally frail and succumb to the cold easily."

"May I see them?"

"Certainly, but they are much too young," Isabel stressed. "Take Alice here. She'll be eight next month and she's a good worker." Mr. Pickett wouldn't be pleased when he learned that she'd taken one of his factory laborers, but she'd deal with her husband later. However, when Mrs. Meacham shook her head, Isabel turned to Amy. "Wake the others," she said.

The next room was much smaller than the first. Situated on the south side of the building, it had retained more of the day's warmth. Elizabeth studied the faces of the little ones. Satisfied she had not missed any, she straightened.

"You don't have many really young girls here." She didn't bother to hide her disappointment. She would have to keep looking.

"We'd have a good deal more had not the duchess taken so many of the b—" Isabel snapped her mouth shut, the word *brats* hanging on the very tip of her tongue.

"The duchess?" Elizabeth's eyes brightened with interest.

"Took them out of my husband's care without so much as a by-your-leave. She fills their heads with nonsense about training them for positions in fine homes instead of the honest work we provide for them at the factory. But you mark my words, it's one of those passing things with nobility. I've seen it happen often enough. One of them gets a bee in their bonnet about filling their empty hours with charitable works. She'll soon tire of it and the children will be returned. Then I'll be the one who has to deal with teaching them their real places."

"She has taken some of these children?"

"Young, old, any that took her fancy. Why, she even went so far as to have the duke insist that all the sales must have his approval. It's getting so a body can't sneeze without their say—"

"The Duke of Burnshire?" Elizabeth broke in.

Isabel swallowed hard. "Do you know of him?"

Elizabeth had no time for Mrs. Pickett's petty questions. "I do believe I'll take your recommendation concerning Alice."

"Alice?" Isabel asked, vague as to whom she had bestowed with the name. No matter. She'd send to London tomorrow for the blue fabric.

"The older child," Elizabeth reminded her. "Now when can I discuss the matter with the duke?"

Mrs. Pickett's delight was short-lived. "You wish to meet with the duke?"

"You said all sales must have his approval." Elizabeth withdrew a card from her reticule. "This is where he may find me. Please see that he gets the card. Otherwise, I'll be in the neighborhood Thursday and will meet with him then. Good day, Mrs. Pickett."

The study was dark except for the two candles on the large oak desk. The dim light spilled across the open ledgers. Devon dipped a new quill pen in the crystal inkwell and added a collection of miniatures to the growing list of missing items.

His agent waited quietly while Lord Stanton made the entry.

Finishing, Devon gave him his full attention. "Out with it, Giles. What has put that scowl on your face this time?"

"It's her Grace, my lord." The old man shifted uneasily in his chair. "She's been talking with Samuels, the grocer. When he brought our weekly order of fresh fish, her Grace informed him that Burnshire has fish aplenty in its streams and we'd best be using what we've been blessed with.''

"I wager that set Samuels back on his heels. He's been sending lads to Burnshire for as long as I can remember to catch the fish he delivers to our door.''

"He didn't take kindly to it. He demanded we pay up our account in full.''

"You did, of course.''

"Her Grace forbade me to pay him. Said our funds would not go to a thief.''

"I see no problem in that,'' Devon replied, leaning back in his chair. As he saw it, there was a problem, though. Not really caring for the social life that went hand in hand with his new title, Devon had not encouraged Danielle to open Burnshire for guests. Consequently, she'd been occupying herself with household matters—with sometimes disastrous results. "See to it that cook makes no further orders from Samuels,'' he said at last, determined to back his wife up once again.

"Yes, your Grace.''

"And I will talk with Danielle.''

Danielle shoved the thick slices of cheese in among the jugs of cooled milk. "What idiot lets someone sell him back his own property?'' she mumbled as she helped pack the food hamper for their weekly visit to the orphanage.

She was still smarting from her confrontation with Devon. What was all the fuss about anyway? They didn't need Samuels. Tom had become quite proficient with his lines. He and one of the older lads would see that cook was supplied with the fresh fish needed.

"No one offends his largest account,'' Danielle continued to mumble as she wrapped the last loaf of warm bread and placed it beside the meat pies.

Having finished, she went to fetch Devon from the study. Seeing him bent over the estate books again, she wished he would allow her to deliver the food baskets herself. But she knew better than to ask. After the incident with Samuels, she wasn't sure how far he trusted her.

Devon looked up from his work. "Are you ready to leave?"

"They are placing the hampers in the carriage now."

"I must check this last entry; then I will be finished here."

Danielle hated seeing him like this. The long hours he spent in the study were beginning to show on him. He looked tired, drawn. "If you would care to rest, I could take your agent with me."

Devon leaned back and smiled at her. "I'm very much afraid Giles is unprepared to deal with the situation should the Picketts offend you and you decide to take matters in your own hands."

"I would never set out to embarrass Giles," she defended herself.

"And what of Samuels?"

"Samuels was a thief!"

"That was for Giles to determine," he pointed out.

"Then he was lax in his work. Everyone knows Samuels was selling us the fish from our own streams. Just last week Tom caught him near the pond with a string of fish and four rabbits."

"Am I never going to convince you that it's best to stay out of things you don't understand?"

"A thief is a thief. What more is there to understand?" she demanded.

"It has long been my belief that Samuels reports to Nathan."

"Nathan? What could he possibly have to say that Nathan would find of any value?"

"Samuels delivers his catch to the kitchens each day. He hears the servants talk."

"Then all the more reason that we no longer deal with him."

Devon set the quill aside and gave Danielle a long, searching look. "Danielle," he finally said, "if you knew your enemy had a spy in your household, wouldn't you prefer to know who he was?"

He rested his elbows on the arm of his chair and steepled his fingers before him. "Think of the advantage," he continued. "You know he reports everything he hears. All you need to do is make sure he hears the things you wish him to repeat to your enemy."

"Are you saying that Samuels was Nathan's spy and he reported every disagreement we have? But how?"

"Servants talk. If we have an argument, you can count on it being the topic of conversation belowstairs. Samuels made his deliveries every morning."

Danielle sank down into the chair in front of his desk. "Oh. And after what I have done, you can no longer use him."

"Don't worry about it too much. I've suspected for some time that Samuels was not the only one who should be watched. With him gone, we might have a better chance of discovering who the other one might be."

Devon rose and came around the desk. "But let's not discuss it now. Come. We have a lot of children waiting for that food you've packed."

Danielle stood and slipped into his arms. "I'm sorry I acted without taking the matter up with you. I was totally to blame. I wish there was something I could do to rectify my mistake."

Devon wrapped his arm around her. Taking her chin in his hand, he forced her to look at him. "It only means, my dear, that until we discover who else is in Nathan's employ, you will be forced to act the loving wife all the more."

His jest brought an answering smile and he placed a light kiss on her forehead. "Now, let's be off before the Picketts think we're not coming and put the children to bed without supper."

The gentle swaying of the coach soon lulled Devon to sleep, but Danielle seemed not to mind. Her thoughts tumbled over and over in her head. Devon's half of this marriage was not proving to have the overwhelming advantages Danielle had at first thought it would. All the advantages turned out to be hers. He had opened his home to her and the children, but what had she given him in return? Nothing but troubles and headaches. He asked only that she appear to be a loving wife. True, she had complied, but she also fought him on it at every turn. Well, she would try harder to do as he asked.

It was the least she could do for all his help. It was his suggestion that they take the baskets of food each time they visited the orphanage, and it had not gone unnoticed that he always scheduled these visits to coincide with the children's supper. But he had brushed her thanks aside, saying it was the best time for him. She was not fooled by his show of indifference. It was the only way in which they could ensure that the children actually got the food.

Danielle steadied the hampers as the coach came to a stop. She hated to wake Devon. He looked so tired. Would he be terribly upset if she didn't? No, she was bound to say something to upset the Picketts and she had given her word that she would leave that to him. "Devon?" She gently shook him.

He woke with a start. Shoving back the dark curls that had fallen across his forehead, he yawned and asked, "Have we arrived so soon?"

"Yes, sleepyhead, and if you yawn at me again, I shall leave you to sleep and go in without you," she teased.

"And let you have all the enjoyment of annoying the Picketts? No, I'll sleep later."

Devon stepped out of the coach, then turned to assist Danielle. "Smile. We are being watched," he whispered as he took her hand.

Danielle's face broke into a broad grin. "I'm beginning to believe you make up an audience just to ensure my amiability."

"Highly clever of me, wouldn't you say?"

"Highly unfair, I would say. Yet I'll humor you until we are home again. Then I'll find some devilish cruel way to get even."

Devon considered pointing out to her that there was nothing so cruel as the punishment of his own designing. Going to her room each night to lie on the bed beside her, knowing he could never have her, was almost more than he could endure.

He signaled for the footmen to carry in the baskets as he took Danielle's arm and proceeded to the door. "Behave yourself, love," he whispered. Amy answered the door and took them down the back hall. "I'm ever so glad you came," she said to Danielle. "Mrs. Pickett told the children you had forgotten about them. She was about to send them to bed without their supper."

"We are only a few minutes late. We would never forget them."

"Oh, I know that, Miss Danny, but you know how Mrs. Pickett can be," she whispered.

Devon's attention was caught by the familiar use of Danielle's pet name. So this was how his wife had been able to abduct Jeremy. She'd had Amy's help. It might prove of value with his plans later. Up until now, nothing he had done seemed to upset Nathan.

In the past, Nathan had used the orphanage as a source of income. Devon was positive of that. But he was just as positive that even with the new instructions he had given the Picketts, Nathan was finding a way to circumvent them. For this reason, the message he had received concerning Mrs. Meacham had come as quite a surprise. Perhaps she wasn't prepared to pay enough to make the Picketts want to risk his anger. In any event, he had Giles check her out completely. Her reputation as a dressmaker was excellent. She was perfect. But first things first. There were hungry children to be fed.

As they entered the large dining room, his gaze swept down the length of tables until it came to rest on the Picketts. He arched a dark brow.

"A bowl of thin gruel for the children and a plate of fine beef for yourselves?"

Pickett appeared to shrink down in his chair, but his

wife crossed her arms defiantly and stood. "It's too near their bedtime for such a heavy meal."

Devon ignored her and ordered his footmen to place the hampers on the tables. Pickett's wife was upset. Excellent! The more upset she was, the more confident he could be that every word said this evening would find its way to Nathan's ear.

"We are dreadfully sorry to be late, children," he said, purposely leaving Mrs. Pickett out of his apology. "But I hope the supper her Grace has packed more than makes up for our tardiness."

A hearty round of cheers was his answer.

Mrs. Pickett pursed her mouth. "You're spoiling them, you know. When we find positions for them, most employers will be unwilling to provide such a table."

Danielle bit her lip to keep from answering. Devon took her hand in his and gave it a reassuring squeeze. He had warned her that if she wished his assistance, she must allow him to deal with the Picketts. But it was becoming more and more difficult with each visit.

"We will deal with that when the time comes, Mrs. Pickett," he said. "For now, a little extra food will not harm them. Shall we retire to the parlor? I wish to discuss Mrs. Meacham."

Mr. Pickett's eyes shot to his wife. She had told him of her efforts to turn this particular sale to their advantage, and he sincerely hoped that if Mrs. Meacham suspected his wife's plan, she'd keep it to herself. "Yes, I need to speak with you. The child she has selected—"

"Is there a problem?" Devon asked, standing aside for Danielle and Mrs. Pickett to precede him. "The information my agent was able to uncover about her—given the short time—has been most favorable."

Pickett tugged at the neck of his shirt, as if the stiff white fabric had suddenly grown tight. He swallowed with difficulty. "My wife, being the one who talked with her, will be able to tell you more. I know nothing of her myself. It's the child she's selected. She's been

trained to work in the factory, and I'm not sure she's
the one to best meet Mrs. Meacham's needs."

"Are you saying I should pass up this opportunity
to place a child?"

Pickett grew uneasy under his Grace's scrutiny. "I
only thought to point out that one of the others might
be more to her liking."

"I will take that into consideration when I speak with
her."

Mrs. Pickett's brow wrinkled in a dark scowl. "I certainly don't see that any of this is nec—"

"What my wife means to say," Pickett quickly interrupted, "is that you have so many duties that take up
your valuable time. It isn't necessary that you burden
yourself with this as well. When Mrs. Meacham returns tomorrow, I will assist her in selecting another
child."

"Did I fail to point out that Mrs. Meacham will be
coming directly to Burnshire?"

The Picketts exchanged hurried glances. "But . . .
but," Mr. Pickett sputtered, "what of the child?"

"You may rest easy. I doubt that she will take your
worker. Upon checking Mrs. Meacham's references, I
find that she is quite capable at what she does. Since
we plan on entertaining at Burnshire soon, Danielle
will need a new wardrobe. Given what I've been able
to learn of Mrs. Meacham's talents, I intend to offer
her a position at Burnshire as Danielle's dresser."

Devon stood and took Danielle's hand. They said
their good-byes and left. Danielle remained silent until
the coach had left the grounds.

"Well done, Devon. Well done. Did you see their
faces when you announced your intention?"

Devon brushed her cheek with a light kiss. "I would
be willing to wager that someone was on their way to
the vicarage before our coach reached the orphanage
gates."

Danielle found it difficult to keep her thoughts focused on what Nathan might think. Devon had kissed
her. To be sure, it lacked the passion of his other kisses.

But this one had not been intended to embarrass her, nor had it been given for the benefit of others. This kiss was for her.

Other than exhibiting a slight touch of curiosity, Mrs. Meacham's face gave Devon no clue to what she thought of his offer.

"I have done so for my clients in the past," she said. "But it will be several months before my shop is set up."

"Would it be possible to delay the opening for, say, a year?" he suggested. "If you would give us your assistance until Christmas next, I will see that the bonus you receive will enable you to open your shop in a more fashionable district than the one you are now considering."

Not so much as a bat of her eye gave him any indication of her surprise at his knowledge of her affairs.

"While the offer is tempting," she replied, "I'm afraid I cannot promise you a year. There are certain personal matters which cannot be put aside."

Before Devon could push the issue, Danielle swept into the room with Katie in hand.

"Ah, I'd like you to meet my wife, Mrs. Meacham, and Katie." Devon made the introductions, then sat back to observe.

Danielle took a seat next to Mrs. Meacham. "I'm so sorry to be late, Mrs. Meacham, but Katie had been playing in the stables and I fear she was a sight unsuitable for the drawing room."

"I—I did not know you had children." Elizabeth somehow got out the words.

Danielle wasn't sure what she thought of the dressmaker. The woman sat stiffly in her chair, her face suddenly deathly pale. "Are you ill?" she asked.

"No, just a little warm, that's all. I did not mean to frighten you or your daughter."

"Oh, Katie is not mine, Mrs. Meacham. She comes from the orphanage."

"My parents did not want me," Katie added.

Danielle put her arm around the small child. "But we want you, Katie, and that's what's important."

Katie smiled at the stranger. "Are you going to teach me how to sew samplers like a young lady?"

"I hope you like children, Mrs. Meacham, for the house is positively bursting with them. I was hoping you could teach the girls to sew."

"Don't get ahead of yourself, Danielle," Devon said. "Mrs. Meacham had not agreed to my offer as yet."

"Oh! But you are going to, aren't you?" Danielle asked.

There was a moment of silence while Elizabeth focused on the little girl. The vicar had said it wouldn't be hard to work her way into the Stanton household. But things had not gone her way for so long that it was only natural to be skeptical. He'd proved correct, and the bonus the duke promised was a nice addition. Then she smiled at Katie and said, "I would be pleased to accept the position, your Grace."

Chapter 11

❦

"**R**eturn the quarterly stipend from Lord Meade," Devon ordered.

"But, your Grace," Pickett whined, "it is paid each month for the care of the child he placed with us."

"It says here that the child is Catherine Elizabeth."

Wiping his brow with a lace handkerchief, Pickett consulted his journal notes. "That is correct. The child is often sick and needs the continual care of the physician. The stipend is barely enough to cover his fees."

Devon laid his quill pen aside and began sorting through the papers Giles had brought from the orphanage. "I seemed to have missed the bills from the physician. My agent must still have them. Bob!"

The door opened immediately. From the quickness of Robert's response, Devon knew he had been listening at the door. He was worse than an old mother hen.

"Would you please tell Giles I wish to speak with him?"

"No, your Gr-Gr-Grace," Pickett stuttered. "That won't be necessary. Giles does not have them."

"That will be all, Bob," Devon said, waving him away. "I won't be needing Giles after all." Robert closed the door behind him and Devon turned a critical eye on Pickett.

Pickett shifted uneasily in his seat. "What I mean to say is, your agent arrived so quickly. Why, you hadn't been gone an hour when he was there to collect the books."

"And?"

"I was in such a rush to gather the ledgers for him that I failed to include a large portion of the receipts." Cautiously, he reached across the desk and laid the sheaf of papers before Devon. Pickett held his breath as Devon flipped through the large pile. How had he ever let the vicar convince him to be a part of this? "I apologize for taking so long to get them to you, but we've had an epidemic of the measles at the orphanage that has kept us all very busy."

"I see. And I will find the bills I need among these?"

"Oh, yes, your Grace. Everything should be there."

Pickett mopped his damp brow. Lord Stanton didn't look at all pleased with the oversight. Hopefully, his Grace wouldn't study them too closely. Nathan had assured him the alterations of the figures would go unnoticed, but Pickett wasn't as optimistic. Still, as long as his Grace was questioning the expenses, the sham bills were better than none at all. "I must return to the orphanage. The ladies from the parish are bringing the clothing they have collected, and I think it only proper that I be there when they come."

"Yes, of course," Devon said. "I want to thank you for bringing these papers to me. They will be reviewed—thoroughly. Then I will want to discuss them with you." Devon let the man reach the door before he spoke again.

"And, Pickett, her Grace and I will be visiting Thursday next. We may wish to bring Catherine Elizabeth to Burnshire until her health improves."

His face ashen, Pickett bowed. "Yes, your Grace," he mumbled before hurrying from the room.

"That redheaded witch put him up to this," Nathan hissed as he paced the floor of Pickett's office.

"Her Grace? But she wasn't even there." Pickett fretted over his feathered quill, nervously shredding its silky edge. "It was the duke who insisted the funds be returned to Lord Meade. Oh, what are we to do?" he wailed. "What if he wants to see Catherine Elizabeth when he comes Thursday?"

"So how old would she have been had she not died two years ago? Four perhaps? Pick one of the other orphans. Tell her we've just discovered that her real name is Catherine. Who's to know?"

"But I gave him the bills from the physician," Pickett whined. "Lord Stanton will be expecting a sickly child."

"So why are you so worried? There's not a child under your care who doesn't appear to need a good dose of tonic."

"The duke is too knowing by half."

Nathan pointed his leather riding whip at the skeptical Pickett. "You presented him with the receipts I gave you, didn't you?"

"Yes, but—"

The whip came down hard on the oak desk, scattering Pickett's papers across the top. "Then he'll have no reason to question your accounts."

Pickett wasn't convinced. "And what am I to say if he does?"

"He won't."

"You weren't there. You didn't see the way his Grace thumbed through the receipts. It was as if he knew they had been forged."

"Don't ask for trouble, Pickett. Leave everything to me. If all goes well—and I see no reason for it not to— it won't be long before he has so many problems of his own, he'll not be borrowing any others. Then we can sit back and relax. Two months, perhaps three at the most, and we'll see my dear cousin dead, and the beauty of it all is that our hands will be clean."

It was taking all Danielle's patience to wait until Pickett had left to discover how the meeting had gone. Once more, she checked her reflection in the cheval mirror. She had purposely worn her most provocative day gown. There was no telling what Pickett and Nathan might get Devon to believe. She might have to resort to her own brand of seduction to make him see the truth. She tingled at the prospect, then chastised herself. It wasn't as if her husband wasn't intelligent enough to see what was going on for himself. He just needed the proper persuasion to see the importance of looking into the matter, she told herself.

She was certain that funds designated for the orphanage were being spent elsewhere. If only she could prove it, Devon would have to dismiss the Picketts—and perhaps then even the bishop could be persuaded to send Nathan to another parish. Danielle blushed a bright pink. Of course, she could never employ the same methods she used with Devon on the bishop; but, presented with irrefutable proof, the clergyman would have no choice but to replace Nathan.

The front door had barely closed behind Pickett when she rushed down the hall and into Devon's study. "What did he have to say for himself?"

Devon looked up at his wife. The morning sun poured across the room, capturing her in a pool of shimmering light. The sight of her creamy white breasts pushing against the turquoise fabric of her day gown caused Devon to momentarily forget his concerns. He would never become used to her startling beauty, and this morning she was dressed to capture his interest. While he enjoyed playing the game of reluctant husband, he didn't know how much longer it would be before he took what she so bravely flaunted.

"What did he have to say?" she asked again.

Devon reluctantly lifted his eyes from his careful perusal of her turquoise-clad body. "He apologized for not giving me these earlier," he said, picking up the sheath of bills and letting them fall through his fingers onto his polished desktop.

"And what are they?"

"The receipts for the items Giles and I questioned in the account books."

"That cannot be," Danielle said. She reached across the desk, affording Devon a clear view of her décolletage as she plucked one of the receipts from the pile.

After studying it, she tossed it back on the desk. "Blankets were never purchased for the children. Ask any of them. They will tell you that they share the moth-eaten ones the parishioners donate."

She had dropped her role of the seductress. But Devon was not about to let her off so easily. Not after the delightful view she had just presented to him.

"There's not much I can do," he said, hoping his skepticism would lead her to start seducing him again. "It appears he has receipts for everything."

Danielle leaned forward and snatched another from the desk. Was it possible she didn't know how the view she was offering would affect him? It was all Devon could do not to reach out and claim what was his.

"Why, just look at this grocer's bill," she demanded, marching around the desk to thrust it into his hands. "This is more food than the children see in a year. I doubt even Mrs. Pickett could put away this much."

"Without proof, what would you have me do? I can't very well call him a thief."

"Well, I can," she threatened.

Devon pulled her into his lap. "Don't be so hasty." Pushing aside a curl that had fallen to her shoulder, he placed a kiss along the side of her neck. "Perhaps if we both put our heads to the problem, we can discover how they have managed to acquire these receipts."

Danielle's whole body tingled at his touch. It was so difficult to keep her objective in mind when she was near him. Even now she willingly arched her neck at his kisses. Oh, if she only had the willpower necessary to offer her lips to his and still keep her wits about her!

"The receipts?" he asked as his lips moved to the sensitive lobe of her ear.

His warm breath sent delicious shivers down Danielle's spine, and it took all her efforts to concentrate on what he was saying.

"The receipts were more than likely written only for your benefit," she said, surprised that she was able to string together sufficient words to make a coherent thought.

Devon held her closer and buried his face in the silken auburn curls. "Then you are telling me that I should throw them back in Pickett's face, all the while screaming that they are lies."

Danielle giggled at the image. "What I envision is that you hold a sharp cutlass at his throat and make him eat every last one."

"You're a heartless wench," he said. He tugged at the hem of her gown, slowly raising it up the length of her stockinged leg. "If you had your way, I would behead all the evil men who passed my way."

She ventured a glance at him. His bold eyes had become a smoldering blue fire, and she basked in the warmth of it. "And what of the evil women?" she teased.

"You?" he said. "Why, I would carry you off to one of my ships."

"You think me evil?" she asked.

Before she knew it, her gown was up to her waist and his hand had plunged beneath it and up her slim back. "The most evil I've seen in a long time," he whispered into her hair.

His fingers traced a sensuous trail of fiery promise up her back. She knew she should draw away from his arms, but she was too intrigued by his game. "And what would you do with me? Tie me to the mast and watch my skin blister in the sun?"

Devon shifted her on his lap. She gasped as he lowered his head to the creamy mounds of her breasts. "I would not let you off so easily, love."

Danielle's breath came in short, hot gasps as his tongue traced warm, moist circles on her breasts. She buried her face in his glossy black curls and drank in the masculine smell of him. Heaven help her, she was being caught up in her own web of seduction, but she couldn't pull away.

"I would lock you in my cabin," he murmured huskily, "and never let you out."

Danielle trembled at the thought. "You would not tire of me?" she asked. "Or did you merely mean to keep me from your sight?"

"I mean to keep you *in* my sight, love. In my sight and in my bed."

The raw desire in his eyes sent a warning through Danielle. He meant only to have her, not keep her. He said he didn't want a wife nagging at his footsteps when he returned to his ships. But it was so easy to lie to herself and pretend he wanted her, not just for the moment, but for all time. Yet she must not lose sight of her purpose to tease but not take.

"And where would you sleep?" she asked coyly.

"Beside you, love."

A throaty laugh escaped her lips. "It was not so long ago since I came to England that I do not remember how very small the beds on a ship are. There would never be enough room for the two of us."

He kissed the tip of her nose. "Ah, but then you've never seen my bunk. It's more than large enough for two."

"No doubt you speak from past experience," she said coolly, straightening in his lap.

Devon nibbled at her ear. "Let us not dwell on past indiscretions, but concentrate instead on my abduction of you." His hand cupped her breast. "The bed is as soft as a cloud," he whispered. "The sheets are of the finest linen. I will take you there. Slowly, I'll remove your clothes and you'll help me with mine."

His hooded eyes held her. An ache filled Danielle as his fingers fumbled with the buttons at the back of her gown. Her imagination was vivid, and it was all too easy to be drawn into his romantic scenario. She was already there in her mind. She could feel his strong arms as he swept her off her feet and carried her to bed. Her heart seemed to stop as he lowered her onto the sheets.

". . . the wind-tossed sea will lull us to sleep after our lovemaking."

Danielle struggled to wake from the dream, for it

was only that, she admonished herself—a dream he wove with soft, whispered words against her lips and the bold brush strokes of his fingertips against her bare skin. He was a master at the art.

"If you wish to execute a successful abduction, you would have to take me somewhere other than one of your ships. I would imagine that would be the first place the authorities would look for me."

"I would force you to write a note before we left, telling everyone that you had succumbed to your husband's charms and run away with him."

She tossed her head back in laughter. "You'll have to come up with a more convincing story than that. Even Brodie would have a difficult time accepting that."

Danielle suddenly sat up. "That's it!" she shouted, jumping off his lap. "Somehow Nathan was able to force the merchants to pad their receipts."

Devon groaned. He had overplayed his hand. He had hoped for a few more liberties before she grasped the solution. Now she would think him the fool. Of course he had meant to check each one out—but only after the proper persuasion from her.

Danielle sifted through the pile of receipts, her joy slowly turning to disappointment. "Even Nathan couldn't persuade all these merchants to do his bidding. We deal with at least half of these ourselves. I've met them and I cannot believe they would be a party to this."

"I doubt that they were," Devon said, reaching around her to pick up several of the receipts.

"But you suggested . . ."

"I said that together perhaps, we can determine where they acquired them." Devon scooped up the pile and carried it to the table beside the leather sofa. "Come sit with me," he said, "and I will show you where my dear cousin slipped up."

Danielle settled down on the sofa beside him. He handed her one of the bills. "What do you make of this one, love?"

Danielle studied the receipt. "It appears to be a bill for ground meal delivered to the orphanage kitchens." "Do you notice anything odd about it?"

"Only that it is for quite a large amount. The monthly bill for Burnshire isn't nearly this large."

"Exactly! While the orphanage has over forty children, Burnshire has more than three times the servants to feed, and our monthly account has never been this high."

"But why would a merchant agree to pad the bill?"

"Look closer, love. The padding was not done by the merchant."

Danielle studied the bill again.

"If you look closely, love, you can see that it is possible that the *two* placed in front of the number fifty might signify a later addition to the weight of the meal delivered, meaning that the total amount due would have also been changed."

"Then how can we prove that the bill was deliberately doctored?"

"Study the amount due. It is no problem to change the delivery amount from fifty to two hundred and fifty. You merely need to add the *two*. But changing the amount due is much more complicated. I'd guess that Nathan didn't want to risk changing the figures too much, which would call attention to the altered weights. He could only add a *one* in front of the original amount charged."

Danielle nodded. "Then if it was brought to his attention, he could say he had not checked the figures."

"You learn quickly," he said.

Her cheeks grew warm under his praise. It was certainly a pleasant change to have an opportunity to show her husband that she did indeed possess a mind of her own. Every time she was with him, she tended to behave like a ninnyhammer. "Are they all like this one?"

"First, allow me to ask you a few questions. How long has Katie been with you?"

Danielle picked up another receipt and appeared to

study it. "What difference does it make? Katie is mine now. That is all that matters. Where she came from is unimportant."

"Perhaps not," Devon said. He sorted through the stack until he found the paper he was seeking. He handed her the physician's bill.

"This cannot be," Danielle gasped. "Katie has been with me for almost two years now. As far as the Picketts know, Katie died of consumption. Amy was so clever with the deception, they didn't even realize I had taken her."

"I suspected as much when I questioned Pickett about the funds the orphanage continues to receive from Lord Meade. He insists that Catherine Elizabeth is a sickly child and that the orphanage uses the money to pay for the physician."

"I don't know who deserves the greater punishment—Katie's father for denying her his home or the Picketts for their indifference."

"Both," Devon said, watching her frown. "It was a shame you did not see his face when I told him we wished to see the child."

Danielle smiled brightly. "It is no wonder Nathan became so upset when I threatened to tell you that I suspected he was still receiving funds for the support of children no longer at the orphanage."

Devon's fingers dug into her arms. "You accused Nathan of that?" he demanded.

Danielle tried to pull back from his firm hold. "Yes, after the wedding, when he and I were dancing."

"So that was why he left in such a hurry." Devon tightened his grip. "Don't you know what could happen to you if you cross Nathan?"

"Devon, you're hurting me." She tried to pry his fingers off her arm.

He dropped his hand. "I'm sorry. I didn't mean to hurt you. But surely you know that taunting Nathan could be fatal."

"But it was your suggestion to taunt him with our marriage."

Devon could have kicked himself for his stupidity. If he wasn't careful, she would put it all together and realize that he was setting himself up as Nathan's target. Once she suspected the truth, there would be no stopping her. She was just stubborn enough to want to be part of it. His concern for her safety would mean nothing to her. What she didn't realize was that he would abandon all his plans if her life were threatened. The thought took him by surprise. He didn't want her involved, even though his need to thwart Nathan had never been greater.

Devon rose from the sofa and crossed the room to his desk. Opening the humidor, he took a cigar from the box. "If I pursue this now, Nathan will think it was all your doing."

"What does it matter?" she asked. "It's what we do with what we discover that counts."

"You don't know Nathan as well as I do. If he so much as suspects you are the one behind my questions, he will stop at nothing to be rid of you."

"Nathan does not frighten me. Now that I'm married to you, he would not dare try to harm me."

Devon paused in lighting his cigar. How could he make her understand? She was so careful with the safety of the children, yet she thought nothing of risking herself. His eyes met hers and he briefly contemplated discarding his plans to stop Nathan. It was ludicrous to involve Danielle in this. Yet he couldn't back away now. He was committed. If he didn't continue, Danielle would do it on her own. No matter that she'd pledged to leave everything to him. Given the right circumstances, he knew she would find a way to circumvent her promise somehow. She would not break it. He was sure of that. But somehow she would justify her actions. The only course open to him now was to keep her happily occupied with the small things—like the forged receipts—and out of the way on more important issues.

"Would you like to help me with those receipts?" he asked, hoping to turn Danielle's thoughts in another direction. "We'll sort through them and set aside the ones we want Giles to verify."

"And what will you do with what he finds out?"

"You will have to trust that I will use the information wisely."

She tilted her chin defiantly. "Will it be enough to have Nathan ousted from his position?"

"No, but it will be sufficient to request that the Picketts be removed from the orphanage. I'm hoping that once his job is in jeopardy, he'll be persuaded to enlighten us on Nathan's other enterprises."

Danielle flashed him a bright smile. "What should I look for, then?" she asked.

Devon joined her and they began studying the bills. He would have preferred to let her try to persuade him to do as she asked. He certainly enjoyed her methods. But to her it was all a lark. She taunted and teased, never realizing she was in danger of being caught in her own game. Well, he was more than willing to play by her rules—for now at least.

"And what have you to report?" Nathan asked as he handed over the leather pouch of coins.

Elizabeth drew her cape close about her. She was fast regretting her arrangement with this man. When he had first approached her, she had been pleased. Not only would she be able to supplement her income with the extra coins the vicar was willing to pay, but she would also be helping to bring down one of the *ton*. Hadn't her own husband been more worried about what others thought than the welfare of his own child? The bitterness rose in her throat.

Even after she had discovered the truth, he had not regretted his action. He had merely insisted he had only done what was best. Their child was better off with people who knew how to deal with that sort of thing. Better off, hah!

The only thing to benefit had been his pride. But to tell her that her child had died, when in fact he had given it over to a servant to dispose of, was unforgivable.

After that, what did she care if another unfeeling lord was toppled from his exalted position? Even so, Elizabeth felt her stomach tighten at reporting to the vicar.

She clenched her gloved fists and blurted out the words. "They maintain an excellent facade in front of everyone, but it's obvious she keeps him at arm's length when they are alone."

His smile was etched with malice. "You've done well, Mrs. Meacham. It won't be much longer before you can return to London a wealthy woman."

The evil on the man's face sickened her. Why did she feel so guilty? The welfare of her child was all that mattered now, and she must concentrate on that. What did she care about the others? Still, she couldn't help wondering what the vicar was planning. She had a vague idea, and it scared her. She must not get any more involved than she already was. She must force herself to think of the child and the money, and put everything else out of her mind.

"Her Grace is planning quite a large party to open Burnshire," she mentioned casually.

The sly smile on Nathan's face quickly faded and was replaced with agitation. He ran his thin fingers through his carefully combed hair, and the brown locks fell in wild abandon around his face. "Find out when they are planning this farce," he hissed.

Elizabeth drew back, frightened by the maniacal look in his cold gray eyes. "I believe late June is the date they have picked."

"How dare he do this!" Nathan screamed, shaking his fist in her face.

"But surely you realized it would be expected of them." She tried to leave, but the vicar grabbed her arm.

"Burnshire is mine!" he ranted. "That senile old fool should have left it to me."

Elizabeth pulled away from him. What had she gotten herself into? The man was mad.

Robert slowly crept away from the vicarage window. He wished he could have heard what they were saying, but he had seen more than enough. Mrs. Meacham was definitely working with Nathan. Devon would not be pleased.

The night was dark and he found himself stumbling over the endless bushes and rocks along the way. Sometimes being one of Devon's closest friends had its drawbacks.

Yet he had to admit there was another side to the coin. He recalled the time they had seduced the chief's daughters on that obscure island—that had turned out to be quite an adventure. Even though the girls had bedded nearly every man on the island, the old chief swore his "virgin" daughters had been violated. Robert grinned. The old reprobate had hoped to obtain a wealthy sea captain for a son-in-law. It was quite a fight they'd had before they were able to return to the ship and weigh anchor.

On reflection, his life since meeting Devon had been anything but dull. There wasn't a mate aboard one of Devon's ships who wouldn't lay down his life for the man. Devon had a way of making each of his men feel a part of the venture. Most sailors had nothing but the clothes on their backs, but Devon gave them a sense that the ship was their home. As long as they worked hard and stayed out of trouble, there would always be a place for them. Though other sea captains had predicted Devon would have a mutiny on his hands, he'd made it work.

Robert took longer than he thought it would to reach Burnshire. Even so, he kept close to the stables until he reached the kitchen gardens. It wouldn't do to have Andrews see him sneaking in. The old butler didn't care for Robert's unprofessional manner and was just looking for an opportunity to run to Devon with valid reasons for his dismissal. Once inside, he hurried along the back corridor leading to Devon's study. After two quick taps on the door, he opened it and slipped inside.

Devon lifted his head at the intrusion. The look on Robert's face brought him to his feet. "Danielle?"

Robert grinned. "I've never known a woman to worry you so."

"She's forever pulling some stunt or other. One of these days she's going to go too far, and all hell will break loose."

"Hopefully, we'll be long gone by then," Robert said, pouring himself a brandy.

"That's easy for you to say. It won't be you who receives the notes from Giles begging you to return and take your wife in hand."

Robert studied Devon. "I do believe you would use that as an excuse to return."

"That's nonsense, Robert. If I were ever coerced into returning, the reason would have to be extremely good. But let's not discuss my wife. What brings you sneaking into the study at this hour? Or perhaps the more appropriate question would be, what has Danielle gotten herself into now?"

"It's not Danielle. It's that new dresser you hired."

"Mrs. Meacham?"

"Yes. I followed her this evening." Robert downed the brandy. "She met with Nathan at the vicarage."

Devon slowly sank down in his chair. Danielle's dresser? It shouldn't come as a surprise that Nathan would set up another spy in the household. But Giles had checked her references. What had he missed?

"Have Giles bring me the information he gathered on her."

Robert grinned at the prospect of waking the stodgy old retainer. He could still picture the man's green countenance when he'd stood on the deck of Devon's swaying ship and explained the terms of the old duke's will. Robert had to give him his due. Giles had traveled a long way over rough seas to deliver a message he obviously considered more important than his queasy stomach. ''He'll have both our heads for waking him.''

''Let's hope yours will be sufficient.''

''The mark of a true friend,'' Robert offered as he went to awaken the old man.

Devon leaned back in his leather chair. He had an important decision to make. A spy this close to Danielle was a big risk. Yet if he dismissed the dresser, Nathan would only find someone else to take her place. And if through her he could set up the right situations, perhaps he could get Nathan to show his hand sooner. He thought of telling Danielle about Mrs. Meacham's duplicity, but quickly changed his mind. His beautiful wife was too impulsive by far. She would more than likely challenge Mrs. Meacham to deny it. That wouldn't do at all.

Chapter 12

"I should be home by late tomorrow," Devon said as he pulled on his leather gloves. He'd learned that Mrs. Meacham's references stopped three years ago with Lady Hamilton. Beyond that there was nothing. He was counting heavily on his family's long-standing friendship with the Hamiltons to get a few answers. He'd told Danielle simply that he had to take care of a number of business matters in London.

Danielle watched as Andrews draped her husband's broad shoulders with the multi-caped cloak. This would be their first separation since their marriage, and she suddenly realized she was going to miss him. She had considered asking to accompany him, then dismissed the idea. This might be the only opportunity she would get to have a private conversation with Amy. She had been worried about her since Jeremy's abduction, and for her own peace of mind she needed to talk with her.

Devon reached out for her, and it seemed so natural to walk into his arms. Odd, but she found she no longer did such things for the sake of the servants. It was his startling blue eyes that never failed to draw her to him. She tilted back her head. Curious, but his sun-browned features had not faded under the pale English skies.

Devon raised a questioning brow at her intimate perusal. "Dare I hope you will miss me?" he asked.

Danielle had come to adore that crazy little lopsided grin of his. An ache that was becoming all too familiar prompted her to move closer. She smiled impishly up at him. "Other than your high-handed ways, my lord, what is there to miss?"

"Perhaps this," he said as he lowered his head to hers.

Danielle pushed the presence of the servants from her mind as she willingly returned his kiss. His arms tightened hungrily around her.

Crash!

Danielle pulled away, her face flushed a bright pink.

"Bob," Andrews admonished, "if you've damaged that salver, you can expect the replacement to come out of your quarterly pay."

"I'm sorry," the footman mumbled as he bent to pick up the cards that had fallen across the foyer floor.

"Try to be more careful."

Danielle's eyes narrowed at the glint of amusement she saw Bob toss Devon's way before he lowered his head. She glanced at Devon. He quickly looked away, but not before Danielle caught a glimpse of the answering grin. She turned back to Bob. Odd, she had never noticed the similarities in their coloring before. True, Bob's face was not as bronzed as Devon's, but it was evident he had spent a good many days in the sun.

"How long have you worked at Burnshire, Bob?" she asked.

"Not long, your Grace." The footman set the salver and cards back on the hall table.

"Where did you work before?"

"Bob saved my life in Jamaica, love," Devon said. "That was all the reference I thought necessary. He needed a job, so I brought him back to England with me."

"Oh," she said as she continued to study the footman.

Devon took Danielle's chin in his fingers and turned her head back to his. "You will, of course, behave yourself while I'm gone?"

"If I must," she answered, hoping he wouldn't be too specific in his demands.

"You must." He bent to place a quick kiss on her lips. "I wouldn't wish to return home to find the constable at my door demanding my pretty wife's head."

"You need not worry. If I do anything so heinous, I promise to also do away with anyone who could later point a finger at me."

"And that is supposed to alleviate my worries?" Danielle laughed up into his solemn blue eyes. "Should I also do away with the constable?"

"Heaven forbid that I should return to a bevy of corpses cluttering the front lawns."

"I would never leave them out for you to see. But I would advise you not to look too closely at the grounds behind the stables."

Devon raised his hands in mock surrender. "Tell me no more. When they come to carry you off to Bedlam, I want to be able to declare I knew nothing about it."

"Coward," she teased.

"Yes, and I'd best leave before you decide you might be better off with me buried behind the stables with the others."

Danielle stood in the open doorway until his coach disappeared down the drive. If Devon was to return tomorrow, she only had this afternoon to visit Amy. She hurried up the stairs to change.

The driver pulled to a stop in front of the well-kept lawns of the orphanage. Ignoring Brodie's dark scowl, Danielle stepped from the carriage and marched to the front door. A chill breeze played across the dried leaves of ivy that clung to the facade.

She lifted the brass knocker and let it fall. Amy opened the door immediately. Dark hollows circled her soft gray eyes, and she looked even thinner than Danielle remembered.

"Who is it, Amy?" Mrs. Pickett called from the drawing room.

"It's her Grace, Lady Stanton."

Mrs. Pickett hurried through the large double doors. "Ah, Duchess, how very nice to see you again. But where is his Grace?"

"He left for London this morning. I have been wanting forever to have some new draperies made for the children's rooms and I thought, with Devon away, this would be the perfect time. I've brought Mrs. Meacham with me to help measure the windows."

Mrs. Pickett ignored the dresser. She had failed to get her gown and refused to forgive Mrs. Meacham for the oversight. "You're wasting the talents of your dresser?"

"It was Devon's suggestion," Danielle lied. "He thought the placement of heavier draperies might make the rooms warmer."

Isabel pursed her thin lips. "Amy, show them the rooms."

"Thank you, Mrs. Pickett." Danielle quickly followed Amy to the stairs. "We won't be long," she called over her shoulder.

While Brodie and Mrs. Meacham measured the windows, Danielle pulled Amy aside. "Did they discover the stairway to your room?"

"I fear they must have, for I can no longer open the small door."

"They did not question you about it?"

"No, they've said nothing," Amy answered, carefully avoiding looking at Danielle.

"Then what has happened to overset you so?"

Amy jammed her hands into the pockets of her apron. "It is a personal matter, Miss Danny. You mustn't worry yourself about it."

"Is there nothing I can do to be of help?"

Amy shook her head. "No. There is nothing to be done for it."

Danielle would have put the matter aside had not she seen a silent tear slide down Amy's cheeks.

"What is it, Amy?" she demanded.

Amy lifted tear-filled eyes to Danielle. "It's me sister. She's been sent to the workhouse."

"Your sister? I did not know you had a sister."

"She's much younger than me, Miss Danny, and she's too sickly by far. Why, she's only six and not much bigger than a mite."

"Why didn't you send her to me?"

"We wanted to be together. I never thought they would make her go to that place. Not as long as I worked here for her keep." Amy grabbed Danielle's hand. "Oh, what am I to do, Miss Danny? She will never survive without me."

"Don't worry, Amy. A child of six is too young to be sent to the workhouse. I will tell Mrs. Pickett a mistake has been made and that I wish her returned."

"You don't understand, Miss Danny. None of the children ever return from the workhouse."

"None of the children?" Danielle choked. She had heard about a few of the atrocities that occurred at the vile establishment. To think that there might be children there was beyond belief. "Why didn't you tell me children were being sent to the workhouse?"

"You were doing so much to help them already. I could not ask you to do more."

"But the workhouse. I would never have allowed them to go."

Amy met Danielle's gaze. "There are places more terrifying than the workhouse, and you saved a great many of the children from far worse fates."

Danielle was shaken by the look in Amy's eyes. She knew without asking that Amy had experienced some of those horrors. She couldn't change what had happened to Amy, but she could certainly help get her sister back. Devon would be furious with her for interfering, but she couldn't leave a six-year-old in that awful place. "Don't fret, Amy. I'll go to the workhouse now and fetch her back."

Danielle gathered up Brodie and Mrs. Meacham and left the orphanage. She pulled Bob aside and gave him their destination. Although reluctant, he told the driver, then held the carriage door for the ladies. Danielle stopped and turned to him. "I gave his Grace my solemn promise that I would allow you to accompany me should I leave Burnshire. I don't know why he made me make such a promise and I'm not sure whether I believe his story about you saving his life. But that's neither here nor there. You've always been there for me when I needed you, and I need your help now. But I warn you, should you say one word to his Grace about where I have gone, I will see that you're dismissed immediately.''

"I'll not disappoint you, your Grace," he said with a bow.

"Thank you, Bob. Your loyalty means a great deal to me."

She climbed into the coach. Now if only she could handle Brodie as well.

The ride to the workhouse was anything but quiet as Brodie argued with Danielle's decision. The sun had disappeared over the trees by the time the coach came to a stop. Danielle pounded on the front door. The woman who appeared informed them it would be hours before she expected to see anyone return from the factory. Danielle was livid, and even Brodie relented when she discovered the hours the children were expected to work.

Danielle returned to the coach. "Tom, give over your whip," she demanded. "Someone will feel its sting before this night is over."

Smoothly she caught the whip he tossed down. Before anyone could stop her, she had crossed the bare yard and marched up to the lighted factory.

Robert instructed Tom to stay with the horses and followed her. By the time he got to the door, she had already disappeared inside. Devon would be furious. His only hope was that Nathan was not there.

He opened the door. Despite the clear night, the air inside hung in a thick white haze that tickled his nose. It took him a moment to see that the fog was merely lint from the cloths. His nose twitched and he took a handkerchief to smother a sneeze; then he heard her.

"How dare you work these children at this ungodly hour! They should be home having their supper."

The looms fell silent as a short, stocky man stepped forward. The arms of his coarse shirt were ringed with dark circles of sweat, and his trousers were tied low to accommodate a belly that looked to have partaken of more than its share of local ale.

"I works them how I think best," the man answered arrogantly.

Robert smiled. The man obviously had never dealt with the duchess before.

Danielle raised her arm. The whip hung menacingly in the air above her for a moment before she brought it down. With a hiss, it sliced through the thick air. A murmur went through the workers as they watched their tormentor cringe before Danielle's anger.

Robert hurried across the room. "Your Grace," he said as he approached her, "you shouldn't be here. Please, come home with me and let his Grace handle this."

"Like he's done so far," she said bitterly. "No. I will see to this myself. The children will not work another moment in this horrible place."

"Then let me help you," he said.

Danielle tossed her reticule to him. "You will find a pistol in there. Use it if you must. I want everyone returned to the workhouse. Find Amy's sister and put her in the carriage, then see that everyone receives a proper meal before they are sent to their beds."

Robert stared at the crocheted bag in his hands. He had no qualms about using the gun, but where in heaven was he supposed to find a decent meal? Even if he were able to locate some food, a pistol would not ensure that it was palatable.

"Everyone go with my footman," she shouted. "There will be no more work this evening."

A murmur went through the crowd, but no one moved. Again she instructed them to go with Bob. But still no one moved. They seemed afraid to follow her instructions. Frustrated, Danielle dragged a wooden crate across the aisle and up to a long table that stood beside a vat of dye. Using the crate as a stepping-stone, she climbed on top of the table.

"I am Danielle Stanton, Duchess of Burnshire," she said. "You need not be afraid. My husband will deal with those in charge. He will see to it that you no longer have to work these long hours. Decent meals will be given you, and a warm bed at night."

Although a few remained skeptical, a shout of approval rose from the crowd.

"Oh, Lord," Robert whispered to himself. Devon was in for it now. In one fell swoop, the duchess had taken a tremendous cut from Nathan's profits, and he doubted she was even aware of the fact. Devon had considered doing something about the workhouse sooner, but he had wanted to investigate a few things first. The strange, middle-of-the-night deliveries to the factory were what had first made him suspicious.

Robert waved his hand in the direction of the door. "This way," he shouted. Stepping out of the path of scrambling feet, he attempted to keep a close eye on the man in charge. He didn't care for the way he continued to glare at the duchess. But the workers, in their hurry to get to the promised meal, soon separated him from Robert's watchful eye. Robert tried to look over their heads, but the man had disappeared into the crowd.

His gaze paused at Danielle. She stood on the table, balancing precariously, her arms thrown wide. From the look on her face, the table must be giving way. Devon would have his head if something happened to his lady.

The next minute she disappeared from sight. Frantic, Robert fought his way through the crowd to the table. Danielle was gone. Surely she hadn't been trampled in the melee. He called to her.

Then he heard a splash, followed by a spit and a sputter. Oh, Lord, no! He quickly shoved past the last of the stragglers. There stood the duchess, waist-deep in the vat of dye. Leaning over the rim, Robert pulled her out and sat her on the floor. She was a brilliant blue, from the top of her glorious curls to the tip of her wet toes.

"If you laugh, I'll use this whip on you," she said.

He lifted his hands in mock surrender. "Never would I laugh at the ill fortune of such a beautiful lady."

Danielle's eyes narrowed at his fancy speech. This man baffled her. To be sure, no one knew of his early life, but he was no footman. Truly, at some time in his past, his station in life had been of a higher nature.

"Help me to the coach, Bob, then see to the workers."

"Dev—his Grace would dismiss me without another thought if I let you return home dripping wet. Perhaps one of the dragons at the workhouse has an extra dress I can borrow for you."

He was gone before Danielle could protest. Perhaps Bob was correct. Rivulets of dye coursed down the back of her head and beneath the collar of her gown. She was wet and cold and everywhere she moved she left a puddle of blue behind her. At least Devon was not at home. Facing Brodie's wrath would be more than enough.

By the time Bob returned with the dress, Brodie and Danielle had found a small storeroom in which to change. It was filled with boxes, but there was just enough room for Brodie to help her into the stiff black gown.

"Don't argue with me," Brodie said. "Bob says that awful man tried to drown you and I believe him."

"That's not so," she protested. "Everyone was pushing past the table. One of the workers accidentally bumped it and I fell into the vat. There was nothing sinister in it."

Brodie clamped her mouth shut and didn't say another word. Danielle frowned as she wrapped her long hair in a large scrap of linen Bob had found in one of the crates. She was hard-pressed to determine which was worse, Brodie's wrath or her silence.

Finished, they left the cramped storeroom. Bob had stationed himself atop a crate outside the door.

"What of the workers?" she asked.

"I told the dragon I borrowed the gown from that if they weren't fed a proper meal, his Grace would be back to cut all their tongues out."

Even Brodie laughed.

"But what of tomorrow?"

"I took the liberty of telling them that you would be seeing to the preparation of a new schedule of hours for everyone."

Danielle's shoulders suddenly drooped. "We're not going to be able to keep this one from his Grace, are we?"

Robert smiled sadly at her blue woebegone expression. "I wish I could say there was no way he'd hear of it, your Grace, but the truth is, he will."

"Do you think he will be terribly upset?"

"He'll be furious," Brodie interjected.

Danielle kept her eyes on Bob, her expression a silent question.

He nodded solemnly.

"You've known him a long time, haven't you?"

Bob didn't answer.

"Ouch!" Danielle shouted.

Brodie didn't relent but continued to rub Danielle's arms with the lemon mixture. "It's no more than you deserve. Now hold still or you will be blue the rest of your days."

"Oh, it's not helping, Brodie. You're rubbing my skin raw and I'm still blue."

Brodie straightened her aching shoulders and stood. The bathwater had long since grown cold, and Danielle didn't look much better than she had when she'd stepped into the tub. "Mary, order a fresh bath for Danielle. Mrs. Meacham and I will attempt to do something with this hair while the water is being changed."

Danielle groaned as she crawled from the tub. "Haven't we done enough?"

"Do you want your husband returning to find you looking like a piece of watered silk?"

"If only Aunt Margaret had not left for Scotland, I could go to Bath and live with her until the color wears off."

"With the hornet's nest you stirred up at the factory, he wouldn't be a day in following you. Now sit yourself at the dressing table and let me see what we can do with this hair of yours."

Danielle grimaced at the locks of hair that hung down the front of her bathing blanket. A quick glance in the mirror confirmed her suspicions. The strange lemon concoction cook had whipped up might have lightened the blue on her skin, but it had turned her curls to a bluish purple that faded to green in places.

Brodie lifted the wet hair in disdain. "However are we going to get the blue out?" she cried.

"Cut it," Danielle answered firmly.

"Cut it? Never!"

"I see no other way. Devon will be home by late tomorrow. Do you think I want to confront him with my hair looking like a beribboned maypole?"

"Perhaps you're right. Cutting it might be for the best. Your hair is thick, and with the tight coiffure you were wearing, the coloring didn't get too close to your head. But that will still leave your hair unfashionably short."

"That's a far cry better than unfashionably blue," Danielle pointed out.

"Don't be flippant with me, Danny. It's all well and good for you to instruct me to cut it, but who's to do the cutting? Surely not I."

Mrs. Meacham spoke up. "Perhaps I could cut it for you."

"You know how to style her hair?" Brodie asked.

"Do you think she would volunteer if she didn't?" Danielle turned to face Mrs. Meacham. "Can you do it now?"

Chapter 13

Danielle ran her fingers through her short curls. "Mrs. Meacham, you are an absolute gem."

Elizabeth eyed the creation with doubt. She had had to cut the hair terribly short at the nape of the neck, but the bobbed curls hid the fact. To be sure, the unusual style suited the young duchess, but what would the duke think of the change? "Perhaps a hair switch might do until you become accustomed to the shorter length," she suggested.

"Do you really think it's necessary?"

"Definitely!" Brodie spoke up. "Thank goodness you have one. His Grace will be put out enough by tonight's folly without this. I'm going to ask Mary for it right this moment."

Danielle studied her reflection in the mirrored glass. "I rather like the short style, but Brodie is more than likely correct. Devon will be upset with me enough as it is. Her suggestion is excellent. I will wear the hairpiece." She turned from the mirror. "Thank you very much, Mrs. Meacham."

Elizabeth smiled shyly. "Please call me Elizabeth."

Danielle searched the woman's face. The woman never failed to puzzle her. With most of the staff she remained distant and aloof. Yet Danielle had come upon her many a time entertaining the children with little stories. She took Mrs. Meacham's hand. "It will scandalize Brodie," she said. "But Elizabeth it shall be."

* * *

Devon handed a package to Andrews, then removed his cloak and gloves. "Please send the box up to her Grace's room."

Devon knew that the presence of Nathan's carriage in the drive could only mean one thing, and seeing Robert outside the drawing room door, his lips twitching in a suppressed grin, confirmed his suspicions. Despite her promise, Danielle had done something to put a wind in Nathan's sails, and from the sound of the voices coming from the drawing room, she must have whipped up quite a gale.

Delayed one day and she had already taken matters into her own hands. How was he ever going to get her to be more careful? Well, best go in and see what she'd done now.

As soon as Robert opened the drawing room door the shouting ceased, but the words hung heavy in the air. Nathan was livid and Danielle wasn't far from matching his anger.

Devon stepped into the dimly lit room. Even in the pale light of the few candles that had been lit, Devon could see that Danielle's skin had taken on a dangerously blue hue. He rushed to her side, wondering whether she was about to have a seizure. Why, he had seen grown men tumble to the floor clutching their chests who weren't half as blue as she was. He took her in his arms, then rounded on Nathan.

"What have you done to overset Danielle so?"

"I! What have I done!" Nathan sputtered. "Better to ask your wife what *she* has done."

Devon moved Danielle from him. Her green eyes shone unusually bright for someone on the brink of suffering a heart attack. On closer inspection, he noticed her blue-rimmed eyes. Hell's bells, it looked like someone had painted circles around them. "Danielle?"

"I was merely dispensing much-needed justice," she defended herself.

Nathan took a step forward, shaking his fist in her

face. "Justice, hah! She was messing in matters that do not concern her. Why, she broke into my factory in the dead of night, sent all my workers home, and now she is demanding wages for them before she will let them return to their jobs. Wages. Whoever heard of such nonsense? They are fed and clothed and have a roof over their heads. What more do they need?"

"Why, you . . . you insufferable—"

Devon recognized that look. Danielle was riled enough to scratch Nathan's eyes out. Quickly, he slipped his arm about her waist and pulled her to him.

"Danielle, love," Devon said, hoping he could somehow convey a silent warning to his impulsive wife. "You promised to let me deal with this."

Danielle's lips tightened into a straight line and she continued to glare at Nathan.

"I must apologize for my wife . . ."

She turned in his arms. "Apologize for your wife!" she choked.

Puzzled by what appeared to be a sudden shift in her coiffure, Devon almost missed the fire in her eyes.

"How dare you apologize for me after what you've allowed him to do!"

Devon dragged his eyes from the strange arrangement of curls and patted Danielle's arm. "Now, love, you didn't allow me to finish." He looked at his cousin. "Nathan, my apology was for her haste only. There will be no apology for what she has done."

"You see nothing wrong in your wife's telling me how to conduct my business matters?"

Devon arched a dark brow. "Your business matters?" he repeated.

Nathan paled. "Your father left the factory and workhouse in my hands."

"Did he?" Devon said, thoroughly enjoying Nathan's discomfort. "Actually, I had planned to discuss the matter with you myself, but something arose that demanded my immediate attention. Unfortunately, my wife lacked the patience to await my return."

"What did you wish to know?" Nathan asked warily.

"Please, take a seat, Nathan. There is no need for us to stand here, facing off like two opponents in a ring. Let's discuss this like gentlemen."

Danielle was less than pleased with the seating arrangement. Devon sat her at the far end of the sofa before shepherding Nathan to the brocade chair by the fire. He was purposely leaving her out. Yet to move closer to the fire would only give Devon a clearer view of her blued features, and at the moment it certainly wouldn't do to complicate matters further.

Devon offered Nathan a drink, then settled back in his chair. He had wanted to obtain a few more facts before proceeding with this, but Danielle was forcing his hand.

"Giles has brought some puzzling matters to my attention, and I think you can answer most of the questions I have."

"Concerning?" Nathan asked warily.

"The orphanage and, of course, the factory."

Nathan shifted uneasily in his chair. "The orphanage?"

"Yes. I was going over the records of the children . . ." Devon deliberately let the comment hang in the air.

Nathan's eyes shot to Danielle, and Devon's chest suddenly tightened. Was it really possible that his cousin's hatred for Danielle was every bit as great as it was for him? He must somehow make sure Nathan kept his anger focused on him. "But let's not discuss the orphanage now. It has been brought to my attention that I have been sorely remiss in my duties."

Nathan's gaze slipped back to Devon.

"Giles has pointed out," Devon said firmly, "and on numerous occasions, I might add, that reforms are needed in the way we handle the factory workers. There are some who believe we owe them more than clothing, two meals a day, and a bed to lie on after a hard day's work."

"What more is there?" Nathan asked bitterly.

"Some benefactors believe the workers should be educated and are staffing the workhouses with teachers. After the laborers return from the factories, they have their supper and then go to class."

Nathan's contemptuous laugh chilled Danielle.

"And when are they to sleep?" he asked, his lip curled in a sneer.

"My thoughts precisely."

Nathan leaned back in the brocade chair, a smug grin lifting the corners of his thin lips. "Then you see the inadvisability of proceeding with this ludicrous idea." He brought the crystal goblet to his mouth and swallowed.

Danielle had to bite her lip to keep from laughing at Nathan's naive overconfidence. She knew that when Devon seemed his most reasonable it was best to weigh his words most carefully.

"You misunderstand, Nathan. I agree that the workers would not have the time, nor the inclination, to study after such a long day. I therefore intend to cut their hours to give them the time needed for an education."

Nathan choked on his brandy. "You can't mean this," he gasped.

"Oh, but I do. Not only do I intend to cut their hours, but I'm going to see to it that they're paid a small wage for each day's work."

It took a great deal of effort on Danielle's part not to stand and cheer at the announcement, but the shout died on her lips. Nathan's face flushed a bright purple. The vicar's anger with her before was nothing compared to the hate that burned in his eyes now as he glared at Devon. Suddenly she felt worried for Devon's safety. He was doing this for her. He had made it abundantly clear that it hadn't been his intention to involve himself.

Her heart swelled with pride. He cared after all. It was then that she realized she loved him. She loved him with every fiber of her being. The trembling she felt when he entered a room was not dread, but anticipation. She had lain awake beside him, unable to sleep all those nights, not because of fear that he might touch her, but because of frustration that he didn't. Lord help her. She had become the victim of her own seduction.

". . . and Giles will be contacting you on the details."

Devon was showing Nathan to the door. What was she to do now? How would she ever be able to hide her love from him? She lowered her eyes as he came toward her.

"What happened this time, Danielle?" he asked.

Danielle was forced to look up. Despite the dim light, she could see the anger in him. Where was the understanding—the compassion? Where was the love that should echo her own?

"Why did you do it?" he asked calmly.

Once again she had been the fool. His actions had nothing to do with any feelings he might have developed for her. His only concern was in thwarting Nathan.

She stood to face him. "You mustn't act as if I was the villain in all this. There were children there, Devon."

Devon raked his fingers through his hair. "Of course. It would have to be the children, wouldn't it?"

"Yes, little ones who had been working since early morn."

"Don't you think I was aware of that?"

Danielle was still smarting from her mistaken notion that he loved her, and all she wanted was to return to her room and have a good cry.

"If you knew, why did you let it continue?" she demanded.

"There are a few things I need to explain."

"What could you possibly say that could explain away the fact that you knew what was happening and did nothing to correct it?"

Devon sighed. "What must I do to earn your trust?"

Puzzlement filled her green eyes. "You talk of trust

when you allow that awful man to work those children from dawn to dusk and do nothing to stop it.''

He wanted nothing more than to lean down and kiss that line of stubborn determination from her lips, but he knew that wouldn't accomplish his objective. Until she learned to trust him, she would continue to settle things in her own impulsive way. It was too dangerous to let her continue in this manner.

He strode across the room, opened the door, and asked that Giles be sent to the drawing room. It seemed forever before Giles knocked lightly on the door and then opened it. Vanity prompted the white-haired man to prop his polished black cane against the wall before entering.

Devon motioned for him to take a seat, then began. ''Giles, will you please tell my wife what it is that you have been doing for the past few weeks concerning the factory at Westbryre.''

Giles shifted uneasily on his chair. ''Everything, your Grace?''

''Everything.''

Pleased with his Grace's interest in Burnshire, Giles allowed a smile to touch his dry lips. With great care, he leaned forward in his chair and began. ''The old duke put the running of the factory in Nathan's hands years ago. Even I didn't know whether his Grace had actually given the factory to the vicar. All I was ever told was that there was no need for me to oversee the funds for it or the workhouse, as the vicar was to have total supervision of them.

''It was my understanding at the time that the factory was being built to provide jobs for those at the workhouse. His Grace, the old duke, felt that with the excellent work the vicar was doing at the orphanage, he would do equally well with the factory.''

''Excellent work?'' Danielle asked. ''Was the man blind? Either that, or he never visited the establishment.''

''Oh, but he did. He visited often.''

Danielle looked at Devon. ''Is this true?''

"I was not here, but I have no reason to doubt it. My father would have felt it his duty to at least show an interest, no matter how slight."

"Ever since his Grace's return," Giles continued, "we have been trying to ascertain whether or not the factory was ever given to Nathan outright. We've searched the records thoroughly and can't find any evidence that Nathan owns it."

"Then what is being done with the profits?"

Devon took her hand. "That was my concern also. It was my father's original plan that the profits be used to support the workhouse, but from what I could see when I visited, very few of the funds find their way there."

"Is it possible that your father told Nathan to keep the profits?"

"You have to understand the strict code my father lived by. A gentleman did not soil his hands with industry. He built the factory for the same reasons my grandfather established an orphanage. It was a charitable thing one did in his position."

"But surely there were profits as well."

"That's something I will be taking up with Nathan."

"I want to be there when you do."

Devon made no comment. Dismissing Giles, he turned back to Danielle. "I will be handling this by myself."

"But I want to hear what he has to say for himself."

"Then you will have to settle for my account of the conversation."

Forgetting her reasons for maintaining a distance from her husband, Danielle walked into his arms. Fingering one of the buttons on his shirt, she coyly glanced up at him through her dark lashes. "Please, Devon. I promise to behave myself."

Devon's eyes narrowed. He took her chin in his hand and turned her face to catch the light. "Whatever happened to you?"

He waited for her to explain, but she flounced out of

his arms, her hair tilting precariously on her head. Impatiently, she raised her hands and readjusted it.

"I had a slight accident at the factory," Danielle answered, blushing.

Devon reached over and plucked the curls from the top of her head. It dangled between his fingers like a wet rat. His brows arched questioningly. "An accident?"

Danielle pulled the hairpiece from his fingers. "If you must know. Everyone was rushing to leave. There was a lot of pushing."

"And someone sliced off your hair with a pair of errant scissors?"

"Don't be ridiculous," she said, running her fingers through her short curls. "I merely got in the way."

"Pardon me if I appear a bit dense. But what does this have to do with your missing locks?"

"Well, if you must know, I fell into a vat of dye."

Devon's blue eyes narrowed to slits. "You could have drowned."

"Oh, the vat wasn't deep enough for that," she said. "But I'm afraid I ruined my cloak and one of my new gowns."

"And what of your promise that you would not interfere?"

"Oh, that," she said, arrogantly dismissing her failure to abide by her pledge. "If you recall, that only applied if you were handling things properly."

"And I am not?" he asked gruffly, pulling her into his arms.

Unafraid, she smiled up at him. "I didn't think so at the time."

Captivated by the dimples that appeared when she smiled, Devon ran his finger down her blue-tinged cheek. "What am I to do with you? I thought you were having a heart attack when I first entered the room," he said softly. "I was ready to murder Nathan with my bare hands."

Danielle settled into his arms. Throwing her head back, she smiled up at him. "Had I suspected as much,

I would have called for the smelling salts and fainted at your feet.''

"Vixen. You would have me be sent to the gaol for murdering my cousin.''

Danielle pursed her lips and rolled her eyes heavenward, appearing to consider the possibility.

"Heartless wench,'' he said. "Enough of your cruelty. For that I won't give you the present I brought.''

"A present?'' Danielle's eyes danced in anticipation. "And what do I get in return for my thoughtfulness?''

Danielle perched on her toes and placed a kiss on his cheek.

"You'll have to do much better than that,'' he whispered as his arms tightened about her.

Before she could turn away, his lips captured hers. With the discovery of her love for him, her resistance was short-lived as she caught herself melting at his touch. What would it be like if he loved her in return, she wondered, then put the thought aside as she lost herself in the passion of his kiss.

Devon moaned as her lips parted under his. It was so easy to ignore the warnings that rang out in his head. He knew he shouldn't be encouraging this, but with her willing body in his arms, how was he to stop?

Eagerly, his tongue plunged into the virgin depths of her mouth. Instead of pulling away from him, she welcomed his kiss, her moan of desire matching his. He struggled against the passion she was igniting in him. Best to remember it was only a game with her. To allow her to continue might prove disastrous for the both of them.

Although the thought of a commitment to this fiery lady seemed less and less a threat, he still had his ships to consider. The life of a sea captain did not set well with the restraints of marriage.

But she shouldn't taunt him so. He was only human, after all. Her body moved enticingly against his, and it took all his restraint not to carry her off to his bed.

"All is not forgiven,'' he said.

"Forgiven?" Danielle raised questioning eyes to his, and her budding passion died at the coolly tolerant smile that curved his full lips.

"You broke your promise to me."

Danielle's eyes flashed with indignation. "Is that all that matters to you?"

His hooded blue eyes raked her painfully slow. "No, love," he answered, his voice suddenly husky. "More seems to matter to me each day."

The liquid blue fire of those seductive eyes rekindled an ache deep within her. How much longer would she be able to resist the strange desires he stirred? How much longer would she even care to? "Does this mean I don't get my gift?"

He studied her for a moment. "Could I use it as a bribe to get you to stay out of places you don't belong in?"

"More than likely not."

"How am I to make you understand? This is not a game. If you anger Nathan enough, you'll put your life in danger."

"Do you think I care more for my own safety than that of those poor children?"

"Then think of what your actions are doing to them."

"It was the children I was thinking of."

He took her by the arms and looked deep into her eyes. "Has the thought occurred to you that if Nathan owns the factory, your actions will have only made things worse for the children?"

"I never dreamed he might own it," she said apologetically.

"Don't you realize how dangerous Nathan can be? You've got to curb this impulsive behavior of yours." Suddenly, he pulled her to him. "Oh, Danielle, why don't you ask me before you do these things? What would I do if something happened to you?" he whispered in her hair.

Danielle's heart soared. "You would care?" she asked.

Sobered by the love he saw in her face, Devon pushed her away from him. When had this happened? "Of course I would care," he found himself saying. "After all, it was I who brought you into this situation."

He watched the disappointment flood her features at his casual words. What had ever possessed him to say something so thoughtless? True, the discovery of her love for him came as something of a shock, and he knew he was responsible. Still, he couldn't help but feel that she was partly to blame. She had teased him unmercifully. But each time he thought of making her his wife in every sense of the word, he had always called a halt to it in time. He suddenly wondered when it was that he had become such a saint.

Danielle turned in front of him. Devon was pleased with his choice. The cloak was beautiful, and the rich blue color brought out the green of her eyes.

"Oh, where did you find it?" she asked.

"In a small village south of London." He ran his fingers across the silver fox that trimmed the garment. "The merchant hinted that you can only get this particular shade of blue from France."

Danielle turned in front of her cheval mirror. "Then it must have cost entirely too much."

"Don't worry about the cost."

"But it seems almost sinful to spend so much money."

"I said—"

At that moment Mrs. Meacham burst into the bedchamber, Danielle's damaged gown over her arm. "I'm sorry to disturb you, your Grace, but I have your gown. I'm afraid it's ruined," she said, spreading the dress across the bed. "As you can see, the dye did not take evenly. I don't believe another washing will help."

"Don't waste any more effort on it. Toss it. I surely have enough gowns now. One more or less won't matter."

"Yes, your Grace," she said. But instead of leaving,

she began picking up the other packages strewn across the bed.

"You may leave those until later," Devon told her.

"But it will take only a moment," she stubbornly insisted as she continued to rearrange them.

Devon took her arm and guided her to the door. "The packages can wait. I wish to be alone with my wife."

"Yes, your Grace," she said, bowing out of the room.

"Was that necessary, Devon?" Danielle asked. "You were rude. She was merely trying to do her job."

He picked up the damaged gown and held it in front of her. "Couldn't this have waited . . ." Devon stopped and took another look at the piece of clothing, then threw back his head and laughed.

Danielle grabbed the gown from him. "Whatever do you find so amusing?"

"You are not the only naive one, love."

Danielle's forehead creased in a frown. "I don't understand."

"The color, love. I paid a fortune for a cloak I thought to be unique, and it appears anyone who can afford the price of a bolt of fabric from our factory can own one."

Chapter 14

E ach day grew warmer as the mantle of winter lifted from Burnshire. The snow melted into dark puddles and birds heralded the early arrival of spring.

Danielle pulled her horse to a halt. A family of rabbits nibbled at the tender shoots of new grass that pushed up through the tangled mass of last year's lush growth. Their long ears, like a ship's distress flags, hung at half mast. The sudden appearance of a small black-and-white spaniel sent them scurrying for cover.

"Pepper!" Danielle cried. "Come back here."

"I doubt we'll see him the rest of the morning," Devon said as he moved his horse up beside hers.

"I should not have let him follow us." Danielle turned an apologetic smile on Devon. "But I feel sorry for the poor little fellow. He's yet to catch anything."

"Give him time. He's young. He'll grow into it."

"I'm not sure I want him to grow into it. Jeremy would be devastated to see his dog kill anything."

A warm breeze teased the green feather of Danielle's stylish new riding cap, and Devon reached to tuck it back in place. "You needn't worry. He'll get more exercise chasing them than he'll ever get catching them."

The past few weeks had brought a change in their relationship. Danielle was beginning to trust him, for she no longer drew away when he teasingly kissed her. But the closeness was beginning to take its toll on his frayed nerves. He didn't know how much longer it would be before he cast his good intentions to the wind and claimed her.

Danielle flashed him a saucy smile. "Such a serious face, my lord," she teased as she moved her dark gray mare closer.

His chest tightened. The spring breeze had painted Danielle's ivory cheeks a becoming shade of pink, and with her turquoise riding habit accentuating the brilliant color of her eyes, she was enough to take his breath away. "You look exceptionally beautiful today," he told her.

"And that is the reason for your frown?" she asked.

"The thought crossed my mind that if you continue to sport that devilishly seductive dimple, I cannot be held responsible for my failure to keep my distance," he warned her.

"I trust you implicitly," she answered.

That was where the problem lay. She trusted him to be a gentleman, when, God help him, he was really a cad.

"You needn't worry that your temptation is a permanent affliction," she continued. "It's the new costume. Mrs. Meacham is most proficient. With her skills, I will be the envy of everyone who attends our party next month."

"The clothes are only as good as the person who wears them," he corrected, his voice suddenly husky. "Rest assured, it will be you whom they envy, not your wardrobe."

Danielle looked at him speculatively. She doubted he was even aware of how his teasing was affecting her. If only it was the stirring of love that was motivating the intimate looks he directed at her, she would willingly help fan the embers that glowed within the deep blue depths of his gaze. But such foolish thoughts should be kept buried inside her. His comments were merely in fun, and she knew she'd be wise to keep her thoughts in the same vein.

"Aunt Margaret was right. You, my dear husband, are a rake and an accomplished flirt," she bantered.

"An accomplished flirt?" he protested.

"Yes, and I'd have to look carefully among your compliments to glean whatever small grains of truth they hold. But for now, I'll discount them all and concentrate on our ride."

"Coward!"

"Oh, but yes," she said, the dimple in her cheek deepening. "You have taught me when it's best to retreat."

He reached over and placed his hand on her mount's neck. "Dare I hope that when you retreat to your bedchamber I'll be allowed to pursue you there?"

"Is there no hope for you, my lord?"

"There is hope, Danielle," he answered, his voice thick with desire. "You have but to surrender. The war would be over and we could both share the spoils."

"Why is it that all your plans require that I surrender? Is there never to be one in which *you* do?"

His eyes captured hers and her breath caught in her throat.

"You seem to forget," he said with a seductive grin, "I laid my weapons at your feet the day we married. It was you who refused to acknowledge my surrender. Now I'm merely waiting for you to claim what is rightfully yours."

She answered him with an unsteady smile. Never had he looked more the pirate—or had she felt more the captured maiden aboard his ship. "I take nothing I haven't earned, my lord," she tossed to him as she flicked the reins of her mount.

The mare responded immediately, carrying Danielle ahead. "Race you to the large rock across the meadow," she shouted over her shoulder.

Devon sent his horse after her. "Do I get to name the prize if I win?"

"You must catch me first," she answered recklessly over the pounding of her horse's hooves.

Leaning forward, she urged the mare on. What had possessed her to throw the challenge in his face? Her mare, while fast, was no match for the big black stallion Devon rode. Had she truly hoped he would win so that she'd be obliged to let him name the stakes, knowing full well what they would be?

She ran her gloved hand along the side of her mare's neck. "Don't let me down, girl. You can make it," she whispered to the horse. "We don't have much further to go. Just to the edge of the woods."

She could hear the stallion gaining on them. The mare seemed to understand and a tremor of excitement ran through her. Danielle could feel her mount respond with more speed. Faster and faster they flew over the meadow turf, but still the stallion came. Out of the corner of her eye, she could see the nose of the black horse as it moved up.

"Faster, girl," she urged. "Faster."

In a burst of speed the stallion caught them and they reached the end of the meadow neck and neck. Danielle was laughing breathlessly as Devon leaned to grab the reins of the mare. "You didn't beat us, my lord."

"No, but neither did I lose. The race was a tie." He swung down from his horse.

"A tie it was," she boasted. "Now no one wins."

He lifted her down. The smug smile on her face only served to goad him more. "That's where you're wrong, my dear," he said, his voice husky. "As I see it, we both win, meaning I'm entitled to collect my prize and you may collect yours."

Before she could gather her thoughts, he swept her up in his arms. She struggled against him. "It isn't fair to name the stakes after the race," she protested as he carried her across the damp grass to a wide rock ledge that edged the side of the meadow.

With an exaggerated sigh, he placed her atop the rock, then climbed up beside her. "Are you saying that the Duke of Burnshire would behave as anything less than a gentleman in naming the stakes?" he asked.

Danielle was unaffected by his attempt to chastise her. The twinkle in his eyes belied any innocence on his part. She tilted her chin defiantly. "I have discovered, my lord, that the more exalted a gentleman's position is, the quicker his character seems to sink him beyond all redemption.''

''You have no respect for the title?'' he asked, deliberately leaning close.

She ignored his attempt to threaten her, for he was only teasing and she knew it. She leaned back against the smooth incline of the large stone and grinned saucily at him. ''I'm very afraid my lack of consideration for titles is the reason why I didn't take to my London season.''

''Didn't give those old windbags their due, huh?''

''It's all very well for you to tease, but I fear I was a sore trial to Aunt Margaret. The devil was forever seizing me, and I couldn't help but try to put them in their place.''

Devon's husky laughter echoed across the meadow.

''Laugh if you must,'' she scolded, sitting up beside him. ''But poor Aunt Margaret finally decided that she was doomed to failure as far as my marriage was concerned.''

Devon's mood suddenly sobered. He placed his finger under her chin. ''How very pleased she must have been to have me take you off her hands.''

Danielle jerked her head away. ''And how unlike a gentleman to put it that way. Perhaps I never intended to marry.''

''My father would have said it's every woman's duty. To him it was a person's only destiny.''

Devon's voice had lost its good humor, and Danielle sensed the pain behind his words. ''The terms of your father's will hurt you a great deal, didn't they?''

He leaned back on his elbow and stared out across the meadow. For a moment, she didn't think he was going to answer her. His troubled eyes suddenly met hers.

''I have to admit I never thought he would carry it that far. We were close when I was young, but then Nathan's parents died. The children of one of the tenants had come down with a strange malady and Nathan's mother was nursing them. The children recovered, but within a week Aunt Lavinia contracted it and died. A few days later, Nathan's father succumbed also. Nathan was twelve when he came to live with us. Looking back on it now, I realize that my father must have held himself responsible for the deaths.'' He paused before continuing. ''You see, the tenants were ours.''

''But your father shouldn't have blamed himself for Lavinia's decision to nurse the sick. It's the calling of a vicar's wife.''

''I think my father knew that, but he was never one to take what he thought as his responsibility lightly.''

Danielle stretched out beside him. ''Nathan must have been very grateful to your parents for taking him in. That's terribly young to have lost your family. A child that age would have been devastated.''

''That's what I thought too. Nathan's parents were quite old when he was born, and I'm afraid they spoiled him dreadfully. Nothing was denied him. I was only five at the time, but it didn't take me long to realize my father intended to continue with the travesty.

''At first it was little things of mine—a toy soldier, a book. When it finally occurred to Nathan that he could have most anything of mine he took a fancy to, his demands became greater. It was after Father gave my favorite pony to him that my mother stepped in. It was the first time I had ever seen my parents disagree.''

''I'm sorry,'' she said, taking his hand. ''You must have been terribly upset. What did your father do?''

The gaze that met hers was cold. ''He informed me that the next Duke of Burnshire should be more of a man than to run to his mother with such a trivial complaint,'' he said, the old bitterness spilling out. ''According to him, I was only being selfish in not wanting to give my cousin the pony. Burnshire became a silent battlefield with my mother and myself pitted against Father and Nathan.''

He looked away. It was plain to see he was embarrassed to have revealed so much. Danielle's heart went out to the child he must have been. "And now Nathan wants Burnshire, doesn't he?" she prompted.

"He's wanted it all ever since the day he overheard one of the servants say if it wasn't for my father and me, he would have been the next Duke of Burnshire." Devon stood abruptly, then jumped down from the rock. "And I'll be damned if I'll let him have it now."

The hate in his face was unsettling. She knew in her heart this was why he had married her—to stop Nathan. Danielle quietly slid down from the rock. She wanted to reach out and take the hate from him, but she realized that would only come with time. "I do believe we'd best be starting home," she suggested. "The sky is becoming decidedly darker."

Taking up the reins of her mare, she moved to a fallen tree to mount. But before she could reach it, he was at her side, lifting her up. She was pleased to see the smile back on his face. "If you're game, I'll race you to the stables," she teased.

"And what is the wager to be this time?"

Her heart tied itself in pretty little knots at the devilish roguishness that danced in those blue eyes of his. She took a deep breath and gestured to the approaching storm. "Obviously, the loser will get wet."

She didn't wait for him to mount, but flicked her small whip along the side of the mare. The horse quickly responded, leaving Devon behind, mounting his stallion.

It wasn't long before he drew the big black horse beside hers. They had a long way to go before reaching the stables. Stride for stride, the black stallion matched the gray mare's pace. But neither was a match for the dark clouds that boiled across the sky, and they were soon caught in the downpour.

Devon tapped Danielle's arm, directing her to follow. He turned his horse toward the woods. The rain had turned the meadow into a bog and they were forced to slow down. Reaching the woods, Devon skirted the edge until he found a path leading into the trees. The overhanging branches sheltered them somewhat from the rain as he searched for the woodcutter's cottage he remembered from his childhood.

He found it nestled in a small clearing ahead. Although the day had turned cold, no smoke appeared above the stone chimney that rose from the sagging roof.

"Let's hope someone was thoughtful enough to leave us some wood for a fire," Devon said as he ducked to avoid a low-hanging branch.

"Someone lives here?" Danielle asked.

"It's not much to look at, is it? It used to belong to the woodcutter, but that was years ago."

Devon dismounted, then helped Danielle. The sodden feather of her cap drooped, its silky edges brushing her wet cheeks. She looked tired.

"You go on in," he instructed as he lowered her into his arms.

That strange feeling of anticipation she always got when Devon touched her returned. If only it was the cold that was affecting her. But no, it was the nearness of him, the feel of his strong arms around her. The knowledge that she was helpless against his advances in a situation like this did not cross her mind. Her thoughts ran not to scenes of ravishment, but to ones of gentle seduction—a seduction she would be hard-pressed not to welcome.

"I'll be with you as soon as I've seen to the horses."

Disappointment swept through her when he sat her down at the door of the cottage. She chided herself for feeling peeved that, with him, the horses came first. She'd do better to see to a warm fire.

The cottage door scraped across the splintered floor when she pushed it open and walked in. The inside was surprisingly clean, given the outward appearance. Slats of wood attached to the back wall held the cottage's few possessions. She trailed her fingers along the plank table that sat before the stone hearth. Not a speck of dust. Odd that someone should see to it that the cottage was cleaned.

A sudden clap of thunder sent Danielle scurrying

back to the door. She pulled and it opened with a groan. A scream rose in her throat as a streak of lightning tore the heavens apart, and the rumbling thunder that followed shook the cottage as if it were made of straw. Soot spilled from the cold chimney. Just as Danielle decided to leave, Devon stepped into the doorway.

"You shouldn't have the door open. You'll catch your death of cold. We'd better get you out of those wet clothes. Use the blanket on the cot to wrap yourself. I'll get the fire started."

Devon knelt in front of the hearth. "Look's like someone has taken a liking to the old place."

Danielle remained by the door, feeling oddly uncertain as she watched him prepare the fire. His biscuit-colored corded coat stretched tight across his broad shoulders. Fascinated, her eyes followed the progress of a raindrop as it slipped down his dark hair to drip from the wet curls at the back of his neck. All too soon, the fire was lit and he turned back to her.

"You've not removed your things."

"Oh . . . no, I . . ." she choked, embarrassed that she had been caught studying him. "It shouldn't be necessary. The storm won't last long, then we can be on our way."

"I'll not have you chilled. Either you remove those wet clothes or I will."

In the two months they had been married, she had learned to recognize that stubborn set of his jaw. It meant he'd brook no argument from her. "You must keep your eyes to the wall," she said.

Accepting the compromise, he turned back to the fire while Danielle quickly began to undress.

Devon heard the wet gown drop to the floor. Next came the rustle of wet petticoats. The temptation proved too great and he turned around.

Danielle stood next to the cot, her hat in her hand. Her red hair was a rich display of wet curls, peppered here and there with a shiny green leaf.

Feeling his gaze on her, she looked up. The fingers

that were unfastening the ties of her petticoats halted. Mesmerized by the desire she saw in his eyes, she didn't move as he came to her.

His eyes touched hers and she could feel her body grow warm under his questioning gaze. He reached out and plucked a leaf from her hair. The next from the front of her lacy chemise, his fingers brushing against her breasts. His eyes burned with all the fires of temptation, but she was no longer afraid of the hunger she saw there. Instinctively, she moved closer. *Yes*, her heart silently cried out to him, and he lowered his head to hers.

"Danielle," he groaned, his voice husky with promise. "Do you know how much I need you?"

The question was a soft whisper of pain against her parted lips. The words were all wrong. Need was not what she wanted—love was. But with her body tingling so, she couldn't think about that now. She needed him too—the feel of his arms around her, his kisses teasing her senses. She arched her body into his.

At her eager response, Devon crushed her to him, the wetness of his coat soaking the front of her. His lips captured hers, robbing her of the doubt that still nagged at the back of her consciousness.

"Achoo!" Danielle's sneeze forced her head back.

Devon released her. Reaching over, he pulled the blanket from the cot and covered her, then moved toward the fire.

The cottage door opened slowly and a small head of blond curls peeked inside and said, "Jem?"

"Come in, lad, and shut the door."

"Your Grace!" Jeremy cried in surprise.

"What are you doing here, lad?" Devon asked as he watched the wide range of emotions that crossed Jeremy's face. "Have you run away?"

"Yes . . . no, your Grace."

"Which is it to be, lad?" he demanded.

Danielle stepped out from behind Devon. "Can't you see that you're frightening the boy?" she scolded, kneeling beside Jeremy. "He's soaked to the skin."

Devon's forehead creased in a frown. "It would seem that every time I am with you, my dear, a child appears. Are you perhaps the Pied Piper?"

"Don't be ridiculous, Devon. And don't scowl so." Danielle led Jeremy to a bench in front of the fire. "Why were you looking for his Grace's driver?"

"Katie and me were playing in the orchard when that man from the orphanage come for me. We hid in the bushes. Katie said as how Jem would help if I came here."

Her hand tightened around his. "And Katie?"

"She stayed hid in the bushes."

"Thank goodness," she sighed. "At least she's safe."

Jeremy threw his arms around Danielle. "I don't want to go back. Please let me stay with you."

Danielle looked at Devon. She was pleased to see concern in his eyes. "I promise you won't ever have to go back, Jeremy. Your home is here with us."

The hour was late when they left the woodcutter's cottage. The sun struggled to penetrate the cool depths of the woods, casting shadows across the path. Minuscule bits of its fading light were captured and reflected within each raindrop that dripped from the naked branches overhead.

Devon kept the horses to a sedate pace until they left the woods. With his arm wrapped around the small boy dozing in front of him, Devon flashed Danielle a reassuring smile. "Now who is wearing the frown? I promise you, I will have a talk with Nathan about the lad. Jeremy stays with us."

She gave him an unsteady smile. She didn't know whether to be concerned or relieved by Devon's show of interest in Jeremy's welfare. It was evident that Nathan still wanted the money for the boy.

Perhaps a short note to Lord Carruthers asking him to withdraw his offer for Jeremy would not be out of order. Yes, she would get to it first thing. Without a buyer, Nathan wouldn't be so anxious to get Jeremy back.

Frankly, she enjoyed helping Devon thwart the vicar's schemes. The past two months, playing the loving couple, had put some surprising ideas in her head, ideas that set her fantasizing about what it would be like to actually be the happily married couple they portrayed.

It was becoming more and more difficult to spend the nights lying next to Devon. She hated to think of how many times she'd been tempted to reach out and stop him when he rose to go to his own bed. But despite her growing feelings for him, the children must always come first. After all, one day he would return to his ships and they'd be all that she had.

"Danielle?" Devon called to her again.

She turned to him.

"You seemed miles away," he said. "Dare I hope your thoughts were on me?"

Her cheeks grew pink. "Devon, the boy."

"He can find his own wife."

"You are too incorrigible by far, your Grace. Is there any hope that you will change your ways?"

He leaned toward her and whispered, "Only if you change yours."

Danielle lowered her eyes from the promise she saw in his. She refused to answer him and they rode on in silence, a light mist keeping them company. The gloomy sky reflected Danielle's mood. It was so simple to fall into the easy camaraderie that had sprung up between them. But how could she explain to her heart that it was nothing?

The lights of Burnshire loomed ahead and a great knot grew in her stomach. Each hoofbeat brought her closer to the bed they would share again this evening. If he turned to her, could she continue to lie to herself—and him—and say she didn't want him? Had Jeremy not come to the cottage, there was no doubt she would be lying in her husband's arms now. Yet what was she to do? Devon had made it more than clear that he didn't want any commitments from their marriage. If he glimpsed the feelings that were beginning to grow within her, would he forgo his plans and leave immediately?

All too soon they arrived at the stable, and Danielle had yet to resolve her troubles.

Devon handed Jeremy down to his groom, then dismounted. "I'm afraid we were all drenched. Send one of the stableboys to the house. Have him tell Mrs. Talbut that hot baths are to be drawn for the three of us."

The groom silently withdrew as Devon lifted Danielle from her mount. "Let's get you to your room and out of these wet clothes." Their eyes met and he slowly lowered her down the length of him. A fire that had been smoldering most of the day burned warm between them.

"Step lively, lad," Devon tossed over his shoulder. "There's a bath and supper awaiting you."

"Do you think there will be apple muffins?" Jeremy ventured to ask.

"Apple muffins it is." Devon rumpled his wet blond curls. "Run along now and I'll see that cook includes one on your supper tray."

"You'd best hope cook has some," Danielle whispered as he guided her around a large puddle.

"Cook may not admit it if asked, but the pantry seems to contain an abundant supply of cakes and muffins since the children came. You see, I notice more than you think," he added. "Such as how the rain has an interesting way of enhancing your riding habit."

"Devon!"

"I'm not blind, love," he said, holding the door for her.

She swept by him. "I think this is a conversation best not continued."

In a few swift strides he was beside her. "Safer now than when we reach your bedchamber," he teased.

Danielle stopped. Slowly, she turned to him. "You'd better have your valet help you remove your damp clothes, and then crawl into a hot bath."

Devon hurried after her as she climbed the steps. "I would much prefer to help you get out of your wet gown, and then crawl into *your* hot bath."

Danielle kept walking. "My bath is large, but fortunately, it's only large enough for one."

"A gross oversight on my father's part. I'll have to commission one that will accommodate a loving couple."

Danielle paused at her door. "And what loving couple did you have in mind, my lord? Surely not one in which the role of husband is but a temporary position."

She hurried into her bedchamber before he had time to consider that she might desire a different arrangement. Leaning against the closed door, tears welled up in her eyes. She had all but told him of her love today, yet he wanted only her passion. Why couldn't she accept that? In a few months he would be gone. Wasn't it wiser to take happiness while it was at her fingertips? What would be so terribly wrong with lying in his arms and accepting him as her husband? What was this nagging of her conscience that continually whispered that it must come from love? Wasn't her love for him enough?

Chapter 15

The subtle scent of lavender rose from the warm bathwater as Danielle stepped into the copper tub. It had been a long day and every part of her body ached from the cold, damp rain. It was at times like these when she appreciated the warm bathing room and the large tub the late duke had commissioned for his wife, Lady Julia. Danielle lay back against the copper side and stretched her legs out before her.

She had finished the note to Lord Carruthers. It was up to Tom now to see that he received it. She could only hope that she had been firm enough.

Danielle's concentration on the problem was such that she didn't hear the door open. Unaware of her visitor, she lifted her foot to stab a fat bubble.

Her brow knit in a frown. Perhaps she should pay Lord Carruthers a visit instead. No, she then decided, the note should accomplish what she had set out to do without alerting Devon to her interference. Danielle's lips curved in a smile. For once, she had acted sensibly and no one knew of it.

"And what, may I ask, are you planning now?" Devon asked, pulling a chair up to the side of the tub.

Danielle scooted down in the water. "What are you doing in here?"

"Don't change the subject, Danielle. I know that smile. It means you are planning something I won't approve of. So have out with it. What notion have you got in your pretty head this time?"

"Must I be planning something each time I smile? Isn't it possible that I was merely enjoying my bath?"

Devon sat down. "That smile harbors a scheme if ever I've seen one," he teased. Stretching his long legs out, he rested his arm on the side of the tub. He had purposely hurried with his own bath so that he could find out what she had meant about the role of a husband. If his wife was beginning to question her original decision to keep him at arm's length, he was prepared to help her change her mind.

Idly, he trailed his fingers through the soap bubbles. "It doesn't appear that our efforts to discourage Nathan have been effective."

Danielle shifted uneasily. "What do you suggest we do?" she asked.

"Despite all our efforts, it's obvious Nathan does not feel threatened by our marriage. Either he doesn't care—which I find hard to believe—or he knows the true status of our relationship."

"But how? All of our friends believe us happily married."

"We go through the motions, but do you honestly think we have fooled anyone? Nathan would never have attempted to abduct Jeremy otherwise."

Danielle sat up in the tub, then quickly ducked back under the water. She knew he'd try something like this. "It's what you'd like me to believe, isn't it?" she accused.

"Shall I summon your maid and ask her?"

That wouldn't be necessary. Danielle suspected she already knew what Mary's answer would be. The revealing nightdresses she laid out for Danielle each night told the whole story. It was obvious Mary believed the gowns might help entice Devon to do more than just share the mattress on Danielle's bed. "I've sent Mary to see how Katie is. But surely you can't believe Mary would ever tell Nathan our marriage was a sham."

"She need only mention her concerns to one of the other maids for it to become common knowledge among the servants."

"Well, I don't have time to discuss it now," she said.

"Mrs. Meacham should be here any minute to help me dress. You had better leave before we scandalize the servants."

Devon stood and kicked the chair away from the side of the tub. "Scandalizing the servants is just what I have in mind, my dear." Bending over, he plunged his arms into the water and scooped Danielle out of the tub.

"Have you gone mad? Put me down this instant!" she demanded.

"Hush, love," he whispered into her ear. "That's Mrs. Meacham now. We wouldn't want her thinking you were fighting off your own husband, now would we?"

Before she could answer, he covered her parted lips. Careful that he not release her from his kiss, he slowly lowered her wet body down the front of his own. Still warm from her bath, Danielle seemed to melt against him. Hungrily, his arms closed around her.

The small gasp from the doorway, followed by the click of the shutting door, only brought a feeling of relief. Mrs. Meacham had come and gone.

Danielle tried to push away from him, but her determination to deny her growing love was shattered as his hands moved up her back. Her whole body seemed to burn with her need for him. She could no longer fight him. She wanted him every bit as much as he wanted her.

Danielle slid her arms up the front of Devon's shirt and behind his neck. Pressing herself boldly against the hard planes of his magnificent body, she hungrily returned his kiss.

Devon moaned at her eager response. Sweeping her up in his arms once more, he carried her into the bedchamber and laid her down beside him on the bed. Propped on one elbow, he reached up to pull the pins from her hair. The rich dark curls tumbled around her face. He ached at the silken feel of her, the touch, the scent of lavender. Oh, how he wanted her. He cupped the side of her face in his hand.

Didn't she know a man could take only so much? He buried his face in her hair. This had to stop. He was almost to the point of no return and he'd be damned if he'd take her this way. Danielle would never forgive him—not to her dying day.

She would want love—and commitment. The thought was sobering. He wasn't ready for that type of commitment—not to anyone.

He rolled away from her and sat on the edge of the bed. "Devon?" she said, confused.

Suddenly they heard the sound of hurried footsteps. Careful to avoid looking at her, Devon stood and tightened the belt on his robe before tossing Danielle hers. She had no more than secured it about her when her maid threw open the door.

"I can't find her anywhere, Miss Danny."

Danielle's heart froze. Mary would have to be terribly upset to enter without knocking. She reached for Devon's hand. "Katie?" she finally managed to say.

"I've looked everywhere. No one's seen her."

"Where's Brodie?" Devon asked. "Perhaps Katie is with her."

"No, she just this moment returned from delivering the new draperies to the orphanage. She's alone." Mary buried her face in her hands. "It's all my fault," she wailed. "I should have checked on her earlier."

"Calm down, Mary," Danielle soothed, although her own heart felt as if it had turned to stone. "Katie could be with Mrs. Meacham. They were working on a dress for her doll this morning."

Mary lifted tearstained eyes to Danielle. "Mrs. Meacham left for the orphanage. One of the draperies didn't fit proper and she went to adjust it."

Danielle could no longer keep her own fears in check. Katie was missing. She looked at Devon. "The man who tried to take Jeremy," she choked.

He wrapped his arms around her. "Hush, love. Burnshire is a large house. She could be merely hiding. I'll have Andrews organize the servants to search for her."

But he doubted she believed a word he had said. He didn't.

* * *

Elizabeth turned from the curtain she was sewing. She wished she had taken Brodie up on her offer to return to the orphanage and help with the final adjustments. At least then she would have been spared the vicar's company. If he grabbed her arm again, she'd stab him with her needle. "It should be perfectly clear," she said. "I've fulfilled my part of the bargain. Now our agreement is at an end."

Nathan shoved his face into hers, his ragged breath misting in the cold room. "It is at an end when I say it is."

"You got the information you paid for," she said. "What more do you want?"

"I want to know everything. Everything! Do you hear me?" he shouted.

"The whole of Westbryre can hear you."

Nathan suddenly released her and she stumbled back against one of the small box beds. Elizabeth had been so certain when she had taken the vicar up on his offer that she would not get involved. She would take the money he offered her, and once she could arrange it, she and her daughter would be gone. She had been so sure that Danielle would not object to finding a good position for the child. Now she knew better. Danielle was raising Katie as her own. Elizabeth had considered leaving. After all, as Danielle's ward, Katie would have all the advantages Elizabeth was no longer able to give her. But each day it grew harder and harder. Finding Katie had been an obsession with her for too long. She couldn't leave without her child.

". . . I'm warning you. Keep them apart!"

"And how would you suggest I do that?"

"You'll have to manage somehow. That's what I pay you for."

"Hah!" she scorned. "The small amount you pay me wouldn't keep her Grace in bonnets."

Nathan's fingers dug into her arm again. "It's my money she's spending on those bonnets. Keep that in mind. Even the wages she pays you are mine." Nathan shook Elizabeth in frustration. "It should have all been mine," he whined like a small child. "It was my mother who was the oldest. Devon's father should never have been born. Don't you see?" He shook her again. "Can't anyone see?"

Elizabeth cringed at the madness she saw in his eyes.

"But it won't be long now," he said. "Burnshire will be mine. All mine." He twisted her arm tighter. "Until then you will see to it that there is no child to rob me yet another time."

"But what would you have me do?" she asked. "If his Grace dismisses me from Danielle's bedchamber, I have no choice but to leave."

"Best dig deep into your imagination and come up with something." He leered at her. "You wouldn't want the duke to discover that you lied about your references, now would you?"

Elizabeth paled. "I—I did not lie," she said.

"That isn't what Lady Hamilton's kitchen maid tells me. She says you were never the good lady's dresser. You were a friend with a past you wanted to forget." He paused for a moment. "A past perhaps I should try to discover."

"Wh—what do you want from me?"

"Ah, that's how it should be. I pay you and you'll do as I say." His thin mouth pursed into a sneer. "For now, I want you to keep my cousin and his wife apart. If nothing else works, create a distraction."

"Such as?" she asked bitterly.

Nathan tugged at the lace cuff of his shirt, waiting until he was sure of her attention. "Such as the disappearance of one of the children."

"You've taken Jeremy?" she gasped.

"Is that what they think?" he asked, a broad grin slashing his evil face. "All the better. Then it might be some time before the little girl Danielle seems so taken with is missed."

"Katie?" she choked. "You've done something with Katie?"

"Don't look at me as if I'm some kind of fiend. My men only meant to give Danielle a fright. The child was released hours ago. She should be walking into Burn-shire any minute now. Granted, she might be a tad tired and a wee bit hungr—"

Elizabeth didn't wait to hear more. She pulled away from his grip and ran out of the orphanage.

Her child! What had he done with her child? She must find Katie before it was too late. The servants would help. Frantically, she stumbled through the woods. The lights of Burnshire never looked so wel-coming. Bursting into the kitchen, Elizabeth was brought up short. It seemed the entire staff was in chaos. Pitchers of steaming water were being rushed up the stairs as fresh pots were placed on the fire.

"Hurry with that water," Mrs. Talbut shouted. "The bricks, Tom, are they warm yet?"

"I'm wrapping them now. Should be enough to warm the whole o' England."

"Bring them along, then," she called over her shoul-der as she left with the large bathing blankets. "I want that bed nice and toasty by the time she's finished with her bath." She paused in the doorway. "As soon as the physician arrives, send him up."

Elizabeth's knees felt as if they were going to give way. "Who is the physician for?" she asked one of the maids who stopped to refill her pitcher with hot water.

"That sweet child was out in this awful weather most of the day. Her Grace was fit to be tied when she learned of it."

"Katie?"

"Yes, and this time the little angel will not be imag-inin' her illness. She's burning up, she is."

Elizabeth stumbled up the stairs. It was all her fault. If she had been honest with Danielle from the begin-ning, the vicar would never have been allowed near the children. A tear slipped down her flushed cheeks. Greed had brought her to this. Now that the vicar was suspicious of her past, she was trapped.

By the time she reached Katie's room, tears were running unrestrained down her cheeks. Pausing at the open door, she quickly wiped them away. The chaos was even greater here than in the kitchen. The room was as hot as an oven, and the servants were still bringing wood to stack beside the hearth.

"That's the last of the water we'll be needin'," one of the maids said. "She'll be done with her bath soon."

" 'Scuse me, Mrs. Meacham," Tom said as he and several children brushed by her with the warm bricks. The covers had been turned down, and the warm bricks were soon distributed on the soft sheets and the counterpane pulled up to cover them.

Elizabeth leaned back against the doorframe. How could she have ever been so naive as to think she could have offered her child more than Danielle was willing to give? The door opened and everyone stood aside as the duke carried Katie to the bed.

"Has the physician arrived yet?" Danielle asked Mrs. Talbut as the small child was placed in the semicircle of wrapped bricks.

"No, your Grace. It seems he was called away on an emergency, but you needn't worry. We've sent one of the stable lads after him."

Danielle tucked the covers around the trembling child. "See that the other children get a warm supper, then put them to bed. I'll not have any more of them sick."

"Yes, your Grace," the housekeeper said. "I'll leave one of the maids here to fetch anything you might be needing."

"Thank you, Mrs. Talbut." Danielle wrung a cool cloth out to lay on Katie's head.

"May I help?" Elizabeth asked.

Danielle was pleased by the offer. "Could you hand me that extra coverlet by the fire? We need to keep her warm."

It seemed like hours before the physician arrived. Danielle restlessly paced the floor as he examined Katie. Devon took her in his arms. "She'll be fine, Danielle."

Tears glistened in the tortured eyes she raised to his.

"If only I been to home, none of this would have happened."

Devon looked across the room to Mrs. Meacham. She appeared to shrink before his eyes. Perhaps it was time he took a hand in seeing that the children were removed from Burnshire. He hugged Danielle close to him. It would be a fight from Danielle at every step of the way, but he would see to it that good positions were found for them. Danielle continued to sob in his arms.

"Oh, why did I ever suggest the ride?" she sobbed. "If only I had been here, Nathan would never have dared to take the children. If Katie dies, I will never forgive myself."

"You cannot shoulder the blame for this. There is no way—"

Danielle's brow furrowed in a frown. "Why did Jeremy run looking for Jem?" she asked. "Why not Brodie—or Mary?"

"Apparently Jem has become quite a hero to them. He fills their heads with all manner of tales."

"I've made quite a botch of this, haven't I?" she asked. "How did I ever expect to be able to protect the children if I don't even know what they are doing?"

"You can't be expected to watch all the children all of the time."

"But I wasn't even aware of this growing friendship with Jem." Danielle suddenly grabbed the front of Devon's shirt. "Could he be working for Nathan?" she whispered.

Devon led her out into the hall. Standing so he could keep a vigilant eye on the physician and Mrs. Meacham, Devon drew Danielle close. "You can rest easy on that. When I noticed the amount of time the children spent in his company, I had Giles check him out thoroughly." He glanced over Danielle's shoulder to the dresser. "Trust me, Jem is not the one working for Nathan. He's too afraid of his own shadow to be of much use as an informant."

Danielle followed his gaze. Devon had an uncanny

way of judging people, and she could see no reason to doubt him now. Everyone seemed to genuinely care for the children. Especially Mrs. Meacham.

When the doctor finished with his examination, he left a small potion of medicine and told them not to worry. He promised to call again in the morning, but it did not set Danielle's heart to rest. She placed another cool cloth on Katie's head. When it grew warm, Mrs. Meacham handed her a fresh one. Danielle studied the dresser. It seemed a shame Mrs. Meacham had no children of her own, since it was evident she would have made a fine mother.

Nathan paced the length of the drawing room floor again. He had not been surprised that Devon had summoned him to Burnshire. And providing that bitch, Mrs. Meacham, had kept her mouth shut, he didn't doubt his ability to bluff his way through this meeting with his dear cousin. He paused at the sideboard and poured himself another drink. What was taking so long? He had been here the better part of an hour and Devon had yet to appear.

"His Grace is otherwise disposed," Andrews had informed him haughtily. Well, the butler's tone would be more respectful once Burnshire was his. Nathan would toss him out on his ear soon enough if it wasn't. He paced the drawing room one more time before stopping in front of the marble fireplace. He gazed thoughtfully at the painting over the mantel. He regretted that he had not thought to add the oil to his own collection before Devon returned to England.

He allowed a grin to lift the corners of his lips. Soon, he thought, Burnshire would be his, as it should have been from the very beginning. Then all the treasures he'd taken could be returned. The months of planning were almost at an end. Soon the jaws of his trap would close—

"Pleased with what you've accomplished?"

Nathan swung around. Devon stood in the doorway, his anger filling the room. The dark look brought a fine sheen of perspiration to the vicar's lips and he pulled out his lace handkerchief. It was enough to cause the devil himself pause to reconsider his sins.

"Good evening, cousin," he finally managed to say.

Devon didn't answer, but slowly walked toward him. Suddenly Nathan was aware of how very slight his own frame was compared to that of his cousin.

"It's over, Nathan," Devon said matter-of-factly.

"What do you mean?"

He grabbed the front of Nathan's waistcoat and pulled the man roughly toward him. Nathan's breath came in tiny little gasps. "Never again are you or one of your men to endanger one of my household. Do you understand?"

"I've done nothing, I swear," Nathan protested.

Devon lifted him up by the front of his coat until their eyes met. "I've had enough of your scheming and cheating—and your lies. When I was young I had to put up with them, but I'm grown now and I'll have no more of it at Burnshire. Aside from the Sunday services and the comfort you may give your parishioners, all your other duties as vicar will be directly overseen by my staff."

"You haven't the authority to do that," Nathan bellowed, twisting in Devon's tight hold.

Devon pushed his face into Nathan's. "You forget, my dear cousin. I no longer live in your world—by your rules. You made sure of that when you set your torch to that tenant's cottage and laid the blame at my door. You forced me to leave England."

"It was merely a harmless prank," Nathan mumbled. "You didn't have to leave. Your father was willing to put everything aside if you married Lady Emily."

With a shove, Devon released him, sending the man stumbling backward. "A harmless prank? Well, I've had enough of your harmless pranks and I'll not have another child harmed because of your greed."

Nathan opened his mouth to speak, but Devon silenced him with a raised hand. "Don't waste my time with your denials. As long as I am the Duke of Burnshire, neither you nor your men are to come here unless invited. Nor will you be allowed near the orphanage without my permission. Is that understood?"

"But—but you can't do this to me. What will everyone say?"

"If you do as you're told, no one need know but the two of us. Now you'll have to excuse me. I have more important matters to take care of." Devon turned and walked away.

"You'll never get away with this," Nathan shouted after him. "You don't have the right to take away my duties as vicar."

Devon turned back slowly. "The right? I make my own right, Nathan. I live by the rules of the sea now, and a sea captain needs no one's permission but his own."

Nathan stood trembling with rage as Devon left the room. "I'll see you dead for this," he muttered to himself.

When Devon reached Katie's room, Robert pulled him aside.

"I must speak with you."

"Can't it wait?" Devon asked. "Danielle may need me."

A roguish grin split Robert's face. "Nathan's man, Chilton, has taken up with one of the local wenches. Seems he's been digging deep in his pockets lately on the expectation of having a healthy purse soon—that is, as soon as he takes care of a certain duke. The woman's agreed to meet me in an hour and I mustn't be late."

Devon shook his head. "I should have known a woman would be the reason for your impatience to be off. Have out with it, then. What did you want to tell me?"

"Her Grace had one of the stable lads deliver a note to Lord Carruthers at White Oaks."

An unfamiliar ache tugged at Devon's heart. "You've taken to following the duchess?" he asked sharply.

"I was following her Grace's maid. I heard her tell the lad the note was from your wife and he was to make sure no one saw him. Had the maid not appeared so secretive about it, I wouldn't have followed the boy."

"And the note?"

"I'm sorry, but there was no opportunity to discover what it said."

Devon stood staring at the door, unable to meet his friend's gaze. Why would Danielle be sending a message to Carruthers? "Thank you, Robert," he finally said. "Now off with you. The wench may not be so moved by your charms if you're late."

After Robert left, he reached out to open the door, then stopped. Giles had always dispatched Danielle's notes up until now. Why not this one? He dropped his hand and walked away.

A supper tray was brought to Katie's room as Danielle prepared to spend the night. She sent Mary off to bed, but Elizabeth refused to leave. Danielle was pleased with her display of concern.

Katie tossed and turned most of the night. It proved quite a task to keep the cool cloths on her head, but Danielle was not to be discouraged. Thank heaven for Elizabeth's tireless help. She left Danielle's side only to fetch more water for the cloths.

Devon made frequent visits to the sickroom. At first it seemed awkward to have him fetch a hot cup of tea or a blanket or a book to while away the hours, but he appeared to want to help and Danielle took courage in his quiet strength.

By dawn of the second day, Danielle was exhausted, but the night without sleep didn't appear to bother Elizabeth. Automatically, Danielle took the fresh cloth Elizabeth handed her. Katie appeared to be resting easier this morning. But she looked so small in the big bed, her skin like fragile parchment. Hot tears welled up in Danielle's eyes and she couldn't stop them from spilling onto her cheeks.

She wasn't aware of Devon entering the room until she felt his hands on her shoulders. Gently he pulled her to her feet.

"It's time you both got some rest."

"I can't," she protested. "Katie needs me."

"Katie is sleeping. Which is what you and Mrs. Meacham should be doing. Brodie will look after Katie while you rest."

"But I can't leave her."

"You're no good to her this way. Here is Brodie now. If anything should change, Brodie need only step across the hall to fetch you."

Danielle wiped the tears from her cheeks. She was so tired it was difficult to keep a coherent thought in her head. But of course, Devon was right. Katie needed someone who had the strength to care for her. Brodie would do an excellent job while she snatched a few hours' sleep.

Seeing that the covers were tucked securely around Katie, Danielle left her in Brodie's care. She leaned heavily on Devon's arm as he helped her to her chamber. Never had a bed looked so inviting.

Clumsily her fingers fumbled with the buttons on her gown, but she couldn't seem to get them to work. It was no wonder, for every bone in her body cried out for sleep.

"Let me help you," Devon offered.

For the life of her, she couldn't dredge up the strength to protest. It was as if once she had made the decision to rest, her body was not going to let her renege. Indeed, it appeared to have gone to sleep before her. Unable to stand on her own, Danielle sagged against her husband's broad chest.

"Although under different circumstances I would be the last to complain, it's rather difficult to help you unbutton your gown with so little room between us."

Danielle smiled wanly. "You'll have to make do."

Devon turned her around. Deftly, he undid the buttons. By the time he had finished, she was asleep in his arms.

He grabbed her as she started to follow her gown to the floor. Carrying her to the bed, he placed her on the sheets. She would be more comfortable in the gown Mary had laid out for her, he told himself as his fingers made short work of the fastenings on her undergarments. He lingered over each tantalizing curve, then pushed the fragile material from her. Lord, but she was beautiful.

Before he realized his intention, he had shed his own clothes and joined her on the bed. Pulling the covers over them, he reached for her. She came willingly as he gathered her in his arms. "This was the way it was meant to be," he sighed.

Danielle awoke to a strange sense of loss. Her hand touched the empty pillow beside her. She marveled at the bizarre things exhaustion could do to a person. It had only been a dream, yet her body still ached with the desires stirred by her visionary lover.

Tossing aside the covers, she stared down at her naked body in horror. Had it not been a dream after all? Had she lain in her husband's arms, welcoming his intimate caresses? Surely not. She would never become so tired she couldn't keep her wits about her.

Hurriedly, she dressed. No one had woken her. Perhaps Katie was better.

Her hopes were quickly dashed when she opened Katie's door. The room was stifling and smelled of garlic and spices she couldn't name. One of the children was feeding wood to a fire that was already blazing. A tent constructed of linen sheets had been placed over Katie's bed. Danielle crept close. Lifting the edge, she walked into a cloud of pungent steam.

"Drop the sheet," Devon instructed.

Danielle let it fall behind her. One look at their faces and she knew that Katie was much worse.

Devon stood over her bed, the sleeves of his shirt rolled up in the heat. He nodded to Mrs. Meacham. "Tell the lad to keep the fire going. We'll have to remove some of the blankets. They weigh too heavily on her chest.''

"What did the physician have to say?" Danielle finally asked.

"The man's a fool," Devon said.

"She's going to die," Mrs. Meacham sobbed.

"Any more talk like that and you'll have to leave," Devon threatened. "I won't have Katie hearing it."

The sheets were lifted and Mrs. Talbut entered with another bucket of steaming water. An odd slick of oil swirled on the water's surface. Mrs. Talbut sat the pail on one of the small tables and took one of the buckets that had cooled.

"We'll need more, Mrs. Talbut. Have one of the footmen bring another small table from the attic."

The ominous rattle of Katie's breathing lent emphasis to Devon's whispered words.

"The water's cooling too quickly," he muttered to himself, then rearranged a few chairs and ordered another sheet. Soon he'd built a smaller tent directly over Katie. It filled quickly with the odorous vapor. It wasn't long before Katie's labored breathing improved.

Devon smiled shyly at Danielle's questioning gaze. "I learned it from a physician on one of the islands. Of course, he placed the patient in a tent outside. It works much more efficiently when the water is set directly on the fire, but I felt having a fire built in the center of her bedchamber might not be the wisest idea."

"That's a point well taken."

It was good to see her smile again. He was beginning to feel as if he was bungling everything. The only thing he had done so far that had had any effect on Nathan appeared to be the changes at the factory, and Danielle had forced him into doing that. Well, from now on he would do everything possible to deepen the wound made in Nathan's calm facade.

Katie stirred on the bed. The sound brought Mrs. Meacham to the bedside.

"Is she going to die?" the woman asked.

"No!" Danielle whispered emphatically. "But she

will need some nourishment. Have cook send up some warm broth and I'll try to get her to drink some.''

Mrs. Meacham hurried to do as she was bidden, leaving Danielle with a few unanswered questions. To be sure, the dresser had formed an attachment to Katie, but her concern seemed to go much deeper than that. Danielle had often wondered what her life had been like before coming to Burnshire, but Elizabeth had always carefully avoided talking about herself. Well, she wouldn't let it worry her in the future. After all the hours she'd spent helping to nurse Katie, Elizabeth had convinced her that she could be trusted completely.

It wasn't long before the dresser returned with the broth. Despite Katie's tossing, they were able to get her to drink a portion of the warm liquid. The rest of the day was dedicated to keeping the buckets of steaming water changed and trying to get Katie to drink the rich broth. By evening Danielle's shoulders ached horribly. She marveled at Elizabeth's resolve. The woman rarely rested, and each time Katie became fretful she was by Danielle's side, helping to keep the warm blankets on the fevered child.

It wasn't until late the fourth evening that the fever finally broke. Katie drank a full bowl of the broth before slipping into a restful sleep. Brodie sent both Danielle and Mrs. Meacham to their beds. She would sleep in the chair should Katie awake during the night.

''Drink this,'' Devon demanded, shoving the brandy at Danielle.

She eyed the amber liquid dubiously.

''It will help you sleep comfortably,'' he assured her as he placed the crystal goblet in her hands.

''My bath will do the same and it's almost ready.''

''Just trust me, love. This will warm you from the inside out.''

She searched his bold blue eyes as she slowly raised the glass to her lips. She was too tired to argue.

''Drink it all.''

Danielle took a healthy swallow. The liquid burned all the way down, leaving her gasping for breath.

"Another," he said, refilling her glass.

She shoved it at him. "No more," she choked. "My insides are quite warm enough now, thank you."

Patiently, Devon cupped his fingers over hers and gently guided the glass to her lips. "Finish the brandy, Danielle. It will help you sleep."

How could she argue with him? Already she could feel a warm fire flowing through her tired body. Standing straight, she prepared herself for the burning liquid as she took another swallow. The drink seemed to have mellowed since her first glass, and Danielle welcomed the numbing warmth that glided down her throat.

Devon put his arms about her. He wanted nothing more than to stay and hold her like this until the stress of the past few days melted from her body, but unfortunately, what she needed was sleep, not him. Reluctantly, he released her. "Mary is waiting to help you with your bath. I'll be back when you're finished," he said.

Danielle slipped into the warm tub. Whether it was the brandy or the hot water, she didn't know. All that mattered was the easing of her aching body. Her thoughts kept returning to the dreams she had of lying next to Devon, her body every bit as nude as his. The picture of them together brought those stirrings of desire that seemed to occupy too many of her waking hours of late. But instead of pushing them aside, she let them linger at the edges of her mind, savoring each warm tingle.

Devon had been so understanding about Katie's illness, even going so far as to put himself out for her welfare. Neither his nightly visits to the sickroom nor his thoughtfulness in making sure that they had everything they needed had gone unnoticed.

After her bath she offered no protest to the thin negligee Mary laid out for her. She stood by the fire as Mary picked up the clothes from the bathing chamber. Skeptically, she eyed the brandy decanter Devon had left on the table, recalling the languid warmth the liquid sent through her. How odd that she had never heard of the therapeutic qualities of brandy before. Well, no matter. She knew of it now. After the horrible experiences of the past few days, it was the very thing she needed. A blissful void of cares. She poured her glass full to the rim.

By the time Mary returned to brush out Danielle's damp hair, she was well into her second glass. As her curls were drying, Danielle let her imagination dwell on each touch, each look, that Devon had given her. It was so delicious to fantasize about a marriage in which he loved her as much as she was beginning to love him. She became so caught up in her thoughts that she didn't notice when Mary left the room and Devon entered.

One look at his wife and he knew he shouldn't have left the decanter. Reaching across her, he took the glass from her hand. "Much more of this, love, and you'll be sporting a royal hangover in the morning." He smiled at the unsteadiness of her gaze. "What did I marry," he teased, "a lush?"

Danielle returned his smile with a lazy one of her own. She had done nothing but dwell on his kisses for the last hour, and here he was, fresh from his bath, looking ever so handsome. She took him in from the top of his damp curls, lingering a moment at the tantalizing glimpse of a furred chest through the open throat of his burgundy robe, to the . . .

My, but didn't the robe fit admirably across his broad shoulders, tapering so cleverly to his slim waist and hips. Her hungry eyes rose to study the bronzed features of his face. The rugged planes never failed to bring that catch in her throat.

She grasped the arm of her chair and stood. Carefully, she walked to him. "What you married, my dear husband, is a wanton woman." She said the words slowly, precisely.

His dark brows shot up. "Wanton?" It was on the tip of his tongue to ask her if she even knew what the word meant, but the predatory gleam that leapt to her green eyes stopped him. "You need to be in bed."

Before he knew what was happening, she was in his arms, with her silk-clad body moving against him.

"I'll help you," he murmured, his voice thick with desire.

Danielle leaned invitingly against him. Slowly, she moved her body up his until she was standing on her toes. Devon held his breath as she placed a moist kiss on his throat. If he didn't stop her soon, he would never be able to summon the strength to do so. Not with the passion she was stirring in him now.

Her kisses became bolder and he tightened his arms about her. She lifted her eyes to his. His breath caught in his throat at what he saw. Her eyes were like the green pools of a hidden cove. The waters were deceivingly calm, but to dip into them would be to discover that they were teeming with life.

He knew that to give in to this aching need for her now would mean the end to all his plans—his ships, his freedom. He could not merely sample her delights as he had with so many other women and then leave. To have touched heaven and turned your back on it was to live in hell.

Her eyes held him captive as she lowered herself against his body once more. The moan she drew from within him surprised even him. Stepping back, he tugged at the belt that held the front of his robe closed. The sides fell apart and he pulled her back to him. The silken feel of her nightdress tore at the last of his reserve. Game or not, he had to have her.

Hungrily, his lips sought hers, feasting on the sweet nectar of her kisses. She tasted of lavender soap . . . of brandy . . . of stormy seas . . . of all the temptations down through the ages.

Her arms went about his neck and she pulled him down to her. "Love me," she whispered against his neck.

He scooped her up in his arms and carried her to the bed, then stood her beside it. He towered over her, his face a bronzed mask of passion. The fires in his smoldering blue eyes held hers while his fingers pushed her gown from her shoulders. A whisper of silk fell to the floor. Danielle swallowed hard. She was drowning in a whirlpool of desire and she was pulling him in with her.

The brandy had made her bold. She lifted her trembling hands and laid them against his chest. Taking her example from him, she pushed his robe from his shoulders.

She flinched at the raw desire she saw in his face. But there was no turning back as his robe joined her gown on the floor. Reaching up, she placed a kiss on the corner of his lips, her naked breasts brushing against him.

He pulled her into his arms. Burying his face in her hair, he whispered huskily, ''Danielle, God help you if this is only a game.''

In one swift movement he had laid her on the bed. Danielle felt a moment of apprehension as he stood over her, his eyes burning a bright blue. Slowly, painfully, they raked her body. His warning about never having been mauled by a pirate flickered across her mind, but then was gone when the rugged planes of his face softened with poignant desire.

Devon knew with a certainty that once he touched her silken body, it would only be a matter of time before he would have to return again and again to dip into the waters of her intoxicating beauty. But he refused to merely take her to satisfy his needs.

Face up to it, he told himself. To make love to her would mean closing the door on a life he had grown to love. Sea captains did not make good husbands, and he would want nothing less for the beautiful creature who lay on the bed before him.

He looked down at her. Her green eyes were heavy with passion, her lips blushed from his kiss. Never had he wanted a woman so terribly much.

''Hell and damnation!'' he swore and joined her on the bed.

Danielle trembled as he came to her. He took her in his arms and the rest of the world was lost to her as his lips captured hers. The kiss was passionate, demanding, yet she wanted more. Wantonly, she moved against him. He parted her lips, plunging his tongue into the depths of her mouth. His finger dug into her back and she arched into him. An agonizing moan poured from him, and her body answered with an aching need of its own. He moved down her, laying a languorous trail of kisses where his eyes had raked her before. She burned with sweet agony.

His fingers moved down the length of her, sending warm rivers of desire from her head to her toes. Like a cat rolling in catnip, she writhed against him. His mouth covered hers and she hungrily drank of his kiss.

Her whole body filled with the essence of their lovemaking, aching for release from this bittersweet ecstasy, yet another part of her wanted it to go on forever.

"Take me," she whispered against his lips.

Her plea was like an echo from his own heart. Never had he known anyone like her. She was fire and passion, begging him to put an end to something she didn't understand.

It was up to him to temper her needs, but she wasn't making it any easier for him. All he wanted to do was bury himself deep within her. Didn't she realize how difficult it was for him to remember that she was a virgin trapped in the body of a seductress?

"Easy, love," he murmured against her breast. "I don't want to hurt you."

Gently, he eased her onto her back. Then he used his knee to slowly spread her thighs apart.

Danielle couldn't control the trembling that shook her body as he settled between her legs. "Oh, Devon," she cried. "Please stop this ache inside me."

Lord help him, he couldn't deny her. He lowered his head to cover her body in the wild kisses of his own need.

Danielle groaned in sweet agony as his lips laid a path of fire down one side of her and up the next. With each touch, each burning kiss, the ache curled inside her. When she thought she could stand no more, his lips found hers.

No more the gentle lover, his hands boldly explored

her body as his tongue ravished her mouth. She gasped when he touched her in places which up until now had remained solely hers. With each secret piece of her body she relinquished to his skillful fingers, the ache grew until it was tearing her very soul apart, demanding release, and she found herself plundering his mouth in return. With each bold stroke of her tongue, his fingers teased her unmercifully.

Suddenly, the teasing stopped and he pulled away. She started to protest, but his burning blue eyes told her he was not through with her yet.

"Wrap your legs around me," he said, his voice husky.

She did as he asked, instinctively knowing that everything her body cried for was within him to give. She trembled again as the evidence of his own need thrust against her.

"Don't be afraid, love," he whispered. "It will only hurt for a moment."

He kissed her then, swallowing her cry of pain as he buried himself in her. He tried to be gentle, but they were like two storms meeting head on.

Over and over, their bodies clashed on a sea of passion. She was lightning, he the thunder. Waves lifted them up and crashed them on the shore, only to collect them again and sweep them away. They rode the wind-tossed sea, explored its mysterious depths, and followed the call of a sea gull as it soared across the sky. They were dreams and reality, hopes and promises—love wrapped in a crested wave.

Then the sun suddenly broke through the clouds and the lovers lay in each other's arms, content in the knowledge that though the storm had passed, love was but a touch away.

Chapter 16

The hour was late when Danielle woke and rolled over in the big bed. Devon was gone. She vaguely recalled him leaving at first light, when she had been too pleasantly exhausted to reach out and stop him. Her lips curved in a broad smile. Despite all she had heard to the contrary, the foul duties of a wife were most enjoyable—and definitely worth future exploration.

She climbed out of bed and rang for her maid. First she'd check on Katie, then her husband. Her husband—strange how she now thought of him in that way. But last night had changed everything for her—and hopefully for him too. After all they had shared, surely he could not longer be entertaining the idea of leaving. He belonged to her now, and she would do everything possible to see that he didn't regret his decision.

By the time Mary arrived, Danielle had been through her wardrobe several times, trying to decide which gown she would wear. Something special, she told herself. Something to rekindle the fires of passion in her husband's blue eyes. She finally settled on a white muslin day dress trimmed with deep green velvet ribbons and tiny embroidered flowers.

Danielle was anxious to complete her toilette. Unfortunately, the staff did not share her desire, for everyone appeared to be moving extremely slow this morning. Recalling the diligent service everyone had given when caring for Katie, she refrained from saying anything.

Ready at last, Danielle took a final turn before the mirror. Mary had woven a green velvet ribbon through her curls and Danielle was pleased with the effect. Hurrying from her chamber, she made her way down the hall to Katie's room. The tents had been taken down and the extra tables removed. Brodie sat reading a book to Katie. It was a joy to see the child sitting up in bed.

Brodie marked her place, then laid the book on the coverlet. "Our little girl looks much better this morning, doesn't she?"

Danielle smiled and sat down on the bed beside Katie. "She certainly does." She placed her hand on Katie's cool cheek. "And how do you feel, young lady?"

"Ever so much better, Miss Danny," she said brightly. "After lunch, Mrs. Meacham has promised Jeremy and me a puppet show."

Danielle looked at Brodie. "Whatever's become of our little hypochondriac?"

A smile tugged at the corner of Brodie's lips. "Recovered nicely, didn't she? The physician was certainly surprised at her progress when he called this morning."

"As well he should be. Did you tell him it was due to Devon's skills and not his that she recovered?"

"Oh my, yes. And he was most disappointed that his Grace had left and he could not speak with him on the methods he had used."

Danielle reached over and picked up the book Brodie had been reading. "Devon is gone?" she asked casually, trying to keep her disappointment from showing.

"I thought you knew. His Grace left for Portsmouth early this morning."

It took all Danielle's efforts to keep a smile pinned on her face. "He must have said something and I merely forgot," she said brightly, despite the heavy stone that seemed to have lodged in her heart.

"He left you a note," Brodie offered. "He was afraid he'd wake you, so he left it on the table there."

Danielle glanced at the sealed note but couldn't bring herself to open it in front of Brodie. She opened the book instead. "I'll read it later," she said, picking up the story from the place Brodie had marked.

Danielle read until Katie's lunch arrived; then she picked up Devon's note and carried it to her room. With trembling fingers she broke the seal. The bold handwriting seemed to leap from the page. She was almost afraid to read the words. She had known when she asked him to love her that she was taking a risk. And now he had gone to Portsmouth. Was it to be over so soon? She forced herself to read.

Something urgent has come up that requires my immediate attention. Trust me when I say nothing less could have taken me from your side after last night.
                                                Yours always,
                                                Devon

By the way, I've asked Andrews to hide the brandy until I return. It wouldn't do to have you tumbling into someone else's bed while I'm away.

The words, written to tease a smile from her lips, brought forth a bittersweet one. She couldn't help but wonder if he had given her the brandy knowing the effect it would have on her, but she refused to dwell on it. Devon had not returned to his ships. And although she was happy that his absence was only temporary, she knew in her heart the scare she had been given this morning was only a small sample of the pain she would suffer if he decided his ships meant more to him than she did.

As she went about her morning duties, the image of him bending over her, his eyes filled with passion, stayed with her and she found herself smiling at the tiniest thing. She refused to think about what his trip to Portsmouth might mean. Perhaps, given enough time in her bed, he would not even want to leave. Her heart sang with happiness at the possibility and she decided then and there that she would do everything in her power to make him want to stay.

"Treason!" Devon bellowed the word. His mount sidestepped at the thundering expletives that followed. "The fools. My men are all loyal Englishmen. They would never sink one of his Majesty's vessels."

"My duty is to escort you to see the Lord Chancellor," Captain Winslow said with reluctance.

"Dammit, Edward, you know I'm not guilty of this. What's it all about?"

"At the moment, it appears to be only rumors, but knowing of your situation with Nathan, we thought we should warn you."

"We?"

"The Lord Chancellor and I."

"Why would the Lord Chancellor concern himself with proving my innocence?"

"Seems a dear friend's son took it into his head to run away to sea. You signed him aboard your ship. The boy writes home often to his mother, praising you."

"And the boy?"

"He's aboard the *Liberty*. It's the ship rumored to have sunk *The Queen*."

"So the Lord Chancellor has a personal interest in seeing my shipmates exonerated."

"Yes, but I wouldn't count too heavily on that were I you. His position obligates him to relay the rumors to the Prince Regent. I know you've secured a few rare treasures for Prinny in the past, but other than that, how good are your relations with him?"

"We might have a problem there," Devon said, leading his mount around a dead limb the spring winds had torn from a nearby tree. "Although the Prince Regent appreciates the unusual things I bring him, I truly think he honestly believes I acquired them by some nefarious means."

"Nefarious? You?"

"Everyone knows of Prinny's passion for oils. Last trip out, I acquired one reported to have been taken from Napoleon's palace in Versailles. There was quite a bloody story behind it. I thought only to amuse him with the acquisition, but he assumed that I'd done some throat-slitting to get it."

"That's splendid!" Edward shouted. "If he believes that, surely it stands to reason that he also believes you to have no loyalties to Napoleon."

"That would be the case had I not been able to convince him otherwise. Unfortunately, when he finally accepted the truth, his imaginative mind leapt to the suspicion that if I was not somehow connected with the theft itself, I must surely have been dealing with the coastal smugglers who are making his life so miserable."

"My Lord Chancellor will not find that very encouraging news."

"Neither did I."

The rest of the ride was conducted in silence as Devon mulled over what Edward had told him. The false charges had every earmark of being Nathan's handiwork. There had been too many similar incidents in the past to discount his suspicions. The older Nathan had grown, the more elaborate—and dangerous—the schemes had become, and the higher the stakes. But this time the stakes were too high. This time, if Nathan succeeded, Devon would hang. It was no wonder Nathan had not seemed overly concerned with the changes at the factory. With no heir to take over Burnshire, Nathan would get everything, without even dirtying his hands.

The plan was brilliant. Nathan was hitting him with the one thing it would be the hardest to disprove. Human nature being what it was, it was much easier for people to believe Devon had acquired his wealth through acts of treason than by the hard work it had actually taken.

The logical solution was an heir, but was he ready

to take on the commitment that came with it? After last night, he no longer worried about Danielle's cooperation. The love he had seen shining from her eyes was all the encouragement he needed.

Then why did the thought nag at his conscience so? It wasn't as if Danielle didn't love children. She absolutely doted on them. But the fact that she was beginning to look at him in the same way was the problem. Besides, he argued with himself, there were no guarantees that if he did manage to give her a child, it would be a boy. Was he willing to stay until their lovemaking produced an heir? And was he then to become the type of husband who filled his wife's belly each time his ship was in port, then coldly sailed away?

She wanted him. He wanted her. But what did she expect would become of their lovemaking? He would tell her he wanted a child, then let her decide.

"I'll take what you've said into consideration," Devon told the Lord Chancellor as he made his farewells.

"It's a grave situation, your Grace. But if what you say is true, the ship's log should go a long way in clearing up the rumors. If the ship was not in the area where the vessel went down, then the crew could not have committed the crime."

"I appreciate your understanding," Devon said. "And now I must be off. I must get word to my ship. They'll be needing to find a safe harbor when they dock, or the ship's log will never make it to London."

"Godspeed, your Grace."

Devon nodded solemnly, then turned and left.

On reaching the outskirts of London, he urged his mount to a gallop. The meeting with the Lord Chancellor had not resolved the problem as he had hoped. The situation was much worse than he had anticipated. The rumors—while unfounded—were spreading rapidly, and Devon feared for the safety of his crew should they try to put ashore before the matter was cleared up. His wouldn't be the first ship to have its crew murdered because of an unfounded rumor. Tempers ran high when it came to treason.

As it stood now, there weren't many men in England whose loyalty he could claim. He had been at sea too many years. He'd learned that even his neighbor, Lord Carruthers, was pressing the House of Lords to request an accounting of Devon's activities.

Devon's eyes narrowed. Lord Carruthers' name had a way of coming up a lot lately. Danielle's note. And that night in the stables. Danielle had been angered and had mentioned a Tom as her champion. Devon's first thought at the time had been Lord Thomas Carruthers, but he had quickly dismissed it. Yet Danielle had sent a note to him. What could their relationship be? It occurred to him that Carruthers was involved in Nathan's scheme. But treason. It was not to be taken lightly. Men were hung for treason.

Devon spurred his mount on. It was a long road to Portsmouth and he refused to spend the entire ride questioning the loyalties of his wife and Lord Carruthers.

Suddenly, though, a cold chill crept up Devon's spine. If Nathan was capable of pulling off such a diabolical hoax, what was to keep him from stopping with only Devon's life? What of his mother—or Danielle?

Arriving at Portsmouth, Devon soon located a man he felt he could trust to deliver the message to his crew. Then, dressed as a seaman, he walked the docks trying to determine the source of the rumors. One thing was clear. Nathan had done a good job of getting them started. Those who knew Devon's reputation as a sea captain merely laughed at the rumors. It was the scum of the sea that took them seriously—the drunkards, loafers, malcontents, all those accustomed to laying their own troubles at another's door. No amount of reasoning would deter them when they'd already decided what they wanted to believe.

* * *

Devon handed the reins of his mount to one of the footmen and wearily climbed the front steps. After four long days he was happy to be home again. He had missed Danielle even more then he'd thought possible.

She was coming down the stairs when he walked through the door, her face flushed as if she had been watching for his arrival from one of the windows. The skirt of her day dress swirled gracefully about her as she descended the stairs, a vision of lavender and lace. Her hair pinned high on her head fell in soft curls down one side. The love in her wide, innocent eyes tugged at his conscience.

He hadn't meant for this to happen, yet he couldn't seem to muster the strength to speak the words that would dim that light. Instead, he basked in the warm glow. He had wanted her body and he had gotten so much more. Perhaps when this was all over, he could stay a bit longer. The decision lifted the heavy weight from his chest. Perhaps he would even take her with him on one of the voyages. She stepped up to him and all thoughts of leaving vanished.

Dared he hope she had missed him? "How have things been with me gone?"

She tilted her chin up and grinned. "Wonderful," she lied. "I hardly knew you weren't here. The household has never run so smoothly. Why, even the children have been perfect angels."

He planted a kiss on the tip of her nose. "Then you might want to send Bob with a large bucket of water to the east wing of the house. Two of your perfect angels are trying to set it afire."

"Holy Hannah!" she exclaimed, lifting her skirts and darting around him for the front door.

He grabbed her arm and swung her back to him. "The house can wait, but I can't." He lowered his head to hers, but she pulled away.

"Are you daft? We can't just stand here and let them burn the house down around our ears."

"The last time I checked, stone didn't burn all that well. Besides which, Jem took immediate exception to the prank and sent a footman to dispense punishment."

Taking her by the arm, he led her to the drawing room. Once the door was closed behind them, he didn't allow her protests to stop him as he covered her mouth with his. He'd been dreaming of this since he left London. The lavender fragrance of her bath filled his head, sending an aching need scorching through him. She felt so right in his arms.

Danielle wasn't blind to the need growing in him. She longed to show him that her own need was every bit as great as his, entwining its tentacles of desire deep within her. But the front drawing room was no place to display her appetite. Reluctantly, she withdrew from his arms.

"I trust you were able to complete your business successfully?"

Devon cocked a dark brow. "Were you worried that I would not return?"

"Why, of all the self-centered, egotistical . . ." she blustered. "Had I my way in the matter, I would have instructed your ship's captain to weigh anchor the moment you stepped aboard."

"And who would warm your bed at night?" he asked, pulling her back in his arms.

She leaned back so she could quell the laughter in his bold blue eyes. "A warm brick should suffice," she said solemnly.

The laughter he'd suppressed burst forth from him. "The next time you drag me to your bed, I'll remind you of that."

Danielle stamped her foot in frustration. "I knew, given the chance, you would attempt to lay that at my door."

"A man can withstand only so much temptation before he takes what is offered. And so willingly, I might add."

The teasing smile was too much. "You are certainly no gentleman."

He was not put off by her anger, but placed a kiss

along the side of her neck. ''That seems only fitting, since the woman I made love to cast aside her mantle of lady for the evening.'' He nibbled at the lobe of her ear. ''And I must say, it made for a most enjoyable time.''

Danielle refused to give in to the passions that warmed her. ''You ply me with brandy, then you take advantage of me,'' she accused, her pride fanning the flames of her irrational anger. ''Is that the way it is to be?''

''It can be even better,'' he murmured huskily in her ear. His hands skimmed down her slender back until they rested on the rounded curve of her buttocks; then he crushed her to him. Her green eyes widened in surprise when he moved her hips against his parted legs. He smothered her protest in his kiss. ''I want a child,'' he whispered against her parted lips.

She pulled away from him. Had she heard correctly? He wanted her to have his child. She searched his face. It was all there. He desired her, of that she was sure. But love? Did he even know what that meant? One part of her wanted to accept being in his arms, for whatever the reason; but the sane part, if there were indeed such a part left of her, warned that this was only a fleeting moment of passion she would live to regret.

''You want another child when this household is already overrun with them?''

''But this one would be ours. Yours and mine.'' He searched her face carefully. Their entire future lay with her answer. Happiness lit her face as she smiled up at him.

''I think I would like that.''

Devon wrapped her in his arms. ''I can't tell you how much your answer pleases me.'' His arms tightened about her. Even though she had agreed, he was left with the disheartening feeling that he had just betrayed her. She would have never consented had he stated his true reason for wanting the child, but he had to stop Nathan at all costs.

Devon grimaced. It sounded so harsh when put in that light. The fact that it was exactly what he had hoped to do did not make him feel any better about suggesting it. Perhaps he should reconsider.

He glanced down at Danielle. Her trusting smile tore at his heart. Lord help him, but if she kept looking at him that way, the question of a child would be answered immediately. Taking her hand, he led her up the stairs.

As the weeks passed, Danielle could not shake the feeling that something was troubling Devon. She tried to discuss it with him, but he always put her off with the excuse that he had a lot on his mind. Each day dawned with him in his study, working feverishly. A constant flow of messengers passed through the doors of Burnshire.

Her heart twisted in pain every time she neared his study. He was planning to return to his ships. She was sure of it. What other explanation could there be? After all, hadn't she heard him sending the stable lads to the docks to await their arrival?

A suspicion began to grow in her fertile imagination. Had Devon wanted the child for the sole purpose of thwarting Nathan? Each night as she waited for him to come to her bed, the suspicion grew and festered. If only he would say he was staying, she could lay her fears to rest. Each time he came to her, the question trembled on the tip of her tongue, but she couldn't bring herself to ask. Then Devon would take her in his arms and all would be forgotten—until the morning.

It was a bittersweet dilemma. Her body ached for his touch, but her mind branded her a fool. In all the nights she had lain in his arms, not once had he told her he loved her.

She didn't care as long as he came to her, she told herself. If he was determined to leave her, there was nothing she could do to stop him. Instead, she threw herself into the management of Burnshire. The details of the house party Devon had planned needed attending to, and she busied herself with the preparations.

The larger her doubts, the harder she worked. With the party less than four weeks away, it wasn't difficult for Danielle to find other things to keep her mind occupied.

She went over the guest list again and again. It was Devon's belief that the festivities would serve to discomfort Nathan, and she intended to do her best to plan the function to that end. Rooms were opened and cleaned. Silver was polished. Huge orders were turned in to the grocers for the special items they would need. Now with the guest list finished, Danielle was forced to intrude on Devon in his study.

She tapped lightly on the door before entering. Devon sat at his desk, buried behind a stack of papers, a glass of brandy in his hands. She was surprised to see Bob at the side table, pouring another glass from the crystal decanter. He appeared discomfited, but quickly resumed the stoic facade of a footman. Returning the decanter to the table, he placed the second glass in front of Devon on the desk, then left the room.

The change in Devon took her aback. Why hadn't she noticed before? With the flurry of activity centered around his study during the past week, she had expected him to be tired, but the dark circles under his eyes worried her. He did not look like a man who was happy with the decisions he had made. Was it possible he really wanted to stay but his pride would not allow it? As soon as the thought formed, she put it aside.

No, something else was worrying him. It was on the tip of her tongue to ask what, but she didn't. Her impulsive nature had always been a curse, and her restraint now surprised even her. Brodie would be pleased. Perhaps there was hope for her after all.

He smiled at her and suddenly she felt shy. "I—I have the guest list ready f-for your approval," she stammered. She quickly laid the list of names before him, but he didn't take his gaze off her.

He didn't say anything. His hooded eyes seemed to

burn into her very soul. The rich blue fire in them
melted her insides and left her trembling. How could
he look at her that way and still consider leaving?

"If you would just look it over and see if I've
missed . . ."

He pushed his chair back and stood up, his eyes
never leaving hers. Danielle's heart jumped to her
throat. He came around the desk and stood over her,
his nearness taking her breath away. For the briefest
of moments, time seemed to stand still. Then, with
butterfly softness, he ran the backs of his fingers along
the side of her cheek.

The pounding of her heart rang in her ears as his
hands slipped behind her, pulling her against his hard-
muscled frame. She waited for his lips to touch hers as
he wrapped his arms tightly about her, but he just held
her close. She knew she should ask him what his plans
were, but at the moment, nothing was as important as
being in his arms. She rested her head on his chest.
She breathed deeply, committing to memory the feel
of his strong embrace, the smell of his magnificent
body.

Danielle sat at her writing table and stared out over
the sweeping lawns. Twirling the dyed quill, she let
her thoughts drift back to the study. What would have
happened had Bob not returned?

Angrily, she tossed the quill on the desk. A pox on
servants! A pox on the account books! A pox on all
estate business!

Danielle's heart fell to her toes. Devon was surely
preparing to return to his ships. Why else would he be
working day and night to put things in order?

"Are you ready to start on the invitations?" Brodie
called from the door.

The invitations. Danielle had forgotten her anger
over the guest list. Her brows dipped in a frown.

"Pox on the invitations!" she suddenly shouted as
she jumped to her feet. Irritably, she paced the floor.
"Why should I invite a herd of strangers to my home?"

"I would think the reasons would be obvious, Danielle. Not only does your husband want to introduce you to his friends, he wants to parade everything Nathan has lost before him. With all the changes his Grace has already made to frustrate the vicar, this party should be most interesting."

"Oh, it will be interesting. There's no doubt about that," she said, waving the guest list as she continued to pace the length of the room. "Do you know whose name has been added?"

Brodie stepped in front of her and took the list from her fingers. Her eyes quickly dropped to the bottom of the page, where Devon's bold hand had added several names.

"Oh, my, " Brodie exclaimed. "He's invited Lord Carruthers. But he is a neighbor, after all. Devon was more than likely confused by the omission."

"Not that name," Danielle said, stabbing at the next on the list. "He's invited Lady Emily."

Brodie feigned ignorance. "I see nothing wrong with inviting an old friend of the family."

"Friend! She was more than just a friend. She was to be Devon's wife."

"But she's not. You are."

"Only because of a twist of fate. Had not our coach overturned moments before he came along, he would now be married to her."

"Hah!" Brodie snorted. "Let's be fair. Had you not opened your mouth and told the vicar you were to be the next Duchess of Burnshire, Lord Stanton would now be married to Lady Emily."

"A mere technicality," Danielle said.

Brodie shook her head in wonder. "You blithely dismiss the fact that your stubborn, impulsive ways got you into this marriage."

"I see no reason to dwell on that point. It no longer matters why he forced me to wed him. What matters is that he may be regretting his choice."

"And can you blame him? He can hardly be expected to be pleased with the wife he has—or doesn't have, would be more to the point. If he were to take up with Lady Emily again, you would have no one to blame but yourself."

"I've kept my part of the bargain."

"And what exactly was your part of the bargain? Was it the carriage load of children you provided as your dowry? You recall the ones, I'm sure. The thirteen extra mouths to feed. Thirteen extra—"

"You've more than made your point, Brodie. But with the children, I had no other choice. They had to come with us. And you must admit he can find no fault with our agreement. I've played my part well."

"Perhaps therein lies the problem."

"I don't understand."

"Being a wife is not playing a part. And a marriage should not be a charade enacted for the benefit of others."

"The idea of this marriage was not mine."

"The idea may not have been yours, but that does not mean you cannot accept it now."

Danielle wished it were that easy. Devon did not want a true marriage. Oh, he was willing to come to her bed, but was she prepared to settle for a marriage without commitment? Why was she even asking herself that? She had already made her decision. To even contemplate life without him was more than she could deal with at the moment. If only . . .

There were no *if only's* to it. She would have to accept Devon on his own terms. If his ships were that important to him, she would settle for what he was willing to give. No commitments. No begging him to stay. She would do all she could to make his home a place he would want to come to when he felt the need for her.

"Give me one of the invitations. I'll write Lady Emily's personally."

By the time Danielle had sealed the last invitation, it was time to dress for supper. The day had grown unusually warm for May, and she was happy for the new summer gowns that Mrs. Meacham had ordered from

London. The one she had laid out for the evening was especially becoming with its border of embroidered forget-me-nots. She hoped Devon would be pleased with the choice also.

Taking one last look in the mirrored glass over her dressing table, Danielle went in search of Giles. After she had entrusted him with the task of posting the invitations, supper was announced.

She was surprised to learn that it was being served in the intimacy of the small breakfast room. The doors to the garden were open, and the smell of the spring blooms filled the room.

"You look lovely this evening," Devon said as he led her to the chair next to his.

Danielle eyed him suspiciously. For the past few weeks he had spent almost every waking hour in his study, and now here he was dressed to start her heart to racing. "Have you finished with your business?" she asked.

Well, at least he had the sense to look guilty, she thought as he lowered his eyes.

"I've been meaning to apologize for that," he said. With a quick snap of his wrist he unfolded his napkin and placed it across his lap. "Now that I've finished, I hoped to explain what it is that has occupied so much of my time."

Danielle took a sip of her wine and waited for him to continue.

"After what happened to Katie and Jeremy, I realized that it would be impossible to see to the children's safety without a constant watch on them. Even you must agree that would be a task too large for any household." Her nod was slow in coming, and he knew she was weighing each word carefully. "I think it's time we tried to find positions for them."

She started to protest but Devon held up his hand. "Hear me out first. I know what happened with Katie was my fault. I foolishly believed Nathan would fear me too much to risk my anger concerning the children when there were so many larger issues at stake. I was wrong. I've turned it over and over in my mind and I see no other way. If I can find positions for them, they will be safer away from Burnshire."

"What of Katie? Her father cheated her out of her birthright. I will not compound that by turning her into a maid."

"I am not including Katie in this. Her situation is unique, and it would be ludicrous to try to place her."

"Katie will be raised as if she were my own."

"I have no objections to that."

He was being too cooperative. Why? Was he that anxious to be rid of the children?

"And Jeremy?" she asked.

"He is too young to place. Tom will be staying also. My groom has need of him in the stables."

She ran her finger around the rim of her wineglass. "Will you give me time to think about it?"

"There is no hurry. It will take a while to place them all." He raised a brow and looked at her. "This won't take as long as it took for you to decide to be my wife, will it?"

She tilted her head and smiled at him. "Will you be resorting to blackmail again if it does?" she asked.

"I was thinking more in the line of a decanter of fine French brandy."

Danielle's throaty laughter filled the room.

Chapter 17

The emerald-green silk ribbons hung in graceful swirls from the snug bust of Danielle's new gown as she turned in front of the cheval glass. "Do I look the part of the Duchess of Burnshire?" she asked the dark figure behind her.

Devon stepped back and studied her, and she immediately regretted the seductive perusal she had unwittingly invited. He looked entirely too handsome in his waistcoat of forest green, and she tried not to look at the snug fit of his buff-colored breeches. But it wasn't any safer to direct her gaze to the fullness of his lips, nor to the unruliness of the dark curl that had fallen across his forehead. Eyes the color of the blue haze of a foggy dawn touched hers, and the strange effect it had on her breathing was unsettling to say the least.

She quickly turned from him. Picking up her wide-brimmed straw bonnet, she made a great show of arranging it just so on the auburn curls. Her eyes strayed involuntarily to her reflection in the mirror. Her cheeks were pale, and when she looked closely she could detect the dark circles under her eyes. Well, no wonder. What with the strain of all the preparations for the party, she hadn't been getting enough sleep. And the nagging stomach upset she'd suffered again this morning was enough to get anyone down. Well, it would be over soon, and she would be able to sleep the day away if she liked.

Devon stepped up behind her. "There seems to be

something missing," he said. "Your eyes lack a certain sparkle."

"If my eyes lack anything, it is sleep."

Reaching around her, he placed a jeweler's box in her hands. "Will this atone for my insensitivity?" he asked.

She opened the box cautiously. "Devon, it's lovely!" she gasped at the sight of the delicate strand of emeralds that spilled across the black velvet.

He reached over her shoulder and plucked the necklace from the box.

"Not nearly as lovely as you," he said, draping it around her throat. After fastening the clasp, he turned her to him. "With your eyes, you should always wear green," he said as he placed a lingering kiss on her throat.

Danielle could not calm the frantic beating of her heart. "The emeralds I will wear," she said, attempting to keep the moment light as she stepped away from him. "But since our guests are scheduled to arrive at any moment, it would be better if I weren't wearing your kisses as well."

With one long finger he moved aside the lace ruffle that trimmed the bodice of her gown and traced the plunging neckline. "You shouldn't scold me so. I was merely practicing the part of an attentive husband. And I'm sure you'll agree I need the practice."

A telling blush swept over Danielle's body and she swatted at his errant hand. "To my mind, the part you're rehearsing is that of the lecher."

"For that I'd need no practice," he teased.

The tantalizing smells of warm breads, roast pork, and spice cakes wafted across the lawns from the multi-striped tents that dotted the gardens. Very few of the invitations had been refused, and the drive was clogged with carriages of every size and description. Devon and Danielle stood at the front steps to welcome their guests. Everyone was anxious to meet the new duchess, and the line seemed to stretch forever.

By the time she had greeted the last guest, Danielle was ready to drop. Devon tucked her hand in the crook of his arm and led her out across the grass.

Games had been set up on the lawns, and the tenants and local gentry alike shared in the festivities. Danielle and Devon were stopped several times on their way to the refreshment tables. It wasn't until they were almost there that Danielle noticed the children. Dressed in the Stanton livery, each carried a tray with glasses of lemonade and ale. She took one of the glasses of iced lemonade Jeremy held out for her.

"Thank you," she said, but the smile on her face froze as Nathan stepped up to her.

"What a cunning woman you are, Danielle."

There was no mistaking the threat in his voice. She turned to reach for Devon's arm, only to find that a tenant had him deep in conversation. There was no escaping now. "Good afternoon, Nathan. I'm so pleased to see that you could come." She purposely honeyed her words.

Nathan's eyes were pale chips of granite. He lowered his voice to a rough whisper. "How dare you parade these orphans in Stanton livery? And under my very nose!"

"It was a surprise to me also, but so clever of Devon. Don't you agree?"

"Don't think you have won, dear lady. Burnshire is mine."

"Burnshire belongs to Devon," she said firmly.

"A temporary condition only," he sneered in her face. "Fate denied me my inheritance with the birth of Devon's father and once again when Devon married you. But you mark my words. Fate will not intervene a third time."

Danielle trembled with the chill of his words long after he had left her side. The man was obsessed with his need to own Burnshire. Seeing the tenants pay their respects to Devon must be eating Nathan's insides. Did Devon even realize the effect this party was having on his cousin?

"What do you think of the children?" Devon asked as he rejoined her.

Danielle jumped. Frantic, she threw herself into his arms. "Oh, Devon, Nathan was furious when he saw them. It is not safe. You must order them back into the house."

He steered her into one of the arbors bordering the lawns. "Then my plan was successful," he said.

Danielle pulled away. "You knew Nathan would be upset?"

"I had hoped."

"You purposely risked the children's welfare to infuriate Nathan? Do you think that was wise?"

"Look around you, Danielle. Each child has been paired off with one of the servants. They've been instructed to stay with the children at all times."

"But why would you do such a thing?"

"It's really quite simple. Homes have been found for most of them. By Friday next, they will be scattered all across England. Nathan will never find them."

"But that is too soon. I cannot ship them off like so much baggage."

"Look at their faces, Danielle. Do they look unhappy? They've known for weeks. They want you to be proud of them. This was to be their surprise."

She had to admit they didn't appear sad. "I know we discussed this, but I didn't think it would happen so soon. How did you manage?"

"Lady Bradford and Mother took care of the details. They've been writing letters from Scotland for weeks. Most of the children will be going to the homes of their old friends."

Devon took her in his arms. "Trust me, love. It will be better this way. It was becoming too difficult to watch over them. This way, they will be out of Nathan's reach."

"I don't know, Devon. It's all so sudden. I can't help but worry."

He pinched her cheek. "Mother even agreed to take

two of the girls," he said, trying to coax a smile to her lips.

"You swear, they're all going to good homes?"

Devon placed a kiss on her forehead. "I swear."

"You'd swear to anything to be rid of Pockets," she accused, smiling up at him.

Devon grimaced. "He presented a bit of a problem. No one wanted to take on a servant with that name. Thought the lad would rob them in their sleep. I tried to reason with him about taking another name, but you know how adamant he is about keeping it."

Danielle's soft laughter filled the arbor.

"I fail to see the humor in this," he admonished. "I was dead serious. I even offered the lad a monthly allowance, but he turned me down cold."

Tears filled her eyes and her sides ached with laughter. "The mighty sea captain brought to his knees by a mere street urchin."

Devon grabbed her by the shoulders and pulled her against him. "And what would it take, love, to bring you to your knees?"

She searched his deep blue eyes. "Would it truly please you to bring me to my knees?"

His lips brushed hers. "Only if it meant you had placed them on each side of me in my bed."

"Devon!" she shouted, her face a bright red.

"Oh!" squealed a matronly woman passing the arbor.

He laid his forehead against Danielle's and they laughed until tears ran down their cheeks.

"We'd better return to our guests," he told her as he wiped the tears from her eyes.

Although Devon stayed at her side, it was some time before they could look at each other without laughing. Resolved to enjoy herself, she put Nathan's bitter words from her mind, and it proved one of the best afternoons she could remember.

The children were kept entertained with games, a puppet show, and a magician Devon had brought all the way from Spain. As sunset neared, she looked around for Devon but couldn't find him among the guests. They would all be moving inside to the ballroom because the dancing was scheduled to start soon. Then the evening would end with a supper served in the dining room. As tired as she was, she hoped she would not embarrass Devon. It was difficult to remain gracious when your every bone ached and all you wanted to do was crawl back in bed and cover your head.

She felt a tug on her skirts and looked down. Katie's blackberry-stained lips smiled up at her. Mary hovered in the background. "It's past time you were in bed, Katie," Danielle said.

"I know, but there are so many things to do. Isn't it just too lovely, Miss Danny?" she replied sweetly, batting her long dark lashes.

Danielle looked at Mary, who only rolled her eyes.

"She's been listening to the young ladies flirting with their beaus," Mary explained.

"Heaven help us when she's ready to make her entrance into society," Danielle said as she led them into the house. "Mary, take her upstairs and get her ready for bed."

"Oh, but the dancing, Miss Danny," Katie protested. "I simply must go to the dance. My beau will be expecting me."

"Your beau?" Danielle asked.

"He's the young dandy with the canary-yellow britches and lemon-yellow waistcoat," Mary threw over her shoulder as she dragged the protesting child up the stairs. "He let her retrieve his quizzing glass from the fountain."

"Off to bed," Danielle said firmly. "Your beau is invited to spend the night. You may apologize to him tomorrow."

"Your Grace," Bob interrupted. "I've been looking everywhere for you. His Grace needs to see you in the study. It's very important."

* * *

Devon slammed his fist down on the desk. "Dammit, Edward, you know I'm not guilty of this."

Captain Winslow shook the dust from his hat. He had slipped out ahead of his Majesty's troops and had ridden most of the afternoon.

"Even the Lord Chancellor is aware of that, but charges of treason have been brought against you and your crew. He doesn't believe them any more than I do, but with Napoleon threatening to land on Britain's shores, the entire country has gone crazy. Lord Carruthers has produced witnesses who have testified to your guilt."

"It's no wonder he declined my invitation. But Lord Carruthers is wrong, though why he would even give credit to these lies is more than I can fathom. Nathan has to have his hand in this somewhere." He stood. "I'm going to talk with these witnesses. I'll make them tell the truth."

"If you stay at Burnshire, the Lord Chancellor worries for your safety. He feels his Majesty's guard would be your best protection."

"His Majesty's guard? Will they will be placing me under arrest?"

"The Lord Chancellor thinks it's best."

"The Lord Chancellor doesn't have to do this to protect me," he shouted. "My men are the only protection I need."

Captain Winslow leveled a stern gaze at Devon. "Do you really propose to ask this of your household? The men who resort to the type of butchery the Lord Chancellor fears are not gentlemen. They'll come with clubs and knives. They'll overwhelm you with sheer numbers."

"You forget, Edward. These are the type of men I'm used to dealing with."

"Not five months past, a ship's captain and crew were thought to be aiding Napoleon. In the dead of night, the ship was boarded, the crew slaughtered to the last man, and the ship burned. Devon, you've been gone from England for seven years. They will question your loyalty to the Crown. With tempers riding high, the Lord Chancellor thinks the Tower offers the best safety.''

"I won't be locked up where I won't have an opportunity to search out those who are guilty.''

"I cannot tell you what to do, Devon. But bear in mind, even his Majesty's men could not stop the last assault.''

"Do not think me unappreciative, Edward. I know what you risked by coming here. Tell the Lord Chancellor I cannot agree to what he's asked. But I will do this. The *Liberty* is due to dock any day now, and I will stay in hiding until then. It will be up to him to see that my ship is met and the logbook turned over to the Crown before the riffraff at the docks destroy the only hope I have of proving my innocence.''

"Wherever you plan on going, do not delay. They will be here at any moment to arrest you.''

Devon shook Edward's hand. "Thank you, friend. I will not forget what you have done for me.''

A light tap on the door cut short their farewells. As Edward made his way through the French doors to the shadows on the garden path, Danielle entered the study.

"It's you, love,'' Devon said.

"Is something wrong, Devon? Bob said you wanted me.''

He pulled her roughly into his arms, holding her as if it were for the last time. "I'm going to miss you,'' he said.

The pain in his voice tore at her heart. "Devon, you're scaring me. What's wrong?''

He led her to one of the chairs. Seating her, he knelt at her knees, her hands in his as he explained what had happened—his sudden trip to London, his preoccupation of late, and Winslow's news.

"This is all Nathan's doing,'' she said when he finished. "Surely the Lord Chancellor can see that.''

"The Lord Chancellor does not believe me guilty,

but the charges have been made and I must disprove them."

"Why should you have to prove your innocence?" she cried. "Let them prove your guilt."

Devon stood and pulled her to her feet. Gathering her in his arms, he tried to explain. "To most people the evidence appears clear. To them I will always be guilty. Do you want to spend the rest of our lives having fingers pointed at us? Could you endure the constant whispering behind your back?"

Tears fell silently down her cheeks. "What do I care what others say of us?"

His arms tightened around her. "There is always the possibility that I will not be able to prove my innocence," he pointed out. "If that happens, I will be a wanted man. And then, Danielle, I will have to leave England forever."

"Then I will go with you," she said through her tears.

He tipped her chin up with his finger. "What is this? Could it be that my beautiful wife cares for me?"

"Devon, don't tease."

He wiped his thumb across her wet cheeks. "Don't cry, love. As soon as the *Liberty* docks, we'll have the proof I need. Until then I must go away."

"Go away?"

"It won't be far," he said, smiling down at her. "I'll be hiding at Seabrook. It's the estate my godfather left me. If you need me, Bob knows the directions." He cupped her chin in his hand. "Other than you, love, Bob is the only one I trust to know where I will be hiding. You are not to tell anyone else."

"Not even Brodie?" she asked.

"If you decide to tell Brodie, be careful that no one overhears."

Danielle stroked his cheek. "If you are worried about my maid, you needn't. Mary would never betray you."

"It is not Mary's loose tongue that I fear. It is your dresser."

"Elizabeth?" Danielle backed away from him. "But

she never gossips among the other servants. Who would she tell?''

"Nathan," Devon stated coldly. "Your dresser has been meeting with Nathan from the very beginning."

"You have to be mistaken, Devon. Elizabeth seems such a caring person. Why would she do this?''

"For the same reason anyone would. The coins she pockets.''

"Well, I'll talk with her," Danielle said as she turned to the door.

Devon grabbed her by the arm and pulled her back to him. "That's the last thing I want you to do," he demanded, then grinned down at her. "I only told you to warn you, not so that you'd take matters into your own hands. Remember the grocer? Don't send Mrs. Meacham away."

"Devon, must you always remind me of my mistakes?''

"Only to keep you from making others. As long as Nathan feels he has someone safely established at Burnshire, he'll rely on her to give him the information he wants and he won't try anything foolish while I'm gone."

"Oh, Devon," she cried, throwing herself into his arms. "What will I do if he finds you?''

"Careful now, love. I might get the impression you're going to miss me, and that would never do. It wouldn't do to have the Ice Princess melt on me now."

"Ice Princess!" She pushed away from him. "You dare to compare me to that . . . that . . . woman? Why, you . . . insufferable . . . contemptible . . . miserable excuse for a husband. You . . .''

"Dare I hope you'll get around to 'adorable,' 'wonderful,' and 'magnificent lover'?" he teased.

"Magnificent lover, hah!" she sniffed.

He smiled down at her. "Save some of your wrath for his Majesty's men."

Her green eyes widened in surprise. "They are coming here?''

"Were it not for the Lord Chancellor's warning, they

would be hauling me off to the Tower to cool my heels until the *Liberty* docks.''

"Then you must leave right away."

"The fireworks display should begin at any moment. I will leave when everyone's attention is occupied. Captain Winslow will appear to arrive during the festivities. When the soldiers come, let him do the talking.''

"Why can't I go with you?"

"Who would be here to see to our guests?" he teased.

"Our guests won't even know I've left."

"No, Danielle. I don't know how long I will need to stay out of sight. Once word spreads of the charges, I'll be a marked man. The danger is too great.''

It was clear his warnings only piqued her interest the more. He had been justified in keeping the news to himself all these weeks. There was no telling what she would have done. A spark grew bright in her eyes.

She brushed her body invitingly against his. "A magnificent lover would remain near his mate lest she have need of him.''

He gazed into her emerald eyes and his loins tightened. "You brazen vixen. Had I the time, I would make you act on what you are suggesting.''

"Then take me with you.''

Reluctantly he released her. "I cannot. But promise you will keep a place warm in your bed for me until I return.''

She turned away from him. "Husbands who leave their wives behind do not deserve to have their places kept warm.''

"Uncaring wench," Devon bantered. "I could always shackle you to your bed until I return.''

"If you were to do that, who would see to your guests?" she stubbornly replied.

He held her close. "I wish I didn't have to leave, but I have no choice. I know it won't be easy facing everyone.''

"Do you think I care about that?"

He searched her eyes. "Your best friends will turn from you. They'll ridicule you behind your back."

"Then they are not my friends, are they?"

Her bravery tore at his heart. He had not meant to hurt her in his efforts to expose Nathan. Why hadn't he realized it would eventually come to this? The answer was simple. He had wanted her as his wife and refused to acknowledge, even to himself, that he was not being fair to her. What would happen when she realized it for herself?

Hungrily he covered her parted lips. He loved her, and the realization shook him to his toes.

"I love you," he whispered, but the burst of the first fireworks covered his words.

Danielle pushed him from her. "You must hurry," she said. Despite all her arguments, she would not delay him now. She knew where he was hiding. She would go to him later.

She watched him leave before joining the guests on the lawn. The fireworks held no interest for her, and she tried to gather her thoughts. As soon as the dancing started, Devon would be missed. A sudden illness that had taken him to his bed would answer the inevitable questions, but what of the soldiers? They would be arriving soon. They would not be turned away as easily by her excuses for Devon's absence.

By the time the fireworks display had ended, Danielle had formulated a plan. Slipping into the study through the garden door, she hurriedly scrawled a note on a piece of paper she found in one of the bottom drawers of the desk. Once finished, she crumpled it and dropped it on the floor.

She could hear the guests making their way to the ballroom and she hurried to meet them. Although disappointed, they easily accepted her excuse that Devon had taken ill and could not join them.

Captain Winslow stepped forward and offered his services to open the dancing. Danielle placed her hand upon his and moved to the center of the ballroom.

The musicians poised their bows above the violins.

At a nod from Danielle, they drew them down across the taut strings.

Captain Winslow whirled Danielle across the floor as the melodious strains of a waltz filled the room. Danielle couldn't help but recall her reasons for starting the dance with the controversial step. Her first dance with Devon had been a waltz. If she closed her eyes, she could almost imagine she was in his arms again. Almost.

"I must warn you," Edward said, breaking the spell. "His Majesty's men will not be turned away by Devon's sudden illness. They will insist on seeing him anyway."

Danielle smiled up at him. "Yes, they will, won't they?"

Although confused by her unconcern, he was somehow pleased by her confidence. Devon was a fortunate man. Despite all Devon's protests to the contrary, Edward was seized with the notion that it was inevitable that Devon fall prey to the lady's charms.

"It won't take them long to realize that you're lying," he pointed out.

"I'm counting on it."

At the sight of Andrews gesturing frantically from the doorway, Danielle paused in her steps and let Edward lead her from the dance floor. She could hear the whispers follow them from the ballroom. Danielle held her head high. She mustn't dwell on what others thought. However, despite her resolve to remain unmoved, the faces of the soldiers waiting in the foyer sent a sharp stab of fear racing up her spine. They believed her husband guilty. Danielle suggested they step into the drawing room.

The lieutenant bristled at her offer. "The butler should not have bothered you, your Grace. It is your husband we wish to see."

"My husband is ill, Lieutenant."

The rigid muscles of his face twitched. "So your butler informed us," he said tightly.

Without looking, Danielle knew that several of her

guests had gathered in the hall behind her. "Lieutenant, we are in the middle of a party, and the presence of you and your men is disturbing my guests. I must insist that you leave now and return tomorrow, when my husband will feel up to speaking with you."

"You don't understand, your Grace. We will see your husband now, ill or not." He pushed her aside and mounted the stairs, his soldiers following.

"How dare you invade my home in this manner!" she shouted after them. "Devon will have your head for this!"

Edward groaned.

The lieutenant paused on the steps. Slowly he turned. His face was an unyielding mask of hatred. "He'd do best to look to his own neck."

Danielle started to answer him when she felt Edward touch her arm.

"That will be enough, Lieutenant Ames," Edward barked.

"Stanton's room is the last bedchamber to your right. Get your business over with, then be gone from here."

The lieutenant touched his hat, mounted the last of the stairs, then disappeared down the hall.

"He'll be back as soon as he sees Devon is not there," Captain Winslow whispered.

Danielle nodded. She couldn't get the lieutenant's hatred out of her mind. This was not as simple as Devon would have her believe. Oh, Lord. Did they truly hang those accused of treason?

The sound of running footsteps echoed from the hall above. "Search all the rooms," she heard the lieutenant command. She clasped her hands together to keep them from trembling. She mustn't let these men frighten her. They were doing exactly as she had hoped.

She let Edward lead her into the drawing room to one of the chairs by the fire.

"What is this?" Nathan demanded from the doorway. "What are those soldiers doing upstairs? They have the guests terrified. Why, it took forever to assure them nothing was wrong and that they should continue with the dancing."

Danielle's heart plummeted to her toes when she spotted the woman behind him. She hadn't seen Lady Emily earlier, and had begun to hope that she was not going to come. She was wearing a pale blue silk gown trimmed with white lace that matched her sapphire eyes and set off her blond curls to perfection. But Danielle knew she couldn't let jealousy cloud her thoughts now.

"That really wasn't necessary, Nathan. I am perfectly able to see to my own guests."

Emily stepped around Nathan. She was smiling, and rather pleased that the party had taken a bizarre turn.

"I'm Lady Emily Chalmers," she said, taking a place on the sofa next to Danielle's chair. "May I call you Danielle? After all, it was I who was to have married Devon. That should make us some sort of relative, shouldn't it?"

Danielle stiffened. Her hope that Lady Emily was no more than a harmless, spoiled kitten was shattered. This cat had claws.

"Don't be offended," Lady Emily said, a hint of tearfulness in her voice. "If anyone should be upset, it is I. If Devon has done something foolish, I will be blamed for driving him into the life he now leads."

The gall of the woman! Devon was on the verge of being arrested, and all she thought of was herself. "And why would that be, Lady Emily?" Danielle asked sweetly.

"Devon and I were engaged."

Danielle arched a delicate brow.

"Oh, but I bear you no grudge," the blond hurried to say. "It was so many years ago." She leaned toward Danielle. "Devon had to leave England before the announcement. You know, the fire and all. Silly boy. My father would have taken care of everything. After all, it wasn't as if the man who died was of any significance."

The Ice Princess. Devon had named her well. "Is

that so?'' Danielle asked, looking right at Nathan. ''I heard that someone set fire to the croft in the hope that Devon would be blamed.''

Her arrow hit its mark. Nathan rushed to the side table for a drink.

Lady Emily blithely continued. ''Why else would Devon have left?''

''Why else indeed?'' Danielle said, her eyes on Nathan's stiff back.

Misinterpreting Danielle's intent, Lady Emily hotly replied, ''We were very much in love.''

Danielle turned to her. ''So much so that you married someone else not three months after Devon left.''

Tears misted Lady Emily's sapphire-blue eyes. ''Well, you couldn't expect me to sit on the shelf until he returned.''

''No. One couldn't expect that, now could one?'' said Danielle sympathetically, her impassive face concealing her true thoughts. She was fast losing patience with Lady Emily Chalmers.

''With Devon gone, I had to cancel the engagement. The old duke was furious with Devon.'' The blond woman paused and distractedly removed her lace gloves. ''It pained me so to be the cause of further friction between Devon and his father. If it hadn't been for the support of Nathan, I don't know what I would have done.'' She cast the vicar a warm glance.

''How fortunate for you, Lady Emily. But then I would imagine Nathan was more helpful than you even realized.''

When Nathan claimed a seat next to Lady Emily, Edward took Danielle's hand and squeezed it in warning. It wasn't necessary. At the naked hatred in Nathan's cold gray eyes, Danielle swallowed the words.

Suddenly the door burst open. The lieutenant strode across the room, Danielle's crumpled note in his hand. ''Thanks to this note we found on the floor of his study, we know where the traitor is hiding.''

''Traitor?'' Lady Emily shrieked. ''Nathan, whatever do they mean? Who is a traitor?''

"Now, now, dear, you mustn't let it upset you." His gaze fell on Danielle. "I'm sure her Grace can explain."

Danielle stood, bringing Captain Winslow to his feet also. "I am as totally baffled as you," she said calmly. "I know of no traitor."

"What is the meaning of this, Lieutenant Ames?" Captain Winslow demanded.

The lieutenant stood at attention. "We have been instructed to arrest Lord Stanton."

"That is ludicrous. For what reason?"

"Treason, Captain."

"You're mad," Danielle said firmly. "My husband would never do such a thing."

"You may believe what you like, your Grace, but the Duke of Burnshire has been charged with treason. There are witnesses."

"You would take their word over that of the Duke of Burnshire?"

"The witnesses are two of his own men, your Grace."

Had not Captain Winslow held her arm, Danielle knew she would have collapsed on the floor. Devon's own men! It could not be.

Chapter 18

D anielle tossed and turned, her thoughts making a mockery of any hope she might have of sleep. The militia had searched all of Burnshire since the note Danielle had planted for them to find had said he'd be hiding somewhere on the grounds. Then they went to the factory, only to return with the special dyes Nathan had been using on the cloths woven there.

She was horrified to learn that the dyes had come from France. The colors were of a special formula that had been introduced just in the past year. So far, only the colored fabrics were known to have been smuggled into England. It would take someone with powerful connections to actually obtain the dyes. Frantic, Danielle tried to explain that Devon knew nothing of the matter. But since his Grace was now in charge of the factory, they argued, the dyes merely confirmed their suspicions of his dealings with Napoleon. She couldn't forget that it was because of her interference that evidence was building against her husband.

The next few days were a nightmare as guests who had come from London for the house party suddenly remembered engagements elsewhere. They left, only to be replaced by the gossips who were curious to see how the duchess was holding up under the strain of the treason charge.

At first she had greeted them all with a bright smile and hoped her gracious manner would convince them she was not worried about the vicious rumors. But then she realized that no matter what she said, they left with their own tales. Well, she'd not be home to any more of them.

She sat up in bed and fluffed her pillow for the tenth time. Would this night ever end? Like swirls of an elusive fog, sleep seemed to drift close, then push away again as she agonized anew over what had happened.

Treason? Could he have been responsible for the lives of all those men? Surely not. But what was she to believe when even his own men turned against him?

No, she could not accept that. She had to see him. As long as there was a chance he was not guilty, she owed it to him—to her love for him—to discover for herself. With her resolve came blessed sleep.

It was late when she woke, sleep hanging heavy upon her. She rang for Mary, but when the breakfast tray arrived, she found that the very sight of food made her stomach roil, sending her to her washbasin. Then she took a dose of laudanum and returned to bed. Pulling the covers over her head, she waited for the medicine to take effect. If only it could numb her thoughts as well as her stomach.

Tomorrow. She would go tomorrow and see Devon. Hadn't he always set things right? The workhouse. The orphanage. He had even secured appropriate positions for the children.

He would take her in his arms and hold her close. He would kiss her until she forgot everything else but the two of them. She'd not let pride stand in her way any longer. She loved him and that was all that mattered.

She snuggled down in her pillow, her eyes heavy. Her queasiness was beginning to recede with the languid waves of sleep that crept over her. In time, he'd come to love her too, she thought. In time . . .

Danielle slept all day, waking for only a light supper, then went back to bed until the next morning. She was surprised to see Brodie sitting in a nearby chair when she at last awoke.

"I've rung for your chocolate," Brodie said as she put down the book she had been reading.

Danielle sat up and smiled. For the first time in days, she was hungry. "Good. I'm famished." Despite her words, the arrival of her breakfast tray sent her hurrying across the room for her washbasin again.

Brodie stood patiently until she had finished. "A little under the weather again this morning?" she asked sternly.

Danielle rinsed her mouth. "Yes, but don't let Katie hear of it. She's been out of sorts enough since her beau left without saying good-bye after the party. We don't need her thinking she's ill on top of everything else."

"She'd have a hard time convincing us she had your ailment."

"Katie's very good, Brodie," she reminded her.

"But she'd tire of the symptoms before her time came."

Danielle brows creased in a frown as she looked at her old governess. "Her time?" she asked, confused.

Hands on her hips, Brodie allowed a broad smile to brighten her face. "Everyone will be pleased to learn their suspicions are true."

"Suspicions?" Danielle was fast losing patience with Brodie's cryptic remarks. Her head was spinning, and if she didn't sit down soon, she'd be forced to make use of her washbowl again. "Will you please tell me what . . ."

Suddenly her face pinked in understanding. "Me?" she said, stumbling to her dressing table.

"You," Brodie answered confidently.

"But how?" She sank down in the chair.

"You're married," Brodie said matter-of-factly. "That's what I've always believed caused it. If you want a more detailed explanation, you'll have to ask his Grace."

Holy Hannah! How could she have been so blind to

the symptoms? It wasn't as if they hadn't been there
for her to see. The sickness had been coming regularly
each morning. Even her monthly time had come and
gone without the usual inconvenience, but she had told
herself she had lost track of the days. Now there was
no denying it. She was going to have Devon's child.

"I don't wish anyone to know," she warned her
companion. "Not until I tell Devon, at any rate." And
how would she do that? She could just imagine herself
telling him, *Oh, by the by, since you don't have enough
worries, with his Majesty's men scouring the countryside for
you, I thought I would inform you that you're going to be a
father.*

Brodie continued to smile. "I'll tell everyone to contain their celebrations."

"You've told the entire staff?"

Brodie removed a note from her book. "I almost
forgot. This arrived from one of the children this morning."

"Brodie!"

"I didn't tell everyone."

"No one knows for certain, then?" she asked.

Brodie pulled her chair close to Danielle's. "They'll
all know if you continue shouting."

"I was not shouting," Danielle protested. Her eyes
narrowed. "How did you find out?"

"I noticed that you've been wrenching your gut out
every morning. But you mustn't look so displeased.
We were bound to find out sooner or later. This is not
a condition that is easily kept secret." She shoved the
note at Danielle. "Why have you waited to tell
Devon?"

"How could I tell him when I didn't even suspect it
myself?"

"He'll have to be told soon." Brodie said. Danielle's
obvious reluctance puzzled her. Anyone with one good
eye could see they were in love. "He will be very
happy," she assured her.

Tears scalded Danielle's throat. "He says he wants

a child, but he also says he plans on returning to his ships.''

Brodie gathered Danielle in her arms. ''That may have been his intention from the beginning, but I've seen the way he looks at you. He's in love and there's no changing that.''

''But to have a child now . . . With this charge of treason over his head, he may no longer wish one.''

''I'll admit it's not the ideal time to be starting your family, but he'll not be wishing the babe gone. It's only a matter of time before he'll be able to prove his innocence. He'll be home then, and once he's held his child in his arms, he'll soon forget his thoughts of leaving.''

''Do you really think so?'' she asked.

''I'm certain of it.'' She wiped a tear from Danielle's cheek. ''Trust me, child. Tell him, and you'll see that I'm right. He loves you and he'll want this child every bit as much as you do.''

Her eyes still bright with tears, Danielle managed a smile. ''Have Andrews order the coach. Pleased or not, a man should know about his child.''

The coach came to a stop. Danielle lifted the drape at the window. Surely they had not reached Seabrook so soon. Bob opened the carriage door.

''This was the shop Lady Montgomery recommended. They have the best display of herbs in all of England,'' he said in an overly loud voice.

Confused, Danielle took his hand and stepped from the coach.

''We have been followed,'' he whispered, then said aloud, ''Will you be long, your Grace?''

''No, not terribly,'' she answered, quickly picking up his cue. ''I need only inquire after an herb grown back in the colonies, then we can return.''

''Very good, your Grace,'' he said, then added in a whisper, ''We can't continue with an escort provided by Nathan.''

Danielle nodded her agreement and then left him standing by the carriage while she entered the shop.

The clerk hurried forward to assist her. Drat! Her mind was a complete blank. For the life of her, she could not recall the name of an obscure herb. Holy Hannah! Why did she even try? Anything would do. It wasn't as if she wanted the blasted thing. "I'll take a peck of your monkey-wart root."

Oh, Lord, from the look on his face, she wished she'd put a little more thought into the herb.

"When dried and ground into a powder," she continued, "the root is used in the colonies to ward off colds."

He continued to stare at her. She could only pray that it wasn't an aphrodisiac or something equally ungenteel.

"I—I'm sorry, my lady," he finally said, "but we don't carry that . . . that item."

"Very well. I shall try elsewhere." She swept out of the shop. "Head the horses for Burnshire, Jem. No one in England appears to have what I need. We'll have to order it from the colonies."

The ride back to Burnshire seemed to take forever, and once there, she was relieved to be able to stretch out on her bed and relax until tea.

She curled her fingers around the coverlet Mary had placed over her. There was no doubt. Whoever had followed her carriage had to be someone who thought to learn of Devon's whereabouts. But how was she to see him if she was followed everywhere? She closed her eyes. If she'd only had her pistol, she could have given her pursuant a small sample of her displeasure. She'd not forget it again.

The fog from the Channel had found its way to the caverns beneath Seabrook and left a moist pattern on the stone walls. Devon took a deep breath and rose from the straw mattress he'd stuffed in the corner of his hiding place. Would he ever rid himself of the stench of the damp chambers? Even his lungs were filled with it.

He chanced a look at Robert, who stood stiffly beside

the only chair, unloading the provisions he had brought from Burnshire. When the man's nose twitched, Devon laughed. "Robert, the higher you hold your nostrils above me, the more of my odor you will breathe."

"Well, hell's bells, Devon. Can't you at least bathe?"

Devon scratched his week-old beard. "I've yet to decide which would be more to my advantage—rotting here without a bath or returning to Burnshire for one last one before they haul me off to London to hang me."

"Don't get your ire up with me. I was only thinking that once it's dark, you might be able to sneak down to the shore and have a quick dip."

"You forget about the towers. The coastline along here is dotted with them, and every one is staffed with volunteer militiamen who avidly watch the sea in case Napoleon attempts to land his troops on England's shores. It would be ironic, wouldn't it, if one of them were to turn me over to the Crown? I was the one to issue the orders that the towers be built, maintained, and manned."

"Bloody efficient, weren't you?"

"You'd think that fact would count for something in my defense."

"Those things are quickly forgotten when treason is mentioned. The only one who appears to think you innocent is the duchess."

"How is she taking all of this?"

"She was upset that she couldn't see you earlier."

"You were followed?"

"From the moment we left Burnshire. But you would have been very proud of her. She carried it off beautifully."

"This isn't proving too much for her, is it?"

"At first it appeared to upset her. I thought the little talk she had with the vicar and Lady Emily would be the last straw, but the duchess handled it well."

Devon scowled. "I would have tossed them out on their ears."

"I took the liberty of suggesting that very thing to her, but she feels that it would only have made things look worse for you if she had turned them away. And she insists that by displaying no concern over the false charges, others will begin to question their validity as well."

"It's a shame I missed her performance with Nathan and Lady Emily."

Robert paused in his work. "The duchess has spunk. There's no doubt about that. I wasn't able to hear the conversation, but she must have given Nathan a royal earful, because when your cousin left, he looked as black as a thundercloud and Lady Emily's face was as white as the good vicar's starched cravat."

"Have any of the servants given notice?"

"Only the ones who haven't been with the family long. But they'll regret their actions soon enough. The *Liberty* should be docking soon. The ship's log will prove your innocence. Then they'll be back, begging for their positions."

Devon's laughter reverberated off the walls. "If you think Danielle made Nathan's ears burn, just wait and see what she does to them."

Having emptied the leather bags, Robert pulled a wooden crate up beside the chair and sat down. "I wish you could have seen the duchess when one of your neighbors arrived. I doubt the woman had so much as taken her seat when she must have said the wrong thing. Your wife had her out the door in less time than it had taken the good lady to remove her bonnet."

Robert folded the empty bags and tossed them over his shoulder. "You needn't worry about the duchess," he said. "She plays the part of an enraged wife better than any actress I know. The stage has been deprived of a great talent." He studied his friend for a moment. "If I didn't know better, I'd say she was in love with you." His brows raised questioningly. "What would you say?"

Devon lowered his eyes from his friend's and cleared

his throat. "I've got a letter for you to deliver to Captain Winslow. Once you do, go straight back to Burnshire. You know as well as I that Danielle cannot be trusted to keep her nose out of Nathan's business." He caught Robert's gaze. "You need to be there to see that she stays out of trouble."

"For all the good it will do," he mumbled. "Once the duchess sets her mind to something, the best I can hope for is that I can follow close enough to see that she doesn't get in too deeply."

"Like you did at the factory?" Devon grinned.

"Much like that," Robert said before rising to go.

"Do your best," Devon called after his friend.

The room seemed to shrink after Robert left. The confinement was beginning to wear on Devon's nerves. Perhaps Robert was right. Surely there was a way to rid himself of this grime. It had been a week and the militia had yet to visit Seabrook. Was it possible that Nathan had forgotten its existence?

Picking up his candle, he carefully made his way up the narrow stone steps to the wine cellar. He doused the light, then opened the small wooden door hidden in the paneling behind the large wine casks. The fit was tight, but he managed to squeeze through. He searched the closets of the old servants' quarters until he came across some clothing that might serve his purpose.

Although the previous owner had clearly been tall, the pants were several inches too short. The rough woolen shirt fit no better, but once he'd tied it in front, it accommodated the breadth of his shoulders without tearing. He was forced to loosen the cords, leaving a broad expanse of his chest exposed, but what did he care? He needed to see Danielle, even if only for a moment.

She didn't know how long she slept, but when she awoke the sun was beginning to set. She was ravenously hungry, and considered asking Brodie to join her for supper, but then remembered that her governess would have eaten earlier with Katie. It was a habit she had gotten into, stemming from her insistence that Danielle dine alone with her husband.

Cook served Danielle in the smaller breakfast room. Roast partridge served with vegetables followed the smoked salmon and a bowl of warm broth. By the time the apricot tarts arrived, Danielle's appetite had been thoroughly satisfied. She sent them back to the kitchen and ordered tea to be brought to the drawing room.

"Pardon me, your Grace, but will you be wanting me to send the rest of Jeremy's things to the orphanage?" Mrs. Talbut asked. "He left so quickly this afternoon that I forgot to include the new coat Mrs. Meacham sewed for him."

Fear crept up Danielle's spine. "Jeremy was not to return to the orphanage."

"But the note said—"

Danielle grabbed her arm. "What note?"

"A messenger brought it this afternoon, not long before your return. It was from his Grace," she said. "A position has been found for Jeremy, and he was to return to the orphanage until he is sent for."

"Are you positive it was from Lord Stanton?" Danielle found herself shaking the poor woman. She dropped her hands. "I'm sorry, Mrs. Talbut. I did not mean to alarm you, but I worry about the note. It could have been from the vicar."

"It's possible," the housekeeper said. "I did not see it myself. Andrews and I were reviewing the staff. I believe Mrs. Meacham spoke with the messenger." She pressed her finger against her chin thoughtfully. "As I recall, she seemed rather upset and asked that we await your return before letting Jeremy leave."

"I wish you had," Danielle said.

"I'm sorry if I've done something wrong, your Grace. To be sure, only Andrews read the note. But both he and I agreed that it was foolish to keep the messenger waiting."

"Have the carriage ready to leave within the half hour," Danielle ordered.

"Certainly, your Grace."

Her promise to let Devon handle such things hung heavy on her conscience, but what was she to do? Her coach had been followed earlier. It would more than likely be now. She could only pray that, if they were Nathan's men, they would not interfere. She thought briefly about ringing for Bob, realizing she hadn't seen him since returning from the herb shop. But then she changed her mind. She wanted to be on her way as soon as possible.

She went to her room. The day had grown cold, and Mary helped her change into a warmer gown. It wasn't until she looked in the mirror to adjust her bonnet that she noticed Brodie behind her.

"Where are you going this late in the evening?" Brodie asked.

Danielle dismissed Mary. Once her maid had left the room, she turned to face Brodie. "I'm going to the orphanage."

"Have you gone mad?"

"While I was out earlier, someone from the orphanage came and took Jeremy."

"But how? Every servant in the house knows your feelings on that matter."

"The man had a note requesting Jeremy's return. The handwriting appeared to be Devon's, and whoever sent it used his seal."

Brodie didn't ask why Danielle was so positive the note was not Devon's doing. For all Danielle's denial of her feelings for Devon, she remained loyal. Brodie was pleased. "Do you think Nathan forged the note?"

"Who else would want Jeremy so badly?"

Brodie's forehead wrinkled in concern. "You think it wise to risk Nathan's wrath now? With Devon in hiding, there's no telling what Nathan might do. Perhaps you should try to get word to his Grace. He will know how to handle the situation."

"That's exactly what I can't do. Don't you think that's why Nathan took Jeremy? I'm sure he expected me to run to Devon the moment I learned of the note.

The most frightening thing about it all is that that was my first thought. It was on the tip of my tongue to order a carriage to take me to Seabrook when it suddenly occurred to me Devon would never have written the note. It had to be a part of Nathan's scheme to get me to lead him to Devon."

"I'll not let you go by yourself," Brodie said. "In your condition, you shouldn't be running all over the countryside."

"I'm merely going to the orphanage. That hardly constitutes running all over the countryside."

Brodie stood firm, her arms crossed in front of her. "What of your earlier trip?"

Danielle deliberately ignored her. "Hand me my cloak, Brodie."

"If you insist on going, I'm going too."

"Brodie," she exclaimed. "Why are you being so stubborn?"

"I intend to see this baby born."

"There's no reason to fly into a pet. It's not going to arrive today."

Brodie tapped her foot on the floral carpet. "I'm going."

"Then you'd best hurry. The carriage is waiting."

Brodie fetched her own cloak and followed Danielle downstairs.

"Just a moment," Danielle said and left Brodie standing in the hall.

The former governess was beginning to think Danielle had somehow slipped out without her when she came hurrying down the hall stuffing something into her reticule.

"Let's be off," Danielle said.

At the orphanage, Amy answered the door, but before Danielle had the chance to talk with her privately, Mrs. Pickett appeared in the hallway.

"Your Grace, what a surprise."

"Is Mr. Pickett home?"

"I expect him any moment. Would you care for a cup of tea while you wait?"

"I haven't the time, Mrs. Pickett. I'm here concerning one of the orphans."

"Nonsense. Amy has only this moment brought the tea." Isabel was not about to let the duchess deprive her of the chance to gloat. After all, the duke was wanted for treason, wasn't he? It was no more than he deserved after giving them notice to be gone. She straightened her broad shoulders and waved her hand toward the drawing room. "You might as well have some while you wait for my husband."

Danielle reluctantly followed her into the parlor. Brodie, stubbornly refusing to be parted from Danielle, took a chair beside her. After several pointed glares, Mrs. Pickett chose to ignore Brodie's existence. She poured Danielle a cup of tea. Uncovering the warm dishes on the tea tray, she held one out to her guest. "Would you care for a broiled sausage?"

Danielle's stomach tightened at the plump sausages reposing in the slick puddle of grease. "No . . . no, thank you," she managed to choke out.

Mrs. Pickett plopped hers across a plate of blood pudding. "You're missing a rare treat," she said. "What with Mr. Pickett expecting to be late this evening, cook made this tea special. I can have her bring you some of the sugar biscuits we had for lunch if you would prefer."

"No, the tea is enough. How late do you think Mr. Pickett will be?"

"Not too late."

Danielle set down her cup of tea. "I've come after one of the orphans. If you would just have Amy fetch him, I will be on my way."

"Oh my," Isabel exclaimed. "I don't think Mr. Pickett would approve of me letting you take any of the children."

Danielle stood. "I'm in a bit of a hurry, Mrs. Pickett. If there's a problem, I'll fetch Jeremy myself."

"Jeremy? Oh, you mean the lad that's been sold."

"Sold? To whom?"

"His Grace arranged the sale a month ago. I'm surprised he didn't tell you." She leaned forward and grinned. "But then with all the goings-on—you know, treason and all—perhaps it slipped his mind."

Danielle jumped to her feet. "Mrs. Pickett, my husband is not a traitor."

"I think it's time we were leaving," Brodie urged, stepping between them.

Isabel stood and glared over Brodie's shoulder at the duchess. "It's what he'd like us all to believe, isn't it?"

"You forget yourself, Mrs. Pickett," Danielle said between clenched teeth. "But my husband will deal with you soon enough. For now, I only wish to know where the boy has been taken."

Isabel crossed her arms stubbornly across her ample bosom. "If the vicar wants you to know, he will tell you."

Before Danielle could answer, Amy stepped into the room. "He's gone to Lord Carruthers, Miss Danny."

"Lord Carruthers?" Danielle could feel the room spinning around her. It couldn't be true. Devon had promised her Jeremy would stay.

The dizziness passed as quickly as it had come. She took a slow, steadying breath. "Where is Lord Carruthers' home?" she asked.

"You'll not be a-bothering Lord Carruthers on the word of a lying wench, will you?" Isabel whined.

Brodie took Danielle by the arm. "We should be returning to Burnshire," she said firmly.

Danielle refused to back down. "As soon as Mrs. Pickett recalls that her husband's wages are paid from Burnshire's coffers, she'll give us the directions."

Brodie only shook her head in defeat.

"Now, Mrs. Pickett, where will I find Lord Carruthers' estate?"

Isabel did not answer for a moment. "It's not far. It borders on Westbryre, you know."

"The directions, please."

"Yes, of course," she said, already anticipating Nathan's wrath. "But Mr. Pickett will be here soon. He knows much—"

"The directions, if you please."

Isabel relented. She had done all she could. "Take this road until you reach Hampton Crossing. Have your driver turn left. It's three miles down the road. You can't miss the entrance. Large iron gates bear the family crest. The gatekeeper's getting a mite deaf. Your driver will have to speak loudly when he calls to him."

"Thank you, Mrs. Pickett," she said, then turned to leave. "Devon's agent will be here in the morning to relieve you of your duties. In the meantime, Amy will come with me."

Chapter 19

Danielle's hand trembled as she lifted the knocker. Surely Lord Carruthers would see her.

The door opened, and the butler stood aside for her to enter.

"Would you please inform Lord Carruthers that the Duchess of Burnshire is here to speak with him."

It was evident from the arrogant manner of the butler that he had heard the rumors about Devon. Danielle had forgotten how very pompous servants could be.

"He's at supper, your Grace"—he paused—"with guests."

"I'll wait, then."

She wasn't about to let him intimidate her. She swept past him and entered the sitting room. Rose silk brocade chairs flanked the fireplace and she crossed the room to sit in one. Lord Carruthers didn't appear immediately, and her attention wandered to the display tables artfully arranged around the chamber, their surfaces covered with miniature figures of dancing ballerinas. The numerous paintings covering the walls echoed the motif. After all she had heard of his harsh treatment of his servants, she wondered at the decor. How could a person sensitive enough to love the ballet be completely insensitive to the needs of others?

"What may I do for you?"

Lord Carruthers' quiet entrance startled her, and it took her a moment to compose herself. "I'm so sorry

to take you away from your supper, Lord Carruthers,
but I have just learned that a boy we had working for
us at Burnshire was taken to the orphanage by mistake
and, I believe, sold to you. I've come for him."

"You must be referring to Jeremy."

She didn't like the cruel lines that etched his thin
lips when he smiled. "Yes. Jeremy is so terribly young,
and the duke and I have taken quite a liking to the lad.
We would never have sent him to the orphanage."

"But, dear lady, the duke was the one responsible
for my purchasing the boy."

Danielle would not allow herself to believe Devon
would break his promise, nor was she going to let Carruthers change her mind. "You are wrong, my Lord. I
don't know who was responsible for the mistake, but
I do know that my husband would never have allowed
Jeremy to come here."

"Mistake or not, the boy is mine now. I paid good
coin for him and intend to keep him," he said, dismissing her.

"Devon will see that you are reimbursed."

Lord Carruthers took her by the arm and guided her
to the door. "His Grace had best keep his coin. He
may have need for it."

She jerked her arm from his grasp and whirled to
face him. "You would not say that if Devon were here.
But I am and I can promise you that you have not heard
the last of this. I will get Jeremy back."

Lord Carruthers reached around her and threw the
door open. "You will have to excuse me, your Grace,
but I have guests who must be wondering about my
absence. My butler will show you out."

Danielle pulled her blue cloak about her and swept
past him and out the front door. Pox on his guests.
The door slammed behind her. She paused on the
steps. Lord Carruthers obviously did not know her,
but that was probably for the best. She would save
Jeremy even if she had to . . .

Danielle's face lit up. It was perfect. Lord Carruthers

was more concerned about his guests than he was about dealing with her.

"Well, let him stay with them," she mumbled, a smile on her lips. "It couldn't be better."

Hurrying down to her coach, she shouted to the driver to head for home, then climbed in. As soon as they were out of sight of the main house, Danielle tapped on the coachman's door. After a few tries, it slid open.

"Stop the carriage and douse the lamps," she said. "I will be out in a moment."

The door shut and Danielle turned to Amy. "I'll need your clothes."

"Her clothes?" Brodie said. "Danielle, what are you planning now?"

"I need to get into White Oaks. Dressing as one of the servants is the only way I know I can do it without being stopped."

"You said there would be no problem convincing Lord Carruthers to return Jeremy."

"I did not think he would be so stubborn."

"So you plan to walk in and snatch the boy," Brodie sneered, "in front of all his servants?"

"Lord Carruthers is entertaining. They will be too busy with their duties to notice me."

Brodie didn't appear convinced, but Danielle was relieved that she didn't offer any more objections.

She wasn't all that convinced herself that she would be able to find Jeremy. White Oaks looked terribly large. It must have almost as many rooms as Burnshire, but she'd not leave Jeremy there. Amy had told her that to go to Lord Carruthers was one of the worst things that could happen to a young boy. Well, if he was so hard on his servants, she was not going to leave someone as fragile as Jeremy to work for the man. Why he had chosen someone so obviously unsuited for hard work was beyond her. But who was to say? Perhaps Lord Carruthers was sadistic. It was possible he had selected the boy purposely, knowing it wouldn't take much to break his spirit.

With much twisting and turning, she was finally out of her gown and into Amy's. The front of the dress didn't quite meet, but thankfully the bib of the white apron covered the gap. Next, she stuffed her curls under the dust cap.

"Would you take me for a maid?" she asked.

Amy looked up from the silk dress she was now wearing. "Your face seems a mite clean to have been working all day, but you'll do." Her hands ran nervously over the patterned silk gown. "H-how do I look?" she asked shyly.

Danielle hugged her. "You look like a fine lady."

Brodie could remain silent no longer. "We shouldn't be doing this, Danny."

"Would you rather Jeremy stayed with Lord Carruthers?"

"Oh no, Mrs. Brodie!" Amy cried. "He can't be left there!"

Danielle wondered at Amy's vehemence, but this was no time for solving another puzzle. She opened her reticule. Reaching in, she pulled out her pistol and slipped it into the pocket of her apron. It hung like a stone against her legs. Before Brodie could offer another objection, Danielle was out the door.

"Wait here until I return," she whispered to Jem.

Jem nervously searched the woods beside the drive. "You won't be long, will ye?" he whispered after her.

"I'll be quick as a ghost in a graveyard," she tossed over her shoulder.

"Oh, Lord," Jem muttered to himself.

The moon lit her path as she made her way back to White Oaks. Her heart was pounding in her ears. She stopped and waited a moment, sensing that someone or something was nearby. Her conscience nagged at her, but it wasn't as if she were going to be dealing with the vicar, she told herself. That was what she'd promised not to do. She quickened her step, sending the apron swinging. The pistol beat against her leg, but she refused to slow her pace. Another cold chill ran up her spine, and she was surer than ever that someone was out there.

Devon kept to the trees as he watched her progress along the drive. What was she up to now? She might be dressed in a maid's clothing, but he had undressed her enough in his mind to know the woman moving among the shrubs was his wife.

Did she even realize the risks he was taking following her? Did she know how difficult it was to do so without being seen by her other escort? He had almost missed her at Burnshire. Then, when she had stopped at the orphanage, he had been furious. Had she not come out when she did, he would have done away with Nathan's man and dragged her out by her pretty little head.

But what was she doing at Carruthers'? The night in the stables kept returning to haunt him. *Tom*, she had said. Had his suspicions that night been right all along? His heart twisted inside him. Danielle and Carruthers? No! He refused to accept that. She loved him. He was sure of it. There was only one logical explanation. Someone had told her that Lord Carruthers was the one to demand Devon's arrest. He frowned at the thought. If she had come to confront Carruthers, he would have more problems than ridding himself of Nathan's man, Chilton. Lord Carruthers had an enormous staff at his beck and call.

He would stop her now before she reached the house. But before he could move, Chilton stepped out of the bushes beside him.

Danielle stopped and listened. Had she heard something? The branches overhead groaned in answer to her fears. She shrugged off her doubts and hurried along, but the feeling that someone watched her persisted until she rounded the corner at the back of the house.

Quickly, she slipped through the servants' entrance.

She leaned back against the door. Luck was with her. It led to the back stairs.

She started up them, only to have a young maid step onto the landing above her. Danielle lowered her head and moved to one side to let the maid pass, when another idea came to her.

"Where 'ave you been?" she demanded.

"I've been tending to my duties, I 'as. Mrs. 'Atch 'as me runnin' 'oles in me shoes."

Danielle couldn't believe her good fortune. Without a query of her own, the girl had supplied her with what surely was the name of the housekeeper. "Well, I've been looking everywhere for you. The new lad's done got sick all over 'isself. Lord Carruthers is in a real lather, and Mrs. 'Atch says as 'ow you were to bring warm water to the lad's room."

The young maid sank wearily against the wall. "I finished cleaning from 'is bath not an hour ago. If 'e keeps this up I'll never get the other rooms ready."

"Mrs. Hatch never was one for dwelling on our troubles," Danielle said sympathetically.

The maid pushed away from the wall. "Ain't that a mouthful of truth."

"I 'ave a few minutes before I'm needed in the kitchen. Show me where the lad is and I'll clean 'im up."

The maid eyed Danielle suspiciously. "I don't rightly remember seeing you before. You new 'ere?"

"I come in to help cook when she's a need for me."

The girl shrugged her shoulders and pointed to the top of the stairs. " 'E be in the west wing. Next to Lord Carruthers' room. Same room 'e always keeps them young boys." The maid snickered. "Likes to keep 'is fancies close, 'e does."

Danielle wondered at the strange comment. Lord Carruthers was keeping Jeremy in the room next to his own? Her imagination exploded with possibilities as she mounted the steps to the second floor. She recalled the cruel twist of his lips when he mentioned Jeremy, then hurried down the hall, staying close to the far wall. It wouldn't do to have one of his footmen catch her now.

Reaching the end, she rounded the corner into what she hoped was the west wing. Heaven help her. There were at least eight doors along this hall. She would need to locate the one Jeremy was behind before she encountered another servant. The next one might not be as easily dispatched as the first.

She listened at each door as she made her way along one side of the hall. Coming to the end, she started back on the other side. At the second door, she heard the sound of someone crying. Slowly, she opened the door. Hundreds of candles lit the room, and her eyes were immediately drawn to the ceiling. Scantily clad figures of beautiful men danced across the brightly painted surface. When she realized that the candles were situated to draw the visitor's attention to them, she lowered her burning face to the silk-clad bed that was so much like her own.

The sight that greeted her there shocked her. Sitting up in the far corner sat a small boy, his little body racked with sobs.

"Jeremy?"

The lad lifted his face to her, and Danielle swallowed the gasp that rose in her throat. Tears streamed down Jeremy's face, streaking the cosmetics that darkened his blond lashes. Someone had used a liberal amount of rice powder on his cheeks. Two round circles of rouge reddened his cheekbones, and more covered his lips.

Holy Hannah, he was painted up like one of those ladies she had seen on the docks when she had arrived in England. But why would . . . ?

Her eyes widened in horror. "Jeremy, come with me. We must get away from here."

The boy hiccuped a sob. He stared at her for a moment as if he didn't believe she was truly there.

"We must hurry," she urged him.

Quickly he scooted off the big bed and ran to her. "I knew you'd come," he said.

Danielle grabbed a cloth from the washstand and knelt before him. She wiped the rouge from his face as best she could.

"Jem has the carriage waiting," she chatted, trying to appear cheerful.

Jeremy stared past her to the door, his eyes wide with fright.

A tingling of fear crept up Danielle's spine. She reached into the apron pocket and withdrew the pistol. Hiding it in the folds of her skirt, she slowly stood and turned.

Lord Carruthers' tall form blocked the doorway.

"How dare you sneak into my house like a thief!" he bellowed.

She straightened her shoulders. "I told you. I came for Jeremy."

"I paid for the lad. He stays."

"Take that up with my husband's agent."

"I don't want the money. I want the boy."

"And you think I would leave him here after what you've done to him?"

"I've done nothing to the boy. Why, I've—"

"Spare me your lies. We both know the truth. The point is, do you want others to?"

His face twisted in rage. "You . . . hussy! How dare you come into my home and spread your filth!"

Danielle backed away from him. His vehement denial was frightening. If she had not seen Jeremy, she would have believed him, but she was not to be deterred. "Either stand aside and let me leave with Jeremy, or you will force me to go to London with my story."

"Who would believe the wife of a traitor?" he said, stepping into the room.

"Devon is not a traitor," Danielle shouted.

Lord Carruthers smiled indulgently. "That is not what the House of Lords decreed." He took a step toward her. "Jeremy, go to my room."

The boy clutched at Danielle's apron.

When Lord Carruthers took another step into the

room, Danielle raised the pistol from the folds of her apron and leveled it at his heart. "The lad goes with me."

His face paled. "Surely you would not use that," he gasped.

"I will if I have to."

She motioned him to sit in a chair. It took only a few moments to secure Lord Carruthers' hands and feet with two of his own shirts. Next she pulled his cravat from around his neck and used it as a gag.

She checked the hall. No one was there, but they must hurry. It wouldn't be long before his guests questioned his prolonged absence and someone went to look for him.

It seemed like forever before his footman found him, and Lord Carruthers was furious by the time he was untied. The footman backed away from the black look on his face.

"Get out!" Lord Carruthers shouted. With the click of the bedchamber door, he leaned over the nearest table and cleared the polished surface of its fragile treasures.

"She will pay for this," he shouted.

Lord Carruthers' dissipated good looks smoldered as he returned to the dining room. Although his guests were only Lady Emily and the vicar, he was careful to replace the scowl before he rejoined them.

"And who was your visitor?" Lady Emily asked coyly. "Or should we ask?"

Her passion for gossip was no secret, and Lord Carruthers wondered if he could use the fact to his advantage.

"Lady Emily," he began, "must you see a liaison in every meeting between a man and a beautiful young lady? Her Grace and I—"

"Devon's wife! Devon's wife was here?" she shrieked.

His spirits lifted at the light that seemed to burn in

her eyes. It couldn't have worked out better if he had planned it. He lowered his gaze to his plate. "You mustn't get the wrong impression, Lady Emily. Her Grace had a small matter of business she wished to discuss."

"She came rather late. Does she always take care of business at such odd hours?"

His head shot up. "I'll not have you casting aspersions on Danielle's character," he said. "She is a lady and has always conducted herself as such."

"Of course, Thomas," she simmered sweetly. "With Devon gone, she must feel overwhelmed by the responsibility of running a household as large as Burnshire. The poor child. Such a shame these things always seem to fall to those least capable of handling them."

Carruthers watched her carefully. She was fairly bursting with this little gem of gossip and looked most anxious to impart it to the next sympathetic ear she encountered.

"For Devon's sake," she continued with a dramatic sigh, "I feel I must lend his wife my assistance."

Nathan shot Thomas a look of concern. "That's very generous of you, my dear, but what with Prinny's party only next month, do you truly wish to tie yourself down with another's responsibilities?"

Emily puckered her lips in thought. She was looking forward to the event, but then again, she had yet to receive her invitation. Drat Devon anyway. If he had married her as he should have, she would not be fretting so over whether or not she would receive one. The Duke and Duchess of Burnshire were always included. Yet after what Devon had done, perhaps she could afford to be a bit more generous to his wife.

"Of course, you are right, Nathan. I was only thinking of the way she inconvenienced Thomas at such an inopportune moment."

Lord Carruthers leaned forward and placed his hand over hers. "That was very thoughtful of you, my dear, but I enjoy Danielle's companionship too much to consider it an inconvenience. She is delightfully refreshing."

Lady Emily had heard this exact assessment of Danielle too often of late to be pleased to hear it again, but she smiled sweetly at her host. "Devon will be most pleased to know you have taken his dear wife under your wing."

The butler entered with the port for the gentlemen, and Emily dutifully retired to the drawing room, leaving the men to their drinks.

Nathan turned to Lord Carruthers. "Whatever were you thinking? Surely you are aware that Lady Emily now believes you to be harboring romantic feelings toward the duchess."

Lord Carruthers leaned back and sipped his port. "I truly hope so, since I went to such great pains to establish the possibility. Having planted the seeds of infidelity in such fertile ground, I need only sit back with you and watch them grow."

"Have you gone mad? If Devon has indeed developed a *tendre* for his wife, he will not stand idly by while you besmirch her reputation."

"And what will he do, Nathan? Come out of hiding?"

Nathan beamed in understanding. "Ah, just so."

Lady Emily paced the drawing room floor. Those unfamiliar with her vindictive nature would have wondered at her malicious smile.

She came to a stop before the hearth. Whatever would Devon think if he only knew his little bride was not such a bargain after all? If Danielle was having an affair with Lord Carruthers, it would only serve Devon right. He should have chosen *her*, not that twit from the colonies. Emily couldn't deny that she had had her own share of liaisons, but she had always been discreet about them. She knew how to conduct herself.

Thoughtfully, Emily ran her fingers over a silver candlestick on the mantel. She had to admit Danielle was shrewd. The young duchess had a wealthy husband and a wealthy lover.

One could certainly see that Lord Carruthers didn't stint in spending his wealth. Emily would have considered Thomas for herself if she had been certain there was no justification for the rumors about his private life. After all, she did have some standards, and she would never allow herself to look like a fool. Perhaps, though, Danielle looked the part.

A fool! That was what she had been. Danielle, still dressed in Amy's attire, stepped down from the coach and walked past her astonished footmen. After what she had seen, she should have shot the man. It was no less than he deserved.

Of course, no one would agree with her. Ever since her marriage she had been letting Devon tell her what she could and could not do. They all treated her as if she were a child. Well, now Devon needed her, and she had proved she was capable of handling a few things herself.

"Danielle, wait for me," Brodie called after her. "You haven't told me what happened."

"That's not important now. Have Amy take Jeremy up to his bed. Then pack a small bag. We're going back to the orphanage."

"What of your promise to Devon?"

"After what I've just done, it's already broken. I've got nothing more to lose now. I might as well finish what I've started."

Brodie clamped her mouth shut. There was no arguing with Danielle when she was in one of these moods. It was best to go along with her in the hope that she could temper Danielle's actions.

Within half an hour Brodie was back at the front door with a small portmanteau. Danielle had the entire household in an uproar. Another carriage had been brought around and was being loaded with baskets of food. Brodie held her tongue until they were in the coach and on their way.

"Would you mind telling me what all this is about?"

"I am getting rid of the Picketts."

"You're what?" Brodie shouted.

"I am sending the Picketts and their servants packing. Devon should have done it ages ago."

"But Devon asked that you not interfere with the orphanage. It's just too dangerous. Especially now he's in hiding, and there's no one to stop Nathan."

Danielle's green eyes blazed. "I'll stop him. As long as I'm Duchess of Burnshire, he will not interfere again. It's due to him that Devon is in trouble."

"Which should serve to warn you not to cross swords with him now."

"What more can he do, Brodie? If Devon can't prove his innocence, he will be hung." Tears welled in her eyes. "I'll not let Nathan win, Brodie. I can't."

The old governess gathered Danielle in her arms. "You're in love with Devon, aren't you?"

"Oh, yes," she sobbed. "Don't you see? I've got to do something or I'll go mad. Taking the orphanage away from Nathan isn't nearly as much as I'd like to do. I wish I could call the man out and be done with it. Putting a bullet through his heart would do me a world of good."

"Tut, tut," Brodie crooned. "We'll have none of that. You rid the place of the Picketts and I'll take over the running of the orphanage."

Danielle sat up. "You would do that for me?"

"It will be for me also. With most of the children gone, you don't have much need of me at Burnshire."

Danielle threw her arms around the older woman. "Oh, Brodie, I love you so."

Isabel stepped back to avoid getting trampled by two men carrying her trunk out the front door. "Do something!" she shrieked at her husband.

Mr. Pickett seemed to shrink under her anger. "What would you have me do?"

"Well, I'd not have you stand there like a whipped dog. Send for Nathan."

"I'm afraid it will do you no good, Mrs. Pickett," Danielle said calmly. "You see, I've brought enough men from Burnshire to see to it that Nathan is never allowed near the children again."

"You little nobody!" the woman snarled. "Your husband is a traitor. He killed his Majesty's men and you think you can dismiss us. Nathan will never allow it."

"My husband is innocent, and as long as he remains Duke of Burnshire, Nathan has no say in what I choose to do."

Mr. Pickett put his arm around his wife's shoulder. "Come along, Isabel. We'll leave this in Nathan's hands."

Isabel let him lead her to the door. Once there, she stopped and turned back to Danielle. "Your husband cannot stay in hiding forever, and when he is found, I'll take great pleasure in watching him hang."

"Leave, Mrs. Pickett."

"I'll leave all right, but you won't be so high-and-mighty when your husband is dead and Nathan is the Duke of Burnshire."

"Shush, Isabel!" Mr. Pickett warned as he hustled her out the door.

White and shaken, Danielle felt her knees give out and she slipped to the floor.

"Oh, Danny," Brodie cried as she knelt beside her.

Mrs. Pickett paused on the step. Curious, she turned to see what had frightened the older woman. The duchess lay on the floor in the foyer, Brodie leaning over her.

"Get a glass of water," Brodie shouted to one of the children on the steps. She loosened the button at the top of Danielle's gown. "I warned you not to overtax yourself, Danny," she said. "You keep this up and you'll lose the baby for sure."

Isabel's brown eyes flew to her husband's pale face.

Chapter 20

Nathan walked into his office and slammed the door. "I pay you too much for mistakes," he hissed at the thin woman standing in front of his desk.

Elizabeth stepped back. "What have I done?"

"Not only have you failed to fuel Danielle's distrust of my cousin, but now I discover her Grace is expecting."

"I had no idea," she said. But thinking over the past few weeks, Elizabeth Meacham suddenly knew she should have realized what was happening. All the signs pointed to it.

"Well, now you know." He shoved a packet into her hands. "And I want no mistakes this time."

Elizabeth stared at the linen packet. "What am I to do with this?"

"Slip a small amount of the powder into her morning chocolate."

"What is it?" she asked, a knot forming in her stomach.

"That's not important."

"It won't kill her, will it?"

"Let's just say it will make her very ill. Perhaps ill enough to bring on a miscarriage."

She shoved the packet back at him. "I'll have no part of it."

"Now, now, Mrs. Meacham," he said as he closed her fingers around the herbs. "You'll be paid well. Very well."

Elizabeth fingered the small linen square. She needed the money. The duke was wanted for treason. The chances of her receiving the bonus promised her were slim. Even the few extra shillings the vicar had been paying her would not be sufficient to care for both herself and Katie.

She squared her shoulders and met the vicar's hard gaze unblinkingly. "Five hundred pounds."

"F-five hundred pounds?" he sputtered.

"Five hundred pounds," she said, standing firm. If her suspicions were correct, he would pay anything to see that the child was never born. With enough coins, she could take Katie and get away from this wicked affair.

"I don't have that much money with me."

"You may bring the coins tomorrow, and I will see that she gets the potion."

Nathan considered saying no. Mrs. Meacham was becoming entirely too greedy. He paid her well. Too well for her not to have known about the child earlier. But at this late date, he couldn't afford to antagonize her. Her kind tended to lean toward blackmail. The only bright spot was that this would more than likely be his last dealing with her. Once the child was no longer a factor and Devon was swinging from one of his Majesty's stout ropes, he would see to Mrs. Meacham's fate—permanently.

"Very well, Mrs. Meacham. You shall have your money." Pulling out his pouch, he tossed it to her.

She opened it and ran her fingers through the coins. "There's not nearly enough here."

"Sixty pounds is all I have with me, but you'll get the rest. You have my word."

His word was about the last one she trusted. She emptied the pouch, then returned it to him. "Have the rest delivered to me before I retire for the evening and I'll see that the powder is in her chocolate in the morning."

She turned abruptly and was gone, leaving the vicar staring at his empty leather purse. Disgusted, he tossed it on the desk. Her high-handed ways were beginning to grate on him. He loosened his silk cravat and pulled it from around his neck. Knotting and unknotting the scarf in his hands, he envisioned it around Mrs. Meacham's throat, her face turning purple as he tightened it.

Rain pounding on the leaded panes of her bedchamber window woke Danielle to memories of her nights with Devon. She reached for him, but he wasn't there. Once more she had to swallow the truth. He might never be beside her again. But it would do no good to lie here and bemoan her fate.

She slipped her legs over the side of the bed. She must see Devon. If she was careful, perhaps she could avoid being followed. She needed to try. She had to tell him of her love.

The door suddenly opened, and Mrs. Meacham came in with Danielle's breakfast tray.

"I found this sitting on the side table getting cold and brought it with me," Elizabeth said. She set the pot of chocolate on the dressing table and helped Danielle with her gown.

The white dress with small pink ribbons scalloped down the front served to help lift Danielle's spirits. She could wait no longer. She had to see Devon. There were so many things she wanted to tell him. It would be difficult. Nathan was sure to have men watching. But surely she was skilled enough to evade them.

Sitting at the dressing table, Danielle watched Mrs. Meacham pick up the last of the discarded garments. Elizabeth's appearance had changed greatly since she'd come to Burnshire. Except for the dark circles under her eyes, the dresser appeared to have shed years from her age. It was still difficult for Danielle to believe she was part of Nathan's schemes.

"Would you be wanting me to do up your hair this morning, your Grace?"

"I would like that," Danielle answered, pouring the chocolate into the porcelain cup. She paused when she noticed the woman's cheeks blanch. "Is there anything wrong, Elizabeth?"

"N-no," she stuttered, picking up the brush and running it briskly through Danielle's curls. She couldn't drag her eyes from the cup. Would the powder have a bad taste? she wondered. The vicar had said it would only make her ill, but . . .

Danielle looped her fingers through the cup's fragile handle, and Elizabeth knew at that moment that she couldn't go through with it. Not for any amount of money. She and Katie would survive somehow.

She reached for the cup.

"Please lay out the blue cloak Devon brought me from London," Danielle said. If she was going to successfully evade any pursuers, perhaps she could use Mrs. Meacham to her advantage.

"You'll be going out?" Elizabeth asked, her hand hovering over the cup.

Danielle spun around on her chair. "Now, you mustn't tell anyone, but I'll be leaving in an hour to meet my husband."

"Do you think that's wise?" Elizabeth asked.

It wasn't the answer Danielle had expected. Didn't the woman realize that was what Nathan would want her to do? "I know I'm taking a great chance, but I miss him terribly."

"But . . ." Elizabeth paused. If Danielle were to lead the vicar to the duke, then all would be settled and perhaps he wouldn't be so upset with her for not making sure Danielle drank the chocolate.

The chamber door swung open, and Mary backed in with a breakfast tray. "Sorry I'm late, but the tray I prepared for you earlier disappeared and I had to make up a fresh one." She swung around and spotted the other tray on the dressing table.

"I brought it up," Mrs. Meacham apologized.

"I'll just take this one back, then."

"Oh, no. I mean, her Grace's chocolate has grown cold." She stepped around Danielle and took the cup from her hands. Setting it down, she scooped up the tray. "Please take this one back to the kitchen, Mary."

"Nonsense," Danielle protested. "I only poured the

cup just now and it appeared warm enough. Mary, you may have the other tray for your own.''

Elizabeth plopped her tray down on the bed and took the fresh one from Mary. ''You're too generous, your Grace. 'Tis your breakfast tray and you shall have your chocolate hot. Besides, Mary has had her breakfast. You wouldn't want to see her turn into a fat little goose, would you?''

Danielle looked at Mary and grinned. If Mary ate day and night she would likely stay as skinny as she was at that moment. She winked at her maid. ''Take the old tray back with you, and don't let me hear that you've been nibbling at it. I won't tolerate a fat maid.''

Mary rolled her eyes. Danielle's dresser was truly developing some strange habits, she thought. First she stole the breakfast tray; then she insisted that it be changed for the fresh one. Mary picked up the cold tray and left. Now that his Grace was gone, Mrs. Meacham must be worried that Danielle would have no further need for fancy dresses.

Danielle appeared to study the sky as she stood poised on the front steps. Assuring herself that everyone who cared to notice had gotten a sufficient glimpse of her, she turned and went back inside. It would have been much more convincing had not someone misplaced her distinctive blue cloak, but no matter.

Chilton signaled to Faris. The duchess was preparing to leave again. He hoped this trip wasn't going to be another waste of time. The vicar had ranted and raved enough over their last failure. If she didn't lead them to the duke soon, Nathan would be demanding their heads.

Both men groaned when Danielle changed her mind and went back inside. But within a few moments she emerged again. The hood of her cape was pulled up against the cool afternoon breeze.

''Must o' forgot 'er gloves,'' Chilton whispered to his companion.

With a nod to the driver, the duchess climbed into the coach. A snap of the whip and they were off.

Chilton, hidden from the coach by the trees that lined the drive, silently berated Faris for not having checked his gear before they started out. His saddle had broken, and now the duchess was leaving, meaning Chilton would have to follow her by himself. He quickly mounted his horse and moved out after the coach.

Faris continued to grumble after his partner left. It wasn't his fault the girth on his saddle had chosen this moment to split. If the duchess had only waited a few minutes, he would have shown Chilton that he could ride his mount, saddle or no.

"Now if this blasted buckle would only . . ." He sighed as the buckle finally released the cinch.

Faris tossed the saddle into the trees, then grabbed the horse's mane and pulled himself up onto his mount. It was then that he spied the other coach. He studied it thoughtfully. It was a small, rather shabby affair. The horses weren't much to look at. A couple of nags, he sneered silently. And the only passenger appeared to be one of the servants. He debated whether he should try to catch up with Chilton or follow this other coach. He stayed in the trees as he kept it in sight. It was going much slower than the first. With no saddle, he didn't relish the jousting he would get if he tried to catch up with his partner. He would follow this one.

Danielle pulled the white dust cap down lower as they approached the small village outside Burnshire. Her plan had worked well and she didn't want to jeopardize everything now. She had told Elizabeth of her intended trip. Devon had been right. She must have somehow gotten word to Nathan, for, sure enough, someone had been waiting to follow her carriage. Danielle's lips curved in a smile. She wished she could be there when he learned that the coach they followed to London carried only her maid.

She watched the passing countryside. This would be her first trip to the southern coast of England. At the rate the horses were going, it would be nightfall before she reached Seabrook. But she mustn't mind their lack of speed. They had helped get her away without one of Nathan's escorts.

The sun had cast its shadows of dusk across the road by the time the small coach pulled to a stop at the front steps of Seabrook. Tom helped Danielle down. She searched the dark windows. Perhaps they should have driven around to the servants' entrance, but it was too late for second thoughts. She shook the dust from her skirts and started up the stairs.

"Whoa there, young lady," an old man called as he hurried across the lawn. "What be you wanting 'ere?"

It hadn't occurred to her there might be a caretaker. "I'm Lady Stanton, the Duchess of Burnshire. I've come to Seabrook to stay for a few days."

Although Danielle had removed the dust cap from her auburn curls, the caretaker eyed her skeptically. "Ye 'ave, 'ave ye?"

He circled her slowly, setting her already frayed nerves on edge. He came to an abrupt stop before her and shoved his unshaven face into hers.

"Ye know yer 'usband be wanted fer treason, don't ye?"

Danielle stood her ground. "And you are?"

"Tabor, miss. Willie Tabor. Been caretaker 'ere for nigh on twenty years now." He swept his arm across the sky dramatically. "Along the coast you sees it all. Ain't been a one of 'em 'asn't sworn they was innocent right up to the time the king's man slips 'at 'ere noose o'er their 'eads."

"You better hope they never hang my husband. Because twenty years or no twenty years, I'd cut your disloyal tongue out and feed it to the gulls for the lies you've hinted at today. Now step aside."

The old man's face broke into a toothless grin as she stomped past him. Devon had one fine wife. That he did.

Danielle and Tom searched the rooms but could find no clue to where Devon might be hiding. The house had grown dark and their candles cast eerie shadows across the sheet-covered furniture. It was obvious Devon had chosen his hiding place well. The house was filled with lonely corridors and dark passageways. Try as they might, they could find no evidence that anyone had been here in the past few years, and it was much too late to search the grounds. They would try again in the morning.

Availing themselves of the well-stocked lunch basket they had brought with them, Danielle and Tom prepared to spend the night. Danielle chose the large bedchamber overlooking the cliffs, but Tom insisted on making his pallet on the floor in the front foyer.

The night was warm and Danielle opened the glass doors to the balcony. Stripping down to her shift, she climbed into the big bed and pulled the linen sheet over her. The sound of the water beating softly against the rocks below soon lulled her to sleep.

Devon doused the oil lantern before he opened the cellar door leading up to the kitchens. Even though he knew Willie would be keeping a sharp eye outside, he carefully avoided the windows as he crept across the kitchen floor to the stairway that led to the rooms above.

The stairwell was dark and the wooden steps groaned under his weight, forcing him to pause after each one. It seemed to take forever to reach his bedchamber at the back of the house.

Devon stood by the bed and watched the steady rise and fall of her chest. Her hair was the color of fine rosewood as it lay against the pillow. Lord, how he'd missed her, but what was she doing here? He had wanted to come as soon as he'd heard she was here, but Willie had insisted he wash some of the smell from him before he presented himself to such a fine lady. A smile touched his lips. Danielle had woven her web over that old sea horse as well.

He hadn't seen her since the night outside Carruthers' estate, when he'd run into Chilton. It had been easy enough to knock the fellow out, but afterwards he'd gone straight back to Seabrook. He'd been a fool to risk venturing out of his sanctuary in the first place. He reached out to touch her. He had dreamed of her so often of late, but this beautiful woman wasn't a dream. She wasn't an apparition. She was real. She was here. And she was in his bed.

Almost afraid to breathe lest she disappear, Devon quietly removed his clothes. Pulling aside the sheet, he slid into bed beside her. She turned into his arms.

"Ah, love," he whispered into her hair. "I've missed you so."

Danielle opened her sleep-drugged eyes and smiled at him. She slid her arms around his neck and whispered, "I've missed you too."

Devon rose on one elbow and made a great play of sniffing the air. His eyes returned to hers and he arched a questioning brow. "What, no brandy?"

"No brandy."

She searched his face. Could it be possible that he could ever come to love her too? But she hadn't come to find that out. She had come only to tell him of her love.

"I find I've acquired quite an appetite for the brew," she said as she moved against him.

"The house has been closed too long. I'm afraid there is none I can offer you," he said huskily, his body already responding to her touch.

She looked into his hooded eyes. "You will be my brandy tonight."

"I hope I prove as intoxicating as your last taste," he whispered against her lips.

Her reply was lost in his kiss. There was no denying the heat of their passion as he gathered her in his arms. His hands found the neck of her nightdress, and before she could protest, he ripped it from her. His lips continued to hold hers as he pushed the remnants of the gown off her shoulders and down her arms.

He parted her lips and plunged his tongue into the depths of her mouth. Her tongue met his, alternately teasing, then boldly mating with his. She was like a fiery swallow of whiskey, burning the length of him as he drank from her cup. Never had his raw need for someone climbed to such heights, demanding satisfaction.

He lowered his head to the silky ripeness of her breast and traced the swollen nipple with his tongue. Her skin was like creamy alabaster in the moonlight.

Danielle moaned beneath him. His tongue carved a path down the length of her. She was on fire, a slow aching trail of fire that threatened to consume her. Wantonly, she arched her body. "I need you," she cried.

He took her then. Fast, hungrily. With all the pent-up fury of a summer storm on the seas. And she matched him with a burning hunger of her own. With each thrust of sweet pain, she dug her nails deeper into his back. Greedily, she rose to meet him until her body was trembling with her need for release.

His mouth covered hers, and with a final plunge, he buried himself deep within her, swallowing her cries of passion as her body shuddered in explosive release. He could hold out no longer; he spilled his warm seed.

Afterwards, she snuggled contentedly against him, basking in the warm afterglow of their lovemaking.

"I came to tell you I love you," she whispered against his furred chest.

Devon drew back and smiled down at her. "The brandy proved to be more potent than I thought."

He was making light of her confession. The temptation to grasp the way out he had handed her was great, but she had not come here for a tumble in the sheets. She had come here to tell him of her love and of the child she carried. She knew the risks. He was a man who wanted no part of marriage. When his vendetta against Nathan was finished, he would be gone. But this was no time for second-guessing her decision. She swallowed her pride and looked into his blue eyes. The need she saw there almost made her change her mind, but she rushed forward. "I want you to know I understand your feelings for me."

"Do you truly?" he asked, his eyes smoldering blue pools of passion.

"I accept that you consider our lovemaking only that of two people sharing a moment of passion . . ."

He buried his face in her hair. He needed to tell her that he had been a vain and selfish man. Only thinking of his own needs, his own life. He loved her too and he whispered it against her neck. He could never give her up.

His warm breath made it difficult for her to form her thoughts. Had he truly said he loved her? "You need not say that, you know. I give you my promise," she added, "that I lay no claims on you with our marriage vows."

He lifted his head and studied her thoughtfully. "Oh, Danielle, what have I done to us?"

Her heart ached at the pain he'd just expressed. "I only came to tell you of my love," she said, tears welling in her eyes. Taking a deep, shuddering breath, she continued. "And also of our—"

The sound of angry voices and the deafening thuds of heavy fists at the front door brought the couple upright in their bed. Danielle clutched the covers to her. Devon cursed the fear he saw in her green eyes.

After slipping on his breeches, he left to check on their visitors. Within a few moments he was back. "I must go," he said. "The militiamen are here."

"But how? I was so careful not to be followed."

She looked so upset. His little sea maiden. He kissed the tip of her nose. "Do not fret, love. I doubt your coming here had anything to do with this. It was just a matter of time before Nathan recalled the place."

She didn't look convinced.

"I must go," he said regretfully.

"Be careful. I could not bear it if you were caught."

He wiped the tears from her cheeks with his thumb. "Willie will keep them busy until I'm gone."

"Not the Willie I met."

Devon touched her lips in a brief kiss. "He loves you too," he whispered, then was gone.

Danielle dressed hurriedly. She didn't have the faith in the old caretaker that Devon had.

* * *

Devon crept along the rocks. Someone had told the soldiers about the secret entrance to the caves, and he was forced to seek a new hiding place. He couldn't stay where he was. The moon would come out from behind the clouds soon, and he would present an easy target to anyone looking along the shore.

One of the towers blocked his way. Even in the poor light he could make out the outline of a man at the top. Perhaps he could slip by unnoticed.

Hugging the side of the cliff, he carefully followed the rugged path to the base of the tower. A ledge jutted out from the sea wall, and he was forced to drop to his hands and knees.

Footsteps dislodging a shower of stones brought him up short. A soldier was headed along the path down to the beach. Devon had no choice. He either took his chances in the tower or surrendered now.

Slowly he made his way to the door and slipped inside. He had no sooner shut it behind him than the soldier shouted to the guard above.

"Have you seen that traitorous Stanton lurking about, man? We've reason to believe he's been hidin' in these parts."

The moon broke through the clouds, bathing the stark tower in light. The local perched on the platform above Devon stared down at him.

Devon returned the bold stare. He was innocent and he'd not cower on his own land.

"Ain't seen a soul all night," the guard shouted over the edge.

"Well, keep a keen eye out. We mean to have him, and there might even be a few coins for the man who spots him."

Devon climbed the ladder until his head was level with the guard's heavy boots. "Why didn't you turn me in?" he whispered.

"Could 'ave turned you over to them when you first come 'ad I a mind to," the man answered as he continued to search the waters below him.

"Then why didn't you?"

" 'Tain't a one of us hereabouts that thinks you guilty, yer Grace."

Devon swung up onto the platform and held out his hand to the guard. "I appreciate your faith in me. I only wish there were some way I could repay you for your help. Fleeing from the militia doesn't give a man much time to collect his purse."

"Don't need no pay. Nor expect it," the guard said haughtily. He lowered his eyes to study the man at his feet. "Thought you loved this old place, I did."

Devon was baffled by the sudden hostility in the guard's voice. "I do."

"Then why you fixin' to sell?"

"Sell?" Devon hissed. "Why would I sell Seabrook? It probably holds more memories for me than Burnshire."

The old man beamed. "Told Willie as much, I did. Told him you wouldn't let the ol' lord down by selling the place."

"Whatever gave Willie the notion I would want to sell?"

" 'Twas last fall 'bout harvest time. Yer cousin shows up with this gentleman. Wouldn't say who 'e was. Said it was none of Willie's business who you sold Seabrook to. Now, Willie's been 'ere long enough, 'e figures 'e 'as a wee stake in the place. Well, 'e listened close enough till 'e learns that bloke's name, then 'e set the dogs to 'em." The guard chuckled to himself. "Worked right pretty, it did. They ain't been back."

Why would Nathan be trying to sell Seabrook? Devon wondered. It made no sense. To be sure, the view across the Channel was magnificent. But until the situation with Napoleon was resolved, this particular stretch of coastline couldn't be considered an ideal purchase. The towers alone were enough to put off a prospective buyer.

But what was he thinking? Nathan could never own Seabrook. Even if something were to happen to him, the property would go to his mother.

A hard knot formed in Devon's stomach. Unless

something were to happen to her too. His mother's
near fatal accident now made sense. With both of them
dead, Nathan could lay claim to this estate. But why
would he want Seabrook? Surely the sale of the property wouldn't net him all that much. The land was too
rocky to grow a decent crop.

Devon stiffened. The towers! Whoever owned the land
controlled the towers. With the towers unmanned and
the coastline virtually unprotected, Napoleon would have
no difficulty landing his ships on British soil.

"You said my cousin brought a buyer for Seabrook.
What was the man's name?"

The guard scratched his beard in thought. "Lord
Carruthers, I think it were," he said.

"I'll be needing your help," Devon said. "I must get
to London tonight."

Since Captain Winslow was preparing for a trip to
Seabrook at first light, he was surprised to discover
Devon, tired and dirty, pounding on his door at two
in the morning.

The *Liberty* had docked the previous evening and the
log had been turned over to the Lord Chancellor. But
there was no way Devon could know about that.

"You look like a sailor who hasn't seen a port for a
year," Winslow exclaimed. "Let me ring for some
warm water, then we'll talk."

When Devon had finished freshening up, he sat
down to a hot breakfast.

Winslow waited until Devon had finished most of his
meal before telling him of the *Liberty*'s docking. "The logbook is in the hands of the Lord Chancellor. It will be presented before the House of Lords at noon tomorrow."

Devon smiled over his cup of coffee. "Can you take
some more good news?"

"Such as?"

"Such as what Lord Carruthers hoped to gain by my
conviction for treason."

Winslow leaned forward. "What have you learned?"

"It was really quite simple once I discovered Lord Carruthers was trying to purchase Seabrook." He went on to explain about the towers that overlooked the Channel.

"And with Seabrook, he could ensure Napoleon's ships a safe crossing," Winslow finished for him.

"It was the reason my death was not enough. Seabrook would have gone to Mother. That's why Nathan's men tried to force her carriage off the road. It was the only way he could inherit the coastal property." Devon paused. "But I suspect there's more. Do you recall when you came to Burnshire the day after my wedding? You had someone watching Nathan and his men and you gave me a report of your findings."

"Nathan's man was watching the docks for their comrade to return. Of course, they didn't realize at the time that he was dead."

Devon waved that aside in his excitement. "Do you recall the incident with the two lads he had with him? How they picked a man's pocket who turned out to be the king's courier?"

Edward's eyes lit with understanding. "The lads weren't after coins. They were after official papers. That means . . ."

"Exactly," Devon said. "They were not there to spot their comrade. The courier was their reason from the very beginning. That's why they didn't return."

Edward smiled. "If this proves true, it won't be long until we have the real traitor."

"It'll not be too soon for me." Devon suddenly grew quiet, his earlier excitement turned to concern. He still worried for Danielle's safety. What had she been doing that night at Lord Carruthers'? He might as well admit it and be done with it. Despite every argument he presented to himself, despite her protestations of love just a few hours ago, he still couldn't manage to shake the jealousy that was burning in his heart. Lord help him, he'd never had to deal with this kind of doubt before he met Danielle.

Chapter 21

I t was late afternoon before Captain Winslow's coach deposited Devon at his London town house. The draperies were drawn back and as Devon approached the front door, it opened. The news of his day in the House of Lords must have traveled quickly.

"Lady Chalmers awaits you in the drawing room," the butler announced.

"Has my driver arrived from Burnshire?"

"He's been waiting since two, your Grace."

Devon frowned. He was tired. He hadn't slept since yesterday morning. The meeting with Winslow and the Lord Chancellor had taken longer than he had expected, and all he wanted to do now was change his clothes, have a light supper, and be on his way back to Burnshire. He needed to talk with Danielle. He cursed himself for not being able to shake this nagging doubt about her and Carruthers. It was not often his instincts were wrong. He prayed they were this time.

"Do you wish me to tell Lady Chalmers you're not at home, your Grace?" the butler asked.

"No. Order hot water to be sent to my room for a bath. If Lady Emily cares to wait until I'm through, I'll see her."

"Very good, your Grace," he said with a bow.

Devon shrugged into his waistcoat, tucked the ends of his cravat in place, then went downstairs. A few moments with Lady Emily should tell him whether the *ton* was accepting the proof of his innocence. Still he stood outside the drawing room door, debating the necessity of seeing her. Reluctantly, he opened it.

Lady Emily watched him cross the room. His broad shoulders still had a way of turning her thoughts to lust. "I was so relieved to hear that those silly charges had been dropped that I felt I must come and offer my congratulations."

"That was very kind of you. I hope all my friends feel the same."

Emily patted her blond curls and threw him a dazzling smile. "Good heavens, Devon, you are the Duke of Burnshire. Of course everyone believed you were innocent from the very beginning."

"It's so comforting to know my friends remained loyal," he replied dryly.

Lady Emily coyly lowered her eyes. "Your butler said you were leaving for Burnshire this evening."

"I have a few moments. What was it you wished to speak with me about?"

"I know you're most anxious to return to your lovely wife," she said, stepping so close she had to tilt her head back to look into his face.

She peeked at him through lashes that looked suspiciously like they had been trailed through a black smudge pot. Shamelessly she toyed with the button on his shirt. "But . . . I hoped I could lure you away for the evening to celebrate your victory. After all, you must eat, and Lady Cromwell sets the most wonderful table. We—"

"I'm afraid I must disappoint you. I have been gone too long from Burnshire. My wife needs me."

She tapped Devon's broad chest with her fan. "So like a husband to feel that his wife cannot manage without him. But you needn't worry about the duchess. She's being looked after, and very well, I might add."

Devon arched a dark brow. "Yes?"

The rigid line of his jaw set her heart racing. Heavens, how could she have forgotten that the man was every bit as enticing as his wealth? She fluttered her long lashes. "Now, Devon, don't be too hard on Danielle. You know we ladies get lonely. And no matter what he says, I truly believe Lord Carruthers is but a mere diversion."

"Lord Carruthers?" As soon as he said the name, he regretted it. If only he could rid himself of the memory of Danielle sneaking into White Oaks.

Emily was decidedly vexed at his calm acceptance of her news. "Don't be coy with me, Devon," she said. "Are you going to tell me you've been in London the entire day and haven't heard what's being said about your wife? Apparently, in your absence she and Thomas have become quite the best of friends. Why . . ." Lady Emily paused. The scrutiny of those piercing blue eyes cut to her soul. ". . . she calls on him for the most trivial of things," she finished, suddenly forgetting the rest of her speech.

Devon's gut twisted into a knot. He should know better than to listen to anything Lady Emily had to say, he told himself. He knew she was a terrible gossip. Still, he couldn't seem to banish the pain that tore at his heart. But he'd not let her know how much her words hurt him.

"I think you misunderstand, Lady Emily. Lord Carruthers is one of our closest neighbors. I asked him to answer any questions Danielle might have concerning the estate. He did me a great favor."

"It was a favor?" she asked, disappointed that more could not be made of it. "Why, he never said so. What with their secret meetings and all, he seemed quite taken with her."

Secret meetings? It took every ounce of his strength not to smash the table beside him. There had to be an explanation for all this, he kept repeating to himself. "Perhaps he only meant to tease you," he said, forcing a smile.

"And after all the details he confided to me. Well, you can believe that when next we meet, I'll have a few words with him." She turned and scooped up her cloak from the sofa. "And you may tell her Grace I think it most unfeeling of them to make me the object of their little joke."

"Will you please accept my apologies for her? She will be devastated to learn you took to heart what I'm sure she meant only in fun."

Devon's nonchalance gave Emily pause, but it only took until she'd stepped into her carriage for her to decide that Devon was the one being duped. After all, she knew what she knew. There was no mistaking what Lord Carruthers had confided that evening. The man was positively smitten with the duchess. Well, no matter. Emily had done her duty. Devon was apprised of the situation. Let that little red-haired hussy try to lie her way out of this.

The wind was kicking up quite a summer squall, but it was nothing compared to the storm that brewed in the eyes of the Duke of Burnshire as he drove his horses to the gates of White Oaks. His promise to the Lord Chancellor to do nothing until they could bait a trap for Carruthers battled with his need to know if there was any truth to Lady Emily's gossip.

With the ease born to one who knows his animals, he brought the racing team to a stop in front of the stone house.

"I won't be long, Jem," he said, tossing the reins to his driver. As he jumped down, a cold drizzle began to fall.

"Where is he?" Devon demanded of the startled butler.

"The drawing room, your Grace."

He pushed past the butler unannounced and banged the drawing room doors so hard it set the pictures to rattling.

"I've been expecting you," Thomas said. He held out a crystal brandy decanter. "Would you care for a drink, Stanton?"

The muscle along Devon's jaw twitched. "I make it a policy to drink only with friends."

Thomas poured himself a generous glassful. "Such a shame you don't have many of them."

As God was his witness, Devon would find a way to bait the trap himself. "My friends didn't question my innocence, and as you saw today, their faith was not misplaced."

Lord Carruthers lowered his glass. "Ah, yes. The ship's log. So fortunate for you the *Liberty* docked before the Crown saw fit to hang you."

"Disappointed?" Devon asked, hate boiling in him.

"What are you saying? That I would wish to hang an innocent man? You forget, Stanton, there were witnesses. Your own men, I might add."

"Men you hired."

Lord Carruthers' eyes shifted to the door.

"Oh yes, I know of your lies."

His face flushed red at Devon's words.

"I—I d-don't know what you mean," he stuttered, suddenly struck by the overwhelming presence of his visitor.

The promise Devon had made to the Lord Chancellor was the only thing that kept him from bringing White Oaks down around this man's ears. But he had come here about Danielle. He would deal with affairs of state later.

"You deny any knowledge of the lies Lady Emily is bandying about?"

Lord Carruthers visibly relaxed as he set his glass down. He slowly ran his tongue over his moist lips. Stanton was upset. There was no doubt about that. The hint of an affair had been a stroke of genius. Perhaps even more than he had hoped.

Quickly he reviewed the possibilities. Did Stanton value his lady's honor enough to fight for it? A duel might succeed where the accusations hadn't. There were not many men who could stand up to Thomas' skill with either the sword or the pistol. He knew the consequences should knowledge of the duel become known. But he was willing to take the chance if it meant he could put an end to the life of this arrogant bastard.

"You married the woman to claim your inheritance. Surely you didn't expect her loyalty also?"

"I asked you about Lady Emily's lies," Devon stated flatly.

"Lady Emily happened to be here when her Grace paid a visit. Danielle was worried about you. She was lonely. You cannot hold me responsible for whatever conclusions Lady Emily may have drawn."

"According to her, you provided the conclusions."

Devon didn't miss the feral gleam in Carruthers' eyes. He took a step forward. Pounds to pence, whatever the man said next would be a lie.

The corner of Thomas' lip lifted in a smile. Jealousy did strange things to a man. It suddenly seemed a shame that his bullet would put an end to Stanton's pain.

He threw up his hands in mock despair. "Danielle is a beautiful woman. I can hardly be expected to toss aside what she so willingly offers."

Before he could restrain himself, Devon planted a punch along Carruthers' jaw, sending the man flying into one of the many tables that crowded the drawing room.

Thomas shook his head in an attempt to clear the ringing in his head. He looked up at Devon from his position on the floor. Hate burned within him. A pistol was too quick. And this pirate deserved nothing less than the slow death caused by a sword twisted in his gut.

"Give her up, Stanton," he shouted. "It's my bed she seeks now."

Devon removed his gloves, a finger at a time. With powerful hands he reached down and pulled Lord Carruthers to his feet. A triumphant smile played across his opponent's lips. The realization that Lord Carruthers was deliberately baiting him caused Devon to pause. It was then he noticed Danielle's blue cloak draped over the edge of the sofa. All emotion drained from him. His gloves slipped to the floor. Suddenly he no longer wanted to fight Carruthers.

Thomas sensed the change in Devon. He would not allow Devon's rage to slip away so easily, not when the man was on the verge of challenging him. "Ask your wife whose idea it was to have you arrested for treason."

Devon could only stare at him.

With another triumphant grin, Thomas pushed his advantage. "It was the only way she could be free to marry me."

Devon shoved Lord Carruthers, then stumbled from him. Lies. All lies, he repeated to himself. But betrayal branded him like a hot poker. He picked up Danielle's cloak and turned to leave. He had to talk with Danielle, to hold her in his arms, feel her heart beating against his. But most importantly, he wanted to hear her say Carruthers was lying. He had reached the front door when he heard Lord Carruthers shout.

"Stanton!"

He didn't bother to turn but stood poised in the doorway. Somehow he knew he didn't want to hear what Carruthers had to say, but his feet wouldn't move.

"Even now she carries my child."

Devon stiffened. With his shoulders squared, he continued through the door and down the front steps. Wearily, he climbed into the coach.

A child. Why hadn't she told him? She had lain in his arms at Seabrook and not said a word. But the militia had arrived. Perhaps she had meant to tell him, but there had not been time. Or could she have been the one to lead the militia to Seabrook? But to accept that he would have to also accept that she had merely made love to him to keep him occupied until they could lay their trap.

Damnation! If he accepted that lie, he'd have to believe his marriage was a lie from the very beginning. He'd have to believe the scene he'd witnessed between her and Nathan about the false engagement had been staged for his benefit.

No, it could not be. He had no doubts that Nathan was working with Carruthers, but Danielle? How would she get word to them? Robert kept a close eye on the comings and goings at Burnshire. Other than the one note and the visit, she would have had no opportunity. The only one who met with Nathan was Danielle's dresser. Devon's chest tightened. It would have been so easy.

Jem almost didn't hear the tap on the coachman's door above the howl of the wind. He was soaked and could only hope the summons meant his Grace was of a mind to stop at the inn up ahead.

He slid the door open and could hardly believe his ears when the duke told him to do so. He laid the lines along the broad rumps of the coach horses and leaned back. A glass of ale would do much to warm his insides.

Devon hardly noticed the cold rain as he stepped from the coach. His thoughts were much too crowded with pain for mere physical concerns. Danielle and Carruthers. She had lain in his arms and loved another. A harsh, cynical smile darkened his handsome features. She had always been such a good little actress.

He entered the inn. The sharp smell of ale permeated the crowded common room, and a fireplace covering the far wall belched ashes with each gust of the wind. He strode across the wood plank floor, stopping at a small table along the wall that had just been vacated. Devon lowered his lean, hard-muscled frame into a chair. Waving aside the innkeeper, who came rushing up with a fresh tablecloth, he tossed his beaver felt onto the wine-stained one.

"Bring me your best brandy."

Devon's sharp words sent the innkeeper scurrying back among the tables, his short, round body stirring up the swirls of smoke emanating from the clay pipes of the local patrons. Devon crossed his long legs under the table.

A tight smile was his only acknowledgment to the barmaid who brought the bottle of brandy. She leaned across the table and filled his glass.

"Would you be caring for anything else, my lord?"

He looked at her for the first time. She flashed him a bright smile. Like most of the tavern wenches of his experience, she wore a puff-sleeved blouse designed to hide none of her attributes.

His dark, heavy brows drew together in a frown as he seriously considered her offer. The chit is comely, he thought, and it would be no more than what Danielle deserved.

Hell, what was he thinking? No wench could heal the injury Danielle had done to his heart. She was a part of him he could never cut out. He waved the barmaid away. The brandy would be all he needed to get him though this night. He tipped the glass.

Finishing it, he had another, and then another. Patrons of the tavern came and went, but Devon remained seated at the table. Danielle was expecting a child? No. The implications of that were more than he could handle now. He took another swallow of the brandy.

He drank until he couldn't see her emerald-green eyes laughing up at him anymore. Then he drank until he couldn't feel the pain.

"Me wife left me too, she did."

Devon forced an eyelid open and looked across the table at the man who shared his bottle. He didn't recall when he'd ask the farmer to join him. Lord, he felt awful. He licked his dry lips and tried to concentrate on what his companion was saying.

"Me own brother, it were." The farmer leaned across the table. "Kick 'er out, I say. I mean, wha' choice do ye 'ave? This lord . . ." He waved his hand about. "This friend done ye a favor, the way I sees it."

Devon tried to pull his thoughts together. "Wasn't a friend," he slurred.

The farmer's head shot up. "Not a friend!" he shouted. Expending so much energy tired him and he took another drink. "Well, 'e's not an enemy, 'cause enemies never do a fella a favor," he said, pleased with this sudden insight. "If 'e's not an enemy, then 'e be your friend."

Devon's brow wrinkled in concentration. Somehow it seemed important to make his companion understand, but his tongue kept getting in the way of his words. "Man's a foe," he finally managed to say.

The farmer sniffed indignantly. "Can't be a foe. A fella don't listen to a foe. Ain't no trustin' 'is words."

No trustin' 'is words. No trustin' 'is words. What the farmer had said bounced around like butterflies inside Devon's head. He tried desperately to catch them and hold onto them long enough to determine what they meant, but the brandy won out. For the first time in his life, he was drunk.

" 'Tis time we were leaving," Jem said as he tried to help Devon to his feet. The storm had let up, but it was black as the devil's eyes outside and they still had a way to go. He hoped his Grace was sober enough to hold his seat, for he'd not be sparing the horses on a night like this.

Jem draped Lord Stanton's arm around his shoulders and helped him out.

Devon stopped at the steps to the coach and whispered, "Did you know a foe will lie to you, Jem?"

Jem frantically searched the shadows along the roadside. He had no time for silly questions. Lord only knew what was out on this road tonight, and him without so much as a footman to help him should a dastardly spirit present himself.

"I heard something like that the other day," Jem said just before shoving the Duke of Burnshire into his coach and slamming the door.

No trusting his words.
The farmer had known what he was talking about. After hearing Robert's explanation of Danielle's escapade, Devon felt like an utter fool.

Devon held his pounding head between his hands. This was surely God's punishment for his lack of trust in his wife. In the light of day, it was obvious that what Lady Emily had told him was a lie. And he had been so quick to believe her. Carruthers' collaboration should have been proof enough. After all, the man had conspired with Nathan to have him hung. What was one more lie? He bowed his head in disbelief. Had there ever been a bigger fool?

His eyes fell on the blue cloak. There was only one way Carruthers could have gotten it. Mrs. Meacham must have given it to him. But why was it important that everyone believe the rumors? Did they hope he'd hear of them and march back to Burnshire and demand an explanation from his wife? The plan had its merits. If he'd come out of hiding, a shot from an overzealous militiaman might have saved the hangman the trouble.

He raked his fingers through his dark hair. That still didn't explain Carruthers' parting comment. To be sure, he could have mentioned the child out of spite, but Devon suddenly worried for Danielle's safety. Now the child, if a boy, would also stand between Nathan and what he wanted. Why did they appear so unconcerned? Had they expected him to return home in a rage and beat Danielle? Or was public denial all they hoped for?

His dark brows snapped together in a frown. If he had believed their lies and something were to happen to Danielle and the child, who would protest their untimely demise?

Devon shot off the bed and rang for his valet. He couldn't wait for the Lord Chancellor to bait a trap. Danielle and his child could be dead by then. He had promised them he wouldn't interfere with their plans. Well, he wouldn't, but that didn't mean he couldn't lay a plan of his own.

Devon had to wait over an hour before Danielle returned to her room to freshen up for lunch. With his hand on the door of her bedchamber, he hesitated.

What he was preparing to do might very well mean the end of her love for him. Even though her life depended on his ability to carry his plan through, could he really do this to the woman who was carrying his child? He had considered telling her what he intended to do. Her acting abilities were good, but no one was as good as she would have to be.

Mrs. Meacham was helping his wife into a lemon-yellow day dress when Devon, carrying the blue cloak, pushed open the door. As soon as Danielle saw him, she stepped out of the gown and ran to him.

"Devon, it's over," she said, throwing her arms about him.

He stood stiff in her embrace. "Are you saying you're pleased?" he asked dryly.

She stepped back and studied his face in confusion. "Of course I'm pleased. I wanted to wake you when I found you had returned last evening." She smiled up at him. "But someone celebrated a wee bit too much."

To say more would only tell him of her disappointment that he had not come directly home. When he didn't smile, she tweaked his cheek playfully. "My, but we've been bitten by the bug this morning, haven't we?"

Devon caught her hand neatly in his. She lifted her eyes trustingly to his, and his heart twisted in regret for what he must do.

"Don't ever touch me again," he snarled.

Danielle stepped back from the hatred etched on his face. "Whatever is wrong?"

"This is wrong," he said, shoving the blue cloak at her.

"Oh, you've found it," Danielle cried. She grabbed it from him, then paused. "This is why you're upset? Because I misplaced your gift?"

Stretching up on her toes, she placed a kiss on his rigid jaw. "I'm truly sorry," she said, handing the cloak to Mrs. Meacham. "For the life of me, I couldn't recall where I might have left it."

"You should have tried White Oaks."

"Oh," she gasped. "I could not have left it there. You see . . ."

His eyes were blue chips of ice and she could feel the frost touching her heart. He knew of her broken promise and he didn't appear ready to forgive her this time. "Nathan returned Jeremy to Lord Carruthers. I could not leave him there."

"You could have sent Giles," he said gruffly. "Or was Jeremy but a ruse?"

Mrs. Meacham used the opportunity to slip out, but Devon noticed she left the door ajar.

Danielle could only stand and stare. This was ludicrous.

"You did not need to go yourself," he shouted.

"But I could not send Giles, you see, for the instruction that Jeremy was to be returned to the orphanage appeared to come from you."

"I sent no such instruction."

"I was sure of that, but don't you see?" she pleaded. "Giles believed it came from you and would never have gone against it."

Devon held out his hand. "Give me the note," he demanded.

"I—I don't have it."

She had never seen Devon like this, and he was beginning to frighten her. Why was he so upset? "Perhaps Mrs. Talbut kept it. Or perhaps Andrews. Or Giles," she cried. "What does it matter? Nathan must have sent it."

She grabbed at his sleeve. "Don't you see? He thought I would run to you. He hoped I would lead him to your hiding place."

"Yet you thought nothing of coming the next day. You had no qualms about directing them to Seabrook then," he said, grabbing her arm. "To think, all this time, I blamed Nathan. I thought him my enemy. But it was you from the very beginning. It was your idea that I be hung for treason, wasn't it?"

Heaven help her. He thought she had betrayed him. "How can you believe that?"

"Your lover informed me."

"Lover?" she gasped, her voice barely a whisper. All she could see through the black curtain that threatened to close in on her was the unforgiving line of his jaw.

He caught her swaying body roughly against him. He hoped she'd faint before she heard the rest of the words he must say.

"Your lover!" he shouted in her face. "The father of your child."

"You are the father of my child," she choked.

"That's what you would like me to believe, isn't it? Consider yourself fortunate. A child will serve my purpose well. The threat of an heir is just what I need to stir Nathan's ire. He need not know it's not mine."

Feebly, she pushed against him. "Y-you're mad," she said, swallowing the hot tears that burned her throat. "I'll not let you condemn my child—no, our child—in this manner. I'm leaving."

"To run to your lover? Like hell you will! You will remain here until I am finished with your services."

Danielle could only stare at the stranger he had become. "My services?" she echoed.

Devon saw the door open a fraction more. He had to finish what he had started. His only prayer was that someday he would be given the opportunity to heal the hurt he was inflicting today. He took a deep breath. "Don't act the innocent, love," he said with a sneer. "This child may be your lover's, but I'll make sure the next one you carry is mine."

She twisted in his arms. "I'll not play the broodmare for you."

"Oh, but you will, love." He laughed cruelly. "And once you've given me a son, you may leave with my blessing. I'll even allow you to take your *love* child with you."

She lifted her hand and slapped his smug face. "You bastard!"

Chapter 22

Devon tossed the whiskey down, welcoming the fire that burned his throat. It would take a lot more of the same to wash away the memory of Danielle's horror at his accusations. He set his empty glass on the desk. He must keep his wits about him.

He ran his fingers through his dark hair. The argument he'd had with Danielle would only serve as a brief respite for Nathan's anger. With his greed he could never afford to let the child be born. A few days would be all Devon needed. He hoped their belief that he refused to acknowledge the child as his own might give him the time he required. He had never meant to place Danielle in danger, but in his reckless desire for revenge, that was exactly what he had done.

"May I speak with you a moment?" Mrs. Meacham stood in the doorway of his study, her hands clasped tightly in front of her. Curious as to what she might want, he motioned her to take a seat.

Elizabeth twisted the handkerchief she carried in her fingers. She couldn't live with her part in this any longer, even if it meant losing Katie. Danielle would raise Katie as her own. Her pain now was more than Elizabeth could bear. How was she to begin? She took a deep breath and rushed forward.

"Pardon me for saying so, your Grace, but you're making a terrible mistake. Lady Stanton would never have an affair with the likes of Lord Carruthers."

Devon frowned. "What would you know of the matter?"

"I saw Jeremy when she brought him back," she confessed. His Grace's black look almost took her breath away but she forced herself to go on. "The lad was painted as brazenly as a lady of the evening," she continued, feeling her face warm under his close scrutiny.

Devon arched a dark brow. "You're saying Lord Carruthers' taste runs to young boys."

She fastened her gaze on the crystal inkwell. "I have heard it does happen sometimes, your Grace." She took another deep breath. "But there's more."

Just how much was she willing to reveal? he wondered. "Yes?" he prompted.

"I was the one who gave the cloak to the vicar. So it stands to reason if Lord Carruthers had it, he must be conspiring with the vicar to make you think there was an affair."

Devon leaned back in his chair. "And why would he do that?"

"I—I don't know," she admitted. For an instant she considered the possibility of dropping it there. No, it was time she washed her hands of the entire mess.

"The vicar's man let it slip that they had conspired to prove you guilty of treason and were furious to see their plan fail."

"And you are a friend of one of the vicar's men?"

She dropped her eyes before his accusing ones. "The vicar pays me to report on what is happening at Burnshire. On occasion I meet with one of his men."

"You are a spy?"

"Y-yes," she answered, finally looking him in the eye.

Her quick reply surprised him. He wondered whether this confession was another one of Nathan's games. "And you tell them what?"

Once again she dropped her gaze. "I report on the intimacy of your marriage, your Grace."

He studied her bowed head. It was obvious the admission embarrassed her immensely, but how could he trust her? "How do I know that Nathan didn't pay you to say this?"

Her head shot up. "You don't, but you must believe me when I say her Grace is in danger."

"Why should I trust someone who is working for Nathan?"

Elizabeth withdrew a small linen square from the pocket of her gown and placed it on the desk. "Because the vicar paid me to slip this into her morning chocolate."

"What is it, a poison?"

"He assured me it wasn't, but in her Grace's condition, it might not have to be."

She explained then how she had prepared the cup of chocolate, only to change her mind and send it back to the kitchen.

Devon closed his fist over the packet. "Danielle would have lost the baby," he said. "And possibly her own life as well."

"That's why I felt I had to tell you. Don't you see, that's why the affair has to be a lie. If the baby were Lord Carruthers', why would they wish it dead?"

Devon rose from his chair. "You realize, of course, that I can no longer allow you to stay at Burnshire."

"I'm aware of that, but I could not stand it anymore." She tore at the corner of her handkerchief. "I lost my own child, your Grace, because my husband could not live with something he did not understand. Perhaps someday I will have her back, for I love her deeply. And if you love Danielle, please don't turn your back on her. Talk with her. Trust that her explanation is the truth."

"You've given me a lot to think over, Mrs. Meacham. But before you leave, I need you to deliver another bit of information to my dear cousin."

Devon outlined his plan for her to tell Nathan of the quarrel. She readily agreed. After she left, he sent Robert to follow her, then went to the kitchens.

All the food that Danielle ate from this point forward would be prepared by the cook personally or sampled before it was brought to the table. He considered sending for Brodie and taking her into his confidence, but decided she was too close to Danielle. She would be too tempted to tell Danielle of his plans to draw Nathan and Carruthers out.

He would guard Danielle constantly. She was napping when he reached her room, and he made himself comfortable in the chair beside her bed. Her eyes were swollen from the tears, and he hated himself for what he'd done. He should be holding her in his arms, celebrating the wonder of the child they had created, not causing her pain. Would she ever forgive him?

Damn Nathan's greed!

He had learned at an early age that Nathan was evil. His jealousy knew no limits. There was the favorite colt that came up lame . . . the strays Devon took in, drowned or poisoned . . . the deeds laid at Devon's door.

He buried his face in his hands. How had he allowed himself to forget? Well, Nathan would not have Danielle, not if Devon had to remain at her side forever.

Danielle fought the worries that were pulling her from her nap. How could he believe the awful lies about her? Was his memory so short that he couldn't recall that when he had been accused of treason, she had stood by him? The answer was simple. She loved him, but he could never bring himself to care for her. He would always believe she had betrayed him with another. A tear slipped down her cheek.

"Are the false tears for me?" Devon asked cruelly.

Her eyes flew open. Quickly she wiped her fingers across her cheeks. "I waste no tears for those without hearts."

"Then do not keep me waiting. Andrews will be announcing supper soon. Mary will help you dress."

She turned her back to him. "I'll eat in my room," she said.

"And have the servants think I'm mistreating my wife?"

"And you think they did not hear you ranting at me earlier?" Danielle snapped back.

"It makes no difference. We'll dine together. If you are determined to eat in your room, I'll eat here also."

Danielle's eyes narrowed suspiciously. "Why are you doing this?"

"I don't enjoy being the cuckold, my dear. Until I can find a way of disposing of your lover, I'll not have you slipping away to be with him."

The tears gone, Danielle's eyes darkened with anger. "Although I have no objections to your putting a bullet in Lord Carruthers' black heart, I do resent being a prisoner in my own home."

He steepled his fingers before him. "I believe that aptly describes the situation."

She slipped off the bed. "If I am to be plagued with your constant companionship, my lord, I'd rather it not be in my bedchamber. Please leave so I can change."

He stubbornly remained in his chair. "I don't think you understand, love. I plan on staying by your side."

"At all times?"

"I or someone I trust."

"But that's ridiculous."

"But that's the way it will be."

His cold eyes mocked her, but she refused to give in to the tears that stung her eyes.

"Be a dear and get dressed. I'm famished."

She opened the door to the armoire.

"It's a rather warm evening, love. Your yellow gown with the blue ribbons will be your best choice."

She pulled out her light blue gown. Tossing it across a chair, she slipped into the bathing chamber.

Devon jumped up to follow. Danielle had moved the chair aside and was struggling with the large bathing screen. Determinedly she tugged at it until the hand-painted panels reluctantly slid across the glass tiles.

"What's this for?" he asked as he helped her guide it through the door and across the bedchamber to the fireplace.

She retrieved her gown from the chair. "I learned when I was a small girl never to parade in front of raging bulls or fools," she said, adjusting the screen.

"I am not raging," he protested.

She slipped behind the screen. "I wasn't counting you the bull, my lord," she said over the panels.

He smiled to himself. At least as long as she was ranting at him, she wasn't crying. He made himself comfortable on the bed as he waited for her to finish.

"Do you need my help?" he asked.

"I learned as a small girl—"

"Can I be the bull this time?" he shouted before she could finish.

He was sure he'd heard her giggle before she turned it into a cough.

She stepped out from behind the screen. "I was going to say I learned as a small girl to dress myself. But if you want to be known as a bull also, I'll not argue with you." She patted a stray curl in place. "I'm ready now. Shall we go?"

"I've yet to change," he told her.

"I'll meet you in the drawing room."

"Oh, no, you don't," he said, taking her by the arm. "You'll stay with me."

"But I have no wish to sit around while you dress."

"I promise you'll not be bored."

She eyed him skeptically.

He leaned down and whispered, "You see, I don't have a screen."

A warm tingle crawled up her back, but she shrugged it away. The man was past all redemption. He accused her of betraying him, then, in the next breath, attempted to seduce her. Worst of all, she found herself enjoying it.

When they reached his room, he dismissed his valet. He stood in front of her as he shrugged out of his waistcoat. His cravat came next; then he slowly unbuttoned his shirt. His eyes never left hers. She didn't dare lower her gaze, for she knew it would go directly to his furred chest. The shirt slipped off his back. She could see the muscles work in his broad shoulders and she knew without looking that he was unbuttoning the corduroy breeches that hugged his slender hips.

Desire darkened his blue eyes and Danielle was sure she had stopped breathing. She swallowed the lump in her throat. Her heart was racing and the room suddenly grew warm. She unbuttoned the first few pearl buttons on her gown, but that did not cool the fires he ignited within her.

He held out his hand. "I want you," he said, his voice a husky whisper of desire. Would he ever have the strength to follow through with what he must do?

Heaven help her, but she stepped into his arms.

"He'll not touch you again, Danielle," he whispered against her lips. "You are mine now. Now and forever."

His words were like a bucket of cold water. He had not meant to apologize for his jealousy. He only meant to punish her further.

She pushed him away. "You think me a fool?" she asked through clenched teeth.

He cupped her breast and ran his finger over the taut nipple. "You definitely don't look like a bull."

She lifted her hand to slap him, but he caught it and pulled her back to him. His arm went around her. He released her hand and began to unfasten the rest of the buttons on her gown.

"You want me too," he whispered.

"Desire is not love, Devon."

He lowered his head to hers. "When did I say I wanted love?" he said cruelly.

Although she didn't pull away from his kiss, he could taste the salt of her tears. God save him. He wanted her too much to release her, but he loved her too much to continue. He only needed to make sure she understood how it would be.

"I'd take you now, but we shouldn't be late for supper."

She glared up at him. What kind of game was he playing? Despite all he'd said, she knew with a certainty he would never have touched her if he truly believed she had taken another man to her bed. He could lie to himself, but he couldn't lie to her. It was a game—a game she was all too familiar with. Hadn't she played the same game of denial when they were first married? But how long would he treat her in this manner before he realized what he was doing? For both their sakes, it had best not be for long. With trembling fingers, she refastened the pearl buttons. "I'm famished, too," she said, pasting a smile on her face.

He did not even bother to turn the other way as he finished unbuttoning his breeches. It was clear he meant to discomfort her. She waited until he began peeling them off. Boldly she allowed her eyes to rake his body like he had done to her so often.

"When you've finished strutting your nakedness," she said, "you may join me for supper."

She swept out of the room, leaving Devon stumbling in the leggings of his breeches.

"Hell and damnation," she heard him shout, and for the first time since Devon's return, she understood what he meant.

Each bite she took turned to dust in her mouth, but she forced herself to swallow it. His foolish pride was making him act this way. And everyone had always accused her of being the impulsive one, of always doing things before she thought them out. Well, she would show them all. She would be the rational one in this marriage. It was up to her to teach him the error of his ways.

Devon choked on his bite of pastry. Oh, Lord, what was she thinking now? he wondered. That smile could only mean one thing. She was scheming again. Whatever it was, he'd have to see that she hadn't a moment alone to carry it out.

With dessert cleared, he carried his port into the drawing room. Danielle frowned when he took the seat next to her. But she ignored him, picked up her book, and began reading. He watched her slim fingers turn the pages, all the while imagining them stroking his back.

Suddenly an icy fear gripped him. What if she never forgave him? He downed his port in one swallow. This was nonsense. He couldn't continue like this. He got up, excused himself, and left Danielle to her book. He stepped out into the hall and signaled Robert. After a few words of instruction to keep an eye on Danielle, he went to talk with Mrs. Meacham.

She had spoken with Nathan.

"The vicar appeared pleased with your denial of the child's parentage," she told him. "But I still fear he will never allow the child to be born."

"I will take care of it," he assured her. "In the meantime, I've changed my mind about your leaving. I may have further need of your services."

He wished he felt as confident as his words. He left Mrs. Meacham with an even greater weight on his shoulders. He had yet to figure out how to arrange it so that Danielle and the child no longer posed a threat to Nathan's hope of inheriting Burnshire someday. He could not wait on the Lord Chancellor's investigations. A plan would have to be formulated immediately. In the meantime, he would stay close to Danielle. Except for the strain of not being able to hold her, how difficult could it be?

His confidence took a tumble when he reached the drawing room, only to discover Danielle was no longer there. He took the stairs two at a time.

"Why did you allow her to leave?" he demanded of Robert.

Robert continued to lean against Danielle's door. "No one allows the duchess anything. You should know that better than anyone."

"Is she alone?"

"Do you think I'd be standing in the hall if I were welcome in her bedchamber? And since I haven't developed the talent of seeing beyond closed doors, how am I to know who she might have in her room?" he asked indignantly.

"She trimmed your sails a bit, Robert?"

"Well, if you continue in this manner, she'll do the same for you too."

"Got a bit testy with you, did she?" He raised his hand to ward off Robert's glare. "I only wanted to know if one of the servants was with her. You can return to your duties now, but keep a sharp eye out. I'll take over from here.''

The maid had forgotten to close the draperies and soft moonlight filled the room. Danielle lay sleeping, her hair a blood red against the white pillow. The night was warm and she'd pushed her covers aside. Her legs, tangled in the sheets, dredged up painful memories of their time together. Lord, he'd have to resolve this soon. He had thought to get her out of his mind when they had made love, but he only wanted her more. He took one of the chairs next to the fireplace. How could he ever leave her when it was over? Placing his booted feet onto the other chair, he prepared for his night's vigil. If he didn't find some way to stop Nathan, nothing would matter.

He thought about the problem late into the night, the solution coming to him with the first light of dawn. With the last of the details still to be worked out, he slipped into sleep.

Danielle awoke to find him slumped in the chair. Seeing the dark circles under his eyes, she suppressed the impulse to wake him and demand his reasons for watching her every move. He shifted restlessly and Danielle's attention was caught by the ripple of muscle beneath his opened shirt. Longingly, she drank in the sight of the crisp, dark hairs curling over the edges of the linen.

How could he be so stubborn as to persist in this farce? He had told her that he loved her, and more and more she suspected the cruel words he'd thrown at her had been spoken out of jealousy and hurt. Love was not something that was cast aside so easily. Even now, after all he'd accused her of, she still loved him. She bent over to kiss his cheek.

Through the slits of his sleep-filled eyes, Devon watched the desire grow within her. When she leaned down, he reached out for her. She gasped at his touch, but he feigned being still lost in sleep to pull her into his lap. He buried his face in her hair, a long sigh escaping his lips. She tensed, but soon relaxed when she thought him asleep.

Although his heart beat at an alarming rate, Devon managed to keep his breathing even. She shifted in his arms. Damn. If she did that again, she'd soon discover he was more than just awake. There were certain things a man couldn't control.

She parted the edges of his shirt.

His heart picked up a pace.

Breathe, man!

In, out. In, out.

He wasn't prepared for the soft touch of her lips against the hollow of his neck. A groan, wrenched from deep within him, spilled out. He opened his eyes and looked at her. She peeked up at him. Her lips trembled despite the boldness of her actions.

There was no help for him. He crushed her to him, the silkiness of her thin nightdress burning his chest with its cool fire. His lips sought hers. She was satin and lace, and a hint of lavender. A treasure he was about to lose.

His tongue skimmed her lips roughly until she opened them to him. Without mercy, he plundered her honeyed mouth. She struggled against him, but he ignored her protests. She would hate him for what he was about to do.

His kiss suddenly turned tender, and Danielle could feel herself responding to the bittersweet need in him. He still loved her. She was sure of it. Her heart twisted for the agony he must have suffered to have thought her guilty of giving herself to another. But he could not be kissing her as he was and still doubt that she loved him. She would show him that she forgave him for not trusting her. She buried her fingers in his dark hair and returned his kiss.

He swept her up in his arms and carried her to the bed. Danielle's heart beat with happiness. He had come to his senses. He knew she loved only him. He laid her on the bed and stepped back.

The smile froze on Danielle's face when she saw the

hurt that suddenly distorted his bronzed features. He wasn't going to let himself love her. She inched away from him.

"You play the strumpet so well, love," he whispered.

Danielle stiffened with anger.

He reached down and grabbed her wrist. "I should take you here and now," he snarled. "But I'll not spill my seed next to his." With that he turned and left the room.

Danielle curled up on the bed. Tears burned her throat, but she refused to give in to them. Damn his arrogant pride!

She didn't know how long she lay there, reviewing everything that had happened. But she couldn't rid herself of the suffering she had seen in his face. Their marriage was over. Despite his threats of retaliation, she knew in her heart he wouldn't remain in England long enough to carry them out.

She made herself get up and ring for Mary. Her mind was numb, her body a shell that stood stiffly while Mary dressed her. But her heart was twisted with pain. With nothing to hold him, Devon would surely return to his ships. He would never lay eyes on their child and know that he had been wrong.

Having finished with her toilette, she dismissed Mary. She spent the morning at her window, staring out at the hills beyond. Her heart continued to bleed until there was nothing left. No tears. No hurt. Only emptiness.

Then something deep within her stirred. It started out as a tiny bubble of self-pity that burst almost at the moment of its conception. Then suddenly it formed again in her mind, billowing and ballooning.

Why was she punishing herself? This was his fault, not hers. Yes, she had broken her promise by going to the orphanage. And she was willing to admit that she should have sent Giles, instead of rushing headlong into a dangerous situation. But what if Jeremy had Giles not been able to persuade Lord Carruthers to return him? No, in this instance she had done what she had to. How was she to know that Lord Carruthers would use it against her? She was not guilty, but she had surely been acting like it, sitting in her room.

"Damn his arrogant pride," she said aloud. "He may push me from his mind, but I'll not let him forget his child."

Danielle searched the unused rooms in the east wing until she found a suite that would suit her needs. Bob dogged her every step, but she chose to ignore him. If Devon wanted her every move noted, then he should find today's activities most interesting.

She took the tape from her pocket and made a few measurements. Yes, this should do. Satisfied, she crossed to the door and pulled the embroidered bell cord. Tapping her foot impatiently, she waited for her summons to be answered.

"Oh, it's you, Miss Danny," Katie called as she peeked into the room. She motioned to someone behind her. "You may come in, Jeremy. It's only Miss Danny."

Danielle knelt in front of the small girl. "You sound disappointed."

"We were a mite," Katie said, her lips in a pout. "You see, we were hoping you were the spirit."

Jeremy nodded his blond head in agreement.

"A spirit?" She'd have to have a talk with Mrs. Talbut. She couldn't allow the servants to frighten the children with tales of ghosts. "Burnshire has no spirits."

"Oh, but Jem says there's a right mean one."

Jeremy nodded again, his large eyes furtively scanning the room lest they be caught unawares.

"Katie, listen to me. There are no spirits at Burnshire."

"But he came and took the old duke. Jem says so. Jeremy and me came to ask the spirit to give the old duke back. Lord Stanton is ever so sad. If the old duke were back, he might smile again."

Danielle had thought there wasn't anything that would bring tears to her eyes again. She was wrong.

Chapter 23

Andrews stood watch outside Danielle's bedroom door while Robert relayed the day's happenings to Devon. The fact that Danielle had taken a new suite of rooms didn't bother him as much as what Katie had said about the spirit Jem swore he had heard. Devon did not believe a spirit had taken his father, but where would his driver have gotten such a notion? And obviously, the man believed it. Could it have something to do with the cottage in the woods?

He sent for Jem.

Devon looked up as his driver entered the study.

"Please take a seat, Jem. I have a few questions I'd like to ask you."

The driver looked at the chair dubiously, then shrugged his shoulders and sat down.

Devon leaned forward and continued. "One of the children tells me we have a ghost at Burnshire."

Jem shifted in his seat and nodded.

Devon tried again. "You'll have to help me out, Jem. Why do you think Burnshire has a ghost?"

The old man's hands twisted and untwisted his cap, but he didn't answer.

"Are you afraid if you tell me I'll dismiss you? Because if you are, I can promise you whatever you have to say will not jeopardize your position."

"I see'd 'em, I did," Jem blurted out. " 'Twas the

369

night the ol' duke died. More'n a year, it be now, they been walkin' the grounds of Burnshire.''

"You still see them?" Devon asked, his thoughts immediately turning to his fear for Danielle's safety.

"One of 'em tried to snatch the lad."

"Jeremy?"

"Would o' got 'im too iffen 'e 'ad not o' 'id like 'e did.''

Devon's mouth was suddenly powder-dry. "Tell me about the night my father died,'' he somehow managed to say.

"I 'ad a right bad ache in me bones that night,'' Jem said, warming to his story. "I was lying awake when I 'ears these two spirits saying as 'ow they was going to squeeze the life out o' the ol' duke. I was 'oping it were only the wind, but when I learns the next morning the duke 'as passed away, I knew it were them spirits all right. I packed me things and moved to the ol' woodcutter's cottage.''

Devon sat in his chair and continued to stare at Jem.

"You'll not be making me return to me ol' rooms, will ye?" Jem asked.

It was a moment before Devon answered him. "No, Jem. The cottage will remain yours for the time being.''

Devon dismissed him, but couldn't shake the certainty that what Jem had heard was the actual planning of his father's death. His father had been old. How much effort would it have taken?

He pulled out a sheet of paper. He would have to move quickly with his plan. The note to Captain Winslow was soon finished and posted off to London.

He took out a fresh sheet. Everything depended on the letter, and he agonized for the rest of the morning over the wording until he was sure he had gotten it right. After Andrews and Robert had witnessed the final draft, Devon sealed the letter and scrawled his solicitor's name across the papers.

He summoned Elizabeth.

"I asked you to come here because I need your assistance. I have something you must deliver to Nathan immediately.''

Elizabeth reluctantly took the sealed papers.

"After all that has happened, I cannot stay here any longer," he continued. "I'll be leaving in the morning for Brighton. My ship sails in two days."

After receiving Devon's final instructions, Elizabeth left the study. The duke watched her go, feeling confident that she'd do his bidding. At last, the wheels of his plan were turning.

Danielle turned around quickly enough to catch the look of sadness in Devon's eyes a split second before it turned into one of disgust. If he could stubbornly deny his love, so could she.

"All the furniture must be moved from this room," she instructed Mrs. Talbut.

The housekeeper looked at Devon. Danielle did not miss his nod of approval.

"This will make a fine nursery for our son, don't you agree, Devon?" she challenged him. Mrs. Talbut stepped from the room. "My bedchamber is next door, and the nurse will take the small sitting room for hers."

"You went to a great deal of trouble for nothing," he said. "I am leaving in the morning. The *Liberty* sets sail in two days. I'll be on it."

She refused to acknowledge the pain his news caused her. Instead, she busied herself with the fabric swatches.

"What do you think of this one?" she asked, shoving a green-and-white sample at him, wondering how she had managed to phrase the question, given the lump in her throat.

Devon was not fooled by her brave smile. She was hurting. He could see it in the tears that rimmed her large green eyes. After all he had done to her, she still believed in his love. But unfortunately, the greatest test was yet to come. Then the pain would be his. He turned and left.

Every bite she took seemed to lodge in her throat. Danielle took another sip of wine. Time was running out. She only had tonight to convince Devon once and for all that she had not betrayed him.

She was past caring that she might be making a fool of herself. She loved him, and if she wasn't able to make him see that he loved her also, he would leave and there was no saying when or if he'd return.

Devon couldn't bring himself to meet her questioning glance. The hurt and confusion there was more than he could bear. But it would be over soon, he kept telling himself. If his plan was successful, Nathan would be forced to show his hand before the *Liberty* sailed.

After eating what he could, Devon went to his study. He declined the port Andrews brought him and poured himself a brandy instead. Danielle's safety was now in Robert's hands. He had learned early enough that he could not watch her. The temptation to forget his plans was too great when she was near.

While Devon drank his brandy, Danielle made her own plans for the evening. She would sleep in her old room this one last time. Dismissing Mary, she stepped into the lavender-scented bathwater. The water felt good after the long day she had spent supervising the decoration of the nursery. She was tempted to stay for a while, but there was no telling when Devon would retire for the evening. She hurriedly washed. Wrapping a towel around her wet hair, she climbed out of the tub.

It seemed to take forever to comb her hair dry, but thank goodness she finished before she heard Devon in his room. It wasn't often someone was given one last chance. She could only pray that she'd be able to carry out her scheme. She sat down to wait.

Devon took another swallow from his glass, then refilled it. He had been lying awake for hours in the dark when he heard Danielle's door open. The thought that whoever had killed his father was coming to do the same to him passed through his mind.

The door opened wider and he relaxed. If someone were coming to murder him, they'd not carry a candle. But he was not prepared for the vision that stepped through the doorway.

A shimmering green negligee covered her body from shoulders to sandaled feet, and candlelight appeared to pour over it like cool water with each step she took. She said not a word but reached up and pulled the jeweled pins from her hair, releasing the auburn curls. They tumbled in wild abandonment about her shoulders and face.

"Don't do this to me," he warned.

She took a step closer. "And what will my punishment be if I do?" she asked, her voice a sultry whisper.

Devon could already feel his body responding to the invitation. "I'll not bed a wench who's so free with her favors."

"I've saved all my favors for you," she answered, taking another step. "But then you know that, don't you?"

Had he been so transparent? She was close enough now that he could see the gown caress each tantalizing curve of her naked body, and the ache grew within him.

Devon's hand tightened on his glass. "You'll regret this decision when I leave in the morning."

She reached up and caught the ties of her gown. With a gentle tug the ribbons unfurled and the gown slipped to her feet. Boldly, she leaned over and ran her finger down his broad chest. "*If* you leave in the morning."

Before he could stop her, she crawled into his bed and straddled his torso. Never taking his eyes off her, he reached over to place his glass on the bedside table. Her fingers closed over his and she brought them to her mouth. Her lips pursed suggestively, she sipped from the brandy, her eyes offering him anything he was brave enough to take.

Slowly she lowered the glass to settle the stem between her breasts. She closed her eyes and arched her back. With painstaking care, she guided his hand to tip the glass—ever so slightly—toward her. The dark liquid spilled across her breasts, then trickled down the valley between them. Devon found himself holding his breath as his eyes followed the moist path down her silken skin until it disappeared in the rich red hairs that brushed against his stomach. He could feel the trickle of brandy seal her to him as he lifted his eyes to her.

The green fires of passion he saw there tore a moan from his throat. She leaned down, her hair spilling around them. She brushed her body invitingly over his as she reached across him to place the glass on the bedside table. Brazenly, she sat up.

"Tonight *I* will be *your* brandy," she said with a husky whisper as she offered her breasts to him.

With a groan, he cupped them to his lips and pulled her down to him. Gathering up her hair, she lowered her body to his, boldly washing him with the brandy. Then she eased her breasts from his suckling and gently guided them down the length of him, her tongue licking at the sweet trail she left behind.

"Damnation!" he cursed. "It's my turn now."

Grabbing her by the waist, he brought her back up to him. He rolled with her until his body covered her. With a sigh, he settled between her legs.

Hungrily, he licked at the brandy that coated her breasts. With tiny nibbles, he followed the trail of nectar down her body.

Danielle buried her fingers in his dark curls and bit back the screams that rose to her lips. She was on fire. A hot, burning fire that soared each time he sucked at the sweet liquid. She moved against him and demanded that he take her before the fire consumed her and nothing remained but a pile of smoldering ashes.

When she thought she could stand no more, he covered her mouth with his, forcing her lips to part. The screams she had thought to hold back ripped from deep within her.

Devon let her screams fill him. He waited until the trembling that rocked her subsided, then slipped his tongue into her warm mouth. His moans mated with hers as she suckled the brandy from his tongue just as he had suckled it from her breasts. Suddenly he could take no more teasing from the tigress arching beneath him. He lifted his head from hers and looked into her half-closed eyes.

"Heaven help us both," he said, then gently he entered her.

Danielle ran the warm, wet cloth down his furred chest, lingering on the scars that scored a path beneath the crisp black hairs.

"You were wrong," he said. "Your tub is large enough to accommodate one loving couple."

She lifted the wet cloth to swat him. He grabbed her arm and they struggled in the soapy water. Slipping and sliding, he twisted and turned, refusing to release her until she lay atop him. Her hair formed a tent around them as he lifted her to place a kiss on the creamy white mounds that peeked enticingly out of the lavender-scented bubbles.

"Had I known you were going to take over my bath, I would not have ordered it," she teased.

"Don't you think I deserved some compensation after you wasted my brandy?"

"Wasted!" Danielle shouted. "Why, you . . . you . . ."

He closed her mouth with his kiss.

Much later Devon watched the firelight from the hearth play across her naked body as she lay exhausted beside him on the bathing blanket.

Danielle stared into the flames. "You're still leaving tomorrow, aren't you?"

He took her chin in his hands and forced her to look at him. "I wish I could stay, but I can't," he said. He ran his thumb across her lips. "I want you to know, though, that I love you."

She turned to him, her eyes bright with unshed tears, and he gathered her in his arms, burying his face in her hair. "No matter what happens," he whispered, "always remember I love you."

The white ground fog and blood-red lining of Devon's cape curled around his muscled legs as he approached the waiting coach. He settled the plumed hat over his dark hair and stepped into the coach.

"Keep the horses to a walk until you are free of this fog," he shouted from the window.

Devon dropped the drape back in place and frowned. He was a fool to have let her stay last night. But, Lord help him, he couldn't have turned her away, even knowing that her life and that of his child depended on it.

He was being overly dramatic, he chided himself. If all went as planned, Nathan would show his hand. Winslow had gotten his message. Everything was in place. Even the fog might prove to be in their favor.

"Blimey!" he heard Jem curse as he pulled up the horses. "A tree's fell across the path. Be on our way in a moment."

Devon's heart pumped with excitement. "Take care, Jem," he warned. "This is highwaymen's weather."

Jem jumped down from the box. "Got me a brace o' pistols, I 'as," the old man claimed.

"I'll give you a hand, Jem," Devon shouted.

The door opened, the steps swung down, and a dark figure encircled by a black cape got out.

Devon laughed. "Fog so thick you could serve it for cream. A shame I—"

A shot rang out and he fell to the ground, the mist quickly covering his lifeless body.

Danielle extricated herself from Robert's arms as the footmen carried Devon's body into the foyer.

"Wait," she cried. This could not be the husband who only last night had held her in his arms and told her he loved her. God could not be that cruel.

The men paused at the foot of the stairs.

Her hand hovered over the bloodstained sheet that covered her husband's body. "I want to see him," she said, more to herself than to them.

Robert covered her hand with his. "His face is gone, your Grace." The pain in her eyes tore at his conscience and he gathered her in his arms.

"Take the body to his bedchamber," he instructed the men. "Don't let the maids touch it. Andrews and I will prepare it."

"What will I do without him, Bob?" she sobbed.

He held her away from him. "Begging your pardon, your Grace, but you have yourself to worry about now. Whoever shot his Grace may have the same fate planned for you . . . and the child."

He was right, of course. Devon might have doubted their child's parentage, but Nathan clearly knew who the father was.

Danielle finished her note to Lady Julia and handed it to Giles. "I'm sorry you have to make this trip in a storm," she said, "but Lady Julia must be told. She is still in Edinburgh with my aunt, Lady Bradford. Also, a notice must be put in the *Gazette*, but it can wait until your return."

He bowed and left.

The rain beat against the windows. She could hear Mrs. Talbut in the drawing room, supervising the moving of the furniture to make room for the casket.

Danielle closed her eyes against the tears, recalling how she'd gone to his room determined to make him set aside his foolish pride and allow his heart to judge her innocence or guilt. There had been no bitter words between them then, just passionate loving. It would be the memory she locked in her heart.

Danielle stood at the window, her emerald necklace the only bit of color to relieve the black of her widow's weeds.

"We mustn't delay it any longer," the visiting vicar

said. "With the rains washing out most of the roads, I doubt they'll be able to make it through."

Danielle glanced out at the dark sky. She had hoped that the break in the storm would make it possible for Lady Julia to be there for the funeral. She was fortunate that the vicar from a neighboring parish had come as soon as he got her message. The heavy rains that had fallen for the past three days had quickly brought a halt to all travel. But she would have spoken the final words over Devon herself before she let Nathan do it.

"They'll need to finish digging the grave before the rains start again," the clergyman reminded her.

Danielle nodded numbly as she reached out to stroke the casket beside her. For the thousandth time, her fingers traced the intricate carvings. The man she loved lay in this cold, wooden box. Never again would he come to her bed or hold her in his arms. Gone was the lopsided grin that never failed to tease a smile from her own lips. Gone were kisses that . . .

Danielle closed her eyes against the pain.

Always remember I love you.

Desperately, she held the words to her. They were all she had.

If someone had asked, Danielle would have said that she didn't recall when they came to take her to the burial grounds. She only knew that she was standing beside her husband's grave and that it had started raining again. She shivered as the vicar spoke the eulogy. She shut out the words. What could he ever say that would comfort her? It was much safer to concentrate on the raindrops than on the inadequate words of someone who would never know what it was like to be held in Devon's arms.

"May I help you with that?" the vicar asked.

Danielle stared at the handful of dirt he had placed in her hand.

"You're to toss it onto the casket, your Grace," he whispered.

"Yes. Yes, of course." She stepped up to the grave as a tear slipped down her cheek.

"Always remember I love you," she whispered.

The dirt slid through her fingers, and before she could stop it, her heart followed.

The door slammed back against the wall. "What are you doing here?" Danielle asked as she strode across the study.

Nathan lifted his head from the estate books. Even in mourning, the duchess was enough to take one's breath away. A shame he had no further need of her. It wasn't often a woman's beauty summoned a physical need in him, but it would be a pleasure to take Danielle. His thin lips twisted in a smile. In memory of his dear cousin, of course.

Leaning back, he thoughtfully tapped the feathered quill against his chin. "I was just deciding what best to do with you." He paused. "Now that I'm the Duke of Burnshire, that is."

"You will never be the Duke of Burnshire. Devon's child will take his place."

Nathan lifted a brow. "You're sure it will be a boy, are you? Lord Carruthers will be pleased."

Danielle grabbed the back of a chair for support. "The child is Devon's," she said calmly. "Now leave at once before I summon the servants to see you out."

"Yes, please do." He pulled a sheaf of papers from his coat. "Then they, too, can hear Devon's letter to his solicitor."

"Another forgery like the last, Vicar?"

"He said you might try to say that, so he went to the trouble of having it witnessed by Giles and . . ." Nathan opened the papers and read the last signature. "And Bob. I believe he's the footman who saved Devon's life in Jamaica. Of course, I'll see to his dismissal immediately."

"We'll settle this here and now." She turned and walked to the door.

"Bob, would you please come in here for a moment?"

Bob approached the desk with her.

"Nathan has a letter from Devon to his solicitor. He says your signature is there along with Giles' as a witness. Would you please verify it for me?"

Robert grimaced at the pain he saw in her face. He had warned Devon not to do this. Surely there had to be another way. Reluctantly, he leaned across the desk. "This looks to be them."

"Thank you, Bob. That will be all."

Danielle reached for the papers. Nathan smiled triumphantly as he placed them in her outstretched hand. She vowed that no matter what the papers said, she would not become upset in front of Nathan, but nothing could have prepared her for the damning words Devon had written.

If you are reading this document, then you already know of the treachery that has brought an end to my life. My wife has taken a lover, and it is my belief she will stop at nothing to be rid of me. Since she has taken everything from me with her betrayal, I leave all my possessions to my cousin, Nathan Holmes, and the title of Duke of Burnshire as well, for the child my wife carries is not my own. The true father . . .

Danielle let the pages slip from her fingers onto the desk. She told herself Devon had written them in haste. She knew now that he loved her. He could not have believed she had betrayed him, not after their last night together.

She started to protest, then stopped. What did it really matter? With Devon gone, her heart was nothing more than a stone around her neck. Nathan could have it all.

Proudly, she turned and walked away. "I'll be leaving in the morning," she called out as she reached the door.

''There is more,'' Nathan said, coming around the desk.

Danielle swung around. ''You have everything. What more could you want?''

Nathan held out his hand. ''The necklace,'' he demanded. ''It belongs to the estate.''

She reached up and unhooked the clasp. She was surprised her hands did not tremble when she dropped the stones into his hand. ''Will that be all?'' she asked through clenched teeth.

''No. There is one thing more. The children. They will be returning to the orphanage.''

She walked out the door and didn't look back.

Chapter 24

"I 'll do that myself," Danielle said, refusing Mrs. Meacham's help.

"But there's so much to pack."

"I won't be taking much with me."

"All these beautiful gowns. Surely you don't intend to leave them?"

Danielle laid the nightdress she was folding across the lid of the trunk. She straightened and faced her dresser. "Perhaps if you ask Nathan, he'll give them to you. After all, he would be the last to say you haven't earned them." Mrs. Meacham's gaze dropped to the floor. "Now get out and leave me to my packing."

Danielle surveyed the contents of the trunk and decided to include only her day dresses. The more elaborate ball gowns Devon had insisted she have would be of little use in Virginia. In a few months they would be too small for her anyway.

Danielle ran her hand over her still slim waist. The child growing inside her would become her life. Their son. The tears that she had held at bay all day spilled silently down her cheeks. She had her child. He would serve to remind her of how wonderful her husband had been before he had let his jealousy tear him apart. It was that Devon she would hold in her heart. All she had left of him was memories, but no one could take those from her. Not even Nathan.

She would look to her future now. Past the pain. Past the cruel words Devon had written in anger to a time when, if she couldn't find happiness, at least she could have peace.

A light tap on her bedchamber door brought Mrs. Meacham into her room again.

"Yes?"

Mrs. Meacham checked the hallway before closing the door. "The vicar has dismissed me, so I haven't much time."

"Surely you did not expect him to keep you on once he had no further use for your spying."

"Please, your Grace, hear me out. Tom and I are going to help you leave tonight."

"Why tonight?"

"Because if you sneak out tonight, you will be able to take the children with you."

"Why would you want to help? I have no money to pay you."

"I care nothing for your money, your Grace. Katie is the one I care for. She's my daughter."

"Katie, your daughter?" Danielle asked. "But if you're her mother, you gave Katie up at birth. Why do you want her now?"

"My husband, Lord Meade, took her to the orphanage. He told me Katie was stillborn, and I had no reason to doubt him. He was a proud man. He couldn't face the shame of her birthmark.

"It wasn't until a year later that I overheard him discussing a quarterly payment to be sent to the orphanage for her keep. As soon as his man of business left, I got the pistol from his study and confronted him. He admitted he had placed my child in an orphanage, but he refused to tell me which one. I think I went a little bit crazy. I waved the gun in his face, screaming that I would have my child even if I had to kill him to get her. He grabbed my arm. The gun discharged. I killed him," she finished matter-of-factly.

Danielle put her arms around Elizabeth.

"Thank you for helping. Katie is very fortunate to have a mother who loves her so much."

Elizabeth's shoulders slumped. "I've searched for so

long to find her. Do you think she'll forgive me for letting this happen?''

"Katie is a very forgiving child.''

"Would you take her with you when you leave?'' Elizabeth begged. "She loves you, and I want her to have that.''

"I've already sent Aunt Margaret a note telling her of my plans to take the children to her home in Bath. She's more than likely on her way there now.'' Danielle squeezed Elizabeth's hand. "You see, I care too much for the children to allow them to remain here.''

"The vicar is going to request your presence at supper tonight.''

"He wishes to gloat over his success,'' Danielle said.

"But you must accept the invitation. If you can keep him occupied for the evening, Tom and I can get the children out of the house and into your coach.''

"How much time do you need? I cannot keep Nathan entertained for long. He would surely suspect something was afoot.''

Elizabeth grinned. "I will get cook to serve as many courses as it takes.''

True to her word, Elizabeth managed to adjust the menu. Nathan, who spent the time pointing out all the changes he intended to make, did not appear to notice.

Danielle kept her eyes fixed on her bowl of soup. She refused to let his words upset her. Now that Devon was gone, the vile things Nathan had to say no longer mattered, she told herself. A few more hours and she would be gone from here forever. She took another spoonful of the soup.

"Of course, the Picketts will be returning to the orphanage,'' Nathan said, hoping he could stir her anger. Her passivity was beginning to wear on his nerves.

Danielle continued to concentrate on her food. Her calm mocked him and he tried again. "Such a shame to lose someone as valuable as Amy, but after her display of disloyalty, I cannot allow her to remain at the orphanage.''

Ah, now he had her attention. "I thought perhaps the workhouse would suit her talents better."

Forgetting her promise not to let him upset her, Danielle tossed her napkin on the table.

"Is that all you can think about, how you can make someone suffer?"

She marched out. It was not until she had reached her room and saw Elizabeth struggling with the trunk that Danielle recalled the plan.

"I've gone and done it now, Elizabeth," she said. "I've lost my temper and ruined everything."

"This trunk was the last thing we had to put on the carriage. We could still try to leave while Andrews serves the vicar his port."

"That's much too risky. Have Tom put the trunk in the bedchamber next to the back stairs. We will have to wait until Nathan has retired for the evening. Have the children sleep in their clothes. Once we're sure he's asleep, we'll leave."

Danielle posted a note to the orphanage warning Brodie of Nathan's intentions.

It was well past midnight by the time they were on their way. Pockets rode with Tom on the box. Katie and Jeremy slept inside with Danielle and Elizabeth.

Due to the sorry condition of the roads, light was peeking over the hillside by the time they reached the outskirts of London. The children awoke hungry, and Danielle had Tom stop the coach while they shared the basket of food they had managed to steal from the kitchen. With six mouths to feed, it didn't go far.

"I'm sorry, children, but that's the last we'll have until we reach Aunt Margaret's house in Bath. The vicar did not leave me with so much as a single coin to call my own."

"Would this help?" Pockets asked shyly, tossing Danielle his gold coin. "His Grace gave it to me."

"Are you sure you wish to part with it?"

"It may not get us passage to the colonies," he answered, "but we won't starve on our way to Bath."

She gave him a big hug. "Thank you, Pockets."

"Ouch!" he said. He reached into one of his pockets and pulled out the emerald necklace Nathan had taken. "I almost forgot," he said, handing it to Danielle.

"I won't even ask how you got this," she said, "but if I can get just a fourth of its value, it will buy passage for all of us."

Danielle stood in front of the jeweler's shop and ran her hands over the front of her traveling gown. She frowned. The wrinkles were still very much in evidence, but she would just have to hope the jeweler didn't notice. Devon would have noticed, she thought, the old pain twisting her insides. Straightening her shoulders, she gave a deep sigh and walked through the door Pockets held open for her.

She paused. The elegance of the shop made her even more aware of her rumpled gown.

"May I help you, ma'am?" the clerk asked.

Danielle stepped between two tables, their white linen tops covered with displays of ornately jeweled snuffboxes. Carefully she made her way across the shop to the counter.

"I have a piece I wish to sell."

"May I see it, please?" The clerk kept a wary eye on Pockets.

She opened her hand and the necklace spilled out onto the swatch of velvet covering the glass case. The many-faceted cuts of the dark emeralds caught the morning sunlight.

His tongue stroked his dry lips as he lifted the jeweler's glass to his eye. "A very fine piece, ma'am," he commented. Much too fine, he thought, for the lady who stood before him in her rumpled gown, her dubious companion hovering over the display cases at the door. The superb piece was more than likely stolen. But business had been slow of late, and the profit he'd make off this little acquisition was too much to pass up.

"If you will excuse me a moment. I must show this

to Mr. Smithers. He handles all acquisitions of this size.''

Pockets discreetly followed him to the curtain that separated them from the back room. He listened intently to what was being said.

''Blimey, your Grace. 'E's telling the man ye stole the necklace. We'd best be off afore 'e drags us afore the magistrate and ye 'ave to explain why yer 'avin' to sell them baubles what 'is Grave give ye.''

''I'll not leave without my necklace,'' Danielle said. She pulled her pistol from her reticule.

''Blimey!'' Pockets breathed. ''You can't go shooting the proprietor.''

But it was too late. The clerk stepped from behind the curtain.

His face went white at the sight of the pistol. He dropped the necklace. ''Ma'am,'' he choked. ''Please. A few moments and I'll have your money for you.''

Pockets scurried around the counter and snatched up the necklace from the floor. ''Let's be off,'' he shouted to Danielle, waving the emeralds over his head.

She followed him out of the shop and hurriedly climbed into the carriage. If Nathan found out she'd tried to sell the necklace, there wouldn't be a jeweler in all of England who would touch it. She instructed Tom to head on for Bath.

Once clear of Burnshire's gates, Chilton spurred his mount. The vicar had made it clear that the papers he carried must be at the coast tonight if Napoleon's man was to be back across the Channel before first light.

''Can't wait fer a fella to get 'is supper,'' Chilton grumbled to himself as he slowed his mount to skirt a broken wagon on the road.

''I'll take the message you carry,'' the man on the black stallion said, reigning his mount in beside Chilton.

Chilton could feel the hangman's noose tighten about his neck. Damn Faris for up and disappearing when he needed him most. He swung his horse around, but another rider closed in from the other side. "I've got nothing ye'd be wantin'," Chilton shouted at the uniformed officer.

"Not even this?" Captain Winslow asked as he plucked the sealed missive from Chilton's pocket.

"I'm only paid to deliver 'em," he blustered. "I don't read 'em."

Captain Winslow tapped the note against his thigh. "Then why all the concern?"

Chilton's eyes traveled from one rider to the next, his gaze finally locking with that of the tall man on the black. His blue eyes were like fires from hell and they scorched Chilton's soul.

"B-but you're dead," he managed to say despite the vise clutching his heart. "I shot you."

Devon shoved his pistol under Chilton's chin. "It was one of your own associates who took the bullet you meant for me. But I'm too close to make the same mistake you did."

Sweat beaded across Chilton's forehead. "I only did what I was told to do. Lord Carruthers, it were the vicar. 'E's the one ye want.'E's the one what told me to kill ye."

"Let's tie and gag him. We've yet to offer Nathan our congratulations on his good fortune, and I wouldn't want Chilton here to spoil our surprise."

Nathan shook the white sand from the last of the signatures. "There," he said, handing the papers to Lord Carruthers. "Seabrook is now yours."

"A bit premature, my dear cousin, wouldn't you agree?"

Both men turned at once. "Devon," Nathan whispered.

"Cousin, I'm appalled," he said, stepping forward. "Dabbling in treason. Father would be so disappointed. A shame you had to murder him before he was able to view this side of you."

"You know?" Nathan gasped.

"That and much more."

Devon held out his hand. "Now, if Lord Carruthers would be so good as to hand over those papers? The Lord Chancellor will, no doubt, want to add them to the dispatch Captain Winslow and I took from Chilton."

Lord Carruthers' dark eyes reflected his hate. "And Captain Winslow?" he asked.

Devon's lips curved in a smile. "On his way to London. He should be placing your note in the hands of the Lord Chancellor within the hour."

Carruthers tossed the papers to Devon. Before Devon could catch them, Thomas' fingers found the pistol he kept hidden in his coat. Devon stepped to one side, but the bullet caught Robert in the arm.

"Damn!" Carruthers cursed to himself. He'd missed. Furious, he threw the empty pistol at Devon's head and slipped out the garden doors. "Kill them both," he shouted to his men. "I must get those papers back or we'll all be swinging from the gallows."

Devon had started for the door when Nathan lunged at him. They both fell to the floor.

Over and over they rolled, Nathan kicking and clawing as he scrambled for a hold. Tables fell, sending their contents crashing about the two men.

The vicar was no match for a man who had defended his ships on more than one occasion armed with a pistol and a cutlass. But Nathan's luck had not deserted him. Just when he thought himself beaten, a vase of flowers fell on Devon, the water blinding his cousin for a moment, but it was enough. Nathan buried his fingers in Devon's throat. All the years of hatred and jealousy lent him strength as his pressed his advantage. Lord, it felt good to kill the bastard with his own hands.

Devon pried at Nathan's fingers, but his cousin's maniacal strength was overpowering. He couldn't breathe. Even with the water in his eyes, he could see the black curtain of death closing around him.

"To your side, Devon," Robert called, but Devon had no time to deal with Carruthers' men now. He was dying. If only . . .

Nathan stared in disbelief as Devon's body suddenly went lax beneath him. Elation surged through him. His cousin was dead!

Nathan loosened his hold and sat up, his laughter filling the room.

Devon slowly opened his eyes and, with his last ounce of strength, twisted sideways and brought back his arm, his elbow catching Nathan's jaw. Devon heard the bone snap just before the pistols exploded.

Nathan collapsed on top of him. He tried to move, but a searing pain gripped him. He'd been hit in the shoulder. It hurt like hell.

Two of the servants lifted Nathan from him. He wondered what had become of Carruthers' men. After a few tries, he managed to prop himself up on his arm. Then he saw them, lying on the floor beside him. Two other servants sat atop them. Carruthers' men were not going anywhere. Robert seemed to have taken care of everything.

Devon started to get up when a shadow fell over him as a man stepped through the garden door. He sat back down.

"What's going on here?" Jem asked; then his gaze fell to Devon. Jem's eyes widened in shock. It couldn't be the duke. The duke was dead. Suddenly the old man knew for sure that the spirits had found him and there was no escape this time—not when the devil himself was smiling up at you.

"Lord, keep my soul safe," he prayed, then slumped to the floor.

"You shouldn't be out of bed," Robert exclaimed.

Devon gritted his teeth against the pain and slipped his arms into the shirt his valet held for him. "I can't have Danielle thinking me dead any longer. She's much too resourceful. If I don't get to Bath soon, she'll be on a ship to Virginia."

"Send someone for her."

"And have them tell her what? That the husband who accused her of adultery, staged his own death, then forced her to flee in the dead of night from her home is really alive after all and wants her to return?''

"Put in that light, it sounds like trouble. You'd best take me with you for protection. The duchess will more than likely shoot you herself."

"A lot of help you would be with your arm in a sling."

"You're not in much better shape yourself."

"My wound will not keep me from telling her that I love her."

Robert frowned. "How much explaining do you think you'll be able to do if you bleed to death on your way there?"

"More than I will if she sails before I reach Bath," he tossed over his shoulder as he left his bedchamber.

Devon caught Lady Bradford as she fell to the floor. "Smelling salts and a brandy," he shouted to the butler. Rejoining the living was becoming quite an inconvenience.

Devon held the glass to Lady Bradford's lips. "Sorry I startled you," he apologized.

Margaret took another sip of the brandy. "You're supposed to be dead," she accused.

"I'll not be apologizing for that. I rather like being alive."

"Danielle may have something to say about that once she learns of your hoax."

"So I've been told," he said, helping Danielle's aunt to her feet. "Where is my beautiful wife?"

"She's out walking."

Pleased by the concern she saw on his face, she debated whether to tell him that Danielle was with someone. "A friend of hers came by a few minutes before you arrived. Oh!" she suddenly exclaimed. "Now that I find you are alive, it somehow seems inappropriate to have given him her direction."

"Who?" Devon asked, his gut twisting with an awful suspicion.

"Lord Carr—"

Devon grabbed her arm. "Which path did she take?"

"Along the old king's road above the city."

Devon turned to leave.

"I thought his visit would serve as a welcome diversion," she called after him.

By the time he reached the street, Captain Winslow and a soldier were dismounting.

"Somehow I felt I would find you here," Winslow said as he handed the reins of his mount to Lady Bradford's footman.

Devon grabbed the reins and climbed into the saddle. "Lord Carruthers may have Danielle," he shouted in explanation.

With each strike of the horse's hooves on the cobblestones, a searing pain shot through Devon's shoulder. He placed his hand against the wound and bent low over the horse's neck. Blood seeped through his fingers. Lord, it hurt. He'd have to find her quickly or, in his condition, he'd not be any help to her when he did.

"It is I who have the pistol this time," Lord Carruthers hissed in her face.

Danielle backed against the edge of the hillside. Elizabeth had begged her not to go out alone. She took another step, then stopped when a few stones she'd disturbed tumbled to the ledge below.

"Why are you here?" she asked.

"I've come to kill you."

The cold black eyes told her as much as his words. She glanced over the edge. There was no escape that way. "Why kill me?"

He took a step closer. "You're the only thing left that stands in my way. The old duke stopped me for a while, but I got rid of him soon enough."

"You murdered the Duke of Burnshire?"

"Nathan reserved that pleasure for himself. I merely provided the incentive—and the men to ensure he didn't get squeamish at the last minute.

"It wasn't as easy with Stanton," he continued. "He

somehow avoided my man. He and his mother both have the devil's own luck.''

Lord Carruthers stared through her. Danielle ventured a step to her right, then another. He appeared not to notice. ''You tried to kill Devon and Lady Julia?'' she asked.

''Devon's death would not have been enough. She would have inherited it, you see. I had no choice. Now you'll be the one to inherit.''

Keep him talking, she told herself. ''Inherit what?'' Danielle asked, taking another small step. ''Surely not Burnshire,'' she continued. ''As the only living male heir, Nathan gets everything.''

''Nathan is dead!''

''Dead? When? How?'' She returned his bold stare. She'd do nothing to remind him that her child would be the one to inherit. ''I lost everything with Devon's death. How can you hope to acquire Burnshire through killing me?''

He shook the pistol at her. ''You don't understand. Why should I kill you to get Burnshire? When France conquers England, Burnshire will be mine. It's been promised to me for my loyalty. Not a bad payment for a few ships, a few of the king's couriers, and a safe harbor for Napoleon's fleet. You see, Napoleon is most generous to those who aid him.''

''Seabrook! You had everyone murdered because you wanted Seabrook?''

''It was more than just Seabrook. It was land—and all the power I could ever want at my fingertips.''

''It was you all along, wasn't it?'' she said. ''You had *The Queen* sunk and the blame placed on Devon.''

''You're quite astute, your Grace, but not as astute as your husband.''

''Devon?''

Thomas ran the barrel of the pistol along the side of her cheek. ''He suspected I was the one who had set him up for treason and he came to White Oaks. We would have ended it then and there had your husband called me out. I'm quite good with these, you see.''

He shoved the barrel into her ribs. "But he was a coward. A bloody coward. I told him the child you carried was mine and he walked away. He . . ."

Tears pooled in Danielle's green eyes. Why hadn't she told Devon of the baby when she had first suspected she was pregnant? She could well imagine the pain he must have suffered thinking she had conspired with a lover to prove him guilty of treason.

". . . escaped me once, but he won't again. My men will see to that. Now you both shall die."

She listened to the sound of the hammer being pulled back on the pistol. What was he saying? Devon was dead. She blinked the tears from her eyes. Were it not for her unborn child, she would almost have welcomed death herself.

A sudden movement in the thicket behind Carruthers caught her attention. Hair as dark as a raven's wing could be seen among the leaves. Hair as dark as . . . Danielle gasped. No, it couldn't be. Devon alive?

Lord Carruthers' eyes narrowed. He swung around, his pistol ready.

"No!" Danielle screamed as she tried to push past him.

He grabbed her arm. "You'll be staying with me," he growled. He shoved the pistol in her side. Damn the pirate. How had he escaped his men?

A sneer curled Thomas' lip at the sight of the fresh blood that seeped through Devon's shirt. The duke staggered toward him. He hadn't escaped after all.

"You're dying, Stanton. Drop the pistol. You wouldn't want to shoot your wife when you fall."

Devon straightened his shoulders and leveled the gun at Carruthers' heart. "It will not be me who dies," he said quietly.

Danielle screamed as a single shot tore through the silence. Both men fell to the ground.

Danielle stumbled to Devon's side. Tossing aside the smoking pistol clutched in his fingers, she gently lifted his head. Tears coursed down her cheeks. Had he returned to her only to be lost again?

"Devon, you can't die," she insisted as she rocked him in her arms. She covered his face with kisses. "It's you I love. No one else. Oh, Devon, you just have to hear me."

He grimaced at the pain in his shoulder but managed a sheepish grin. "I've always known you love me."

Danielle lifted her head and stared down at him. Had she heard correctly?

"I pour my heart out to you, thinking you're dying, and you calmly state you've known it all along?"

"I am dying," he said.

There was no mistaking the note of apology in his voice—or the pain. She'd not let him give up now. Not when he'd only just come back to her.

"If you're thinking of dying to escape your punishment, you'd best think again. You're too mean to die."

Then suddenly it came to her. "You planned the whole thing, didn't you?"

The sheepish grin told her she had guessed correctly.

"Why didn't you tell me?" she demanded.

"Not a good enough actress," he teased.

She knew then that he'd live.

"Well, you were wrong about one thing. Elizabeth proved to be on our side after all."

"She worked for Nathan." He'd explain Robert some other time.

"She explained that all to me. She is really Lady Meade. She's Katie's mother."

"She's Lord Meade's wife?"

Danielle managed to reach over him and lift her skirts. She tore a strip of cloth from her petticoat. "Elizabeth was married to Lord Meade. She shot him," she said matter-of-factly. "Oh, but you mustn't blame her, Devon, because she did not mean to. You will help her, won't you?"

Devon shifted his head in her lap. He rather enjoyed the view he had from here. "Since she helped me set up Nathan, I believe I could help her, but—"

"You let her help, yet you wouldn't let me," she

accused. She folded the linen strip and tucked it into his shirt. "If you weren't wounded, I'd dump you on this ground and leave you."

"But, you see, she was not carrying my child."

"That's something else we need to discuss," she said as she adjusted his shirt over the strip of petticoat.

"As soon as I'm better."

"You're right. What you need now is a physician."

"Captain Winslow should be here shortly."

"Well, then you should rest until he gets here. Close your eyes now. I will sit here and think of a suitable punishment for you."

"How am I to rest knowing that your mind is conjuring up all sorts of diabolical things?"

She put her hand over his eyes, forcing them shut. "You're nothing but a scoundrel, my lord, and you'd best not be expecting me to feel sorry for you," she said. "You'll not cheat me of your punishment that way."

"So what is my punishment to be, my little abductress?"

Tears ran unchecked down her cheeks. "I have decided to become one of those wives who uses her children to keep her husband by her side."

"Our children," he whispered.

"Our children," she affirmed. "And I have also decided I will sail with you. I will let you be the captain."

"Are you sure you wouldn't like to be the captain?" he asked.

"No, I'll let you. I'll be your first mate. I'll climb the rig—or whatever it is called—and raise the mast . . ." She paused. "Or is it hoist the sail? Well, no matter. I'll—"

"Say no more," Devon groaned. "It hurts too much when I laugh."

Raising his hand, he traced the sweet outline of her lips. "Best give me something to think about other than my pain, love."

And right before God, she did.